HELLFIRE & HOLY WATER

JONIE NIKOLE

Cover design by JonAlexandra Nickles

ISBN: Printed in the United States

Edited by Book Writing Pioneer

BOOK WRITING
P I O N E E R

HELLFIRE & HOLY WATER

JONIE NIKOLE

TRIGGER WARNING

I would like you to know that this book is not for everyone. One of my beta readers had to step away and did not come back. Please take care of yourself. For the twisted and depraved, I hope you love reading it as much as I enjoyed writing it.

I SEE YOU

For my readers—GraceAlexandra N, Meredith K, Kati J and Melissa H—thank you all for reading through this madness and for your patience and grace as I molded these messy words into something worthy of your time.

To my family, who strapped in and went through all the ups and downs of this ride, I love your guts and thank you.

WE ARE NOT ALONE

PRESENT DAY - BABY

"I f you keep talking, I'll have to kill you myself."

"You sound like my father," she said quickly, forcing out the words. "That's all I'm trying to say."

Her words cut through the silence for about the fourth or fifth time in the past hour. The more I tried to drown her out, the more persistent she became. Her voice filtered through the wall like a cannonball, delivered through gritted teeth as she pelted me with her pain and fear, ensuring I hadn't forgotten she was there.

I could almost feel her body dragging along the stone as she adjusted herself against the wall. She was moving again. This only furthered my irritation, as my nerves were already burned at the ends. But I let her ramble without interruption. It was a necessary aggravation, and I was aware of it. I resisted the urge to snap at her to shut up and stay still.

I could still taste the blood in my mouth. I spit more of it out but shut down the impulse to examine my own injuries. My arms and legs were working just fine as I stretched them out and moved them around. This was the important things, for now. I concentrated my efforts on the young woman on the other side of the wall. I listened to her voice rather than her words, listening for what my eyes could not see. Between the stressed words, she'd pause while gasps of air filled the spaces that the babble did not.

The wall that separated us was made of stone blocks that felt sticky and wet against my back. Ordinarily, I might have welcomed the coolness of the stone, pressing my body against its surface to save me from the heat of a Louisiana summer. But now, it only seemed to amplify the chill that had settled across my skin. I imagined she was suffering similar. She shivered as she spoke. Her teeth chattered between her words. It was also quite possible that she was suffering from shock, along with the other injuries she described. I'm not a professional on that, though. I am, however, an expert on bodily infractions.

"Keep your hands tucked up under your thighs. Or in between your legs," I told her.

"It hurts too much to move," she cried. "I can't even ball myself up or stand."

If she would stop fidgeting, it might help her hurt less, though I understood the urge to switch spots. The floor was doing nothing for my mood. She would need to find an alternative way to generate heat to prevent a full-body meltdown.

"It'll help hold in the heat," I said confidently, considering that if she was seriously injured and in shock, she could die from exposure just as quickly as anything else. It wouldn't take much more for her body temperature to fall below what was needed to stay alive. The cold wall did her no favors, as her shorts and tank top provided little protection.

"Not that you sound like an old man or anything. It's the accent. It's not, well, you know... American. You know what I'm saying, right? It's like the same, but not exactly. You're definitely not from around here. That's all I mean. Wherever here is, anyway."

Even through the wall, I could feel the tension radiating from her. The more she talked, the more I was convinced she was in shock. The notes in her voice came out in a choppy cadence as if she spoke with her lips pressed tightly together.

I visualized the young woman in my mind, pulling out those images that were clear and focused. I could see the freckles that mapped across the bridge of her nose and ran along her rose-colored cheeks. The blush that crossed through her eyes when she was frustrated or concerned. The fiery red of her hair crackled in the sunlight like hot flames, thick and massive in volume when bound up. The flash of fire that lit up her eyes, even as a child, when she was angered. Or the change in hues that often gave the young woman away when she got pissed up or embarrassed.

I'd been around her most of her life and understood her in so many ways. She had yet to put the pieces together. But she was an intelligent girl, so it would only be a matter of time before she reached our connection.

"Oh, for Christ's sake. You know what I'm saying, right? I don't mean to imply that you sound old, either. I'm sure you are quite lovely," she apologized, stumbling helplessly through another unnecessary and useless apology.

The young woman had an educated southern haughtiness about her. There was also a touch of a foreign undertone to her Southern drawl that was unsteady as if it had been broken in her attack. I knew that sound as much as I knew my own breath. It was fear.

Her fear and her pain were causing her to vomit words like a bad reaction to turned fish because she could control neither. Her frustration grew as she continued with more apologies.

I knew all too well that silence was sometimes worse than the physical pain the body suffered. Silence can trap you in your mind and make you wander across a vast, isolated desert for days, all within just a few minutes of thought. Mind games were a part of my work, and I had mastered them. Sometimes, that's where the Boogeyman lived, and he held you hostage in the black of nothing. I was good at being one's Boogeyman, but I was not hers. Someone else had taken up that mantle, and she was slaying him through conversation.

"Baby? Are you still there? I said I'm sorry. Can you please say something? I can't see anything, and the sound of my own breathing is starting to freak me out. It's not Queen's English, for sure. My grandmother was English. She was quite the proper pot she was." This time, when she spoke, her words were delivered with a very confident Queen's English. "Very posh. But yours isn't that. It sounds Cockney? It's dirty, like that old hottie guy from Expendables. That must be it. It has such an edge to it," she said, a little too enthusiastically, which caused her to cough again.

I heard her as she skittered across the wall again. I guessed this time; she was moving to sit up straighter as she struggled to find air. She sounded as though she was choking with each burst of a cough that sounded wet and wheezy. The sound of a punctured lung, perhaps. Or maybe it was just a broken rib or two, irritating her breathing. I considered that if she were unconscious, she would struggle less. Even I would benefit from her silence. Then she gave a light-hearted laugh before she spoke again. I knew I wouldn't be that lucky.

"That scaffy bastard gave me a gammy spell!"

I hadn't gotten the reference but noted the change in her accent again as she attempted to sound like her father. Her cough had subsided, but she still sounded wheezy and exhausted.

"That's from a Disney movie if you didn't know," she said quietly. "Hey, but that was pretty good, right? Though I'm pretty sure I sounded somewhere left of my grandmother and right of my father," she stated proudly. "I knew it was still in there somewhere," she continued, referring to the lack of her father's accent in her voice.

"Baby, can you please say something?"

She did sound like her father. I could hear it in the way she pronounced the word 'You,' as he would.

I had yet to engage her in real conversation. When she first began to stir, I stayed quiet—opting to wait and listen. It wasn't until she began to cry that I knew for sure that I wasn't alone. However, I can't say that finding her was my objective. Just a happy circumstance.

Wherever we were, we were being isolated from one another.

I immediately considered the possible ramifications of continuing any exchange with her. I wasn't sure who might be listening in on all the chatter. Even in the darkness, the wrong set of words could reveal more than I intended. And honestly, the less she knew of me, the better it would be for both of us. The air around me felt heavy with uncertainty, and I wanted to gauge my surroundings before proceeding with her.

One thing was certain—by my calculations—I had already counted us among the dead. Statistically, I had beaten the odds way too many times. It was only a matter of time before my path ended with me tits up. It was bound to happen eventually. But if this were to be my last run, I'd make them earn it. The least I could do was take a few more of them with me on my way out.

"I've lived in Hackney for the better part of ten years now," I said finally, placing a hand flat against the wall separating us. "Dublin before that, and Dallas before that. But I call Hackney home."

As I talked, I ran a hand along the wall and pressed my ear to the stone, trying to hear what lay on the other side. I had already brailed my way through most of the floor and still had two of the surrounding walls. I hadn't found any cords or outlets. There was no sign of electronic devices or cameras, so we were unlikely to be recorded on video. I hadn't felt as though I was being watched. I had a sixth sense about that sort of stuff. That's what made me good at what I do.

But I wasn't so sure about the sound. Those types of devices were easier to hide and required far less setup. A small watch battery could power something as small as a pencil eraser for up to twelve hours—or an opal the size of a pebble, like the one I wore attached to a silver bracelet around my wrist. I was surprised to find it was still in place. They hadn't taken it, which was a mistake and meant that I was running out of time. Someone else would be on their way shortly.

I filled the silence as I told her about my apartment and how it had once been the site of a linen factory built around 1890. The four-story building closed in 1975 after rebranding itself as a furniture factory, a toy car manufacturer, and later a carpet shop. After that, it became a favorite hangout for drug seekers and pop-up rave ventures. Then, around 2008, London entrepreneurs began investing in a new trend: converting commercial properties to residential use. They converted old, abandoned buildings and warehouses into modern structures featuring black-stained timbers of contemporary design.

With its high ceilings and spacious floor plan, it appealed to the gritty urban youth of the area, who loved that the historical elements weren't torn down but embellished as part of the living space.

I had once been a frequent flyer to many of the old buildings' grimy underground scenes and was all too happy to buy one of the new apartments when they became available—one with a balcony that overlooked Hackney. From my perch, I could see as far as the Lee River. It was far enough to observe people from my very own vantage point. I love people-watching. "They fascinate me," I told her—like birds—their habits, migration patterns, and mating rituals. Watching people and examining their lives is one of my favorite pastimes.

Since I'm unable to connect with people, I must study them to learn normal human behavior. I'm told I lack empathy, understanding, compassion, kindness, and tact. I do not possess the ability to care about people.

But as my mind wandered toward my lesser qualities, it struck me that I would have to tell her she'd most likely not make it out of this alive. In the spirit of transparency, I didn't believe I could save us both. Although I really wasn't angling to save her at all. At least, that hadn't been my plan.

It wasn't that I wished her harm, but to my thinking, she wasn't exactly my responsibility. She had her people. I had very little doubt that, at that very moment, an entire community was dedicated to looking for her. By now, they knew she had been taken, rather than just missing. Her loved ones would risk life and limb and stop at nothing—sacrifice everything—to get her back.

Could I save myself and leave her behind?

Yes. Yes, I could do that.

I know what I am capable of. I know I could walk away and not look back. I felt nothing for her. Yet, when it came to the thought of her death, something inside me made me question my own mind. Something inside me made me feel sick when I thought of it.

If I were being completely honest with myself, that thought unnerved me. I wasn't sure why exactly. The thought of her death might have made me feel something close to human, maybe. Somewhere deep inside the pit of my stomach, something churned as if it had soured—like the death of this young woman bore a hole through my middle, making my legs feel weak. It was an unusual and disconcerting feeling.

I have no delusions about myself. More than once, I've been referred to as nothing more than an apex predator. Like a Tyrannosaurus rex, I am built to kill, with no reservations in taking the life of another. It sounded kinder than calling me a murdering psychopath or serial killer. Still, I don't shy away from those words either. Yet, the voice in my head screams for me not to let this girl die. This had happened to me only once before—that was the day my wrath was released upon the world.

I struggle with the planning. It wasn't every day that I had to work in "don't get the girl killed." I never worried about the casualties of my war. I am, of course, excellent at what I do, but mistakes do happen. Once I had it all worked out in my head, I decided she would probably come out with a few scars, but she'd survive. She'd even have a few barbs to write about—or one helluva good story to tell her grandchildren. Hell, maybe even a bestseller would come out of this. If nothing else, and the girl died, I'd have more names to add to my list. With that, I decided to talk to her and proceed with caution.

"My flat is off Mare Street in one of those overpriced historical renos. It faces the Lee River, allowing me to watch people. Do you know the place?"

"I've been there," she blurted out, happy to be conversing with someone other than herself. I smiled, thinking she was like a wind-up toy in desperate need of having her batteries removed.

"Hackney Borough is in London. Northeast London, right? Or is it referred to as East End? I'm not sure, really." Her voice was louder this time. It projected well through the wall, but she still sounded as if her teeth chattered when she spoke.

"When I was in high school, for my senior class trip. My first long-distance outing without my family. I thought I'd be a chicken heart, but I wasn't. I loved being out on my own without them hovering over me, always treating me like a child. I remember Wick and Dalston. There was a music festival near there."

I smiled at the history lesson and her willingness to share the most mundane information. This girl warmed me for reasons that escaped me. It was an unfamiliar experience to want to care about another person.

I had people in my life, but not anyone I felt I had to protect—not like this, anyway. When she spoke, I felt a gooey comfort inside, like a rich, warm chocolate. From the way she spoke, I knew she was grasping at survival, trying not to feel alone and scared. That made me feel strange.

"Which is the first? Do you know?"

"The first?" I asked.

"Yeah, the first. What part of London scared you the most? I mean, if Hackney is number four, then there must be a number one."

I thought about my answer. I knew with every fiber of my existence that I was drawn to danger. I lived for it. Sought it out. Created it.

The architecture of London, particularly in Hackney, has grit and strong bones. It's dirty and historically beautiful," I began. "But I'm not afraid of anything. And certainly not a place."

Pondering for a moment, I adjusted myself against the wall, shifting my weight to find a more comfortable position. My ass was numb and cold beneath my dress.

"I think a person's mind is probably the most dangerous place to reside. And teenage girls are the devil," I smirked. "They can be quite deadly. Nothing meaner on this planet than a teenage girl with an audience."

I gave her a small laugh. I had tried my hand at humor, hoping it would slow down her breathing and lower her heart rate. She was struggling, and I could hear it more frequently in the silent moments now.

"True dat!" she commented, using slang that seemed out of character but fit the mood as she returned the laugh.

"That's no joke, seriously. These days, they're like little badgers in yoga pants, 'tudes, and lattes."

As the quiet fell upon us, a light scratching sound could be heard. A faint and distant cry quickly accompanied it.

"We're not alone in here," she whispered.

THE DEVIL WAS IN THE DETAILS

1998 - SISTER MARY CHARLES

"This will be my final statement," I wrote at the top of the paper. I have tried to tell my story before. But my body would shut down, my mind would wander elsewhere, and the words refused to form in my mouth.

After writing the words, I paused momentarily, thinking of the words that would follow this statement, and then continued to draw over them repeatedly, until the paper wore thin and nearly tore, making the letters bolder. With each letter, I hoped I hammered home the point that I would not be doing this again.

Reflecting on it all, as I sat there, pen in hand, at a desk that had become part of my new routine, I realized I had been far more naïve than I could have ever imagined. A flicker of movement caught my eye, causing me to lift my head. The movement brought me back from my thoughts for just a second to see the same lady in the same white dress with the same intensity of a gargoyle watching over me, just as she had for the past year now. My constant shadow. My own private detail. My own Nurse Betty. I saw the question in her expression as she glared at me from the protection of the newspaper she pretended to read. Probably for my benefit, giving me just enough rope to hang myself if I felt so inclined. I waved the pen towards her, nodded my understanding, and continued my task as the woman observed. No one would try to murder themselves again today. I thought, perhaps, maybe tomorrow.

I wrote, "Though no one could have predicted the outcome of what would follow that day, it had not only changed my life forever but also that of those within my circle."

On that day, I sat quietly underneath that big magnolia on my favorite park bench, resting comfortably on the grounds on the east side of the campus. The sky had a pink hue as it welcomed the end of the day, and a gentle breeze had drifted through. I had immersed myself in the last few pages of "The World That Then Was."

I procrastinated on reading the assignment because of a book in another class. I had spent the worst part of two grueling days cramming in all the material for an essay on 'Angels and Demons in Today's World.' It had been my topic of choice, although I wasn't particularly excited about it. It was due that Monday morning. Who would have guessed I would write this instead?

When I finally lifted my head, I noticed the sun setting lower than before. The pink horizon had begun its fade to dusk. The sky took on a deep purple, and the stars twinkled brighter than I had expected. I saw the faint beginnings of Gemini appear in the southern celestial hemisphere. I wasn't sure what startled my thoughts from my assigned reading, but I quickly realized I hadn't been paying attention to the bus. I began to shout and wave my hands frantically above my head, hoping the driver would see me. If not him, then someone else on the bus would stall his exit.

I gathered my things and ran the 100-plus yards to the bus stop. I couldn't miss my ride back to Baptiste. As I ran out of breath, I began chastising myself for not being in shape. I appeared to take good care of myself, but I knew my cardio would fail me if I ever had to run for my life. Noticing the empty concrete bench at the end of the street, I slumped in defeat. I hadn't heard its arrival, but I had witnessed its departure.

As I waded through my internal tongue-thrashing, I already knew the answer to why I chose the park instead, and I felt my anger slip away. I liked the fountain next to the bench where I sat nearly every day. It was near the playground where the ducks often gathered. I enjoyed the rhythmic sprays that jetted out from the fountain. The sounds the ducklings made while playing in the water made me laugh—squawking and pestering one another with little bites from their beaks like children in a game of tag. I watched on as the mama ducks hovered about, on guard for signs of danger. Each one with its nervous tic and expression. Each one rounding up their babies. Sometimes, each other's babies, only to watch them scatter in seconds like breath on the white head of a dandelion pappus.

"This is what herding cats must look like," I said once to a fellow student who had sat anonymously at the other end of the bench one day.

"I wouldn't want that job," he offered with a kind smile. "They look exhausted," he observed and returned to reading his book.

That thought had amused me on more than one occasion as I laughed at the waddling circus that would commence during the duckling round-up each day. Clearly, no one had ever tried herding ducklings. Each mama duck worked unsuccessfully to sort her little ones from the others. They would splash and run through the sprays of beaded drops like children playing in the sprinkler on a summer's day. I remembered doing the same—bickering with my friends and classmates as we played. The baby ducks would bite and quack at one another as much as they rubbed heads and cuddled beneath the security of one another's wings. I liked that they found such joy in something so trivial, filling my days with so much joy.

Seeing no alternative, I dug through my bag, but couldn't find my coin purse.

"Great. Just great," I said again, but this time, I looked up, addressing the Great Heavenly Father. "I'm sure there is a lesson to be learned here, huh?" I said, irritated all over again. "Are you seeking an act of contrition for that Jedi crack?" I asked. "Well, Father, I am properly contrite," I said with a frown, knowing full well that I really wanted those Jedi powers and feeling like God knew it. "Since Jedi powers aren't part of the deal either, can I trade two Hail Marys for a quarter?"

I smashed everything back into my bag and began the trek across campus, back to my dorm. Directly across the street from me was a payphone, of course. But I had no change. At the time, I hadn't considered calling collect. That probably would have been a good idea, and maybe would have saved me from these white walls and the nurse standing guard. With it being a weekend holiday, I knew it would have taken an act of Congress to find someone to pick me up. Baptiste was gearing up to join the state in celebrating Fat Tuesday. You can imagine the chaos that would plague a Catholic church during that time. I had so much to look forward to, and I couldn't imagine missing a minute of it.

St. Constantine's was holding a baby benediction that Sunday morning, and a luncheon would follow that same afternoon. Babies offer the world hope. They promised new beginnings and that life would continue, even after it ended for others. And for those of us who had vowed and sworn our lives over in the service of God, babies weren't a part of the bargain. That made me think of Mama. How hurt she was to hear she'd never be a grandmother. However, replenishing and regrowth without any of us adding to the population were part of the rules. That had always been the most challenging part of my decision to join the church. I wanted to devote my life to Christ, but a small part of me felt cheated by not being able to be a mother.

The luncheon would find over three hundred people in attendance. I had already agreed to help and had the menu all planned out. While some of the other ladies, none of whom I would ever dare to name out loud, because the Lord saw all and knew exactly who needed a few more penances on their walk of righteousness. They shied away from that duty, leaving it to the novice and unprepared. But Mama had been nothing if not diligent in my home training because I was a natural party planner. I just never got to see how it turned out.

I was just about to cut across the grass when a voice called out my name. I honestly wasn't sure that I had heard him correctly. Not until he repeated it.

"Sister? Sister Mary Charles? Hold on there. Please wait."

He waved at me, gesturing for me to make my way in his direction with welcoming hands and a brilliant smile. Two years ago, that smile would have done me in. I made friends easily enough, and people seemed naturally drawn to me before. That part hadn't changed much, except now I was sober. I liked that I no longer demanded to be the center of attention and used booze to achieve it.

With that said, hearing my name on someone else's lips caught me off guard. Not that I was truly ever on guard. It was just that time of night. I had gotten used to being called Sister and even Mary Charles, but it seemed out of place then. I had adopted the name after taking my first set of vows. No one had ever called me by my given name again. Well, no one except Mama. Even my father had started calling me Mary Charles in the proper setting. But Mama still wasn't able to wrap her mind around her only child and daughter trading in a life of high society and political ambition for that of an impoverished nun. Mama couldn't understand, and nothing I could say would ease that hurt. She would never be a grandmother. She'd never see her only daughter walk down the aisle to marry the man of her dreams. She'd never see me run for Senate or become the first lady president.

I often regretted my quarrels with Mama, especially now. They never felt good when I looked back on them, but that had been our relationship. The more she wanted, the less I gave.

"Do you need a lift, Sister?" He yelled from the side of his car.

An expensive-looking rust-colored SUV sat near the sidewalk on the opposite side of the street.

With all my idiosyncrasies and insecurities, tepidness was not among them. I had never met a stranger that I didn't like or a potential new follower of Christ. Mama says that's why I would have made a skilled politician. I think that's what made me a good partier and an even better Sister. Stepping off that sidewalk changed the course of my life.

He eagerly approached me as if we were old friends. His arms were already reaching out to take the bag from my shoulder as if muscle memory had set in to repeat an act he had done a hundred times before. It was so familiar and intrusive. I should have guessed that his forwardness had so much more to it. But his eyes gave nothing away.

I paused to look at him, wondering how our paths could have crossed. There wasn't anything about him that was recognizable. He was charming, a little short, but nice-looking. His brown wavy hair was clean, and he was well-dressed. I imagine most girls in my position would have been more than happy to have a man like himself offer to take them home. I wondered if maybe I knew him from campus Mass. Somehow, that was a vague recollection, but nothing solid I could hold on to.

"I'm okay, but thank you," I replied, wrapping my hand around the handle of my bag, not allowing him to pull it from me and securing it to my side. This stopped him from taking it, but it did not disarm him.

"Philosophy 210, is that right?" He asked.

Then, his arm dipped around my waist and continued to usher me toward the open passenger door of his Range Rover.

"You're heading to Baptiste. I noticed you back at the stop. I'm on my way there myself, and I really don't mind giving you a ride." I noted that those were all statements rather than questions as if he had rehearsed them and had the words at the ready.

"I'm Liam," he continued, "Liam Williams."

He was doing his best to put his best foot forward, to sound like a convincing and sincere gentleman.

"How's Mother Agnes?" he asked, slightly stepping back, but it wasn't right. Something was off about it.

"I meant to call on her last week. My parents are very fond of her. We've known her personally since I was knee-high to a tadpole," he said through a laugh.

This had been his first lie.

I planted my feet like a tree, rooting myself like an immovable object so he couldn't move me.

The hairs on the back of my neck rose at the mention of Mother Agnes Valentine. Who had never, in her life as a nun, ever been referred to as simply "Mother Agnes" by anyone.

Everyone called her by her full title, Mother Agnes Valentine. She insisted on it because she wore it proudly.

St. Valentine was said to have been betrayed by those he served, imprisoned, tortured, and later beheaded on February 14, somewhere between 269 and 272 AD. Pope Gelasius of Rome canonized him in 496 AD. Later, he was removed from the Roman Catholic Church calendar in 1969 due to a lack of evidence of his good deeds. Yet, he is still known as the patron saint of lovers.

History may not agree, but it suggests that he was either a Roman priest or the Bishop of Terni.

There are several legends surrounding St. Valentine, but Mother Agnes Valentine was partial to the tale of a priest who secretly married Christian couples in defiance of either Emperor Claudius II or Emperor Aurelius's direct order.

Whichever emperor ordered the decree, they were of the same mind. They believed single men shied away from becoming soldiers because of their ties to their families. Needing men to fight their wars as a solution, one of these emperors denied all marriage requests across the Roman Empire.

Mother Agnes Valentine was a hard, fast, hopeless romantic.

She also had a fondness for a man who had been cast out because there were no witnesses to his good deeds. "Let not the left hand know what the right has done," she'd often say.

Feeling my senses chime and ding, something uncomfortable came over me.

I hadn't ever really experienced actual danger in my life. But I had grown up in a world of pleasantries, double-cheek kisses, snake deals, and backroom handshakes. My parents had groomed me for success from the time I could walk. And I was seeing what lay beneath those twinkling eyes and dimpled cheeks. His tone was clipped and fake. The words he spoke didn't match what was written in his body language. The bells and whistles were finally going off like tornado sirens on a naked Tuesday. I felt the beads of sweat begin to build on the back of my neck.

Did he think the outfit I wore made me look dumb? Did he think I was nothing more than some ignorant cow? I would know how to answer that now if I were asked. Yes, I was, in fact, that much of an ignorant cow. I was a fool not to be afraid. I still clung to the arrogance of my upbringing. The one that taught me nothing bad could ever happen to me because I was protected by the Queen of over-protective mothers. I think that's perhaps why I didn't balk at becoming a nun if I'm being honest with myself now. Maybe somewhere deep inside of me, I knew that if it didn't work out, I could always run home to Mama.

"No, I'm sorry," I said, again removing myself from his grasp by circling around him and, this time, letting go of my bag. There wasn't anything in there that I would miss if I had to run. The words of warning from Mother Agnes Valentine crept in amongst the bells and sounded louder than ever as they boomed in my head.

"Please be careful. You are getting yourself involved in something dangerous."

I hadn't been afraid before, but I was beginning to understand what genuine fear felt like. Then I thought of Mother's words as they rang through my mind, and everything clicked into place.

"I don't know you, and again, thank you, but I do not need a ride," I said directly and with less pleasantry. Panic bubbled up within me. It gripped my chest, and the air seemed to leave my lungs. It was so powerful. I could barely breathe.

"Come on, Sister, don't play hard to get. I'm a nice guy. You're a nice girl. Honestly, I think I should be wounded," he said, pinning on a hurtful expression and placing his hands over his heart as if he had been shot. "I've never had this much trouble getting a girl. Let's not play games, Kate," he said with a rueful smirk. "I've heard you're a pretty good time."

"Wait, Kate? He called me Kate." Then I covered my mouth.

I hadn't meant to say those words out loud. My stomach was uneasy because I didn't know what to do. Growing up, I had people who protected me from these types of ordeals. But since arriving at St. Constantine, I had shed that life and the luxuries that came with it. I had forged anonymity here. I was so far removed from that protection, and now my new home seemed more dangerous than anything I had ever experienced in my life.

His eyes changed, and I noticed that the generous smile that first lit his eyes like shiny black diamonds no longer showed the warm and inviting expression it had earlier portrayed. I watched the corners of his mouth twitch, and the kind façade evaporated, causing me to let go of my books, and I immediately turned to run.

By then, it had been too late. It had taken me too long to see the threat in front of me. The devil was in the details. Before I knew it, or before I could take another step, it was over. The impact of his weight knocked me to the ground, pinning me beneath him.

"Stop it!"

He commanded such authority that my body instantly froze. Then his hand quickly came across the bridge of my nose and covered my mouth, silencing any sound that could further escape me. As the tears began their journey from the outer edges of my eyes, I heard the screams in my head, loud enough to wake the dead. But no one above ground seemed to hear me. I struggled under the weight of his body and gasped for air. My lungs burned as I punched and kneed at him, to no avail. His hand was cutting off my air and weakening any attempts at fighting back. I stopped struggling when I saw the glint of the knife's blade. I also fell silent. I told myself that if I stopped struggling, then maybe he would let me go. It sounds ridiculous now as I write this down, but I was once that naive.

It felt like it only took a matter of seconds before he had me off the ground and into the backseat of his car. He pulled zip ties off the floorboard, pulled my arms behind my back, and zipped my wrists together, with no one seeing anything. No one to see me vanish from a sidewalk, under a bright streetlight, and in full view of the public.

I sat motionless in the back of his Range Rover, watching the road as he drove. I knew that stretch of the highway, having traveled it about every other weekend for about the past two years. He was heading to Baptiste.

I had considered that it was a practical joke that wasn't funny. Or even maybe Mama's way of teaching me a lesson—showing me I could be gotten to because of how important they were. No matter how far removed I made myself. I could see her doing something like that. She had built a name for herself. In her delusional and desperate way, she often tried to make me believe I could be fodder for those who waited on the sidelines to take them down. It makes me sad now when I think about how I viewed my Mama. I want to now believe that she just loved me that much and was only trying to protect me. It wasn't as if she had been wrong.

I lived the life that only dreams were made of—parties, football games, and more parties. High school had been a popularity contest that I had won. College hadn't started out all that much different. Booze and more booze. Boys and more drugs. Eventually, however, I figured out there was more I could contribute than debutant balls and booze-fueled sex in the backseat of cars with the next boy that made me feel good about myself. I fully admit that I had gone off the rails in my teen years. It had taken some time to reel myself in, realizing that no one would convince me to be a better version of myself. God had called me toward something greater than I had even expected. The more I read, the clearer it became where I was meant to be.

As we drove at a speed not to attract attention, I noticed the car slowed down, and the blinker indicated he was pulling over. There wasn't an exit in sight, and then the car pulled off onto the shoulder of the highway. I thought maybe he had to relieve himself. Didn't men do that all the time? I tried not to panic at the thought of being killed and dumped on the side of the road like trash as that image popped into my head. We were on a quiet, lonely part of the road, with few headlights coming or going. This sped up my heart rate. Unassuming people would be none the wiser. Cars pulled over for whatever reason all the time. Without a reason to do otherwise, anyone would keep their eyes forward and drive on with not a thought twice about what could be happening in the car next to them. Most of the world doesn't see a serial killer around every corner or, in my case, parked on the side of the road.

The man got out of the car. He whistled as he strolled to the rear of the vehicle. 'Life is a Highway' entered my mind. The tune he whistled as he swaggered past the door, hand in pocket like a man without a care in the world. I turned to look over the top of the backseat. Viewing him from the corner of my eye. He rifled through a backpack when he pulled out a bottle of water, a pair of shorts, and a T-shirt.

As he stared at me, a complete view of nothing but water and marsh was lost in a sea of darkness. He looked around to see if anyone could see him from any direction. With no witnesses, he crawled into the backseat and pushed me onto my back. I remember biting my lip to hold back the pain that shot through my shoulders and down to my wrists. As she sat on my chest, his knees pushed into my twisted shoulders, and he held the water bottle above my face.

"Open, Sister," he directed. "Don't make this harder than it needs to be. If I press here," he said, forcing a knee into my shoulder, "I can snap your arm. It will be quite painful, Kate. Please do as I say, and this will go easier for you."

I saw the strength in his expression. He wasn't playing around. He had the look of a man who would do some serious harm if I didn't comply. But I refused to make it easy for him. I squinted up my face like a mulish child refusing cough syrup and pressed my lips firmly together. Refusing to look away, I stared at him, shaking my head, "No."

A sinister smile crept across his face, the sides of his mouth turning up in a devilish grin as if to tell me how much he appreciated my decision. He shifted his weight, further forcing his knees into my shoulders, causing me to cry out.

He was good at masking his anger and hadn't been discouraged. He then cupped his hand under my chin, placing a thumb under my lower lip, and forced my lips apart with a gentle dig of his index finger. When he pressed into my shoulder like a trained seal, I again reacted with a silent whimper, and my mouth opened. He smiled again as he ran his thumb across my teeth. Gently at first, which alone said little, but I found the action nearly sadistic because of how he looked at me. He then quickly jammed his thumb between my teeth and stuffed the lip of the bottle into my mouth. The taste of iron danced on my tongue from the cut on my lip. He had drawn blood.

I felt the water fill my sinuses and run out of the creases of my mouth, soaking down my hair beneath my neck. By then, the tears began to flow hard, spilling from my eyes as they met up with the contents of the bottle, puddling inside my ears and along the backseat. I was soaked and nearly drowned, but enough of the water had made its way down my throat and into my stomach. I knew it hadn't been just water. My mouth felt like dry cotton mixed with blood and salt. I remembered enough of my crazy years to understand that feeling. It wasn't long before I felt my body relax, and I was face down in the backseat, dissolving into the fabric as the world faded away.

VERY BAD BAD THINGS

1998 – SISTER MARY CHARLES

A blanket of dead leaves and wet underbrush covered the path into the trees as I stumbled behind Liam. My body, as much as my mind, disobeyed my commands. As soon as I had one part of my body moving in the direction I had mapped out in my brain, the other part would fail, and I'd end up back in the same direction, following behind him. I had lost all ability to aid in my own escape.

I didn't recognize my surroundings, and my legs shook uncontrollably. I tried to see through the dark, but my brain felt like spaghetti being twisted up on a fork without the assistance of a spoon. My noodles were spinning and flopping all over the place. My eyes saw everything and nothing all at once. I couldn't focus on any one thing long enough to discern its importance. The ground seemed to melt beneath my feet with every step, trying to swallow me whole as I walked. Twice, I stumbled over myself and fell to my knees. Hard, sharpened edges of rock and undergrowth had cut deep wounds into my legs and the palms of my hands.

"Stop messing around! The sooner we get this over with, the sooner you can go home. Just keep that in mind." That was lie number two. It was then, in full venom of the serpent he was, that he reached down and yanked me up by my arms. "I've got plans for you, Sister," he said with a smile that didn't mask his intentions. "And keep your mouth shut. One word, and you'll never leave these trees."

I nodded my understanding, but he might as well have been talking Chinese. I was mostly oblivious to it all. By the smells around me, I had figured out that we were in a swamp. There was little difference between this body of trees and water and the area where I grew up. Of course, it had more creatures lurking in its waters that could kill you than at home. But it wasn't all that different from the snakes and spiders that could haul you off if they had a mind to. Their bites could be nasty and just as deadly. The dark was just dark. Not that I ever had time to really mull over what was hiding in the shadows of my pampered neighborhood. But then, in the middle of my noodled-mind, I wondered just how dangerous the two were when paired together. The pair created an atmosphere of grim prospects. Somewhere out there, very, very bad things were happening that didn't necessarily occur in the light of the day.

A fire was blazing high up ahead, scattering embers that fluttered back down like snowflakes and burned out as they touched the damp earth. The dirt path gave way to white footstones, leading to an abandoned stone building. Standing there between the wildly raging fire and the dilapidated structure were six men who drank and danced like the hunters I had once seen in a village outside Kulb, Sudan, during a mission trip in my third year of college. They spun in a half-circle, advancing themselves forward in a toe-tapping motion as they praised God for the success of their hunt and sought His blessings for their feats of bravery and honor in bringing down their kill. The meat they caught that day would be used to feed the entire village.

Watching their behavior reminded me of a scene from 'Lord of the Flies' when the small boys first started the fire and danced around the blaze like unbridled wild natives, without parental supervision to tether and squash their inner impulses. Left to their own devices, those who had read the book or watched the movie knew how that turned out. This wasn't an abandoned island. This was not the site of a downed plane. This was a swamp in Louisiana. All I could think was that I was watching those lost boys' older versions of themselves, reliving a moment from their past. I was watching the fallout of young boys who had become wild men.

They all smiled and cheered as if they were excited to see me. I remember those cheers from my party days. A compulsion overtook me, and I attempted to raise my arms in celebration and shouted to everyone, "Let the party begin bitches!" Hearing no one respond to me as he held my arms down, I realized that the words had tumbled out of my mouth incoherently, and I had been saved from contributing further to the indignity. As we drew closer, my eyes were alarmed by their faces. They didn't have real dimensions. Each of the men in front of me had something distorting their appearance. Each had a strange and ominous look. "Lord," I said aloud in a giggle – again, forgetting myself, I said in a laugh, "I am as high as a kite."

More than once along the trail, I was sure the trees were laughing at me. Their eyes winked, and their branches pointed accusatorily as they mocked my march. I remembered being high. I remembered that feeling, and this was so much more than that. I found that I didn't exactly hate it, and a part of me was ashamed. I saw wicked trees and demons. That part, I didn't like. In my confused mind, I saw the faces of biblical demons chanting and dancing around me. I no longer saw the little boys who had grown up and once danced like lords. The faces of who I perceived to be Leviathan, Sathanas, Belphegor, Moammon, Beelzebub, and Asmodeus taunted me. I knew that it wasn't real. But the harder I tried focusing on them, the worse it got.

The drugs he had given me had to be hallucinogens. The man set me on the ground. At that moment, I wasn't even sure I had feet, let alone legs, to hold me up. His face dipped close to mine, and I could see him in color. I couldn't help but think how wonderfully beautiful he was. By then, I couldn't recall his name, but he sure was pretty. I know he told me his name before, but it had disappeared from my thoughts like everything else. So then did his face. As I looked into his eyes, fear and panic crept through me like a wave spreading along a beach of rushing tides. I felt my body grip my insides as my bladder released, and urine ran down my legs and into my shoes. I was beyond terrified. Seeing my fear, he laughed and took a beer from a passing friend. It struck me then that God had nothing under control. He had no idea what he was doing. I was staring into the face of Lucifer. There, for the first time in my life, I felt God had abandoned me.

"The God I believed in wouldn't test me in this way," I heard myself whisper. But yet, there I was. I felt broken then and like a fraud as I asked, "Why me?" At a time when I should have turned to God for solace, all I could find was despair.

"God has nothing to do with this, Sister," he said, smiling at me. "And to answer your question— because I can," he whispered back, running a hand down my cheek. "Because I can. You should have stayed out of it, sweet Kate."

"Do it again!" "Do it! Do it!"

The chanting was loud. The words bounced around in my mind, pulling me away from his comments. As the men tossed back the beers, one of them, holding a clear glass bottle, spat its liquid onto the inferno. The fire raged like a dragon's breath as he drew flames from the fire. The cheers erupted as he did it again and again. Sending a hot burst close enough to singe his eyebrows. There were cans all around them, and articles of clothing had been discarded and scattered on the ground. I recognized a stack of cloth on a stump pile near the building. I had seen those jackets around campus. They were the jackets from a local fraternity piled neatly on top of one another. The only thing not in complete disarray. These were fraternity brothers. I tried to make out the emblems, but I couldn't read the Greek letters or focus on the patches. My skin grew cold as I sat alone on the ground. I drew my knees to my chest and, for the first time, realized that he had changed my clothes. The shirt and shorts were in my dresser back at the dorms. I rarely wore them, if at all, lately. I curled up tightly as I wondered what happened to my habit. He had lost interest in me for the time being, and I hoped that if I grew small enough, maybe the devil would forget I was there.

"Let's get this party started," I heard one man yell out as he crunched a beer can to his forehead. I watched him growl deeply and shake his head as if to shake off the pain of the impact. "Damn, that hurt!" he sang out as he danced, flexing his arms and puffing out his chest. Peacocking for the other's benefit, he threw the can to the ground.

"Take it off!" chimed another voice. This stirred the others, and they all began to sing. "Take it off!"

"Where did you find this one?" I heard a voice say as if it were coming from all directions. Then, a short man with a pudgy gut stood over me. He grinned as his eyes undressed me head to toe. "She's pretty lame. Are you sure she's up for this? She kinda lookin' like you got her out of the discount bin. Is she clean? I didn't bring any rubbers."

"Damn Dude!" Laughed another. "You got a crackhead to dress up like a nun? You're going straight to hell."

I watched Lucifer throw his empty beer can into the fire and walk back towards me. Once in front of me, he crouched down beside me. He reached down and removed my white tennis shoes and fed them to the flames. Shouts of laughter rang out across the guys. That action had earned him a round of high-fives from all around. The group was in full approval of his methods of rendering me barefoot. After that, he began to undo my wimple. Two simple pieces of black and white cloth covered my head, hiding my hair underneath. His eyes told me he was laughing at me. I flinched as he raised his hand towards my face. He paused momentarily as if to consider his next move. Then, he reached in and swiped back a piece of hair that had fallen into my face. The tender way of his gesture, as his eyes changed, almost fooled me. I didn't think the gesture was meant to be charitable, but the ease with which he could shift gears with such readiness sent a chill through me. As his eyes moved over me, I felt more like he was appraising me. He had weighed me out and had found me wanting.

"Kinda hard to run through here without those," he whispered with a grin as he shook one of my bare feet. "You really could be pretty, you know? Without all that," he continued, waving at my wimple that had been reduced to ash as it danced among the floating embers. "With a little makeup. A nice dress. I bet you clean up real nice. I'm sure I could get a lot for you," he bragged as he grazed a fingertip down my arm. "I hear you were a lotta fun back in high school. Where did that girl go, huh? Too bad we didn't meet sooner. This may have been a lot more fun for you."

I would have shivered in disgust if I had been able to feel anything. As my stomach churned, I fought the urge to puke. Maybe I should have just let it go. He knew all about me—even why I had become a nun. I want to believe I'd exaggerated Mama's delusions. I often felt like she was the enemy knocking at the door of my life. I'm not sure I truly felt abused by her, but she sure made it pretty damn clear that I wasn't to walk a different path unless she paved it first. This had set me on a head-on collision course with Mama as far back as I could remember. With God taking a holiday, Mama's voice, and all her warnings of what could happen if I didn't heed her words—well, there I was. Kidnapped, drugged, and had a man undressing me, not only with his eyes but with each tug of my clothes. I had hit the trifecta of the many ways Mama had warned would be my undoing. "I told you this would happen," I heard Mama say. The only thing left was to find my body in a trunk on the wrong side of the tracks. As I thought about that, I began to laugh. An uncontrollable, hysterical laugh bolted from somewhere deep inside, and Mama's voice rode it in triumph.

"Dude, my man, what did you give her?" asked one of the guys. "She's bat-shit looped," he laughed. "She's gonna be a helluva lotta fun," he chuckled as he tossed back his beer.

At first, Liam gently rubbed the strands of my hair between his fingers. Then he quickly shifted gears and grabbed a fistful, wrapping the ashy blonde strands around his fingers and pulling my face into his. The viciousness of the pull quickly halted my outburst. If he expected to see fear, it had been replaced. An old familiar stubbornness had seeped in, and "go fuck yourself" had taken root and set a fire in my belly. It had snuffed out any fear as I returned to my old mindset. I had come to realize that nothing I did would keep any of this from happening. Instead, I had decided to let the chips fall where they may and see who survived it.

I stared into his eyes, still unseeing his face, but I saw his soul. It was black and void. When I grinned at him, he leaned in and pressed his lips to mine. I didn't fight back. Instead, I pressed my face into his and took the full weight of the kiss. This seemed to anger him. The harder he kissed me, the harder I kissed back. Then he forced my mouth open with his tongue. It was greedy and violent. I felt him slip something into my mouth. It was another pill. And then another. At first, I tried not to swallow, but then, it just didn't matter, did it? I willingly accepted the pills. Maybe they would numb me to the world. The longer his mouth pressed to mine, the faster they dissolved and disappeared. There was absolutely nothing I could do to stop it, so I embraced it.

"Play nice with my friends," he whispered into my ear. "Or things will get a lot worse for you. That is a promise, Sister."

My arms and legs began to feel like jelly all over again, and soon, I melted beneath him, becoming one with the leaves and dirt. I expected to feel cold, but I was on fire. Like the nerve endings in my body were sparking off all at once. I felt as if warm water had been flushed through my veins, causing me to heat up from the inside out. Before I knew what was happening, he stood over me, removed the shorts and shirt he had taken from my room, and tossed them aside. Then, he lifted me up by my hips and removed my panties. "Do your worst," I said, staring up at him.

"That's exactly what I had in mind," he replied. He grinned sheepishly as he raised an eyebrow at me. "Well, these are curious," he smirked. "You're a naughty girl, aren't you, Sister? I don't believe these are good, godly girl-issued," he winked, twirling them on his index finger with a sinister smile. "You're full of all sorts of surprises." He then raised the lacy material to his nose and took in a deep breath, inhaling the scent of my panties before placing them into the pocket of his jeans.

"She's all yours, boys," he called out and stepped out of view.

I lay there, unable to do anything about what was happening to me. I felt the hands of one man and then another. Each set of hands roamed over my body in their own way. Each had their own personal touch. Some hands felt rough as if they had worked with them—while others were soft and gentle. My mind drifted off, and I wondered aimlessly about unimportant things as the hands roamed over my breasts, grazed my stomach, gripped my buttocks, and cupped between my legs. Mouths tasted my flesh as though I had been served up like a pig from a spit. The jerking of my body caused my head to fall to one side. Eyes wide open, I did my best to hold them there.

That had been the first time I noticed her. My heart sank at the sight of my friend. I hadn't been the only one who had been dragged off to party among the demons. As my eyes focused in on her, her body came into view. She was sitting propped up against a tree. Her face was locked on mine as if witnessing my descent into hell. It took me a moment to realize that her eyes were unchanging. Not even a flutter. They were lost in the dark as the blaze danced in her frozen features. She hadn't been just any girl. She was the reason I was here. She's the one I had confided in, who got the ball rolling that had led us to our death.

As I searched for signs that she could see me, I noticed that her hair was partly pulled from her ponytail, as leaves and grass matted down the strands no longer bound in the mass that rounded her face. She was down to a bra, a pair of cut-off shorts, and her skin showed the details of her art. Blue patches of design that I knew all too well, and my heart sank. I knew that red hair. Those markings. The makeup and the clothing. Tears now spilled from her eyes as recognition was made.

She mouthed, "I see you." I tried to call out to her. But as I opened my mouth to speak, she slowly shook her head. An indication I took to stay quiet. As her eyes slowly closed, she apologized, "I'm so sorry."

At that moment, I understood everything and nothing at all. I had connected the dots that had put us there, but couldn't understand how the seven of them were involved. Was that really how my story would end?—how our story would end? As I watched two of the men eagerly wait their turn with my friend, I couldn't help but ask God again why he would allow this to happen to me. To my shame, as I asked God that question, it was never, "Why had he done this to us?" I had sought the comfort of God's love over the comfort of money. I had sought humility over cameras, lavish parties, and power. I had embraced the life of servitude. As I struggled with how my life would end, my heart began to harden to the idea of God. As I watched my friend being tossed around like a ragdoll, my soul began to fire off in ways that if God could genuinely see my thoughts, I would be spending eternity in the fires of hell. For at that moment, my hatred wasn't for what they had done to me but for what God had allowed to happen.

"To the virgin sacrifices of hell's week," I heard a man call out—interrupting the curses that ran through my mind. They would have tumbled from my lips and burned God's ears, had I been able to form the words in my mouth.

"To the virgins!" the group sang out as one, unifying them in their deeds. They raised their beers to the sky and toasted us as if we were their heroes.

As I watched as the men cheered and clapped one another on the back, as if kidnapping and rape were award-winning accomplishments, I couldn't help but wonder if maybe I had been wrong when I thought I understood why we were there. Perhaps it was some sort of fraternity initiation haze. They were congratulating and welcoming one another into their brotherhood. My mind tried desperately to wrap itself around the words I was hearing. Was this seriously nothing more than a fraternity initiation? Nothing more than a sick and twisted game? As I looked around and saw the men in all their glory, it struck me that the idiots had no idea what they had gotten themselves involved in.

I thought that the virgins of hell's week sounded like one helluva good time, remembering there would have been a time that I would have blossomed in that sort of attention. I'd wear as little as possible, red solo cup in hand, and throw myself at the first boy who wanted to "sacrifice me." Thinking about the symbolism of it all. The virgins. If they only knew the truth, the joke would be on them. The story of the virgin Princess Andromeda had popped into my head then, and how she had been chained to a rock to appease Cetus, the Kraken, so that he wouldn't destroy the city of Joppa. At a pivotal moment, she is saved by her future husband, Perseus, and the Kraken is turned to stone by the headless Medusa. However, I had no Perseus to cut the head from a Gorgon and turn to stone the monsters that lurked in my shadows because I was no virgin. I wasn't innocent of wronging others. It could be God punishing me. Perhaps that's why he had forsaken me. I was a fraud—impure and now, truly unclean. I felt undeserving of my name and vowed that if I made it out of this, Sister Mary Charles would die here in the swamp, and Kathryn Daily would be reborn and set the world on fire.

"These two were really great sacrifices," Lucifer cheered, echoing the other's sentiment as I watched him tuck a knife into his pants and pick up a shirt from the ground. I recognized the shirt—it belonged to Caroline. It had a rock band unfamiliar to me printed on its front. Knowing she would love it, I gave her that shirt from the church's donation bin. She was into brand logos. Looking the part helped her blend in with her assignment, which involved investigating the girls who had gone missing around the parish. The beautiful girl with red hair who lay opposite me was my friend and confidant. We were friends who had joined forces to investigate a potential crime.

I grew concerned when I noticed she hadn't moved for a while. Her eyes had long since closed. I would miss those eyes. They were kind and told a story, in just the way she looked at you. She was better than me in all ways. She had led an exemplary life. One that she could be proud of, unlike me. I had dishonored my family. The only thing I managed to get right was finding God and becoming a nun. And even that did not save me. With the tears splattering down her face, her makeup ran together, creating a beautifully gothic masterpiece. The dark edges of her mask were smudged perfectly. I couldn't help but think I hadn't seen her look any more beautiful than she had right then.

"You comin', man?" The guy with the muscles and clean face called out. He, too, was pulling on a shirt over his head. "The guys wanna make a run to town and pick up more beer."

"Nah, y'all go ahead. Someone's gotta get these girls back home," he shouted back. "I'll meet you back here. And hey, don't forget to bring those rods. I've heard the fishing's been pretty good lately."

"Alright, man. See you back here. Thanks again, girls. You two deserve Oscars. Y'all were great!" The man called out. Then he ran to catch up with the others.

That had been lie number three. Once the others had cleared out, Lucifer returned to my side. As he looked down at me, the peaceful resolve I had found returned, and I could finally hear God's words. That's when I found my voice and recited the Lord's Prayer. I was just at the "forgive those who trespass" part when Lucifer bent over me and gently kissed my forehead. I had felt his lips against my skin that time.

"Against us," he said, just above a whisper, as he bent over me and then quickly inserted the blade of the knife between two of my upper ribs. "You didn't think you could get away with talking, did you, Sister? You should have kept your mouth shut. Those two girls are dead now because of you. They were very profitable, and my bosses don't like having to throw away good merchandise like that. They lost a lot of money, and that's on you. And then you had to go and involve her," he continued, gesturing a nod at my friend. "Not getting into my business shoulda been your business. You got her killed as well. For a woman of God, Sister, you sure do have a lot of blood on your hands."

When it was all over, I felt the blade of a knife enter my body six more times. As I felt the earth warm beneath me, I could only assume that the wounds represented one of each of the seven evils bestowed upon me—all seven sins—each of the men who played a part in killing us.

MOTHER AGNES VALENTINE

ACROSS TOWN - 1998

Mother Agnes Valentine sat at her desk grading papers late into the night. The class had been instructed to write a short paragraph defining Matthew 5:37. She did not want them to simply recite the verse; instead, she wanted them to explain its meaning in their own words. She wanted to know if they understood that using the Lord's name while taking an oath or making a promise was a sin. She wanted them to acknowledge that doing so undermined their own character and honesty as individuals. As she read through the works of the future Hemingways and not-so-very Poes, one thing stood out. She'd have to speak with Sister Mary Thomas about the children's penmanship lessons. By the scribble, she had to work too hard to decipher. Either the sister's lessons were not being put to good use, or she wasn't teaching them at all.

"They are 5th graders," she mused, irritated by children their age unable to form coherent sentences.

Mother Agnes Valentine got up to stretch out her legs. Her mind whirled with concern, and she knew that her worries were not helping her grade the assignments she could not read. Her niece Caroline would be visiting tomorrow night, and she grimaced at the idea of having another Mexican dinner. Of course, this could be an easy fix if they flipped for it. That's how they settled most things between themselves. In truth, her youngest niece had always been her favorite. Understanding that with a sigh, like most things, she'd probably cave into whatever she wanted. She reached over and picked up a roll of antacids, thinking she might need to prepare herself. She just hoped that her niece's unprompted visit wouldn't bring troubling news.

The other concern she had was that Sister Mary Charles had yet to return home from school. It wasn't like her to skip out on her responsibilities, nor was she ever late. This worried her more than the lack of legible penmanship or the prospect of suffering through another Mexican dinner. Even more than the troubling news Caroline may bring. As she popped the antacids into her mouth, she took the need to get up and move about as a message from God. Her old bones had been giving her troubles, and she wasn't having the kindest of thoughts. She looked up at the clock and noticed the time. Her favorite program would be on in ten minutes, and she welcomed the mindless distraction from her intrusive images.

She had few vices, though society would say she were to have none. She wished she could own being the type of nun who looked the part in all areas of her life. But she counted on her devotion outweighing some of her lesser godly qualities. She had always wanted to be a nun, but hadn't grown up in the sort of environment that encouraged the path leading to the almighty. She had reconciled herself to the fact that there would be no feast day to honor her. Besides, she swore too much and, once upon a time, fought the need for a drink. She hadn't become a nun to seek personal glory anyway. She had devoted her life to serving the Lord, hoping that it would bring her some redemption, as she felt she was guilty by association. She hoped to save her family from the same fate she believed had claimed her ancestors. And even the not-so-distant ones. She had devoted her life to the church as a teenager and had kept her vow of chastity through high school, honoring her commitment.

Sitting down in the comfortable green velvet chair, she reached for her pipe. The chair had belonged to her grandmother. It was the only piece of furniture original to the family home. She had taken the chair with her when she moved out and took residency in the church down the driveway beyond the field of flowers. Her brother, Franklin, had married and started his own family. The chair was old and worn. And it did not match the rest of the furnishings that her sister-in-law had picked to replace the old blood that had been a part of the home for generations. Out with the old and in with the new had been her way of thinking. Watching generations of belongings being hauled out and thrown away had broken her heart. For the sake of her relationship with her brother and his children, Mother Agnes Valentine had kept her mouth shut. She ran her hands over the quilt. The quilt had been used to cover the chair over the past few years. It held back the springs and padding that had begun to break down and poke through. But she could still smell her mother in the chair. She imagined that when the time came for her to pass it on, whoever received the chair would do the same.

The pipe had belonged to her younger brother and her father before him. As she filled its bowl, she could smell the aroma of John Middleton's apple-flavored tobacco, which often made her think of her father. She savored the flavors, letting her hair down, and began untangling the mess that had been tucked up and bound all day. Then, she grabbed a brush and waited for the program to start.

The program began as it most often did, with its two most frequently used openers: "Up Next" and "Until Forensic Science Led Police to the Killer." However, a red line ran at the bottom of the screen only a few minutes into the program, interrupting the episode. "Live from Baptiste, Louisiana, in Marie Anjou Parish." She stopped what she was doing to read the emergency broadcast as it ticked along the bottom when a familiar face appeared on the changed screen.

She thought this was odd, considering it was extremely late, and what news outlet would be airing live this time of the night? That meant it had to be serious. The face on the screen was that of a local woman and native Baptiste resident, Jurnee Matthews. Affectionately called "Little Girty" as a child, she was now known as "Jurnee to the Weather," which aired every weekday from 6:30 am to 7:00 am. Seeing her little Girty and former student on the television was a treat every morning. But this was not the norm. Girty had about three more hours before the weather broadcast would set the day's tone.

"I'm currently standing steps away from L'eau Rouge Bayou in an area where the Arcadian Parish and the Marie Anjou Parish intersect," Jurnee began. "MAPS has been dispatched this early morning to a gruesome discovery where individuals had planned a weekend camping trip. This reporter has learned that a barrel was uncovered over in that area," she continued, gesturing at her cameraman. She instructed him to pan his lens in the direction she was pointing. It was clear that she hadn't done many on-location broadcasts before, if ever. She spoke with her hands; her gestures were erratic and wide, while her face bore eyes seemingly too big, and did not blink. As she moved, it was all she could do to keep from toppling over. The hem of her skirt was too tight, and her muck boots were too big. It was obvious that they did not belong to her. "A Med-Air Chopper is said to be arriving shortly, and there is word that a woman's body has been found," Jurnee continued to say.

"My poor Girty," she giggled. Then she placed a hand over her mouth to muffle the laugh as if someone had witnessed her being unkind. But Jurnee had her full attention when she heard that a woman's body had been found. Agnes had spent the weekend worried, and now her stomach had dropped. Almost everyone had noticed Sister Mary Charles's absence, and she couldn't pretend she wasn't concerned about it.

She was now standing inches from the television. She searched each section of the frame, hoping, praying, and pleading. While her eyes were trained on the screen, she reached into her gown and pulled out her rosary. She placed it up to her lips and waited for Jurnee to finish her report.

Jurnee placed a hand over her ear and immediately stopped talking. She did her best to appear professional while posing awkwardly for the camera. She wanted her best features to shine through, though she came across as clumsy and unsure of herself. She listened intently to the person on the other end of the earpiece, receiving information from an undisclosed source.

"Oh My God!" Jurnee burst out loud before she could stop the words from rolling past her lips. She could not hide her shock, and her words cracked several times before she could finish her statement. "I have just been informed that the body found is that of college student Kate Daily. For those of you who have not been paying attention to the news, she was reported missing yesterday morning in Oklahoma after she missed her weekend check-in with her parents, Oklahoma Governor Harrison Daily, and his wife, former Attorney General LJ Daily."

Mother Agnes Valentine's heart sank as she fell to her knees. LJ had rung her phone off the hook for nearly two days straight. But Agnes had no answers for her. She hadn't missed that Sister Mary Charles of St. Constantine's, right there in Baptiste, hadn't been mentioned in the report. But she didn't expect that it would be. Kathryn's parents were people of power and wealth. Mother Agnes Valentine wasn't sure the world would take notice of one missing nun. However, the country would be paying attention upon hearing that it was the beautiful daughter of a power couple. Tears ran down her face, heartbroken at the news of another loss. She reached for a phone and dialed as she continued to listen to the report.

Jurnee, again, covered her ear to listen to the information being disseminated from the earpiece. Her eyes widened, and she turned to look into the trees. "Did you say they are alive?" Jurnee asked, shocked at the voice she heard. "Wait, can you please repeat that? Did you say they found a second body? Please confirm. They are both alive?"

THE WATCHER

NEW ORLEANS – YEARS LATER

The sound of a car's horn blaring and its brakes bringing what sounded like the weight of the Titanic to a screeching halt caused her to stir. By the sound of the car's engine and the way the air moaned under the weight of real steel slowing in the swells, it was clear that the car was old and heavy. He didn't have to look in the direction of the noise to know that he was right. The male voices could be heard throwing swear words at one another while onlookers laughed and added commentary to an already heated situation—further instigating a fight between the two men.

A man's voice could be heard yelling out. His tone, obviously spooling for a fight: "You trying to get yourself killed, you dumb shit?!"

The second man's reply followed, "No, sir! I'm just drunk."

Then, he and others erupted in drunken laughter and male bravado. A few giggles escaped from two different women, whose voices were smoky and heavy on tipsy. What sounded like the beginnings of a street brawl of whisky-fueled testosterone was over in just a few seconds. The drunken twenty-somethings weren't interested in a fight. They were looking to have a good time and hopefully get laid—not trade punches.

Liam groaned at the chaos. When it finally grew quiet, he returned his gaze to the room. It wasn't exactly the kind of peaceful quiet that one might find under the stars where civilization hadn't touched, but it was as quiet as a city of thousands could be during one of the most celebrated times of the year.

A jazz band played in the distance, showing that the city was still in Carnival mode. He loved New Orleans for this very reason, but not for the reasons that most would expect. Most people visited for its culture and beauty—a few for its history and tradition. But most didn't look past the colors and the theater. The underbelly was dark and ugly. Tourist dollars masked the city's violence, and the citizens often paid the price. He was here for that. For the women who wandered too far off Bourbon alone. For the girls whose parents thought they were "old enough" to be left unsupervised. He was a collector.

He watched the woman in the bed stretch, and when the nod of her head began to tap out beats, he knew that the city had once again grabbed her attention. That's when he heard a stereo click, and the sound of Ice Cube's "Frankenstein" cut through the air, drowning out the smooth tenor of Thelonious Monk's "Round Midnight." He saw the expression on her face. The upturned curl of her lips. That smirk that excited him. She looked as if she were about to cause trouble. He could tell by the way she moved that this was her song. Loudly, she began to sing along to the words. He watched as her inner gangster woke, and she stirred to life.

She then pushed herself onto her elbows and slapped away at the tiny cross that had adhered itself to her cheek. It had left a slight indentation on her face in the shape of its likeness. He wondered why the vampire in her hadn't burst into flames. He had a pretty good idea of her misdeeds beyond what he had witnessed for himself. He didn't understand why a woman who was responsible for the things she had done still wore a cross. Envisioning her burst into flames and her ashes scattered to dust wasn't altogether unappealing. He smiled at the thought. Then he chuckled, hearing the irony in the song—this monster he had created.

He wondered if her slow delivery indicated that she'd let her guard down, but when she continued to rock on as she inspected the door, he knew she was still alert, even if she'd had a bit more to drink than he'd noticed before. The door had two deadbolts and a chain latch securing it. He knew, as well as she, that those locks wouldn't keep anyone out who really wanted in. They were purely a source of false security. Silver duct tape had been placed crisscrossed over cracks in the middle of the door.

Management had told him that the damage had been her handiwork. A few weeks earlier, they had accidentally given the room to another customer after she made it clear that it was hers and hers alone. She expressed her displeasure by kicking in the door and dragging the occupants out into the parking lot. This was an accident they would not repeat.

The window was framed in heavy black curtains and held a rusted-out air conditioner. He knew that it didn't work. When he had gained access to the room late last week to plant his camera, he thought he'd suffocate from the smell. The warmth of the room only made the stench worse. Management had informed him that the current tenant wasn't all too happy with the air quality either and issued her complaint by smashing the clerk's face into the counter.

"She threatened to remove my future offspring," he told Liam. "Her exact words! I should have called the cops. I can't even tell you how afraid I am of her. She's fucking crazy, man. She said she was going to feed me my sack. Again, her words." Corky—the man's badge read—wiped at the sweat dripping from his forehead. He looked close to tears. "I told her that someone would be by her room soon. Then she grabbed me by my face and slammed my head into the counter. Look what that bitch did to my face," he cried, pointing at the gash that ran down his cheek and the purpling black eye that had his eye swollen near shut. "She told me that the room made her balls sweat," he continued in near hysterics. "Her balls, man! Have you ever heard a lady talk like that?"

Corky's sweaty demeanor wasn't caused by the office having the same AC problem as her room. This clearly indicated that he wasn't lying when he said he feared her coming back. The thought of her balls sweating made Liam laugh. When he first discovered that she had survived their time in the swamp, he wanted to find her and finish the job he had botched. She had seen his face, and he couldn't risk her telling anyone who he was. Yet after seeing his handiwork, watching her in action, he was excited by her. And he thought he had issues. He was a kitten compared to her. He only killed to protect his marketability and reputation. Even if he didn't mind killing people, it really wasn't personal. It was just business to him. The people he killed were nothing more than a bad investment, and he was cutting his losses. She did indeed have balls. Big brass ones, and he loved the show.

"No, sir," he chuckled, thoroughly amused by Corky's outraged description of the woman. "I can't say I have had the pleasure. But I don't reckon she's much of a lady, do you? I mean, you are renting that shithole to her by the hour, right? Surely, that gave you some idea of her character? And I wouldn't recommend calling the cops. Do you really want to add to the number of patrol cars coming through here? Wouldn't that be bad for business? And take into consideration, I do business here. It would be bad for me," Liam said with a glare. "I can always give you a match to that eye, or worse," he hinted, hoping he made his point clear. "Now, give me the key to her room," he said. "And keep your mouth shut."

The pale pink paint was peeling in different areas of the room, exposing its 70s wallpaper underneath. It's ugly, blotty printed roses and tiny, unrecognizable yellow flowers were tacky and lacked dignity. The bottom half of the room's cheap brown caravan-style paneling had scratches and dents on nearly every visible spot. He could only imagine what that bed was covered in. The room reeked of cat piss, cigarettes, mildew, and sex. And lots of it. Along with the heat, it was a wonder that no one died from toxic fumigation. But this was just her sort of place. She would feel at home here. More relaxed. Just the kind of place she would let her guard down.

"Well, that was fun," she said, looking around the room. Her accent was heavy.

He had to admit, her accent puzzled him, among other things. Perhaps that could explain itself in due time. It was going on 3 a.m. The light on the building underneath him had begun to flash, just like it always did at this time of night. This was the beacon that lit up the street, signaling for taxis to start lining up to collect the patrons who piled out of the bars.

"You ain't gotta go home," a man's voice rang out as he opened the bar's front door. "But you can't stay here." That was Joe. He knew Joe pretty well. Joe was one of her guys; he was just her type: young, dumb, loyal, and nice-looking. Joe had a southern twang cut by Marlboros and Texas. And massive arms built by Gold's. He'd have to be careful around the guy. Joe looked out for her and used his size to her advantage. He didn't think much of Joe. Joe was a meathead, and he'd been in and out of trouble his whole life. But that wasn't what bothered him about Joe. Hell, Joe was an employer's dream. Willing, strong, and dependable. That said, Joe wasn't very bright and was loyal to only one person. The combination made him extremely dangerous. If he were serious about wanting to get to her here, he'd have to kill Joe first. He didn't mind the idea of that, but he wasn't the young man he used to be, and he didn't relish getting himself killed by taking Joe one-on-one.

He watched her hand fumble across the table. Her fingers scrambled in search of something. A phone, perhaps? If that were the case, she wouldn't find a phone anywhere. He knew she didn't have one on her when she entered the room, and she didn't have one on her back at the bar. As far as he could tell, she never had a phone with her. She made no calls to anyone. Unless she was here, she was most often alone. She didn't entertain friends, and those loyal to her kept their distance. She had no people other than guys like Joe and the many nameless unlucky souls she brought back here.

"Lord," she prayed as she sat up. "Not you," she corrected, "The other one." It wasn't a prayer, exactly. It was more like she cursed the man above and then switched to a God of her liking. "Goddess Eir, if you are listening," she countered, "I could use another drink. And an aspirin."

He had been watching her off and on for months now—frustrated that his attempts to locate her outside of New Orleans had not been fruitful. But she always returned here. So, whenever he returned home, he made it a point to stop by the hotel and check in on her. He liked the new her. She was brash and unapologetic. He watched her survey the mess that covered the floor, and then she flung her legs over the side of the bed. Sitting on the edge of the bed, she didn't bother covering herself. He appreciated that. It's not like anyone was watching, right? He smiled as he thought about her time with the stranger. He couldn't look away.

Then he thought back to their time in the swamp and wished that he had taken his turn like the rest of them instead of only facilitating the setup on the fraternity assholes. He had used their function as a means to an end. It didn't take much convincing to rope them in on the idea of nailing a virgin, even if the two women were just stand-ins. A little booze, a brilliant idea, and just like magic, an event for Hell's Week had come together. He needed the two girls dead. It was him or them. And he wasn't going down because people couldn't mind their own business. It had been easier than he planned to make them all complicit in the murders. Well, most of them. But with a bit of twisting, they were all guilty of kidnapping, rape, murder, and an actual homespun cover-up. He made sure they all understood what the cost would be if they spoke.

She collected men like flies. He wondered what it was about her that drew them in. Even he couldn't answer that because he hadn't seen it back then either. There was nothing particularly special about her then. And now, it couldn't just be her beauty alone. Plenty of beautiful women didn't have men falling on their swords. She killed with impunity, and she enjoyed it. Maybe that is what made her stunning. In all her faults, he believed her to be the most honest person he'd ever encountered. Other than her look, there wasn't anything pretentious about her. She didn't give two fucks about what anyone thought of her, who she offended or shocked. He had seen it time and time again. She simply didn't care about any one person's feelings enough to lie to them—even the reason for killing them.

She had a fantastic body, and he liked that she knew it. She wielded it like a weapon. "I am like a brilliant fuckin' Van Gogh," he once heard her tell a man who was staring at her a little too long. She wasn't offended, but she had warned him off. "You can look, Baby, but don't you go getting yourself any ideas." After warning the man against touching her, she then gave the man a coy smile. He knew as well as she what the man had intended. And he knew that smile. If the man were wise, he'd have gotten off the trolley at the next stop. Yet the man hadn't heeded the warning, and he watched as she left the man in a heap in the alley, bleeding from a gash left in his groin. Liam was sure to take credit for that. He had made her into what she was. He was also pretty certain that if he had her body, he'd strut himself naked down Bourbon. Hell, maybe she would, too. Maybe she had. Nothing surprised him concerning her, except that she was still alive. She had seven seriously fatal wounds. He couldn't understand how it was possible that she was still upright.

She barely seemed to register the man sleeping on the other side of her. It was challenging to read her thoughts. She was unpredictable and rarely did the same thing twice. He doubted her indifference to him was a lapse in judgment. She truly wasn't worried about the man next to her. She was always four steps ahead and placed herself between the man and the door. This was usually the point in the show where she decided what to do with them. She reminded him of a kid who collected things in jars. She let the moths go but pulled the wings from the butterflies. Why only the butterflies and not the moths? He figured out this was when she decided who would lose wings or be set free. He wasn't sure how the loser got picked. Who was business, and who was for shits and giggles. There was a possibility that she mixed the two to make her life more interesting.

"You poor bastard," he said aloud. "You don't stand a chance in there. Are you a butterfly or a moth?" He was trapped in that glass jar with her and had no way to escape unless she removed the lid.

As she looked around the room, her focus stopped when it caught sight of what she was interested in. She stretched over the sleeping man to grab his cigarettes from the nightstand. As she did, she placed her bare breasts directly into his face and pressed down. He did not move. She smiled at him, looked around the room again, then put a Camel nonfilter between her lips and struck the match. She examined the flame before lighting the cigarette and then blew it out. Afterward, she held the match to her nose and inhaled. The scent of the match seemed to excite her.

"At least this one has good taste in smokes," she said as she continued to stare at him. "Les filtres sont pour les chiennes. Je ne le tuerai pas aujourd'hui. Il était plutôt bon au lit."

He had to think for a minute. He wasn't the sharpest knife on the block when it came to the foreign bullshit. He had learned just enough Cajun French to make him believable, but it was shoddy at best. He did, however, understand, "bitch and kill." And something about sex. Maybe the little kid in her had decided to show mercy on the winged creature. He had to admit that this had disappointed him. It wasn't like her to play with her food. This meant that he was just for fun, and that had irritated him. He had come to see her in action. Not watching a drunken college boy get lucky. The little shit didn't need the bragging points. Maybe he would do something about that later as well. Take out Joe and this boy.

"Hot damn," she said, pleased with his appearance, as she looked at the sleeping man. Then, she lifted the sheet for another appraisal. She took a long drag of the cigarette while observing him and seemed pleased with what was underneath the sheet.

He could tell by the way she moved that she was wrapping up the night. She quickly gathered her dress and heels off the floor. She had been dressed simply. No bra. No panties. No hose. He had learned a great deal about women's fashion over the years and found that her simplicity worked best for almost any occasion—especially with the girls he dealt with. He could turn a girl out, collect the money, and have her move on to the next client quicker if she had less baggage. As she stumbled, he wondered if he had been too quick in his assessment. Maybe she was a lightweight, and he'd have to adjust just how much to give her when it was time. She had nearly gone ass over teakettle into a chair. "For fuck's sake!" she cried, her eyes narrowing at the sleeping man as she kicked at one of his boots. "I may have to change my mind." She snarled through clenched teeth. "So much for my quiet escape."

She glanced over at the stranger to see if her tumble had woken him. His face twisted a bit at the sound of the chair smacking the wall, but his reaction was minimal. She then dropped to the side of the bed and pulled out a suitcase from underneath it. She opened it up and pulled out a change of clothes. Then, she quickly searched through the case before slapping the top down.

"Uhhh... What the fuck?" she growled, agitated. She reopened the case, stuffed the dress from earlier and the heels inside, pulled off the wig, and placed everything on top of the pile. She then zipped it up and shoved the case back underneath the bed.

He watched her pull the door closed on room 108. It was a bottom-floor unit and visible from his viewpoint. This "No Tell Motel" was poorly lit, and Liam had used it for that very reason on several occasions. It had been fortuitous the day he saw her leave that room. He walked right past her without really looking at her. It had taken him days to remember her face. When he did, a panic welled up within him that he wasn't sure he could choke back. A busted-out street lamp helped to conceal him as he watched her from the third-floor fire escape on the old but not abandoned building across the street. He wondered if she would hail a cab or hitch a ride. He considered offering her a ride and then thought better of it. It wasn't time yet. He got his answer when she drew her fingers to her smeared red lips and whistled. Even still, in her walk of shame, he thought that she was absolutely stunning. Her hair hung naturally, with no wigs or hairdos to disguise her natural hair. Everything else about her was, as he had remembered, just older now. She had grown up and filled out. He liked the blossoming curves. But somehow, she was so much more.

She looked innocent, standing there in bare feet. He assumed that was what had upset her about the suitcase. He traded on that innocent look every day. He did, however, hate the shorts. They were tacky. And the Masters of the Universe T was childish. It read "Hello Ladies" across the top with a picture of He-Man below the writing. Perhaps if he kept her, he'd help her improve her wardrobe. Pick out things like that red dress she had previously piled on the floor. He liked that. Just thinking about her in that dress stirred him up again. Her face sparkled under the light, probably from all that crap she had on her face. Her blue eyes and freckles added to her look. Even when he knew that nothing about her appearance was real. The freckles had been exaggerated, and the long, crazy lashes were not her own. And he knew she had the darkest brown eyes he had ever seen on a woman. They were not blue at all. He thought that taming the monster he had created could be extremely exciting. Or seriously stupid.

He had started his descent from the fire escape to a black Tahoe when he saw her wave. Not sure what to do, he ducked back into the shadows just as Joe exited a doorway off the bar. She waved at him again and gave him a thumbs-up. She was letting him know that she was okay. Joe waved back before heading in the opposite direction away from her. Liam saw the driver of a Crown Vic pull up. She was an older, heavy-set black woman in a large purple hat with gold and green feathers. She was enjoying the night's festivities.

"Oh, chid," she started, leaving out the "L" in her pronunciation of child. "Ain't yous a sight? Why yous ain't gots no shoes on?" He heard the plush cabby ask her. Her head was nearly out the window, as she waved her over. "You get yourself in here! You tryna catch a death?" The cabby's accent was a thick bayou, soaked in genuine sincerity.

She opened the rear door and slid into the woman's cab. Then she wiped the bottom of her foot off with the palm of her hand and plopped the bare foot up along the edge of the front seat. The round-faced driver got a good look at the bottom of her dirty sole.

"Something like that," she said, looking out the window towards the street. "I'm just waiting to see who bites," she added, shooting the woman a cheeky smile.

The woman let out a deep and robust roar of laughter that nearly shook the car and set the cab to drive. "Yous got jokes, Mon Cher. Yous got jokes. Where ya headed to this time?"

"It's a drive. Are you okay turning off the light?" she asked. Then she handed the cabby a small rolled-up tube of bills. "Here, for your trouble and the Mister."

The cabby took the money, and without unrolling it, she tucked it into her bra. Then he watched as the light on the roof of the cab went dark. "Got it, Cher. I'll take you wherever you wanna go."

He followed just far enough away not to be noticed. The distance gave way to a familiar terrain the longer he followed. He nearly had a stroke when the cab pulled up to a perfectly landscaped cathedral-style church. The church sat on an old plantation that had lost none of its former beauty, though it looked empty. He would have thought that her ties to this place had long since been severed. He watched her exit the cab and thank the driver for what he assumed was her discretion. A person didn't spend that kind of money just for a ride. She was obviously paying for the woman's silence.

"Call anytime, Cherie," the driver yelled, waving at her. Then she put the car in reverse and set off back in the direction from which she had come.

He watched her as she quietly circled to the side of the building to a single-entry door. She pulled a key from her pocket, inserted it in the lock, and pushed open the door. She stopped before entering and looked in the direction of the road. Her gaze was far away but discerning. It was like she was seeing ghosts. He wondered if he had been seen after all. Her eyes twinkled as they held tight to the road, and he felt her eyes had locked on him as if she was looking into his soul again. It was only a brief moment before she went inside. But he swore he saw a smile creep along her lips as she turned away.

WE KNOW WHAT WE KNOW

T obias waited in the alley off De La Rue End for his contact to show. "Off The Street" came to a dead end facing a seamless brick wall recently painted white and covered with an elaborate mural. As he watched towards the mouth of the only entrance down the dead-end, cars passed as a few pedestrians waited to cross the intersection, and the meaning of the road finally clicked. His eyes caught the edge of an outline that was only noticeable if you stood in the right spot. De La Rue, a new pub, was named after the street where it was located. It had been positioned strategically at the end of De La Rue End and could only be seen from the street, with its door blending seamlessly into the white brick wall. Its doorknob was hidden within the mural. The mural painted across the brick was comprised of a beautifully constructed funeral procession, a horse-drawn hearse, jazz instruments, black umbrellas, and festive mourners.

Tobias felt mentally and physically drained. The flight from Okinawa, where he'd been working, far from the bayous of Louisiana, had him feeling out of sorts. He hadn't been all that excited when he had been volun-told to return home. The Old Man often tried to come across as though everything was a request, but they all knew better. It wasn't a suggestion. More recently, he had warmed to the idea of calling Baptiste home. Something he wouldn't have thought about in his younger years, as he missed Lockerbie. It had seemed so big to him as a child, but it wasn't much bigger than Baptiste. Over time, his memories of the place had dimmed away. It was now like a once vivid color that had faded to gray and slipped to the farthest parts of his mind.

As he thought about home, he wondered what it was about the swamps of Louisiana that drew in such people. Over the years, Louisiana had been the home of at least twelve known serial killers, possibly sixteen more unconfirmed, and the hordes of pirates, outlaws, and gangsters that had congregated over the past three centuries. Maybe it was its rich history. Perhaps it was the lure of openness and easy access to limitless disposal sites. Who needed a hog to devour a dead body when you had alligators and endless waterways to wash away almost anything one could dream up?

Before joining Interpol, Tobias was part of a Marine recon unit. Being a soldier had given him the opportunity to find himself, but he never felt as though he was making a difference in the world. He had some idea of what his father had done, and that is what he wanted for himself. And like his father, he would have to branch out. The Old Man hadn't wanted him to follow in his footsteps. But Tobias was his father's son after all. He liked the structure the military had provided and the connections it had made for him. Interpol was just a stopping point on his way to something more. He knew he wouldn't get that working in an office, but having a former intelligence officer as a father had its perks. It wasn't so much what he had done but rather who he had done it for. That is what had built his father's reputation.

"Those will kill you," he heard a man with a deep voice say as he passed by him and then stopped. Tobias, who stood with his back resting against the wall, took a deep drag and then pressed the last of the cigarette into the wall before turning to face the man with the voice.

He laughed. "So will getting shot. But you never tried to talk me outta that now, did you?" The streetlamp shone brightly on the man's face as he stepped out of the shadows. With a hefty slap to the back, the men embraced one another in a tight hug.

"Gunny," Tobias said. "It's been a while. You're looking a little gray over there," he teased, pointing to the barely-there gray hairs that shadowed his temples below the still-full head of black hair. "Is that cut regulation?" Tobias asked, noticing Bishop now sported a longer cut rather than the high and tight he was so used to seeing Bishop wear. "Looks like retirement suits you," he said with a smile.

Bishop laughed at the teasing. He had missed the boy who had grown into a fine man, soldier, and friend. They were brothers. Brothers who were united by the camaraderie that only men and women of combat could understand. Bishop hadn't known this squared-away soldier and Interpol agent as a young boy, but he would bet the farm that Tobias had been a force to be reckoned with in his youth.

"Have you seen your father?" Bishop asked, feeling somewhat guilty about having all this done in secrecy and behind the Old Man's back. Bishop almost looked apologetic.

"No. And I don't think I will. I wanted to meet with you first and see what you thought. I don't think it's a good idea for anyone to know I'm here. We need to work out a game plan or something." Tobias ran his hands through his hair, a bit tired but more bemused. "Madness, right? I was hoping to be wrong. When I saw her in Tokyo, I knew it was her. She looked different, though. But it was her. She didn't even acknowledge me. She walked right past me like I wasn't there. I might be overreacting, but I know what I saw."

"That's probably best," Bishop said, meeting his eyes with the same concern. "I've not known you to get worked up over nothing. Besides, we've worked with her for a long time. I think I can trust your eyes to know what she looks like."

Bishop gestured for Tobias to follow him as he turned the doorknob, which had been camouflaged within an image of a saxophone. Once inside, a leftover speakeasy from a bygone era came into view. The small, intimate room was in the process of being renovated in an attempt to reclaim its resemblance to its heyday. It was also an excellent place to meet privately and have a much-needed cold beer.

With its walls sparsely covered in memorabilia and antiques from the 1920s to 40s, the guys slid into a booth along a wall covered in plaster and new red bricks. The attempt at aging the room to fit its intended décor was evident but unfinished. As a young woman approached them, Tobias blushed as she drew closer to their table.

"You boys lookin' to drink an early dinner? I hate to say it, but the kitchen is still closed. But if you're hungry, we have some leftover jambalaya and Johnny cakes. It won't take me but a second to pull them off the food truck. It's only a few hours old. I mean, it's all from the lunch rush earlier today."

"That sounds fine," Tobias said, thinking that he hadn't had anything to eat all day and should probably put something in his belly before filling it up on beer. "I'll have a Blue Moon as well. Thanks."

"I'll have the same," Bishop said, noticing that the girl didn't take her eyes off Tobias as he spoke. "You have oranges, yes?"

"Of course. We don't serve Blue Moon without an orange. That would be criminal," she laughed. "I'll have it right out," she said before placing a hand on Tobias's shoulder. "It's good to see you're back in town."

"An old friend?" Bishop asked with a questioning raise of an eyebrow and a corny smirk.

"I'd like to think we're still friends," he said sheepishly. "I mean, I took her to prom. It was a good time. She's a nice girl. Maybe it coulda been something if I had stuck around. But we ain't here to talk about Crystal."

Crystal dropped off their drinks and placed the food on the table. "Here's some honey butter for those cakes, boys," she said. They nodded their appreciation with a polite smile and waited for her to walk away. After she had left them to themselves, Bishop began to talk.

"You know we can't let this go. She's already killed at least five people, and word is, she wasn't given a green light. I've talked to a few others. I'm pretty sure there's more."

"I just can't believe this is happening. I keep telling myself there's not a chance in hell that my father knows about this," Tobias continued. "No fucking way. But given everything so far, he has to know, right?"

"Look, I know how you feel about her, but I know what I saw. And you know what you saw. She's lost her mind," Bishop whispered, feeling himself getting tuned up as his insides knotted tightly into a ball. "She's not just killing anyone. She's dropping high-profile bodies all over the damn country. And no one has any idea why. Even if she had permission, why is she doing it?"

Tobias sat quietly, staring at his beer and thinking to himself. He knew her, and he loved her. Part of him couldn't believe what was happening, while another part wondered if this had to do with an incident that happened when he was a kid. He could feel Bishop's eyes burn a hole through him while he thought about what to do next.

"I know y'all have your secrets. The Old Man is like a vault when it comes to that stuff. I've never asked because it's none of my business who y'all are, or were, or did for him back then. Or even what you do now, for that matter. But I do know a few things," Tobias said, thinking about how to proceed. He knew what he was about to do crossed all lines; if he continued, his father would have his ass. His head dropped for a moment, letting his decision play out, as he leaned forward and drew out the file folder tucked into his waistband under his shirt. "I took this from his house," he said, sliding a folder over to Bishop. "Don't worry. He wasn't home, and I was in and out."

Bishop took a big gulp of his beer, washed down the remainder of his cornbread cakes, and reached to take the file off the table. As he gripped it, Tobias placed a cautious hand on top of it. "What's in here isn't for everyone," he said, hesitating as he lifted his hand. He felt as though he was betraying not only his father but the people in the file. "I don't know who knows what, and I think it should stay that way until that has to change."

Sitting back in the booth, Bishop opened the file and began to read. As he flipped through the pages, his eyes occasionally drew in Tobias, who sat quietly as Bishop took in the information. As the color drained from his old gunnery sergeant's face, Tobias could tell that Bishop was just as uncomfortable as he was with what he was reading.

"And you were there?" Bishop finally said in a rushed tone. The incredulity in his words were crisp as he shook his head in disbelief. He then closed the folder and placed the file back on the table in front of Tobias. "All four of you? And you found them like that?" Bishop stated as fact rather than a question. His stomach now wished he hadn't eaten as his mind looped around the flood of images. Not only the disturbing details of the women's conditions, but to think that the three young boys and the little girl he knew as adults had witnessed something so horrific happen to the people they loved.

"Yeah, we were there. We were just some dumbasses being where we weren't supposed to be. Of course, the Old Man made sure our names were left out of it. The story was that a couple of poachers got credit for the find. Our names were never brought up. Even Miss Gabby was left out of the final story."

Bishop watched Tobias struggle with his memories as his own experiences with each of the individuals involved flooded through his mind. It explained so much about each one of them. "You wanna tell me about it?" he asked. "I'm all ears. I'll get us another beer."

MOONSHINE &
FISHING POLES

"**B**ack then, we were nothing more than a foursome of mostly shoeless and sometimes feral cats," Tobias said as he began to explain the events that took place when he was a kid. "We were barely double digits and plumb full of piss and vinegar. If we only knew, right? We spent many of those early days just running wild across the southern edge of the L'eau Rouge Bayou. Oftentimes, just looking for shit to get into, if I'm being honest. Just being dumb kids."

He and his family had arrived in Baptiste about six months before that fateful night, and it hadn't taken Tobias all that long to figure out why they called it 'The Red Water.' He had made friends with two of the local boys, brothers Crimson and Bama Monroe. They had taken to the old docks off Pier 16 to earn a few dollars. They had basically pestered their way into work. On that morning, Tobias was sitting on the side of an old fisherman's shrimp trolley, and Crimson shoved Tobias overboard and into the river. After he was finally fished out, his white shirt clung to him like a second layer of skin.

"Anything that goes into the Rouge white comes out pink," Crimson said, laughing at Tobias through a mouthful of cola and a candy bar.

"Titty pink," Bama seconded as he snickered and pulled the top of his bibs to one side, comparing Tobias' shirt to one of his nipples.

"Titty pink," Crimson had repeated it again, just in case Tobias didn't understand what a pink titty looked like.

"That's what Henry Dawson calls it anyway," Bama said.

Crimson and Bama Monroe were named after their father's favorite college ball team. After Tobias figured out what that meant for the boys, he concluded that their father's unfortunate naming choices had contributed to the boys being ready to fight at every side glance or remark thrown in their direction. There sure were a whole lotta Bless their hearts being thrown around whenever the boys were out and about. Tobias, however, hadn't quite grasped the American South's use of kind words to cut someone down. It was an expression he hadn't heard before, but had quickly learned by the way it was delivered that no blessings were being handed out.

Miss Simone, the boys' great-grandmother, Tobias heard his father say, had the misfortune of yet again bringing up another generation of young Monroe boys. He said it had always been the boys in the family that had caused the most trouble and that Miss Simone had spent many days negotiating and keeping cooler heads when things got out of hand—on both sides of the law. She was pretty well respected, and people tended to see things her way.

Tobias remembered her small television that used to sit on top of an old Zenith color set from the '60s—the ones with a record player on one end and a radio on the other—all three sharing the same console. Miss Simone had told him then that her Hank had gotten her the set as a birthday present. She had been so proud of the new color TV, but she had explained that it didn't work much anymore.

"Well, that's a 30-year-old relic, and it ain't got much use anymore," she said. "But I just can't bear to part with it if you can understand that," she continued to say, looking at the fixture as if it held a piece of her.

Tobias listened to her as she told him stories and all the memories that came with them. The TV part of the vintage combo had long since passed away, "but it'll still spin my Loretta's, Patsy's, and Tammy's," she said happily. "The radio side of that old thing will tune in every once in a while, but it's mostly static now."

"Or just as long as Mars and Saturn are lined up just right with Earth," Crimson said, cutting in with a laugh and a grin as he hugged Miss Simone in greeting after entering the room.

Tobias wasn't surprised by the affection the boys showed her. He had often played witness to both their kind gestures and their shenanigans. Both of the boys were loving in that way— just prone to finding trouble too.

"Or if you stand on one foot, hold your breath and scratch your butt," said Bama with a cheeky smile as he hopped around.

"Oh, you," Miss Simone gasped as she hid her smile. Tobias could tell the boy's antics had Miss Simone beaming with pride as everyone watched him make a fool out of himself. Miss Simone had often used the boys as rabbit ears as punishment—knowing how badly standing still in one place would ruin their day. It was torture, especially on those nice days, and even Tobias had been on the receiving end of that punishment from time to time.

Miss Simone mostly let the boys be. She had her moments, those when she'd have to get a switch after them, but it wasn't like she didn't have a whole town as her eyes and ears. If there was anything too serious, she'd just send the sheriff out after them.

"That daddy of yours is sure worth his salt," she'd say.

Tobias had no idea what that even meant. But he got the impression that his father believed her to be worth a lot more than salt. He told Tobias that he wasn't to be fooled by the poor old lady routine, that she had more connections than Al Capone and was probably just as ruthless. Tobias wouldn't understand what any of that meant until much later in his life. As kids, none of them had any idea.

Miss Simone had turned on her TV around eight and was out about 10:30, as Tobias remembered it. At least, that is what was in the report. She'd been watching those Golden Girl reruns with a remote in one hand and a glass of her moonshine in the other. But if he was remembering it all right, that's how she was, most nights. So it made sense that on that night, it would be no different.

It was sometime before midnight when the brothers snuck out and arrived at Tobias's house. He sat crouched on his heels in the shadows behind that large old Magnolia tree out front in the yard. He had been hunched down like a burglar on the prowl, out of view from the front of the house, avoiding his father, who he thought had gone to bed when he retreated to his room. But his light came on, and Tobias could see him sitting in a chair by the window, lamp on and reading through a pile of papers on his desk. When he saw the two starting up the driveway, he stepped out from the tree with a finger to his lips.

"Oh, hell naw!" whispered Crimson. His voice was hushed as he pointed an angry finger at Tobias's little sister and looked up at the window at their father. "You bess be sending her ass back in the house with your pa. We ain't taking her with us. She'll slow us up. And she's a dirty blackmailin' snitch," Crimson shouted in a whisper as he continued, eyeing her accusatorily. The suspicion and annoyance were not hidden in his expression. "You know what we do to those types around here, dontcha?"

"Snitches get stitches," Bama said, chiming in as he eyed Tobias and then dropped his gaze towards her. He was daring Tobias to disagree, and he knew he couldn't.

"She's coming," Tobias said, blowing out his chest in an attempt to make himself look bigger. Crimson had at least twenty pounds on him. But he knew that Tobias was serious, and he stepped back.

Tobias and the brothers weren't exactly friends in the beginning. When he first got to Baptiste, they did just about anything and everything to get at him. Tobias's father didn't like it much when he would get into what he called scrimmages. He wanted Tobias to use his wits and not his fists. He told Tobias that he was to outwit his opponent like a game of chess. But Tobias hadn't been any good at board games. Given his size, his mother knew he would eventually have to defend himself or get his ass whooped. It was crazy for him to think how alike his parents were, but such polar opposites at the same time. Given what his father did for a living, you'd think he'd be different. His mother was cut from something different, for sure. She had grown up in Baptiste. Tobias's aunt had told him his mother had been quite a brawler in her day. "She didn't take crap off anyone," she said. After meeting his mother's remaining living family and the house she had been raised in, he found humor in that.

"She'd let me practice with her when my father wasn't around," Tobias explained. "My parents had skills that most parents didn't, and my mother didn't mind teaching us things like that. This had often caused friction between my folks. My father wanted me to be a scholar, not a soldier like him."

"I met her in Germany once. She was the contractor who was teaching us Farsi. She was a special person," Bishop said, fondly remembering a woman that Tobias had nearly forgotten.

"You need to show just enough to let them know you got something and let them decide if they wanna mess around and find out," Tobias's mother had said, all serious. His mother had a mouth on her, worse than any two sailors.

"My father said because she was raised by heathens, she didn't know better," Tobias said with a light laugh. "I'm sure my aunt would've loved to hear that. He told me that Americans had a different way about them. I think it's because he was raised so proper that my mother just wasn't anything he was used to. I think that's really why he loved her, though. She seemed to be the crazy that fueled his train."

"Nice girly skirt, Braveheart," Tobias heard as he felt a hand on the back of his head. The force had sent him propelling forward into a free fall, landing him face-first into the mud. His insides turned red in anger. The green clan tartan he wore disappeared beneath the murky water of the road. As he lifted his face from the mud, he felt the anger grow through him like a rash that spread across him like smallpox when he heard his sister's cry.

In an attempt to embarrass Tobias, the two idjits had accidentally pushed her into the ditch. She wore a green dress that had this mass of pink tulle bunched up underneath it. It sucked up all that mud and water. All that hair of hers was matted so thick in wet clay that Tobias could only see her green eyes showing through the paste that covered her face. Tobias laughed at the memory when it came to him, but back then, she was really pissed.

"You miserable twats!" she cried out. Tobias had never heard her use those words before, but her fury was as red as her hair. She could have set the world on fire with the flashes that sprang to her eyes. "I can't show my mummy this dress!" She screamed, in a deafening screech, as tears ran from her eyes. "You have ruined my mum's birthday!" she continued to cry as she slapped the water around her. She was like an earthquake that threatened to level the earth around them all.

That was when turning the other cheek came with a fist to the side of Crimson's head, followed by another to his mouth and a direct hit to the center of his chest. As the air left his body, Tobias climbed on his back, locked in a rear-naked choke, and held it for what seemed like an hour. Tobias felt the weight of his body fall to the dirt as he shook, and every part of him wanted to hold out until Crimson's eyes rolled white to the back of his head. Tobias watched Bama's expression shift to shock as he let him know that once he was done with his brother, he'd be coming for him next.

He barely got the words out of his mouth, "Get off of him! You're gonna kill my brother," he cried out in a whiny, shrill. "I'm gonna tell your pa!" Then he turned to run. Tobias saw nothing but his ass and the bottom of his shoes carrying him as fast as he could to get to his father. At that point, Tobias knew that he was in deep shit.

His adrenaline was pulsing through his body so hard and fast that it took him a moment to get a grip on himself. Then he let go of Crimson, as his face took on the same shade as his name. Tobias had the urge to kick him in the face while he lay there passed out. But knowing that his father was probably on his way and wouldn't be impressed by his takedown, Tobias hauled back and slapped him. He sputtered awake and coughed like he was trying to dislodge a hairball. After that day, Tobias and the brothers were as thick as thieves. Tobias would regale them with stories of where he and his family had traveled. He told them about his mother and how she had died. They told him how they lost their parents to a fire. They loved Tobias's accent and took to calling him Braveheart from then on. He didn't mind, really. It was kinda cool after he finally got to see the movie.

Greer was a small thing back then, with her red hair and a mischievous streak to match. She loved nothing more than having something to hang over Tobias's head. After the death of their mother and making Baptiste their new home, the Old Man took to working longer hours. So much for retirement. He said he was establishing himself in his new role as Baptiste's sheriff because he was an outsider. He had to prove himself, no matter who his wife had been. But that seemed like a load of bullshit to Tobias.

"As kids, I truly believed he kept himself busy to avoid us," Tobias said, regretfully. "There was just something there. Maybe he kept his distance out of grief. But I got the impression that he'd rather be anywhere but home. I watched after Greer most days, or she'd sit with Miss Simone, who said she missed having a little girl around. Our mother's family was all too happy to spoil Gears. She was every bit my mother's doppelganger. I'm sure it made it all that much easier for everyone. I can't say she's changed there. She's still sassy-mouthed and still causing trouble."

"But I've never had to put her in handcuffs," Bishop said, pointing at Tobias with a grin.

"Only because she didn't get caught," Tobias replied. "And she was the worst of us," he laughed. "Lord, if you only knew."

"Greer begged me to take her with us that night. She used those sad, green puppy dog eyes on me, and I caved like a chump. I don't know how many times I wished I hadn't given in. But she saw the boys steal Miss Simone's moonshine from the shed, and I didn't have a choice. She had us by the baby short hairs, and I knew it."

"I tried to convince her to leave the dog at home, thinking it would've been best for everyone. But she insisted that he'd be good for our protection," Tobias said with a laugh. "That was a load of crap. That mutt was nothing more than gator bait. However, the fight hadn't been worth the voice I'd have to use to convince her. We'd get caught sneaking out if I had to raise my voice any higher. So, I let her drag the damn dog behind her. And drag she did, let me tell you. I almost felt sorry for him. I ended up having to set the fishing poles down and Greer's blanket, which I'd taken from her bed. My arms hurt from gripping everything so tightly. My body was tense that night, and I honestly couldn't tell you why. It was like I knew something bad was coming our way."

"Hurry up, Greer!" Tobias called out in frustration, again switching between his Scottish tongue to English.

Greer didn't remember the words like he did. He often tried going back and forth between the two languages, hoping that she would catch on. But she never took to it. Tobias didn't know why he still tried to hang on to the words he spoke with his father. And then his mother. No one used it anymore. Not even his father, who seemed to have abandoned anything that tied him to the past.

Tobias rubbed his hands over his face like he could wipe away the night and start over. But all he managed to do was smear bug dope, mixed in with those tiny gnats down his face, further pissing him off in ways that set his teeth on edge. His eyes stung, and that had piled on to just another reason why they never should've left the house. Tobias really wanted to go fishing, but from the start of the trip out, he really just wanted the night to end.

"An donas cù!" he called out angrily. "Let the damn dog go," he said.

Tobias held up the lantern so that Greer could see it. In the light, he could barely make out her form, but could tell that she was no longer moving. Fed up with her shit, he stomped angrily in her direction. He was ready to drag her back home. To all be damned. Being grounded for a month had to be better than putting up with any more of her crap. As he got closer, though, he could hear her crying and saw the dirt-stained tears that ran down her face. The sight she displayed almost made him feel bad for being such a dick. She tugged hard on the dog's rope as he lay out on his back like roadkill. His legs were pointed straight up, creating an immovable force, and he whined in protest.

"Take off the rope," he said as he reached her.

She had given up and was sitting next to the dog. Something about having a dog that could fit inside his football helmet was disappointing. Tobias sighed, giving in. He bent over and loosened the rope from around the dog's neck. Then, he nudged the dog with his foot to let him know he was free to make his escape.

DOCK AT THE END OF THE BAYOU

"L et's go, you motherless bastards!" Bama yelled when he didn't see Tobias or Gears pulling up the rear. His voice was loud as it carried itself across the air like a megaphone belting its way through the trees. "Whoever gets to the dock last has to eat the eyeballs. And you bess not be a titty baby about it!" He growled in a maniacal laugh.

Tobias' irritation began to dissolve as he walked with Gears, and he shook his head at Bama's comment. As he yelled out, Bama couldn't see them from where he was, and his excited voice signaled to every solitary living creature within a mile that they were out there. The trees stood stoic—their branches stiff and without sway. The wind was so close to mute that the bugs traveling the invisible highways seemed to move slowly. Not even a blade of grass wobbled in the stiff air. Tobias shrugged off the memory as he should have known then that the night had something gruesome brewing for the four of them.

Bama was the first to reach the water's edge and pushed open the fort's door. "It was probably some old fart's lady pad," Bama said as he and Crimson explained the place to Tobias.

"What lady would want to stay there?" Crimson said, looking annoyed with Bama. "Maybe whatever woman would want you," he said in a wide grin. "It smells like your farts," Crimson said, wrinkling up his nose.

"A dead old Bama's lady's farts," Tobias replied, appearing inside and stepping back out as he covered his nose. The smell nearly knocked him off his feet as his eyes watered up. Thinking of that, he wasn't so sure he could give up his bed to sleep in there. The shack smelled like a dead goat had been buried inside, and the spiders and bugs had moved in to protect it.

"Just keep the door shut and she'll never notice," Crimson warned. "Don't none y'all open it."

"And if she figures it out, she's gonna have the sheriff beat your ass," Bama said, looking over at Tobias as he held his hands wrapped around his upper arms. "By the size of his arms, you won't sit right for a month if he gets ahost ya ." Again, he grinned at Tobias.

By the time Tobias and Greer caught up to the brothers, they were already dragging the rigged-together dock out to the water. The boys had spent days collecting up barrels and all the items needed to build a floating platform. They didn't like fishing from the land's edge, but twenty or so feet further out, they could swim and fish without getting into the grassy stuff or cutting up their feet on the old stumps and debris that sat on the bottom. Some years back, the brothers' pa had strung up layers of hog wire across the water to keep out anything big enough to eat a small child.

"What the hell is that?" Crimson yelled out, partly puzzled, partly pissed off. "Dammit to beat hell."

Crimson looked menacing when he was upset, but really, it was all bluster. His dirty blonde hair had been buzzed to the scalp. He had big brown eyes and tanned skin that looked funny next to his bright white legs.

"But somehow, the girls fell all over themselves about him. He was too dumb to realize it," Tobias told Bishop. "Hell, we all were just that dumb. But the boy hated bathing. To tell you the truth, that's probably what kept the girls at arm's length," he laughed, thinking about how the girls would all gather and wave at Crimson from afar.

Bama was the youngest of the boys, but he would probably surpass Crimson in size someday. He had the same-colored hair, but he wore his longer, and his hygiene was impeccable. If he had the money, he'd have the wardrobe to match once he grew into himself. He hadn't cared all that much for shoes, though. He'd carried a pair of sandals around with him - just in case he had to get into the water. He hated the mud squishing between his toes.

He was standing on the other side of the platform, struggling under its weight. He wasn't as strong as Crimson. His young muscles strained to hold up the platform, and it was all he could do to keep his side from falling after Crimson's sudden outburst and let go. Bama finally let go and looked at Crimson as if he had lost his mind. Tobias hurried towards them, trying to help, but he had been too late. Then Crimson pointed at the rear of the dock.

"Some asshole stole one of our barrels," Crimson said, scratching at his head. He wasn't convinced there was any other explanation for the disappearance.

Tobias looked over the hole where a blue plastic barrel had once been tied. They had secured it there about three days earlier. They spent the day testing out each of their best feats of engineering brilliance—each figuring out how to construct the barrels together and then attach the platform—without it all sinking into the bayou and losing all the ill-gotten booty they had pirated over those last few months. Crimson said it wasn't stealing if they were only repurposing forgotten items. Of course, Tobias' father strongly disagreed after catching them pilfering Mrs. Poole's old boat for parts.

"We're only taking stuff nobody's usin'," Crimson said confidently to Sheriff McTavish, defending their thievery through his big gappy smile where the left front tooth was missing. That was courtesy of Tobias that day in the mud. "Nobody cares about this old stuff."

"Can't we just use it like that anyway?" asked Greer, eyeing each of the boys and waiting for one of them to answer her. She could tell they were upset, but she thought they were being ridiculous for being upset over just one barrel. "You got seven more of them," she counted. "One, two," and then paused to look at them. "Why don't ya just tear off the other one and make it itty bitty," she said, gesturing with her small hands.

"No retard," Bama said, giving Greer a sideways glance. He agreed with her, of course. He always did. But he hated it when she would follow them around. Her smarty-pants know-it-all bull crap upset him, but he couldn't let her know that she was right.

"You're just a stupid girl," he scoffed. "And this is man's business. Go find a dolly or somethin'."

It was bad enough that Crimson and Tobias had become joined at the hip, completely ignoring him most of the time. It had always been just the two of them before. The Alabama Brothers, from Baptiste, Louisiana, were eleventh-generation Monroes, born and bred. Tobias knew Bama liked him well enough, but he also knew that Bama didn't like being relegated to the baby table with Greer. Tobias eyed him as he wrinkled his nose at her and gave a little shiver that shook him to his feet as if to let her know how gross he found her. Tobias watched her as she first made a face back at him, but then her eyes softened just a bit, and he saw the smallest hesitation fall in. It wasn't anger. Bama had hurt her feelings.

"Don't call her that," Tobias said, stepping towards him. He wasn't sure if he wanted to punch him for the comment or the way she looked at him. He had a fist drawn back, but he paused, thinking about it first. When it came to his sister, he didn't care if Bama was younger than him. He'd take on Hulk Hogan if he had to. Tobias saw the way Bama's expression fell as he backed away, and Tobias dropped his arm.

With his hands raised in defeat, "I don't mean anything by it, man. I give up," he said. It could have been out of fear or the simple recognition that he had been a jerk. Tobias didn't know which, and he honestly didn't care. "I'm sorry," Bama continued, apologizing as he looked at Greer with her slightly turned-up lips.

Greer crossed her arms over her chest and snorted, knowing he wasn't sorry one bit and a little disappointed that Tobias hadn't punched him in his ugly face. In truth, though, Greer didn't find him ugly at all and had been carrying around a slight crush. Still, she wasn't going to let him get away with calling her a retard. With her face scrunched up like she smelled something rotten, she stuck her tongue out at Bama while Tobias had his back turned.

"Don't be a brat, Gears," he said, not looking at her—but knowing damn well she was making that face.

Figuring he'd let them work it out from there, he went to see Crimson, who was still pissed off about the missing barrel. Tobias wasn't sure if an animal had eaten the ropes or if something else had happened. He could see no reason for the broken binds, and he was pretty confident they had secured the ties so that nothing would fall apart. He reached down and rubbed the rope between his fingers—mimicking the way he had observed his father rub dirt or a broken branch between his fingers while out tracking during a hunt. That's when he realized their ties were not frayed, torn, pulled apart, or broken. It was obvious that the binds had been cut by something sharp.

"These are clean cuts," he said.

"What difference does it make?" Crimson said, his tone going from anger to annoyance. "Whatever. This changes nothin'. Let's do somethin' else already," he said, walking away from the dock in search of anything else to do.

For him, it was over. Of the four, he was often the first one to cool the quickest—opting to sweep it under the rug and move on rather than stew on it. He didn't spend too many brain cells or thoughts on things that couldn't be helped. It was what it was, and he was already beyond it. Crimson walked over to his backpack. It was sitting on the ground near his bedroll. He pulled open the flap and retrieved Miss Simone's best moonshine. He was pretty fond of her bourbon, but this batch had been ready and was a whole lot easier to steal since she hadn't gotten around to jarring it. All he had to do was find something to dip into the barrel and get out before anyone saw what he had done.

They had put together a pretty nice camping setup during their trips out to make the dock. It was lined with logs to sit on and a fire bed with an oven rack for cooking. Crimson found a seat, stretched out his legs, popped the lid off, and took a big pull from the jar. His cheeks blew out like a chipmunk at the over-estimation of the pour. His eyes bulged, and he gasped in search of clean air. He could barely swallow the fire that burned through his face like gasoline. The fumes stole all the oxygen from his lungs. The alcohol level was so high that from where Tobias sat, it smelled like the same stuff Miss Simone put on their cuts and scrapes. It sure burned the same.

"Holy shit, opossums!" Crimson yelled out. Now, dancing in a circle like his hair was on fire. As he darted around, he moved to the beat of the Charlie Daniels song, 'The Devil Went Down to Georgia,' as it played on an old radio kept in the fort. "Whoooeeee!" He whooped. They all laughed at that—daring to forget the past day's troubles. "Miss Simone sure put some extra stank on this one!"

As the moonshine and cigarettes circled between them, Tobias watched the boys in amazement as they sat around the fire that night. It wasn't cold out, but the smoke from the fire had kept the bugs at bay. Sometimes, he'd take part in the drinking and smoking, or he'd just let it all pass him by. He even admitted to letting Gears have a taste, though his father would kill him if he knew. They spoke a lot like Miss Simone. Her English was thick, and her Southern was drawn out and lazy. Tobias often had to ask them what in the hell they were talking about. His mother had been a linguist with the American government, and he was sure that even she would have difficulty understanding them.

Tobias found their freedom exhilarating. Short of going to mass or school, the amadans, his father had called them, ran wild. They were nothing like Tobias had ever experienced. He and his sister had so much adult supervision that they couldn't use the restroom without someone knowing about it. As Tobias shared that, looking back, knowing who his father was, he wouldn't have been surprised to find that his father had planted a tracker in his ass cheek.

Startled, Tobias quickly stood up as the cry of a baying dog interrupted their misspent youth. The noise was so loud that it pierced the humid air, making the hairs on his arms stand in attention. As the noise came again, Tobias spun in a circle, trying to get a fix on the noise and its direction. He was really hoping that he didn't look like the P word. He stood up straighter and took a deep breath, knowing that if the brothers saw any hint of cowardice, that would be the word they'd call him. It wasn't a word he could bring himself to say, nor did he like hearing it. His heart had sunk to the bottom of his stomach. He knew he was in the clear when Gears and both brothers quickly joined him, looking just as freaked out as he was. They stared into the blackness of nothing as the shadows from the fire danced.

"What was that?" Greer cried out, running at Tobias.

She leaped so hard into his arms that it was only luck that she didn't knock him down. Tobias wrapped his arms around her, protecting her from the invisible threat that none of them could see. He could feel Gears' heart bouncing off his chest. Their heartbeats collided against one another so hard that he wasn't sure where his began or hers ended. Tobias did his best to stay calm and not react for her sake.

Just as it occurred to him what was making the piercing sound, Greer lifted her head from his neck and looked him dead square in the face. Her heart had begun to slow, and the look of fear had faded from her expression, giving way to one of recognition. "Rory!" she roared as her eyes widened. Then she twisted herself free from his arms. She dropped to the ground and ran in the direction of the howl. The three boys tore out after Greer with their lanterns and torches as the howl grew louder and more persistent the further west they traveled—further from town they got.

"Maybe this ain't a good idea," Bama yelled between deep breaths as they caught up to her.

"What are you doing?" Tobias yelled, panting out the words in a panic. He hadn't ever seen her move like that, and he was surprised at how long it had taken them to catch up to her. "You can't just take off like that!"

"I think Rory's a coon dog," Bama said, bending over to rest his hands on his knees. He sucked in long, deep breaths. As Tobias watched the boys, who were natural athletes, it occurred to him why it had taken so much effort to keep up with Greer. They had all passed the jar around way too many times. "It sounds like he has somethin' treed. Maybe it's a coon. Maybe a jaguar!" Bama continued excitedly.

"You're drunk, you dumbass! There ain't no jaguars in Louisiana, and that mutt ain't no coon dog," Crimson shot back, shaking his head back and forth. "He ain't much bigger than a damn old opossum. Who's the retard now, dummy? Probably just a bobcat. That's the only big cat in Louisiana. And there's sure ins hell ain't no raccoons in these parts. The trash pandas would be further south, like near Texas or something," he said confidently.

"Where is he?" Greer shouted, looking around the area and not seeing Rory anywhere. "Roryyy!" she said in a sing-song voice. He was so close, but they were unable to see him or the reason he was freaking out. His howls grew more urgent.

Tobias panned his torch into the trees. "If it's a bobcat, or a coon, or even a jaguar, would it not be up in the trees?" he asked.

"Maybe it's the swamp monster," Bama giggled, dancing around with his hands above his head. "Boogie boogie!"

"Not funny," Crimson shot back.

"Alright, alright," Bama said in a sorry, not so sorry-like tone. "Y'all actin' like we ain't ever heard a noise in the swamp before. It's the bayou. Y'all are actin' like a bunch of damn chicken titties."

Tobias continued to scan the tree line, still not seeing Rory or anything moving. Then, as if a light bulb exploded in his head, he began to brush back the thigh-high grass that surrounded him.

"I don't know why, really. I couldn't see the ground," he explained to Bishop. "With my arms spread out in a fanning motion, I just walked. I gestured at Greer to do the same. We both raked in a forward until Gears stopped. Her body stiffened up, and the look on her face scared me."

From where Tobias stood, he could see Rory's tail moving rapidly and barely clearing the height of the tall grass. He was circling something on the ground, like a drag mark that looked like a dug-out trench. As they followed it, they came to a dip in the water about ten feet from the river. It was like a spill-out, that had created a small pond. Rory whined and whimpered as he stopped.

"Over here!" Tobias shouted, waving the torch so the others could see.

"What the hell is that?" Tobias asked Gears. He didn't know why he had asked her, but she was the closest. The ground didn't look normal, and it had a smell that hit hard—gutted and rotten.

"A dead gator, maybe?" he said, attempting to answer his own question.

Bama, now standing next to Greer, was so fixated on what he saw that he didn't notice Greer slip her hand into his. She pressed against his leg, fingers locked in a death grip. He couldn't use that hand to cover his mouth and nose unless he shook her off, which he couldn't bring himself to do. He remembered his other hand and covered his face, fighting off the foul smell. So repulsed, he forgot to be upset by Greer holding his hand.

"I could see her trembling next to him, and honestly, I don't think he had the heart to make her feel any worse," Tobias told Bishop as he took another drink and swallowed the lump in his throat at the memory.

SISTER IN A BARREL

Tobias walked out through the muck to the blue plastic barrel with Crimson held tight on his heels. He reached for the barrel and gave it a nudge, not thinking much about it. However, it seemed to be stuck firmly in place. Rory was still barking his fool head off. Tobias was unable to think clearly as his ears began to ring at the painful pitch.

Crimson reached down, scooped up Rory and clamped a hand around his face. Then he hefted the dog out of the sloppy mud. His body was slick and smelled of vomit. At that time, they didn't know how he had gotten so disgusting. Crimson had to squeeze Rory under a chicken-wing-like vise grip just to keep from dropping him. As quickly as he could manage, Crimson made his way over to where Bama and Greer were standing. Both were silent and eyes wide. He sat Rory at Greer's feet.

"Don't let him go," he told her. He met Bama's eyes and recited the same statement to him. Then he walked back out into the tainted water to help Tobias drag the barrel to ground.

The barrel hadn't been all that heavy—at least not at first. But it wasn't as if Tobias had expected to find anything inside it either. When they used it for their dock, it hadn't been punctured. It was perfect for their purposes because it still held air. But now the top had been removed. Its metal ring was gone, and the lip was just sitting on top.

"It wasn't until I reached to pull the barrel out that I realized just how terrible the situation was. I jumped back, and let me tell you, the screech that came out of me could have come out of my sister. My heart was stuck in my throat, and I couldn't get away fast enough," he confessed to Bishop.

"Holy Shit!" Tobias yelled, jumping back with his hands in the air, signifying he hadn't touched a damn thing. At the top, a foot was sticking out from under the lid. It was barely discernible, but it was still a foot, and it had red toenail polish. "I don't know where I found the guts to look inside or to investigate further. But you know, I still can't talk to a girl with red polish on her fingers? How messed up is that?" Tobias said, looking painfully stricken as he continued to recount that night.

Greer's tiny face began to contort. She saw what they saw, and a scream escaped her that pierced the air. The kind of scream that came from deep in the gut—shattering all eardrums within hearing distance. She cried hard and long. "Toe-toe-toe-Toby!" She wailed, using a name she hadn't used since she was able to say Tobias. Plea-plea-please take me home," she cried in a mix of a stutter and hysteria. "I want to go ho-ho-home now, please," she wailed as she pleaded with him. Her face was red and tear-stained, as snot poured from her nose.

"I saw a different side of Bama that night. He pulled Greer into him and tucked her face into his side—shielding her gaze from seeing anything else. It was a gesture that hadn't gone unnoticed, especially by me. I was helpless to do anything to help her from where I stood. Besides that, I was too freaked out myself. How do you wrap your mind around something like that? There was a part of me that wanted to bury my face into Bama's side, too. I think that was the worst I have ever missed my mother," Tobias continued.

"This is fucked up," Tobias heard himself say, unable to find a better way to describe their current situation.

He rarely used profanity back then. His father believed that swear words were used by those who hadn't figured out a more intellectual way to converse. He also ate plenty of soap at Gears' age after repeating the words he had heard his mother say.

"Though I doubt in a million years, my father found my mother unintelligent," Tobias relayed to Bishop.

"She is just colorful," his father would say.

Bama's eyes watered, but he wouldn't dare let any of them see him cry. "We need help," he finally said, choking back a sob. "We gotta get your pa. Can we please go home?"

Crimson couldn't take his eyes off the foot that stuck out of the barrel. He was staring at it stone-faced, and his mouth hung open so far that he caught flies. He was sure he saw it move, but thought he was just seeing things, like his imagination was playing tricks on him, because of all the drinking. He was sure Miss Simone's homemade libations had him floating clouds earlier, but with all the adrenaline coursing through his body, he had to have sobered up with all that was happening. But when Tobias saw a slight wiggle of a toe, he too thought he was seeing things. It was just a light tilt at the arch of the foot. And that was all it took. Crimson lost it. Then, the whole foot kicked up out of the barrel.

"Y'all! Look! Look! Look! Oh, Jesus Help Me Christ! Jeeesusss Christ, Y'all assholes! Are y'all seein' this!" Crimson yelled, jumping up and down and pointing at the foot. "It's moving! It's moving!" They all watched in horror as a slough of water came from the barrel, and the foot became more forceful and deliberate in its movement.

"It was the only thing I could think to do. I took a pounding run and delivered a desperate, hard blow at the barrel, hitting it awkwardly, and sorta bounced off. I wasn't my strong, handsome self as a boy, if you can believe that," he chuckled grimly.

"Oh, I can only imagine," Bishop said, responding with a kind smile. "I saw pictures of you as a boy—all limbs and teeth."

"It was like diving and pulling off a body flop onto the top of a swimming pool. I kinda winced at the blow as it knocked the wind out of me, and I immediately felt like an idiot. A little bit of the liquid in the barrel splashed out and over the edges, but nothing more than that. But I did see something else then. A hand reached out and gripped the top of the rim. I don't know what came over me. Fear, maybe. I don't know. I backed up, and between the two of us, we took another run - this time, digging deep with each step, throwing all our hopes and determination into the blow until the whole barrel toppled over. We watched in complete dismay as the water and all its contents spilled out into the grass, washing all its horrors out in the muck and causing this wave of rotten mess to run close enough to touch Bama and

Greer's feet. The pink water had been thickened with mud and smelled of vomit and something like sewage. From behind us, we heard a voice that scared the shit right out of me, and I couldn't hide it that time."

"Boys, y'all go get his pa," Miss Gabby said as she picked up Greer and held her close.

"She had shown up out of nowhere like a fucking apparition that haunted the swamp. Later, we were told that she had heard Rory's barking and Gear's blood-curdling screams and came floating herself on over.

It was a full-on caldron of death soup made with a woman's body. Worst part, not even two feet away, was another container—a freezer. We hadn't even noticed it. It nearly killed the Old Man when he opened it up. He said it was like seeing his children. I remember every smell and detail of that night. You can't imagine what that did to us as kids. Crimson got pretty heavy into drugs that year. Bama withdrew from everyone, rarely leaving Miss Simone's house unless it was to hang out with Miss Gabby. He was afraid to be alone, but couldn't be with other people, if that makes any sense. Hell, they both already struggled in school, and that shit just made it harder for them. And Gears, well, I think it was nearly two years before she would sleep in her own bed and stop wetting it. She's better now, I guess, but she drinks too much and won't commit to her relationship. She works long hours at the paper and spends most of her free time at that jujitsu studio off Larken. I think she still keeps a bedroll there. It makes her feel safe, I guess.

All of us kids spent a lot of time with Mother Agnes Valentine. A lot of time with her, actually. Probably more than we had when we first moved to town. She was heartbroken. I don't think she ever really got over it. With the death of my mother and the rest of her family gone now, she just crumbled. You'd think God would shield those types of people a little better, right? I know it ain't right to think about, but she devoted herself to God and still saw the worst parts of pain. And my father started drinking. I thought he had changed with the death of my mother, but I was wrong. Something happened that night that he couldn't come back from. And Mother Agnes Valentine blamed him for all of it. Except, I don't know what she blamed him for."

Bishop sat quietly through most of Tobias' account of what had happened that night—only interrupting to seek clarification or to comment on knowing Tobias's mother or how awful he found Miss Simone's moonshine.

As he listened to Tobias' observations on how it affected the others, he finally brought himself to ask, "And what about you? How were you able to get past it all?"

"I kill people, Gunny," Tobias confessed. "None of us made it out okay. We just found ways to deal with it. Me? I live alone, smoke like a freight train, and I really enjoy my job."

Tobias could tell that Bishop wanted to be surprised by his answer. But he wasn't. Tobias was every bit his father's son, a product of his upbringing and his mother's life. Like it or not, nothing would have changed that. Tobias came by his parents' personalities and skill sets honestly, inheriting from a man who made hunting sick bastards an art and a mother who taught him that violence was sometimes necessary.

"My mother was every bit the Old Man's equal. Losing her had crushed him in ways that no one could understand until they did, I reckon. I also saw that in Mother Agnes Valentine. Maybe it made him even more determined to rid the world of evil. Maybe that's why that night nearly destroyed him, I don't know. I thought taking the sheriff's job was supposed to be a sort of retirement. But it turned out to be his cover. I don't think he really thought about it being a real job he'd have to put real effort into."

Bishop reached over and lifted the cuff of Tobias's sleeve. "I hear she was a pretty good investigator and an even better tracker. Your father said she's the one who started the business. He said it was her idea to turn contractor, and well...work outside all the red tape," he smirked with a shrug.

"I see you got some new ink," he continued, nodding at the lines he uncovered beneath the cuff. He wore a look of surprise as Tobias removed his jacket and pulled up his sleeves.

"Eye for an Eye" was written in bold letters down his left arm. And down the right, where the words, "Vengeance is Mine, Sayth the Lord."

"My mother had the same," Tobias said, "the tattoos, I mean. I had no idea until my auntie told me. I had never seen them on her before. She showed me an old photo of my mother, and it wasn't something I expected to see. I don't remember seeing them as a boy. So, I went out and got them myself," he shrugged, unsure if Bishop could understand.

"I'm sure she'd feel honored by it if she were here," Bishop said.

"I doubt that," he snorted, laughing out loud. "She was the 'do as I say, not as I do' type. But I hope she's proud of me anyway."

Then Bishop fell silent as he listened while Tobias chatted on about his mother for a while longer.

"Everyone will be here soon," Bishop said finally, once a lull had fallen on their conversation. He could see that Tobias needed sleep, and he had to get things ready for tomorrow. Your father has called in his whole team." Tobias heard an unspoken tone in Bishop's words and wondered if Bishop had more to say, but instead, he finished, "Let's get out of here. And remember, you need to stay out of sight."

"Sure thing, Gunny. Understood."

ALL THINGS THAT SKITTER

PRESENT DAY - BABY

"Are you all set?" I asked her. "You got your snacks out? Do you have all your potty breaks sorted? Make sure you have your pen and paper ready and your tape recorder running."

The younger woman shifted against the wall and gave a laugh masked behind a soft groan. "What a time to mention food," she said. "I've been dreaming of pizza and beer for hours. "You don't understand what I could do to a cheeseburger and fries right now," she laughed again. "Do you think room service forgot about the two of us? And they got such good reviews on Yelp," she teased back. "It'll be the last time I book to stay here. Have you seen that pool? It looks like herpes."

"A good sense of humor helps," I said. "It'll help keep the mind from diving off into those dark places."

"I'm already in a dark place - figuratively and literally. This better be one hell of a story. I canceled my date with Matt Damon to be here," she quipped. "And my hair was on point. That doesn't happen all that often."

I thought about that night as I looked for a suitable place to start. Remembering every moment in crisp detail. I couldn't explain how I had gotten there. A woman's scream had beckoned me there. At first, it was muffled, but as the cry grew louder and more urgent, a surge of static set through me, and my mind began to flicker like channels on a television. Then, as if I had been living in utter darkness, everything came into focus. The lights, the music. The smells. It was as if I had been plucked out of thin air, and everything hit me all at once in bright, vivid colors.

I followed the screams towards an alleyway. There, I saw a girl sprawled out on the ground, where two men were tearing at her clothes. Her long blonde hair had spilled out from beneath a cap, and it lay uncovered on the filthy cobble. Her dress had been ripped, and her dignity was displayed for the world to witness. Her arms were pinned above her head as one of the men struggled to keep her from moving. Something about that set a fire in me, and my stomach grew hot as if I were going to explode from within.

"I'm thinking the sort of woman who charges by the hour would probably be a better option for you fellas tonight," I said to the men, unzipping my jacket and letting it fall to the ground beside me. "It doesn't look much like from here that she's all that into you. Unless unbathed and drunk are her type?"

The girl's eyes brightened wide as saucers, and she began to wail harder. Although it was a different sort of cry this time. Not at all like before. It carried a note of relief behind it. The man holding her arms adjusted his grip to one hand as he placed the other hand over her mouth to muffle her screams. The hand was grimy and nearly black at the tips of his fingers, as if the man had an aversion to water, and his fingers were rotting away. I found the whole exchange quite repulsive.

"This ain't none your business," the waddling man said, as he pointed out one of his nubby fat fingers at me. Disgust was written all over his expression. As if I were the one who should feel bad for interrupting them. The fact that the man was upset with me for interfering in his rape plans, had hard-baked a rage in me, that caused a fuck you to fester like an ulcer in the core of my soul. All I wanted to do was tear his head from his body.

"Ye'd best be on your way there, lass, if you know what's good for you," he crooned as he tried to pull his trousers up over his belly. He was a fat bastard he was, and his English was appalling. It was clear that he was an illiterate twat, and there was nothing about him I found redeemable. "We'll give you some of the same here," he said, sliding his hand down the front of his underwear and rubbing himself as he smiled. His eyes showed that he was confident in his words. Yet, his body betrayed him as he staggered forward.

"That's right, Missy," the other man braved as he, too, got to his feet and began to inch his way forward. "I got somethin' for ya right here," he bragged, taking his cue from his mate. He spoke through blackened teeth and grabbed his crotch while shaking a fistful of his pants at me. "You can come and play with Big Willy," he chuckled.

The man's teeth were something out of an old 18th-century London play—Oliver Twist-level disgusting—like someone had taken a marker to his teeth and blacked out all but two or three. I was pretty sure that I'd rather take a blunt stick to an eye than have either of them near me.

"Big Willy, aye?" I asked, winking at the man and giving him a welcoming bite of my lower lip.

"You really know how to get me goin' there. I like a man who can take charge and bend me to his Willy," I smirked as bile crept up my throat. While they walked in my direction, this had left the girl unsecured and unwatched. I looked at her sprawled out like a dead fish in a hot pan and then at the doorway, repeating the gesture over and over with my eyes until the girl finally caught on and quickly gathered herself up and moved out of the way.

"Are we at an impasse already?" I said, with my best devilish smile projected. I have to admit, I was enjoying myself, thinking out what I was going to do next. I kept their focus on me. It was the easiest way I could think of to size them up and keep them distracted. Getting no answer, "Oh wait, shall I use smaller words? Was that one too big for you?" I asked, slowly drawing out each word as if I spoke Alien. "Do you need me to use it in a sentence?"

While the two men babbled incoherent garbage between themselves, I took the opportunity to move in closer. Their exchange was clearly directed at me, but they were too pissed to form truly witty comments. They talked about what they were going to do to me as if they were one-upping one another—who got the first go and all.

"You can settle this like gentlemen," I giggled in a girlish way. "Rock, paper, scissors. The winner gets the first go." I said, laughing at their Laurel and Hardy routine. As if either of the eejits had any idea of what they were about to bring their way.

Just as I started for the man, the closest man to me, I saw his eyes dart right in surprise, giving away a third man's approach. I hadn't noticed a third man. It had been too late for me to react. I felt the blow contact with the side of my face and the power with which it was delivered.

"I was watching that," he growled, as if I had stood in front of his telly and blocked out his favorite programming. It had been a rookie mistake. I didn't check the corners. You always check the corners. I wasn't even sure of where he came from. The shot had tipped me off balance, yet I was able to steady myself before another punch could land, and I ducked it accordingly. I surprised myself. I was remembering all that training. My vision was fuzzy, but I'd had plenty of experience in fighting, and I had been prepared. I still had my wits about me, and I would be ready for the next.

I raised an elbow into a sideways swing and planted it firmly into the jaw of the man closest to me. Now, the skinnier and taller of the Dumb and Dumber pair had tackled me, knocking me to the ground. What a gammy bastard he was. As I raised my head to take in the impact, a hot, burning sensation gripped me. His head had connected with mine, sending a squash of blood from my nose and mouth. There is more blood now. So far, all of mine. The dumbass had managed to accidentally head-butt me. I could feel where my teeth had gone through my bottom lip, and the blood filled me. I laughed. All he could do was look at me in shock. He was just as surprised as me. The look of horror on his face was actually quite comedic.

I let him lay on top of me just long enough to get my vision clear. As he began to sit up straighter, he, too, was not feeling his best. He looked as though he was going to find a corner to puke as he pulled away from me. I found my opening then. I was able to sweep a leg around his neck, pull him down, and twist him up. The man was too messed up to stop me. He screamed as a snap rang out, and his elbow gave way. When I let him go, he drug himself away, waving me off in surrender.

"You fucking whore," the voyeur screamed at me as he watched his friend slink away like a wounded dog. "I'm going to kill you, and skull fuck your eye socket."

I had a Spartan fixed blade under my shirt and prepared myself for him. I readied my feet into position and waited for him to come at me. I knew he would, though I hadn't had time to size him up. But he was bolder and stronger than the other two. He was also sober, and that gave him the advantage. As I wiped the blood from my mouth onto the shoulder part of my shirt, I nodded to him that I was ready if he was and gave him the "come and get it" wave of my hand.

It only took a matter of seconds, which had surprised me, really. His size had meant that he had the advantage. And with the blow I took earlier, he definitely had the power, but that had been a sucker punch. Once he had his hands on my shoulders, he stalled, putting too much thought into his next move. In one single movement, not giving him a chance to encroach further, I was able to get in on the inside and rotate my body between his arms and feet. He never even saw the blade. It never left the length of my forearm. As I spun, the knife sliced evenly across his throat, and I was able to break his hold at the same time. The move had me back, facing him. I watched as he slumped to his knees, grasping at the gaping hole that I had left in his throat. As the blood spilled, the light in his eyes turned out.

By this time, Fat Hardy had begun his retreat. He was finally able to get his trousers pulled up, but he only managed to trap himself between a rubbish bin and a parked car. He couldn't escape me, and he was too afraid to move once his back was literally against the wall. I childishly skipped towards him. I felt giddy and alive. Victorious and veracious. As I skipped, a song began to play in my head, and I started singing, 'And another one bites the dust, Aww! And another one..."

"Aw, you seem scared? Are you scared?... of little ole me," I said to him in the stickiest, sweetest voice I could muster as I pouted out my bottom lip at him and tapped the tip of the blade on his forehead. His friend's blood was still visible, and I saw the color drain from his face. Then I winked at him and laughed. He had shit himself. "Bet ya didn't see that one comin', aye?"

My voice was back to normal, and I was excited. "Do you still wanna take that go? Come on, Love, don't be sore. Where's that brave, tough man now, aye?" I took his hand and placed the palm of his hand beneath my skirt and onto my ass. Forcing him to cop a right good tight grip. "You feel that, don't ya? Does it feel good? Does it feel like hers over there? Upon seeing his face grimace in disgust, it ramped me up.

"Wait! What? You don't like older women? Am I not your type? You're a pervy pedo, ain't ya Fatty? Or is it you don't do crazy, aye? Come on now, look at me," I said, as I grabbed a fist full of his greasy hair and yanked his face to meet mine. "Is this not fun for you anymore?"

He was crying by then. "Please. I, I, I didn't mean her no harm," he stuttered out. "We were just messin' around, you know how it is. Just havin' a little fun with the lass is all." He had sobered up a bit now and was making his excuses as to why he was such an appalling human being. He had the look of a man who had seen his life ending and was grasping at great hope. "I have a wife and three little girls," he cried. "Who will look after them? For God's sake. Please have mercy," he pleaded. "Girl, girl," he continued to cry in a hurried panic as his eyes sought out his victim. He was unable to move his head because I had such a grip on him. "You, girl. Please tell her. I didna touch you. Oh, God. Please help me."

The girl said nothing as I waited for her to speak. Hearing no other objections, I continued on. His insistence on speaking to the girl further enraged me. Thought I didn't know that was possible. I couldn't believe he'd actually thought that he'd done her no harm. As I watched his face, the fear and the tears, I felt nothing. No pity. No stay of execution. No regret. I wanted him dead. As I looked him deeply in his eyes, I raised my blade and stuck him three times in his gut. One for each one of his daughters, and then I buried the blade into the side of his neck. "That one is for your wife. They are all better off withoutcha," I said through gritted teeth. "Your God is not here to save you, and the world will not miss another fat fuck like yourself."

I hadn't forgotten about the man with a broken elbow as I let the Hardy guy fall and slide down the wall of the tavern. I was turning to head his way when the girl leaped from the doorway and headed down the alley. I thought she was taking her exit, but when she stopped next to a pile of old frames, I found myself amused and smiling. I wondered what she'd do when she picked through the pile, and after settling on her choice, she turned and headed back towards me. I wasn't sure what she meant to do with the metal rail, but I really wanted to find out.

The girl walked to the man who lay on the ground between us, still holding his elbow but not moving. There was nothing wrong with the man's legs, so I assumed he was frozen in fear as she kicked at him and got no response from his lifeless body. He was playing dead. It might have worked if it weren't for the slight tremble of his body or the quiet groan that rumbled from his throat. Then she stood over him. I could see the man's eyes squeezed tightly together. Before I could say anything, but not like I would have stopped her, she lifted the rail high above her head. The slice that came down, cutting through the air like a hot knife, narrowly missed me by half an inch. It crashed hard onto the man's head. It wasn't sharp enough. In a fury, she hit him over and over, until the man's eyes no longer squeezed shut. I saw his face relax and his hand fall away from his elbow.

I attempted to leave then. But she ran up to me and threw her arms around me. She no longer clutched that dress of hers closed. Her knees were scraped up, her makeup was a mess, and all over her face, but she was alive. And still able to tell one hellva story. Though I thought perhaps she'd leave out the part where she had just caved in a man's head with a bedrail. I reckon I hadn't expected her outpouring of emotion. I wanted to push her off me, but I did nothing. I just stood there like a sod and let the girl wrap herself around me.

"Okay, okay. That'll be quite enough of that," I said, pushing her back. "You're not my sort. That was, however, impressive. Nicely done. What's your name?"

"Charity Martin," she replied in a strong, even voice. She was recovering well, and her voice had very little falter to it.

"Hello, Charity Martin," I replied. "Do you have an ID? If so, can you please hand it to me?"

She left me then and walked over to the fat man. Her demeanor had changed to a touch of indignation. Her posture was upright, and she wasn't afraid anymore. She walked with confidence and purpose. Once in front of Hardy, she kicked him hard in the face, his body toppling over from where he slumped. Then she retrieved a small clutch from his pocket. As she handed it over to me, she asked, "Do you want my cash and cards as well? Take whatever you want. I reckon you've earned it."

"I'm not robbing you, Charity Martin," I said. "I want to make sure you leave nothing behind. Nothing that can come back to me. Or you, for that matter. Because you can come back on me—take everything you had on you with you. We were never here. You hear me? And I wouldn't tell anyone about that either," I said, nodding my head over at the man missing the top of his head. There are no cameras in this alleyway. So, don't call the Garda. Just make sure you leave that way," I directed, turning her to face the open hole of a clear pathway. "Let someone else call this in." I then handed Charity back her clutch and continued," Do you understand? Not a word to anyone."

Charity looked around the alleyway, surveilling the bodies. She felt no shame in what had happened. I could tell that by the way she smirked at them. She could tell her parents that she was attacked, but it would just as easy for her to slip back into her bedroom as if nothing had ever happened—or not to go home at all.

"No one will see me and all this," she said, looking down at her torn dress and the disarray of her, well, everything. I'll tell my boyfriend I had a small tumble, and he'll let me crash with him. He'll believe it if I have another drink or two to sell it." Then she nodded her understanding and took her purse back. "I won't say a word. I swear."

"Good. I need you to ring someone to come and fetch you. You need to wait on the street, under that light over there," I said, pointing to the end of the alleyway again. "There are people everywhere, and you'll be safer in the light." I then gave her my jacket and began walking in the opposite direction.

"Wait," Charity said in an attempt to halt my retreat. "What is your name?"

"They call me Baby."

GETTING THE BAND
BACK TOGETHER

Under-Sheriff Bishop Bohannon watched the Gulfstream G6-Expensive series land on the paved landing strip with a bounce, a couple of hops, and what looked like the ass-end of the plane trying to race the nose to the finish line. Then, it skidded a few yards and came to an abrupt stop. It was like someone had finally had enough, reached over, and pulled the e-brake. The front of the plane lurched forward, and the nose of the aircraft bowed down and kissed the ground. Grateful to have an end to what appeared to be one hell of a ride. Then the nose lifted skywards as it dropped its tail with a heavy thud and leveled off. An image entered his mind of flying drinks, food, and disheveled bodies being tossed around like an animated slow-motion Looney Toons' episode. This brought a smile to his face, and he gave out a chuckle. He knew the souls on board the cushy private rental. Those passengers were used to getting the crap beat out of them. But judging by the looks of that landing, he was pretty sure that with this flight, they'd all rather be back in the desert getting shot at.

When the door finally pushed open, a middle-aged, haggard-looking flight attendant in black heels and a blue-gray uniform stepped out into the fresh air. Though there had been a light fall of rain, she hadn't retreated back into the shelter of the plane. She inhaled deeply, sighed heavily, and smoothed out her graying black hair. She was a little greener than her experience would have suggested, and no matter of deep breathing could hide it. She straightened her neck scarf, pressed down her skirt, gripped the handrail, and wobbled her unsteady legs down the stairs, where she stood statuesque at the bottom. Once there, with a slight shake of her hands, she pulled a pack of cigarettes from her skirt and lit up. Then, she waited for the others to follow. Her big, toothy smile did not match the yellow of her eyes as she greeted each passenger who exited the plane. The flight had rattled her entirely. She had been shaken and stirred without ice. Upon seeing the passengers unload, Bishop exited his Bronco and began walking towards the group. Each of them looked grateful to now be on solid ground.

A small gathering of five men and two women took shape on the tarmac under the grayed backdrop of the muggy night. The running lights on the plane and the four luminaires that sat atop 20-foot lamp posts refused to be extinguished, promising that the day was coming to a close. The rain had slowed to a mist, but the forecast promised a downpour with possible high winds in just a few hours. If they were going to get anything done with what was left of the day, they needed to get a move on it. He was there for the four dressed like a comical mix of Hawaiian tourists and a tactical assault team. A tall Brit was thanking the captain and his co-pilot for a safe landing under the circumstances. Their flight out of Seattle had been fraught with turbulence, severe thunderstorms, and lightning that threatened to drop them from the sky at any moment. While he spoke, a younger, more vocal blonde man, whose accent placed him out of the Detroit area, was wound up tighter than a virgin at a prison rodeo. He was loud and spooled up for a fight.

"Where exactly did you learn to fly?" He demanded. "Is it a reputable establishment? Are they in THIS country? Land of the U.S.A? Because I'm almost positive that you, sir, got your flight license from a fucking Lucky Charm's cereal box." On that note, Silas Holiday, aka Sunshine, wrapped his arms around his wiry friend and carried the man away like a petulant child. "I promise you," he said, over Silas's back, unable to move or point a finger at the pilots, "I will be checking on your airtime and flying credentials. You have not heard the last of me," he continued as he was hauled away from the men who looked taken back by his behavior.

Addison Adler, whose handle was Brick, was dressed in ripped black jeans, a blue Hawaii shirt, and tan unlaced desert boots; he stepped through the group and met Bishop toe to toe. "Boss," he said. His face was so close to Bishop's that their noses were near touching. His eyebrows wrinkled deeply as he held a stern gaze fixed on Bishop. All seriousness and no bullshit was all the expression held. A practiced one, no doubt. He had used that look his entire career. His eyes twinkled mischievously as the wheels turned, and Bishop saw what Addison had worked out. If he were being honest, he wouldn't have moved, letting Addison have his moment. As Bishop stood still, Addison's lips stretched and twisted into a deep creased pucker. Then he quickly pecked a kiss on the tip of Bishop's nose. As he drew back, a grin crept across his hidden dimpled cheeks, buried beneath a thick mass of a black woolly beard that hadn't seen a razor in over a year. When Bishop didn't move, Addison grabbed him into a tight bear hug, squeezing him so hard that Bishop was sure he heard a rib crack. Then, he was lifted off the ground. Addison's deep laugh thundered from his throat, but it had started deep in his belly. A genuine laugh melted the hardest of moods and squashed the most serious of natures.

"I sure did miss you, brov'ver!" Addison said his British accent was thick with love and heavy on respect. Bishop was his best mate. Over the past twenty-five-plus years of their friendship, they had seen the best and the worst of one another on every continent, in at least 32 countries. Bishop was not only his best man at his wedding but also Uncle BB and godfather to Addison's two children.

Sister watched the two men from her place on the ground. She had to take a minute before joining the group. Her stomach was still in the air, and her legs hadn't found ground yet. Her hand still clutched the little white bag that contained her breakfast from earlier. She wondered why she even bothered to take motion sickness medication, as it never made her stomach stop rolling. As she rested her head on her knees, she watched the two. She was happy to have the band back together. Though they'd all worked together off and on for several years now, lately, it wasn't often that they were all in the same place or had the same assignments. It always depended on the task and how many it would take to accomplish that task. However, they had been stretched thin lately. The unit was small, and although they often believed more bodies were needed, they knew most didn't have the heart to do their job. Their line of work took them all over the world, and at times—more often than not, it brought them to the most devastating circumstances.

It had been almost two years since she had last laid eyes on Bishop, and several months since they had last spoken. They had been nothing more than welfare checks and static conversations that made their situation more uncomfortable. Although it had been by design, either by her actions or his, it hadn't sat well with her. Rome had been tough on them. He didn't say why, but she knew something had broken when he left Rome without a word. It was her fault, and she knew that part. She didn't know how she let things get so

far out of control. She was angry with herself more than at him. He wore his hurt like a bad suit. The longer he left her on silent, the further she let him go. Maybe it was the unspoken that had sent them both fleeing to opposite ends of the planet, each taking to their own corner of the ring. Without either returning to end the round. She knew it was for the best, but it was still hard on her and everyone else involved.

After each of the boys had hugged it out and exchanged greetings with Bishop, Sister took a deep breath. It was now her turn. She wasn't ready for it. She really hoped that her stomach would hold up. She told herself that it was just the flight that had made her sick. However, she wasn't only tasting her taco breakfast but also the unease that had crept into all the unfilled spaces. Her insides coiled and twisted at the thoughts that circled around her. She not only had a bad taste in her mouth, but a bad feeling had settled in her bones.

Offering an assist, Silas reached out a hand and yanked Sister to her feet. "You might as well get this one over with," he said. His jovial smile showed no compassion for her condition. He never treated her like a delicate flower. But of course, he knew she'd break his nose if he tried. Once on her feet, she placed two fingers between her teeth and forced a sharp and quick whistle from her lips. Then, she wearily made her way towards the man whose eyes would not seek her out. "One foot in front of the other," Silas whispered quickly into her ear before finding something else for himself to do.

Walking towards Bishop, she hoped that either her nerves would settle or the earth would crack open and swallow her whole. Though the odds of her plane falling from the sky seemed more probable. As she walked, she began to wish just for that. Either way, the fiery pits of hell or a fiery crash and burn felt safer.

At the sound of the whistle, Bishop's eyes finally went her way. His gaze showed warmth but distance. He looked good—really good. She missed him. It wasn't until his eyes met hers that she realized just how much. They had been close once. Thinking back now, she never would have guessed that this would be how they would end up. His face bore an expression that she could only read as sadness. His eyes were different. It was like his soul wasn't reflecting back the energy with which he once viewed the world. Or her. It wasn't exactly coldness she saw in them, but it was something close to it. That made her stomach hurt more as she fought back the tears. Was complete indifference worse than being hated? He was clearly still upset with her and doing nothing to pretend otherwise. He'd never win any awards for his performance today. He was a master liar. Yet, he couldn't fake it and wouldn't try. It was written all over his face; anyone with even half a brain could read it.

When his hands clapped together, she noticed a change in his body language, one that resembled excitement. She followed his gaze and watched as his hands reached out towards the plane in a welcoming gesture. At the top of the stairs, standing confidently, disciplined, and waiting for her marching orders, stood a large black Rottweiler.

"Come on, Girl, go get him," she yelled up at the black beast and pointed. The dog's eyebrow hairs danced in place as her lips curled up at the ends at the sight of Bishop. She always smiled for him. When Sister pointed at Bishop, drawing an invisible direct line between the two, that was all she could stand. She began to bounce in place, her body arching and bobbing side to side. Unable to contain her excitement any longer, she darted down the stairs, ran across the tarmac, and nearly knocked Bishop over as she dove at him head-on.

"Beast, you beautiful girl, you," Bishop said, rubbing her mahogany cheeks and soft ears. Sister watched as he allowed Beast to lick the smell of lunch off his face. This had always grossed her out.

The cheeseburger he had wolfed down earlier was greasy and must have smelled delightful. And Beast was enjoying every last invisible taste of it. She whined excitedly. She was happy to see him. Her unclipped tail wiggled so hard that it vibrated through her body and down to the paws that matched her cheeks. "How have you been, my sweet girl?" He continued, running his hands down her back and patting her sides. "What is all this!" He exclaimed, running a thumb over the top of her nose. "You have gray hair! You are aging, my friend. Becoming an old gal," he teased the dog. "You're an old broad now." When he finished ruffling her fur, he instructed her to sit. Beast looked up at Sister, walked to her side, and sat at her feet.

"You're looking as pretty as ever," Bishop directed towards the clouds. It caught Sister off guard since his eyes were still on Beast. It sounded almost hollow and forced, but also as if he spoke in jest and a half-truth. He then reached out his arms and pulled her to him. The embrace felt awkward but warm. Now, it was her turn. At that moment, everything had been placed on the back burner. She allowed herself to melt into him. He felt like Christmas. She wrapped her arms around him and held on for dear life. She soaked up his heat. She inhaled his scent. His skin smelled of bath soap, sweat, and a hint of cologne. And a bacon cheeseburger. The cologne was probably Old Spice because he was just that kind of guy. He anchored her, even if she didn't want it to be so. They held onto one another longer than either of them had needed to. Or maybe they did.

"Cough, Cough," Addison said, clearing his throat. While Silas and Luke shamefully stared at them like idiots. The three amigos sat near one another on the ground and pretended to pass something back and forth between them.

"Popcorn?" Addison asked, handing over an invisible bucket to Silas.

"Why thank you, kind sir," Silas said, taking the invisible bucket from him. "Salted or unsalted?"

"I'll pass," chimed in Luke. He sat cross-legged between the two others and stared up at them as if he were watching a traumatic cliffhanger. "I'm just here for the train wreck."

"You outta mints?" he teased, pulling away from Sister and ignoring Larry, Curly, and Mo. "By that landing, it looked like a rough flight." A hint of amusement crossed his face, but he held back the laugh. He knew she'd rather cut off her own big toe than be on a plane.

"You know how much I love flying," she told him. Her southern drawl seeped in sarcasm. "If God had intended me to fly," he'd attached wings to these here shoulders and called me Angel." She then hooked her thumbs over her back and pointed at her shoulder blades. He quickly gave her another tight squeeze and a healthy laugh before clearing his throat and stepping away from her.

"What's with the getup, Boss?" Silas asked. "We joinin' the roe-da-o circuit?" Silas cracked up at himself as he tucked his thumbs into the waistband of his long black shorts and started doing a jig. "Giddy up, little doggies!"

Bishop, whose handle had once been Boss, again clapped his hands together, ignored Silas's question, and the jab at his western duds, which he thought were a far cry from BDUs, tactical blacks, and a suit and tie—none of which he missed. "Let's get this dog and pony show on the road, shall we?" He said, smiling at Silas. He then reached into his bag and pulled out four six-pointed gold stars with the words "Marie Anjou Parish" printed in blue embossed lettering on the bottom and "Deputy Sheriff" printed at the top.

"You are all now newly sworn deputy sheriffs of the Marie Anjou Parish Sheriff's Department. Welcome to Baptiste." He then tossed the bag over to Silas. "Well, everyone but you, McQueen. You'll have a different assignment, but we will get to that later tonight."

"You got it, Boss," McQueen said, giving Bishop a German salute.

"You're a dumbass," Silas said before smacking McQueen in the back of the head. "Stop clowning."

"Oh, 'cause there can be only one," McQueen countered. "Got it. You're the only clown."

"Come on, children," Bishop said, giving them a stern look of disapproval that didn't quite reach the top.

"Is Brick my first name or last name? "Addison asked, being a smartass, as he joined Silas in rifling through the bag.

"Does it matter, Addison? There's no paper on you here. You'll be in and out. Get the job done and be back to the fam in no time. Besides, I could always use Addie Adler," he said with a shrug and a grin. "I'm sure that could get things tuned up around here. Given your build and skin color, that'd be like calling you Marion," he chuckled. "Y'all's shirts are in the bag. Load your shit and saddle up, ladies," he said, pointing to an older model crew truck parked at the side of the flight barn about fifty yards off the tarmac. "Sister, I used Charlee Lovejoy for you," Bishop said, hinting at something ill-favored in the tone. "You've used it before, so I just ran with it," he continued, not looking at her. "There are rooms for you in town. They should be ready by the time we get there. You can get cleaned up, and then, we'll go see what the Old Man's up to. There's a press conference scheduled for 8 a.m. tomorrow. There won't be a lot of time to mess around. Sister, were you able to get through the file?" He asked over his shoulder as he pulled a set of keys from his pocket. Then, he lofted the keys over to Addison. "She's all yours."

Before she could answer, McQueen busted in. "Wait, wait, wait! Addison's driving? Do you really trust him to drive again? You sure are quick to put my life in danger." McQueen was beside himself as he picked up his bag and quickly followed behind Bishop. "I'm coming with you. You do remember what he did to us in Argentina, right? Sister, you need to say something!" She held up her hands, signifying her lack of response. She opted to stay out of this ongoing battle.

Luke Kidd, whose father named him after the character Cool Hand Luke, also known as McQueen, was the youngest of the group. He was blonde, skinny, and very unassuming. He was that kid on a skateboard that most people hated but never gave a second thought to —well, other than to call the cops because he saw the same "No Skateboarding" sign just like everyone else, but chose to ignore it.

"Make no mistake, he's a wiry little bastard," Silas said, which he said often. McQueen was deadly with a rifle and a wiz with electronics. If he can see it, he can kill it. If it's out there, he'll find it. So far, no one's been able to hide anything from him. Their hidden assets are not safe. Teaching the boy to shoot had just been a bonus for them. However, they had all agreed later that there were better ideas than that. The boy had a good heart, but he lacked impulse control, which was a poor mix with his short temper.

Bishop scooped up McQueen after he learned the feds were about to arrest him. McQueen was a teenager fresh out of high school, working as a print copier at Kinko's. His side job, however, had been far more ambitious. Whenever a client would bring in a loadable USB drive to load images to be digitized or to offload them for printing, Kidd would secretly insert a command code that would install itself once the device was inserted into their computer. The command appeared to be a broken image, and the owner would be completely unaware that they had just granted him full access to their digital information. Since he had their home addresses from their customer information forms, he would search for the IP address associated with their address and wait.

Most would throw the drive into a junk drawer, losing it in a sea of loose change, pens, cords, and whatever else people toss in a drawer, never to be seen again. But there were those diligent few. Once in their hard drives, he'd search out their misdeeds, bank accounts, and personal information. If he found them lacking in the "upstanding moral character" department, he'd relieve them of whatever he felt should be paid in restitution.

It was the seriously awful ones who paid the highest price. By the time he was done, they didn't have enough money left over to rent ice cream. He'd take a service fee and give the rest to some well-deserving random charity. He never donated to the same organization twice. Until he did, and that had been a costly mistake. Hacking and stealing from a local businessman with many top-secret secrets and deep connections to the U.S. government was no bueno. It wasn't their sort of case, but someone owed a favor to someone somewhere higher up in the food chain. Bishop and Silas had been the ones to pay the young man a visit. They were so impressed with the boy's skills that instead of burying his talents in a 6 x 9 for two slices, they offered him a job. Therefore, while Luke Kidd does his time in FCI prison, Kid McQueen works for McTavish. Or did, at least in the beginning. After McTavish's pseudo-retirement, McQueen followed Silas like a lost dog without a home.

Silas, an English Dane out of Norway and a Florida surf enthusiast, had been listening to McQueen's grievances about Addison's driving. He grabbed McQueen with his big hands, tucked McQueen's head in his armpit, and generously rubbed the palm of his hand along the top of McQueen's head. "Come on, Kidd. You act like you nearly died."

McQueen pulled away, now real indignation caused his eyebrows to meet in the middle, becoming one. "Dammit, Silas, not the hair! You'll pay for that! You have to sleep sometime, you Viking animal! Just so you know, a Kidd always gets payback," he said as he proudly pinched his fingers to the sides of his shirt, showing off the black T with the red lion crest. "Winter is here, my friend!"

As a group, GOT was their favorite pastime, and none of them had missed that he mashed up the different kingdoms' mottos and threw in one of his own. "Silas is right; you are a dumbass," Addison said, shaking his head with a laugh.

McQueen was a true fan and liked a little piece of each family. As they walked, he did his best to put every strand of his hair back where it was—frantically raking through and patting in place every strand. "And yes! Last time, it took three days to remove that seat cushion from my puckered asshole!" He then cupped a hand at his rear and pretended to yank something from the seat of his pants. "His driving is worse than that flight. And he drives on the wrong side of the damn road!"

They all exchanged looks and burst into laughter at his antics and the game of charades, which demonstrated the removal of a seat cushion.

"You can ride with me, Kidd," Bishop said once they had all settled down. "Don't get your panties all knotted up. I have a baby seat in the back with your name on it."

Addison's forearm high-fived Bishop's at that nicely placed barb while McQueen mouthed a "hardy har har" and a "go fuck yourselves" at the two of them. He then waved them a high middle finger salute and tossed his bag into the back of Bishop's Bronco.

"You still have her," Sister said to Bishop before yelling, "Shotgun!" Further sending McQueen down a rabbit hole.

"I get no respect. Absolutely none."

After opening the door, Beast barreled past Sister and took her place in the middle. "She's gorgeous, Bishop. You've done a wonderful job restoring her."

ROME

18 Months Earlier

B y the time Sister was dropped off at Trudy's, she was more interested in the clean sheets on the bed than leaving the room. She'd pull the covers over her head and sleep for a week if she had her way. She sighed, wiping the desire from her mind. It couldn't happen just yet. She had a date with the coroner while the guys got McQueen set up with the department's computers and got himself enrolled at the town's private school. Bishop had a hometown advantage when it came to collecting information, but McQueen was far better at finding things nobody wanted found. She'd meet them for dinner later, and afterward, she'd finalize her report before tomorrow's press conference.

Unwilling to prolong her stay South of the Mason Dixon any longer than required, or the continental US for that matter, she placed her garment bag on the bed, removed the clothes, and changed into a clean, collared, long-sleeved white shirt, blue jeans, and a pair of clean socks. She was more interested in the clean underwear and socks, but what she had on looked like she had been on a stakeout for three days and smelled just as bad. Every inch of her body was exhausted. She was mentally and physically drained and felt as if she hadn't slept in months.

Dressed, she gave herself a once-over in the bathroom mirror, pinching at her cheeks to add a bit of color, hoping to awaken the cells that would make her appear less fatigued. She quickly yanked a hairbrush through her hair and spackled on some face cream. exhausted. Every line and crease of her face looked like a ragged road headed south. She gave the mascara a few strokes and applied a lot of deodorant. Silas, who had ambushed her at home, had forgotten to pack her a toothbrush.

"Daddy called," he said facetiously. "You didn't pick up." Silas was sitting on her couch when she opened the door to her cabin. His beard hadn't been trimmed, and he appeared as though he had been living homeless.

"I love the look," she said, grimacing at him. "You looking to secure the cover of Mountain Man Magazine, or did you miss the shower on your way up here?" She didn't bother asking him how he had gotten in and gave Beast her best "What good are you?" look. "I've taken personal time," she said, stomping her snow boots on the floor. "And he's not our boss anymore, remember? He retired to a comfortable position, and he's supposed to be getting fat and sassy in his old age."

"Don't blame her," he said, petting Beast's head. "She put up a good fight. Nearly slobbered me to death. I don't know about sassy, but he is getting fat," Silas laughed.

"You brought her ham, didn't you?" She asked, accusing him of bribing Beast. She nodded at the newly built fire burning in the wall. It wasn't anything big. Small enough to put out in a hurry but strong enough to stay off the chill. "Make yourself at home," she continued, annoyed that he had come uninvited but trying not to show it. "The coffee is still warm," she said, tossing her head towards the small kitchen. "And I don't answer to Daddy," she shot back while organizing the firewood into a neatly stacked triangle.

"We all answer to Old Man, and you know it. Retired or not. And thanks for the coffee," he said, holding up the only mug in the place while steam rose from its center. "When he calls, we drop what we're doing, and we answer. That's the deal. And if he sent me here, it must be worth the come runnin'."

She noticed him glance at the end table and saw that he had already tripped its top. The couch's end tabletop had a hidden compartment. She should have known he'd look there since he was the one who had given her the table for some holiday or another last year. "And don't worry about old Stella," he said, patting the bag beside him. "She's already waiting for you."

"That for me?" she asked, eyeing the bag he had sitting next to him.

"Yep. I even got your unmentionables," he said, patting the bag again with a smile and a Groucho raise of his eyebrows.

He may have remembered her underwear, but forgetting her toothbrush was most likely payback for the flight north. He hated the Northern weather. He may have looked like he was built for the cold, but nothing about it had excited him. As she ran an index finger across her teeth, given an option, she'd rathered he forget her unmentionables altogether and brought a damn toothbrush.

"There," she said out loud," examining herself in the mirror. She looked and smelled as good as she was going to. She felt like warmed over crap, and she was really putting on too much of a fuss. That had bothered her more than she cared to admit. When she was done, she tapped the star with an index finger. "When in Rome," she sighed.

She hated that expression and what it truly implied. But Bishop seemed to have embraced a simpler life and was comfortable in his new surroundings. She already knew he would, though. He was the type who could adapt to his environment better than anyone. She had to wonder about a uniform's ability to shape a person's persona. Depending on the person wearing the uniform, it could just be another change of clothing. A costume. A disguise. Or was it armor? "Which one is this?" she wondered out loud. She had worn so many faces over the years that she felt none accurately depicted who she was. Everyone had ideas, of course. But deep down — not even she knew the answer to that.

Whether it be a habit, tactical gear, a tiny black dress, or a swanky gown - they were all the same, just costumes. "This has got to be the most authentic form of an identity in crisis," she whispered to the woman in the mirror. Beast whined at hearing Sister's tone, looked up at her as if she was hanging on Sister's every word, and sympathized. "When in Rome," she repeated. Again, Beast whined in response. She shook off the appraisal of herself and swiped at the steamed-over image in the mirror. Everything would be fine. What other choice did she have?

Sister loaded her gun belt with two ammo magazines, a flashlight, two sets of cuffs, and Stella—an XD fitted with a light sight for light or dark and black pearl grips. Stella had been a gift from Bishop. Something that she cherished deeply. As she fastened the belt around her hips, she called for Beast, and they headed for the door. She tossed the green and tan sheriff's shirt in the trash on their way out. There wasn't a chance in hell she'd wear anything that looked like a Coleman tent.

THE AMBUSH

B y the time Sister was dropped off at Trudy's, she was more interested in the clean sheets on the bed than leaving the room. She'd pull the covers over her head and sleep for a week if she had her way. She sighed, wiping the desire from her mind. It couldn't happen just yet. She had a date with the coroner while the guys got McQueen set up with the department's computers and got himself enrolled at the town's private school. Bishop had a hometown advantage when it came to collecting information, but McQueen was far better at finding things nobody wanted found. She'd meet them for dinner later, and afterward, she'd finalize her report before tomorrow's press conference.

Unwilling to prolong her stay South of the Mason Dixon any longer than required, or the continental US for that matter, she placed her garment bag on the bed, removed the clothes, and changed into a clean, collared, long-sleeved white shirt, blue jeans, and a pair of clean socks. She was more interested in the clean underwear and socks, but what she had on looked like she had been on a stakeout for three days and smelled just as bad. Every inch of her body was exhausted. She was mentally and physically drained and felt as if she hadn't slept in months.

Dressed, she gave herself a once-over in the bathroom mirror, pinching at her cheeks to add a bit of color, hoping to awaken the cells that would make her appear less fatigued. She quickly yanked a hairbrush through her hair and spackled on some face cream. exhausted. Every line and crease of her face looked like a ragged road headed south. She gave the mascara a few strokes and applied a lot of deodorant. Silas, who had ambushed her at home, had forgotten to pack her a toothbrush.

"Daddy called," he said facetiously. "You didn't pick up." Silas was sitting on her couch when she opened the door to her cabin. His beard hadn't been trimmed, and he appeared as though he had been living homeless.

"I love the look," she said, grimacing at him. "You looking to secure the cover of Mountain Man Magazine, or did you miss the shower on your way up here?" She didn't bother asking him how he had gotten in and gave Beast her best "What good are you?" look. "I've taken personal time," she said, stomping her snow boots on the floor. "And he's not our boss anymore, remember? He retired to a comfortable position, and he's supposed to be getting fat and sassy in his old age."

"Don't blame her," he said, petting Beast's head. "She put up a good fight. Nearly slobbered me to death. I don't know about sassy, but he is getting fat," Silas laughed.

"You brought her ham, didn't you?" She asked, accusing him of bribing Beast. She nodded at the newly built fire burning in the wall. It wasn't anything big. Small enough to put out in a hurry but strong enough to stay off the chill. "Make yourself at home," she continued, annoyed that he had come uninvited but trying not to show it. "The coffee is still warm," she said, tossing her head towards the small kitchen. "And I don't answer to Daddy," she shot back while organizing the firewood into a neatly stacked triangle.

"We all answer to Old Man, and you know it. Retired or not. And thanks for the coffee," he said, holding up the only mug in the place while steam rose from its center. "When he calls, we drop what we're doing, and we answer. That's the deal. And if he sent me here, it must be worth the come runnin'."

She noticed him glance at the end table and saw that he had already tripped its top. The couch's end tabletop had a hidden compartment. She should have known he'd look there since he was the one who had given her the table for some holiday or another last year. "And don't worry about old Stella," he said, patting the bag beside him. "She's already waiting for you."

"That for me?" she asked, eyeing the bag he had sitting next to him.

"Yep. I even got your unmentionables," he said, patting the bag again with a smile and a Groucho raise of his eyebrows.

He may have remembered her underwear, but forgetting her toothbrush was most likely payback for the flight north. He hated the Northern weather. He may have looked like he was built for the cold, but nothing about it had excited him. As she ran an index finger across her teeth, given an option, she'd rathered he forget her unmentionables altogether and brought a damn toothbrush.

"There," she said out loud," examining herself in the mirror. She looked and smelled as good as she was going to. She felt like warmed over crap, and she was really putting on too much of a fuss. That had bothered her more than she cared to admit. When she was done, she tapped the star with an index finger. "When in Rome," she sighed.

She hated that expression and what it truly implied. But Bishop seemed to have embraced a simpler life and was comfortable in his new surroundings. She already knew he would, though. He was the type who could adapt to his environment better than anyone. She had to wonder about a uniform's ability to shape a person's persona. Depending on the person wearing the uniform, it could just be another change of clothing. A costume. A disguise. Or was it armor? "Which one is this?" she wondered out loud. She had worn so many faces over the years that she felt none accurately depicted who she was. Everyone had ideas, of course. But deep down — not even she knew the answer to that.

Whether it be a habit, tactical gear, a tiny black dress, or a swanky gown - they were all the same, just costumes. "This has got to be the most authentic form of an identity in crisis," she whispered to the woman in the mirror. Beast whined at hearing Sister's tone, looked up at her as if she was hanging on Sister's every word, and sympathized. "When in Rome," she repeated. Again, Beast whined in response. She shook off the appraisal of herself and swiped at the steamed-over image in the mirror. Everything would be fine. What other choice did she have?

Sister loaded her gun belt with two ammo magazines, a flashlight, two sets of cuffs, and Stella—an XD fitted with a light sight for light or dark and black pearl grips. Stella had been a gift from Bishop. Something that she cherished deeply. As she fastened the belt around her hips, she called for Beast, and they headed for the door. She tossed the green and tan sheriff's shirt in the trash on their way out. There wasn't a chance in hell she'd wear anything that looked like a Coleman tent.

PERFECT PRETTY STITCHES

S ister arrived at a large glass building on the outskirts of Baton Rouge, which took over half a city block. There was enough glass in the building to put windows in every home in Rhode Island. Something about glass houses came to mind as she hit the buzzer of the side entrance of the building. And stones. Something about stones. It wasn't that she tried to be cynical, but she found herself always seeing the potential fallout of every encounter. A straw house entered her thoughts as she told herself to think positively. And that was quickly followed up by matches. Then, three little pigs and one very fat wolf. Yep, it was going to be one of those days. A man wearing something close to the same green and tan colors met her at the door and asked to see her credentials. His eyebrow arched hard at the appearance of Beast, who stood quietly at her six, watching her back.

"I'm sorry, ma'am. We don't allow dogs in the building," he said, handing her a clipboard.

"Sgt. Beast, say hello to the man," she said as she signed in.

Beast turned to him and barked. Then she moved between them and patiently eyed the guard, waiting for him to address her.

"Sgt. Beast is a retired veteran of the U.S. military armed services. She is not just a dog. She is a war hero. And I'd appreciate it if you'd show her the same respect you'd show any officer or soldier," she stated directly, putting a blunt end to the tone. She wasn't in the habit of dressing down anyone without cause.

Just because she was tired and not feeling at her best wouldn't change that now. She gave the guard a sweet smile and then reached down and rested her hand on the top of Beast's head. "I have all the appropriate clearances, I assure you. And my partner here is always on her best behavior. So, there's that," she continued, pointing to an identical badge like her own.

The guard, who was only halfheartedly looking at Beast, directed his eyes at her badge and read aloud, "Marie Anjou Parish Deputy. Beast." He chuckled. "Sorry, ma'am. I meant no offense, just the rules," he said, stepping aside with a little bow, allowing her and Beast entrance into the building. By the smirk on his face, she concluded that his apology had not been directed at her but Beast. "The doc is waiting for you," he continued, reviewing the expected visitors, clearances, and appointments log. "He's in five," he said, directing her down the west corridor.

It was a long and quiet hallway. The flickering of the lights was the only sound reminiscent of a zombie movie she had seen a few months back. The walls and floors were all in monochromatic tans, making them appear dull and lifeless. This made the space look tunneling and like an impending death trap.

When she reached exam room five, she ordered Beast to stay outside the door. Beast spun in a circle, sat, and took her post with only a small protest. Sister had been holding her breath and had nearly forgotten how to breathe, as Beast whined, as if to ask, "Are you sure I should stay here?" That's when Sister exhaled deeply. She inhaled and slowly released the energy that had her spun up inside. She felt the oxygen and blood return to her center. Then she reached down and calmly rubbed the top of Beast's head before entering the room.

Dr. Harold Tomlin was the Parish's medical examiner and coroner. He appeared as though he had been performing doctoral duties as far back as North v South. A picture of him in gray with a white apron, a jug of whisky, and a bone saw entered her mind. He had the perfect face for that sort of era film. His posture was slumped, and his eyeglasses were as thick as soda glass, but his hands were steady as she observed him carefully make each stitch with gentle patience. He sat hunched over on a chair, where he was in the process of sewing up a young girl's Y incision. The room was silent. Not just quiet but void of noise of any kind. Not wanting to invade his space, she quietly approached the table with the same amount of stillness.

"My eyes are failing me, girl, but my hearing is superb," he said in a low voice, not looking up at her. "No need to sneak in here like you've missed curfew, young lady. You quite literally won't wake anyone." His lips curled up into a smile at his humor as he continued to stitch.

She slowed her pace and hesitated for a moment. The quiet was so deafening that she felt as though she had been tiptoeing into the room and had to stop and press her heels to the floor, ensuring she hadn't looked like an amateur buffalo trampling across his floor. The lack of sound and the bright white of the surrounding walls made her feel as if she had invaded his sanctuary.

"I'm with the sheriff's department," she offered. "McTavish sent me. I'm here about the girl," she said, nodding at the table as her words trailed off. She felt as though she was intruding as she watched his face. He looked like a man with a deep concern about him. Clearly, the introductions were unnecessary. He had been expecting her, but she saw something different in the way he addressed her. She had considered reaching out to shake his hand, but thought better of it. He had been, after all, elbow-deep in the chest cavity of a body and was gloved up, needle in hand, and fixed to righting his intrusive, albeit necessary, mutilation of her body.

Instead, she watched him sew and wondered how in the world she had made it this far in her career. She felt outwardly like a blubbering idiot and a nervous wreck inside. She had dealt with serial killers, drug lords, and the worst dregs the world had to offer. Never once had she been afraid or apprehensive. Every job had been met with her skills as a trained operative and a brilliant investigator with a doctorate in criminology and human behavior.

However, right now, it was a miracle that she had managed to put her pants on straight. She felt like a bundle of raw nerves; it was all she could do to stand still. Her brain was all over the place—while her insides vibrated at a frequency that made her eardrums pulse so loudly that she wasn't sure she could hear words. Was this a panic attack? Was she literally melting down in front of this doctor?

"This poor girl has suffered greatly," he said. His voice was soft, low, and welcoming. She could hear the calm in his words. "I haven't gotten anything from pathology, so our conversation is strictly just that—a conversation. Are you okay with that?"

He didn't wait for her to respond. She closed her open mouth to stop the words as he continued. "Note the bruising around her wrists and ankles," he directed, using the sewing needle in his hand as an indicator. "She had been tied up for a significant amount of time before entering the water. Whoever dumped her did their best to hide evidence, but by the pure grace of God, there was some evidence that hadn't been washed away. This pattern burns here, for example...are from a cigar." He then paused the sewing and pointed at the girl's torso and upper legs, "are from a cigar. Or multiple. There are two distinct patterns. These fat ones here are a standard everyday Robusto or Toro type. These here are smaller, like a cigarillo. I found ash still embedded in the wounds. This would indicate that the burns had some time to heal, allowing the ash to be encased in the eschar crust. The water had softened the scabs, but they didn't slough off. Which is a miracle in itself, considering she had been in the water for a while and the amount of river critters that would have fed off her, " he said in a grimacing tone, as he reached into the front pocket of his coat and handed Sister a small plastic tube. "Twist that off and give it a snort," he instructed. It'll help with the smell."

Sister twisted off the long cap, similar to a lipstick tube, placed the tip in her nose, and inhaled. A quick burst of menthol shot through her, and she instantly felt awake. With the smell of menthol in her nose, the sourness of the room also quieted down. Before she could ask a question, Dr. Tomlin continued on without a pause.

"However, the body had been washed before finding the Rouge. Her hair smelled of sodium hypochlorite. Not even the worst of what the Rouge has to offer can mask that smell. She also had been sexually assaulted. I'd venture to say that she had gone untouched until meeting her assailant. Based on the bruising here," again, pointing to the girl's inner thighs. There was also bruising internally, as well as rectal tearing," he said quickly as if trying to get past those details and out of his mouth as fast as possible. He struggled with words. "Like I said before, this girl suffered greatly. There were no fluids present. I found no biological information. Not even spermicide."

The old doc dove into the interview without looking up at her as he spoke. He provided a complete play-by-play of the girl's injuries, starting at her feet and working his way upwards. Everything from broken bones to bruised organs. She found it odd that he didn't ask her name. He kept his eyes down and his hands steady as he painstakingly placed perfectly aligned stitches from the girl's collarbones to her navel. They were morbidly pretty, she thought. Each of the threads were perfectly lined up and diligently placed.

Once he had finished stitching and interpreting his preliminary findings, he pulled off his gloves and tossed them, along with a mask, into a bin next to the exam table. He then adjusted his glasses, sat up straighter in the chair, and finally looked up at her. She saw that his eyes were damp, like he was on the edge of a dam break. As she looked at his face, she saw him—the window before the eyes that swallowed her in.

He was definitely an old, soft soul. Maybe that's why he didn't give her an edge to speak. Perhaps he had to vomit out all there was before he could no longer say the words out loud. The sorrow that lay deep in the age of his face made her feel sad for him.

"I remember you," he said, looking deeply up at her and then back at the floor. "It's been a while since I spent my time with the living, Deputy Lovejoy. My eyes aren't what they used to be, so I convene with dead now. But I remember my patients. It's been a long time, my girl. It's good to see that you've done well. What I mean to say is... I'm glad to see you're okay. You are okay?" he asked, his eyes searching hers for truth.

Something in the way he said her name seemed deeply personal. But she couldn't place him. And the way his eyes begged her to confirm that she had turned out just fine made her want to remember him. She wanted to be okay. She couldn't bring herself to tell him otherwise. She did a total memory recall of his name, but nothing came of it. She prided herself on her memory. She could store images, which were used to correlate people, places, events, and things. But there was a brief time in her life when she could not recall anything. Not a smell, not an image, not a name. Perhaps the options or opportunities for recognition were limited to that time. She looked down at him with a questioning expression. Seeing the wheels turning, Dr. Tomlin began his explanation.

"I was in private practice back then. For the living, that is. A pediatrician, actually. A kid's doctor, if you can believe that."

Sister smiled at him, thinking she could believe that, and would bet that he was wonderful with children.

"Can't say as I ever had you in my office back then, but I did so happen to also moonlight as the state's expert examiner. I worked on cases involving sex crimes, child abuse, and violent domestic assaults. I had been called in to collect evidence and document these types of crimes for the Jane Does and alike, who would need to be—well, you know—unnamed. Those who would inevitably be entering into witness protection or something similar."

"Most often, something far worse, of course. They don't all make it out alive, do they? Only a select few of us knew who the victims were, as I'm sure you are aware. Anyway," he sighed, "I was the one they called in to perform your examination—both examinations. I mean, for the both of you. You and, well, your friend."

Tomlin saw the flash in her eyes. The briefest hint of yellow. Like lightning bolts flashing in clouds during a thunderstorm. She hadn't meant to give anything away, and as quickly as it flashed, the expression changed, and the light darkened across her features. She felt it happen. Her body stiffened, and she unconsciously stepped back from him. Seeing it in motion, she adjusted her footing and disguised the movement by removing the cap from the menthol tube and taking another hit. Her body reacted as it always did when she was reminded of forgotten things. It wasn't the memory of what happened that made her nervous. Not knowing who she should be afraid of made her uneasy. Given what she did, it was a ridiculous assessment of herself, but she wasn't scared of those she went after. She feared what she didn't know about herself and the people who got to her. Feeling underwater, she began to tap off numbers across each finger. One, two, three, ... and so on, until she counted down enough numbers to stay in the moment. As she counted, she felt herself steady inside.

If he had noticed her train come off its rails, his kind nature wouldn't have allowed him to speak of it. She could tell by the way his eyes shifted that he had noticed something. The concern he directed at her also gave him away, but being the sort of man she assumed him to be, he quickly continued, ignoring what he may have witnessed. "Although I found nothing biological to indicate how many may have been involved, I can tell you that he... or they have done this before. He waited for a moment. Wiping his hands together, he ran them across the tops of his lap—considering whether he should go further. "Let me show you."

Tomlin stood and selected two sets of latex gloves from a box. He handed one pair to her and snapped the other pair on his hands as he returned to the girl's body. He gently swept her hair back from around her ear, rotated her head to the side, and exposed her neck. Tomlin knew that she would understand once she saw what it was. When he hesitated, she gently nudged him with her elbow before crossing her arms over her chest and waited.

"Go on. Please."

After giving her a reassuring glance, he said, "I'm sure McTavish has his reasons for having you here, but on my life, I hope he knows what he's doing. I don't like second-guessing our sheriff friend; God knows the man is as solid as they come, but I'm not sure he's doing the right thing in discussing this case with you. But I will, however, do as I have been asked."

Deep inside, he wasn't sure he was doing the right thing. His heart ached at what he had firsthand knowledge of. Being a doctor and a decent human being, he wasn't altogether convinced that a person could bounce back from that sort of trauma without having some deep scars. Both physically and mentally. But he was old and tired of seeing the "throw-away girls" on his table. The girls who went missing or were found abused and or dead. The girls who rarely got the sort of justice they deserved. He hated hearing, "At least they are still alive." So many times, he often wondered if death would have better served them. It was an awful feeling. But after attending to several suicides of these poor women, he knew that not all of them bounced back. He did know of her reputation. If she could apply the same amount of dogged determination she applied to her career, then he was all in. He just hoped that in doing so, it wouldn't take her to places she need not to revisit.

She saw the mark immediately, and her hand unconsciously shot up to the scar behind her ear. Nausea crawled up her belly, and she beat it back. The raised indentation was that of a small line cut just behind the ear. Its significance was lost to the universe. No one had yet been able to uncover its meaning. Those close to the case surmised it was a calling card of sorts. The mark wasn't just on the two of them. It had been found on several bodies over the years. And not just on women.

There had been at least five teen boys with the same mark. And this didn't happen in Louisiana alone. There were bodies with this mark all over the U.S. and across the pond as well. Dr. Dylan James of the Tulsa Police Department's forensics lab was the first to make the connection after they fished a girl out of the Cimarron River in Beaver County. And Sister was one of a handful of people who knew that this went beyond the Rouge.

"It's the same as mine," she said, pushing the girl's hair aside to get a better look. "She's so young. I think she's the youngest so far," she said before biting back the words. She hadn't meant to divulge that she knew more than she was supposed to.

"One more thing," he said, walking to a highly polished metal table that ran the room's length and braced itself against a glassed white wall. He pulled open an acrylic bin and removed a small zip bag. "I found this inside the girl's mouth. It was tucked in between her back teeth and her left cheek." In her hand, he placed the baggy. Inside was a round, gold-coin-like button with extraordinary detail.

"It's pretty expensive," he said, turning it over and over in the palm of her hand. "Someone paid a good nickel for it. It's anyone's guess on how it got into the girl's mouth, but I would venture to speculate that it belonged to whoever took her life."

She pulled her phone from her pocket and tapped it open. She took a picture of the button-like object with the tiny screen to send to McQueen. Then she returned it to him: "It's best you keep hold of this. If the image isn't good enough for Kidd, I'll send him to take a look at it tomorrow. If that's okay with you," she said.

She gave the man a once-over and considered asking him the million and one questions that ran through her head. About this girl. About before. But she couldn't form the words. This girl was the youngest so far. And there hadn't been a body in this area for the past ten years that had a link to their murders.

Her ducks—are most definitely—not in a row. Hell, she didn't even know where her ducks were. And before she could ask him anything, she needed to collect her files. If what she suspected was true, then her man was back in the bayou. And she believed Old Man knew it, too.

"Thank you," she said as she turned and headed for the door. "I'll reach out later this week if that's alright?" She asked. "I'm afraid I don't have much to go on. I'm still collecting information, and I'd like to get better acquainted before I set a formal record."

"Yes, that will be fine. It's been less than sixteen hours. This inquiry isn't formal. Pathology will take a couple of weeks, even if I rush it through the system. There is still plenty to be done before my findings are made public," he said. "If I may," he said after a brief pause as if trying to find the right things to say.

Sister could see he was struggling with his words and turned to look at him directly, releasing the doorknob. Every part of her was ready to retreat, but the sadness in his eyes stopped her exit.

"Mother Agnes Valentine," he said softly, not meeting her eyes. Sister saw his eyes reddened softly around the edges and turned glassy. "She was an extraordinary, kind, and gentle woman—a dear friend and confidant. What I mean to say," he said, finally able to collect a thought as he pushed past the lump that hardened in his throat. "My dear, she thought the world of you. Both of you, really. She considered you one of her greatest successes. What happened to the two of you devastated her. She lost a lot that night, didn't she? She never really recovered from it. Her passing touched us all, and I am truly sorry for your loss. I couldn't help but notice that you were not at the funeral." His eyes grew sad, but then he quickly recovered. "I'm sorry. Of course, I understand why you didn't. I just wish things could have happened differently. That's all. I just wish there could have been a better way forward for you both."

Sister wasn't sure what to say. Mother Agnes Valentine was indeed one of the best people she had ever known, and she loved her dearly. She had suffered significant losses, from the death of her family to the destruction that night brought—not many had been shielded from it. One common thing about

Baptiste—everyone seemed to suffer a loss, and Mother Agnes Valentine wasn't alone in her grief.

An awful shame overtook Sister, and she, too, felt herself well up in tears. But she wouldn't dare let them fall. There wasn't time for self-recrimination, and the pain she let settle on others by her absence. There was nothing she could do about yesterday.

"Thank you she said, "I appreciate that. She was an extraordinary woman indeed. And thoroughly missed," she continued. "I miss us all—the way we were. What we should have been. The lives we could have lived. But we are here now. Nothing to do but move forward." Then she gave him a polite smile and left the room.

INTRUDERS & SACRIFICES

S ister's arm slowly crept out across the top of the bed. She felt drowsy and only partly awake. The movement felt more like a reaction than anything else. She felt exhausted, as though she hadn't slept through the night. Her body was slow to respond. Usually, Sister woke to find Beast snuggled up next to her, no matter what time of the day or night it was, with her head buried in Sister's neck or beneath her chin. It was their thing. Beast was part of her—even though it had taken them a long time to get there. Beast had been unhinged and on the verge of being put down in those early days, a lot like how Sister had felt.

Gently, she patted her hand atop the blankets, feeling her way along the covers. Her hand landed on a soft material, pausing as she anticipated the feeling of a tongue, knowing that Beast would lick her hand if it were within striking distance. Like a frog darting at a fly, she waited. With no response, she felt again and quickly realized that although the material was soft, it wasn't Beast. She pulled the material towards her face, squinted through sleepy eyes, and recognized the familiarity of an old pink cashmere housecoat. She had given it to Beast because it wasn't her style. It turned out to be Beast's favorite snuggle.

The housecoat had been on every outing and adventure from here to Egypt. Beast would rub her face all over it, followed by her body. Sometimes, she'd rub so deep that Sister thought she'd rub the material right out of its collective backing. Beast would wiggle and worm her body through the robe, burying herself under it and falling asleep. Her head would often get stuck in the arm sleeves, and Sister would have to help her find her way out.

She vaguely recalled leaving it at the foot of the bed last night. Beast had probably dragged up to the pillows, and it had gotten tangled up in the bedding throughout the night. Sister quickly opened her eyes wide, somewhat alarmed at not finding Beast, and scanned the surface of the bed. Beast wasn't there. The usual spaces were cool to the touch, as if they had long since been abandoned. As she lifted herself up, light peeked through the opening between the white and tan curtains of the eggshell-painted room, letting her know that it was now morning. Beast was not immediately visible. The room was beautifully decorated but smaller than the last place they'd been hunkered down. The part of Johannesburg where they stayed wasn't exactly known for its vast array of luxury hotels or spacious accommodations. However, with that being said, this place was a closet in comparison. There weren't many places in the room where she could hide.

Sister's abrupt exit from the bed was so fast that she startled herself. It was times like these that it didn't make sense to sleep in the nude. It was as if she were asking for a hurricane to blow through while she slept. Weighing out her options, floods and neighbors be damned, she decided she'd risk a nakked encounter with fire rescue rather than feel bound up. Instantly, she realized something was wrong as the hair on her body went on high alert. Panning the room, her eyes caught a glimpse of herself staring back from the mirror above a white eighteenth-century dresser, planted directly across from the end of the bed.

"Yikes," she said grimly as she wrinkled up her nose. Perhaps she should reconsider all that ice cream and cheeseburgers. It probably wouldn't kill her to eat a salad more than once a month, she thought as she shrugged at herself. She really didn't look that bad, but that hadn't been what grabbed her attention in the first place. As her eyes adjusted to being awake, her reflection appeared smudged in the mirror. She raised her hands to her chest and looked down. A coloration of red lines had distorted her image in the mirror. Someone had written on it. "What in the hell," she said. She had slept through an intruder in her room. Why hadn't Beast alerted her? At least a bark or something. It couldn't have been a stranger. Sister would have found pieces of them still lying around the room after Beast ripped them apart. As she played twenty questions with herself, she began to panic and looked for something to throw on. She still hadn't seen Beast.

Sister was now fully awake and in fighting mode. She slid a hand under the pillow and pulled out Stella from beneath it. She then quietly tiptoed towards the bathroom, keeping her eyes on the door. The room was small, and if any unwelcome guests were still there, that would be the only place left for them to hide. The door was closed, and she thought she had remembered leaving the bathroom door open, with the light on above the shower before she'd lain down last night. She heard a whimper as she prepared herself for what was on the other side of the door.

Sister stopped moving and waited for the noise to happen again. Then she quickly yanked open the door, her gun aimed and in firing position. Expecting to find Beast inside, the room was empty, and the light was off. She was relieved to find no one there but still felt uneasy when she heard the whimper again. This time, she heard it clearly. She turned her body to face the chair in the corner of the room. It was small and stood on decoratively carved legs. As she approached, she saw a paw slightly showing out from beneath the chair. It was impossible to register what she was seeing. A rat could barely fit in the space, yet Beast had managed to quietly tuck herself underneath the white Victorian replica.

Beast's eyes followed her intently as Sister made her way across the room, picking up, moving, and examining their belongings along the way. Once Sister had determined nothing had been moved or taken, she placed Stella on the bed. The fact that her backup weapon was lying in plain view on the dresser, untouched and still operational, only added to her worry. Beast still hadn't moved from beneath the chair. She got down on all fours and slowly crawled towards her. She couldn't understand what had happened last night that would send her ferocious friend cowering under the chair.

Beast gave a yip as she slipped out her tongue and nervously licked Sister's face. Sister gently eased her out from beneath the chair and into her lap. Beast's eyes looked uncertain and slightly wild. Sister wondered if she had gotten into the chocolate again. Beast acted almost untrusting of Sister. She hadn't seen this side of Beast in a long time. Though it happened only a few times, it hadn't happened recently. When Beast first came to stay with her at the beginning of their relationship, it wasn't uncommon to find her cowering in a corner, snapping and peeing on herself. Beast had been found in a building, snarling and daring to bite anyone who came near her or the body of the man she had been protecting.

Sgt. Beast and her handler, Monroe, were soldiers attached to MPCs. They had been called in to do a building-to-building search, running grids in a section of Damascus's government district. An anonymous bomb threat had been called in. This was also the same part of the ancient city where an American delegate would be visiting. He had agreed to moderate a temporary truce talk for an upcoming holiday involving several small countries.

There were three of them. They were located north of the city, waiting outside a building just a street over. Monroe, along with Beast, entered the Straight Street building first. They intended to cut through the building and courtyard, emerging on the other side and effectively joining forces with another group to start the search from there. Straight Street hadn't been part of their intel. They hadn't been in the building for less than a minute when Beast alerted Monroe to the dangers of the room they had entered.

"Stay outside. Do you copy? Do not proceed into the building," Monroe called over the radio. "Repeat, do not enter the building," he relayed to the other two, who waited to proceed his way.

The road to Damascus entered Monroe's thoughts as he took a measure of his life. He knew that, for the most part, he had lived right. He stayed clear of the family business and was proud to have put his little brother through college. If either of them had continued the family ways, it would have been his baby brother. However, he had excelled in college and found himself a passion. He finally understood when people referred to their moment on the Road to Damascus. He hadn't been converted in that moment. Nor had he found some grand epiphany, but he had found resolve. He knew it was too late for him, and he was okay with it. He knew it the second he had tripped the device.

"Can you hear me, Lt.?" He said over the radio.

"Go ahead, Kid, I am here. We're both here."

"I fucked up, Lt. I'm not going to make it out of here. Don't let them hurt my dog, okay? I want you to find Charlee Lovejoy. She's with the Brits over at Camp Bastion. She won't be hard to find," he laughed fondly. "She's pretty damn hot. Just promise me you won't let them put Beast down. Charlee will take care of her."

"I promise, Kid. I'll take care of it myself," he said solemnly, knowing there wasn't any way he could help any other way.

Monroe's boot stood steady, but he could feel his body tremble in anticipation of what was about to happen. He shouldn't have rushed in before Beast. He had made a mistake that would cost him his life. As the device clicked, the air in the room evaporated. Acting quickly, Monroe scooped up Beast and threw her away from him. Her body bounced heavily off a nearby wall on impact, but she wouldn't have been in the direct line of the blast. He had saved her life and ended his own. Beast refused to eat. She refused to sleep. For two days, she lay on Crimson's body, refusing to be apart from him and snarling at anyone who had a desire to be bitten and mangled. She wouldn't let anyone come near them. She was inconsolable and on the verge of being put down. On day three, Sister finally decided to tranquilize her.

She hugged Beast, remembering that day, her eyes damming back the tears. She had been surprised and heartbroken to hear what had happened to Crimson. He had grown into a wonderful man, and she was surprised to learn that Crimson wanted her to take Beast if anything happened to him. Beast wasn't the sole property of the U.S. government, and Crimson had the final say on when she would be retired and where she would go upon his death.

They were both so close to starting a new chapter in their lives that it broke Sister's heart. She knew he had found love and wanted to marry and have children. Sister fought back the tears that had been shed so often when remembering that day and the fear in Beast's eyes. Their sadness was still present occasionally, but Beast had recovered okay. She slowly returned to the world and found it okay to love another human. As Sister sang to her, she gently rocked Beast just as she used to. She lightly ran her hands down Beast's side and whispered softly. After a few moments, Beast's ears perked up, and she whipped her tail as if a spell had been broken. She whined excitedly, licking Sister's face with conviction, and began to hop around.

Beast would be okay, but it didn't explain what had happened. Sister placed her hands on the carpet beneath the chair to search for any unforeseen incidents. Beast had clearly been upset, but at least this time, she hadn't messed on the floor. Sister was happy that Beast understood the value of a $400 pet deposit and the concept of armed robbery. Now that Beast was coming around, Sister could concentrate on the message in the mirror. This wasn't the first time this had happened. She had gotten them several times over the years. Disturbed, she sat on the edge of the bed and stared at the mirror. Trying to remember the last time her friend had been around.

"I see you," it read.

THE OLD MAN

T he sheriff's station was just a short distance from their rooms at Trudy's, a charming B&B that felt like a home away from home. The house was a beautifully maintained white French colonial with two stories, black wrought-iron terraces, and large windows. Given the town's desire to maintain a polished landscape, Trudy's had been prominently celebrated and a point of pride in the community. After the last couple of days' shenanigans, Sister and Beast could use some much-needed exercise. It would also give her time to see just how many of the town's residents were still actively pursuing the trade that had kept their community thriving for almost 200 years.

After showering, Sister headed for the kitchen, hugged Sarah Trudeau, Trudy's owner and head chef, and said goodbye to Silas and Luke, who had their mouths full of eggs, hash, and grits like they were having their last supper. They barely pulled their eyes away from their plates long enough to utter any resemblance of an intelligent response. Instead, they nodded and grunted like Neanderthals on a gut pile, gesturing wildly with forks in hand in her general direction as she headed out the door.

When Sister stepped outside, wet, warm air met her at the door. A large lamp hovered high over the house, casting down its rays along the roof, eliminating the gray skies like a gloom that hung over a room and drowned out the sound of light. The only noise was mechanical. No birdsong, no dogs barking, and what human presence she could see along the streets remained mute and somber. With no sign of sun, the storms that had rolled in days before their arrival were threatening to book for an extended stay. She had been so sure the sun was out, with the way the light had peeked and creased, causing shadows to dance on the walls of her room, but it was only an illusion. The lamp overhead peeked directly through her window. She was only imagining a bright and sunny day.

Sister adjusted Beast's vest, ensuring the badge was clear and visible and that the Velcro fasteners were secure. The vest signaled to Beast that it was time to work. Baptiste had a leash law, and Beast glared at Sister as she attached the leash to the vest. "Oh, you'll survive. You big baby. I'll take it off once we get inside the building," Sister said as she patted down Beast's side. "I don't need you upsetting any of these fine folks. They tend to overreact when they feel anyone has threatened their lovely town."

Then she offered Beast the other half of her sausage and biscuit. She really wasn't all that hungry anyway, and it made for a good peace offering. Beast side-eyed Sister as she slowly took the breakfast with a chafing snort and started walking. With her head down and a pouty turn of her eyes, she set out as if she were headed to her execution.

Sister's attention drifted to the scar behind the girl's ear as they walked. If she included Mia Ward, the total count was now about fifty-eight. Approximately a third were found in the United States, while the others were scattered across other countries. Each of the fifty-eight victims bore the same scar, which was two potential links that connected them all. The other connection between the victims was only a theory.

At the time of their deaths, it appeared that each of them had been isolated from friends or family for various reasons, ranging from divorces to runaways. Their ages ranged from seventeen to fifty-one. It appeared that only a few of them had been linked to drugs and prostitution, but at the time of their deaths, they all had drugs in their systems, and evidence of sexual activity had been present. Each individual who went missing and later turned up dead had withdrawn from social connections or was separated from loved ones within months of their death. Although there were a few exceptions, they were not significant enough to disregard isolation as a means of linking them all together. The forensic evidence was all over the place, and the manner of death varied among them, as did their demographics and economic backgrounds.

Sister again resisted the urge to touch her scar, wondering what it meant. There was the obvious interpretation; all the professionals called it a signature.

She would have made the same conclusion had she written her own profile. When it had first been discovered, it meant nothing. It was just another mark that had been left on her body that night, but after the others were found with the same scratch-like scar, deliberately placed in the exact location, she did not doubt that it was important. Instead of running her finger over its edge for probably the millionth time, she gripped the leash tighter.

Sister focused on the back of Beast's head as she walked, fighting the compulsion to trace the scar. She began to count off numbers on her fingers: 1, 2, 3, 4, 5... When she reached number 6, she stopped counting as an image of the Old Man's face replaced the scar in her thoughts. She wondered if he had planned all of this for her benefit. Perhaps he was trying to weed out just how far she had plummeted through the wormhole. She knew that didn't require an honest answer because she already knew it. He had directly forbidden her to chase her own case. And even though he wasn't her boss anymore, he still had that power and could have her eliminated altogether. He wouldn't actually have her killed, but he could have her 86ed. And that would be the same as if he had killed her all over again.

She was drawing lines and dots that had many law enforcement officers questioning her sanity. She was sure a few phone calls had already been made. As far as she knew, McTavish's team had yet to be invited to that party, and she had overstepped a few times. When he found out that she had been tracking down leads on each of the victims, including the three young men, who no one believed to be part of the MO, he ordered her to take a sabbatical. She believed that all of the murders were that of one killer. They all thought that she needed to regroup and clear her mind because she had clearly lost it. He was angry with her for going against him. It was as simple as that.

When he spoke, he commanded such authority that nobody defied him. It wasn't out of fear. He had a well-balanced mix of rugged authoritarian and gentle rearing. His layers never had to be peeled back or stripped away to reveal his true nature or meaning in anything. He was respected. Nothing commanded allegiance more of a leader than that. Those around him loved him because he pulled no punches. He didn't level threats. Only promises. He didn't have to rule in fear. The man was a legend; no one questioned anything he said because he was never wrong. Bishop was the same man; maybe that's why he had made him his number 2 instead of her.

Sister had shown the correct amount of shame and walked away. She promised him that she would wrap up and close the files on two of her remaining cases and step back. The real question now is, how much did he really know? She'd like to think he gave her some space, but she figured it ran more along the lines that he gave her enough rope to hang herself, and he had the only knife sharp enough to cut her down. She knew him better than anyone, and he never did anything without first determining the outcome. And, more often than not, he knew the result of each move before it happened.

There had to be a reason he sent her to speak with Dr. Tomlin, not the others. She had thought about everything they had ever touched. Every case, every file. And knew that, without a doubt, he was an excellent chess master of people. Placing them on the board, he played out in strategy. Her view on the matter wasn't cynical. She revered his skill. It wasn't like she thought he viewed them all as pawns in a twisted game of his own creation. But instead, she thought he was exceptional at figuring out people. Be it the members of his own team or how they functioned best. Or a subject and how to constructively and with minimal fallout, apprehend them. Even if that meant, in the end, they would die. He played this game his way. McTavish knew how to manipulate his surroundings to achieve the best results. She had seen him use this skill in nearly every aspect of his life. She tried not to disappoint him. But she directly lied to his face when she told him she'd leave the deaths alone. But she couldn't, and she wouldn't.

She was surprised to see that from the sidewalk to the lobby entrance, the building was littered with people. On one side, there were the onlookers and the protesters. On the other, cameramen stood shoulder to shoulder, filming a line of news anchors. The mechanical silence missing a block away now rumbled as if crossing the street had turned up the volume, and suddenly, the world woke up. The street was jam-packed with so many bodies that she darted down a sidewalk opposite the front entrance and headed back to the employee parking lot and jailer's entrance. That was where she found one of her merrier men loitering.

Addison was leaning up against the Bronco and watching a less-than-ladylike woman string together a list of swear words that would have made any biker worth his cookie proud. Her handcuffs jangled against her many gold bangles as she struggled with the young man in uniform who hadn't enough experience to fend off her advances and reddened in embarrassment when she fully cupped her hand between his legs and gave him a little squeeze.

"What can Mama do for you, boy?" She asked in a thick Haitian accent. Then she rubbed her body vigorously against him. He groaned as he twisted out of her reach while doing his best to keep both of his hands guiding her toward the entrance of the building. Just as he had been taught. Arm's length kept him out of striking distance. But she was persistent, and he was losing the battle of maintaining control as he awkwardly navigated her across the parking lot.

Addison leaped away from the Bronco and ran ahead of the deputy and his new lady friend. As he reached the door, he held it open for the young deputy, who looked away from the camera, shielding the humiliation on his face as he and the woman entered the building. He had been teased, groped, and accosted in every way possible, with every step along the way and in full view of the cameras. The young deputy knew full well that the exchange had been seen on the security feed and would circulate the building before lunch.

Addison, who had watched the exchange with much amusement, winked at the deputy as he entered the doorway. Noticing his name badge, "Careful with tha' one, Smitty. She looks like she'd give you a run for your wallet."

She stopped abruptly, noticing him for the first time, causing the deputy to fall short and run into the back of her. Her eyes looked over Addison in appreciation. Her expression tilted generously into a sultry smile as it crept along the lines of her face and rested in her heavy eyes.

Tilting her head to look up at him, she said, "I'll be outta here around noon tomorrow, Cherie, if you wanna give it a go. I'll even give you a run for free."

Addison's laughter erupted in the hallway. "You're my kind of excitement," he said with a fast smile, tapping his ring finger. He held his hand up for the woman to view, displaying a black rubber ring instead of gold. "But my woman would gut me tip to stern."

"Good for her. I like where her mind's at. I reckon I still got the boy here," she continued with a grin and reached for the deputy again. Catching him off guard this time, she threw her cuffed hands over his head, anchored him in, and gave him a firm kiss on the mouth.

"Hey, now. Stop it," Smith said, pulling the lower half of his body out of her reach and unlacing her arms from around his neck. His hips swung widely to the left and then the right. "Stop that, Miss Annabelle, I said."

His voice, which tried desperately to be commanding, came out weak and pitchy. He sounded as if he was barely out of high school, and his baby face had backed that up. He was young, and judging by the expression on his face, he hadn't experienced this much attention from a woman in his entire life, let alone from a woman like Miss Annabelle.

"That's the spirit," Addison chuckled. As he laughed, Sister watched the sparkle shine in his eyes. He was enjoying his exchange with the woman. "You foxies really know how to treat a fella," he said as he patted Smith on the shoulder. "Now, you stop givin' him the runabou' and behave y'self. Ya upsettin' the boy."

There wasn't anything special about the building. It was the standard brick-and-mortar style that had been renovated just enough to keep up with modern times, but it stopped short of leveling away at its historical appeal. It was an older structure and one of only a handful of remaining architectural leftovers from the original town, established in 1793 and reestablished in 1807. A fire had swept through in 1936 and nearly decimated the entire town. They quickly rebuilt, but it held tight to its traditions. No box chains or corporations were allowed to set up shop in their town. Everything was locally owned, and the town's council, once comprised of both the Monroe and Doucet families, had provided numerous incentives to maintain this status quo.

Baptiste now had two stoplights. It wasn't unlike many other small towns in the South, but it had some notable differences. For one, the town had been built by criminal enterprise, and the people took a certain pride in that history. The only residents attempting to distance themselves from this past were the families who had invested in the schools and church on the Doucet Plantation. It was the worst-kept secret in town that Baptiste still operated using much of the ill-gotten gains, even though they pretended to have moved beyond that sort of business.

The vice trades were still holding strong, but the two major families were less and less the lead figures nowadays.

Sister was glad to see that at least one of the town's two diners had been upgraded. It used to be a local greasy spoon called Mel's, but now it sparkled as a polished eatery named Blondie's, which offered lattes, bagels, and salads. Sister remembered a time when Mel and Jake, who owned Jake's Mean Pig, had fought for the top spot by lowering their prices to entice customers and forever running a new deal on lunches and family meals. Now that Blondie's was geared more towards the health-conscious residents, while Jake's was probably the best place to get BBQ and gumbo in town.

The gas station had also been improved, with new pumps and vendors inside rather than outside. Coke was now available in cans instead of bottles, and the chips and snacks appeared to be freshly stocked. It was a far cry from the one church and whorehouse setup of years ago. Sister made a note to visit the gas station's owner, Joe Beatty. Back in the day, Joe sold Miss Simone's moonshine out of one of those old vending machines, and that wasn't a secret either. The town council and the sheriff didn't mind as long as Joe kept up with his city chamber's membership dues and paid his sales tax on time.

By the time Sister and Addison reached the front lobby, Silas and McQueen had battled their way through the front doors. Sister hadn't seen Silas come to stand behind her. He was sucking hard enough through his nose, that it had drawn her attention. She couldn't exactly see him, but through the corner of her eye, she caught sight of his head pecking at the air like a deranged chicken. Self-consciously, she caught herself doing the same, hoping to find the aroma of coffee and burgers, but the building seemed void of anything food-related. Her head slightly tilted downwards, and she inhaled. She knew it wasn't her and stood up abruptly. Lifting her elbow, she quickly stuck the pit of her arm into McQueen's face.

"What do you think?" she asked, drawing back and watching as the horror stole his once-relaxed expression.

"Oh God, Sister, that is so gross! You guys are always playing like a bunch of damn kids around here. Why do you have to do that to me?" he asked, disgusted by her actions, and his face twisted up into a scrunch. "And you call me the Kidd," he uttered in exasperation, wiping his face.

"Whoa!" Silas said just as he darted around her. Narrowly avoiding a blow to his gut. "Someone remembered her Teen Spirit." His boyish giggle was infectious, and she joined in his laughter. She loved his laugh.

"Oh, lighten up, Frances," she said to McQueen. "You are entirely too serious."

"Careful now, McQueen!" Addison said, coming up from behind him and hugging him so tight that it lifted him a couple of inches off the floor.

"Why do you always have to be touching me?" McQueen shot back as Addison let him go and began straightening himself together. His feathers were ruffled, and he was just on the edge of losing control.

"Watch that one," Silas teased. "She's in a mood," he continued, referring to McQueen's quickness to get emotional as less than masculine. "He got a call," he said, holding an imaginary phone to his ear, and nodded at McQueen on the sly.

The group was getting a good row at McQueen's expense, and Sister was just about to wallop Silas for his insensitivity to McQueen's current girlfriend situation when a voice cut in, and she dropped her hands to her side. The group had reduced themselves to children who had just been caught by their father and were about to take a tongue-lashing.

"You about ready, Deputy?" she heard a familiar voice call out to her while he eyed the mischievous bunch. They all knew that he was talking to her without having to ask. "How old are you lot, again?" he asked, giving them all a mock disapproving look before he cracked a smile. Then, looking back at Sister, he asked her, "Or shall I call you Doctor now?" he asked, raising his eyebrow. "I see you used your time off wisely," he said. "Even if I know that's a lie, you finally finished that thesis, and I am very proud of you. Congratulations are in order. The rest of you miscreants should be paying attention," he said, pointing at each of them. "There is always time to perfecte your craft."

"I blow shit up," said Silas with a glow of excitement. "I think I got it down, Sir. But hey, I don't mind the practice or the on-the-job training," he laughed. "I could use some classroom work."

"Oh, I'm set," seconded McQueen. "I mean, I'm the smartest one here, so I'm not worried at all. But if you need a tutor, Brick," he said with a straight face, "I can help you get through your ABCs, no problem," he quipped, finishing his joke, deadpanned.

Sister raised her head to meet the eyes of the Old Man, the legendary Alister McTavish. It seemed like forever ago that he had entered her life. He was her rock. The rest may think she had to be dragged back here by her hair, but he was part of why she had returned to this place of misery and gators. Swamp rats and mudbugs. She owed the man. And with all the time in the world, she couldn't touch the debt she owed him.

"Wash out your mouth," she replied, embracing the hug she knew was coming. "Those online classes were from some city in Estonia. It was finished solely for vanity reasons and bragging points only. I bet the diploma isn't worth the paper it's printed on," she teased, knowing he knew better. As he held her, she couldn't help but think that he gave the best hugs. He was solid and sturdy. Like you were being shielded from the world by the mere circling of his arms around you, and nothing could get in. She loved the man for all that they were to one another.

McTavish was an older man with a deep voice and a taste for drink. He had a head full of nearly white hair, but his red beard and mustache were only slightly marked, and he kept them both fashionably trimmed. He had lived in the US for a long while now, but he still boasted a strong Scottish accent. However, she noticed that he had begun to mix in some of the local vocabulary over time. Maybe doing this job as long as he had, he, too, found himself unconsciously switching between accents with different audiences. Most of the ladies around town went to great lengths to be in his company. He was a good-looking man, but all agreed that it was the accent that had lured them in.

"He's a real pannie-dropper, tha' one," Addison had said as he witnessed one woman after another try to gain favor with McTavish. "We need to get that man a book and charge $100 per woman and a dollar a word. We'd be retired by next week."

"I've missed you, my girl," McTavish said affectionately. It's too bad that an old man can't request the presence of such a lovely face without her having to be stolen away and belted to a seat," he finished. His voice sounded hurt. However, his eyes betrayed him, but only slightly. He had always been a teaser. And he also knew how much it took for her to return.

"I'm sorry, I..." she began in response, but he cut her off with a raise of his hand and another quick squeeze.

"Nothing to explain. You are here now. That's all that matters. I have other problems I need to speak with you about," he said quietly, but it can wait until later." Then he walked away from her and gave a brief smile at the others.

As she stepped back from him, she extended out an arm and smacked him with a lengthy brief and a summary before handing it to him, shrugging off the moment that seemed to have McTavish worried but secretive. She knew full well he wouldn't read most of it. He never did. She just hoped he'd take in enough of it to understand the finer points, make notes, and figure out how to work the vultures waiting outside. He was a great speaker. However, he disliked small talk and questions, so she had to write everything to accommodate his lack of patience with the media. It took her only half an hour of reading on the plane to prepare a summary for him.

The rest came from Dr. Tomlin's discoveries. She still didn't understand why he had asked her to prepare. Bishop better understood what was happening around here than she did, and he was an excellent writer. Besides, she wasn't allowed to mention anything about the other victims anyway. So, what could she offer that they themselves didn't already know?

The other two bodies mentioned in the summary had been found recently around the parish. However, they had nothing to do with the girl. They had no branding or scars. They had obviously met an untimely and tragic end, but their murders were not their type of murders.

"Have you slept?" she continued, noticing the black circles that had darkened his usually bright hazel eyes, now dimmed to grey, and looking heavy. She knew he hadn't. They were a lot alike on that front. He slept very little during a case such as this. The expression on his face told her all that she needed to know. And yet, an underlying problem still seemed to darken him.

"There have been over seventy bodies found in the bayous across La Louisiane just this year alone, and it's only fucking May," he said as he picked up a mug off his desk and tossed back the last of its contents. "The gammy fucks won't stop dumping them here. Do you think this state is just full of murdering bastards, or is it just possible the surrounding states have figured out that we have a gator problem that can get rid of their problems? Taylor? Taylor!" he called out. It seemed to come mid-sentence of his rant about using Louisiana as a dumping ground. No one lifted their heads as far as Sister could see. She looked out to see who he was yelling for and wondered if he was losing his grip on reality. "Taylor," he called again. And this time, a woman hurried in from around the corner with a panicked look on her face.

"Yes, I'm here, Sir. I'm here," she said quickly; her mousy finish was off-putting and strange to hear from a woman in uniform.

"More coffee, please," he said. This time, his tone was calmer. But that was short-lived. As soon as Taylor reappeared with his fresh coffee in hand, she tripped and dumped the contents down the front of him.

"God dammit, woman!" McTavish yelled in a voice that startled Sister and several others in the room. He began to aggressively scrub at his pants, at the same time stopping Taylor from trying to help. "For Christ's sake, woman, get off your knees and stop that," he said, gently pulling her up and ushering her to the side. "I can manage."

Sister wasn't immune to the man's voice. She could listen to him talk for days. She loved his accent. The emphasis he placed on certain words made them feel exotic. However, some words gave Sister pause and were like nails on a chalkboard to her ears. Seeing her stiffen and the disappointment on her face, he softened his expression and refocused on cleaning up the mess. Then he ran his hands over his furry face and gently handed the empty cup back to Taylor without a word. But his eyes told her that he was sorry. She thought he was all out of sorts, which was unusual. It truly wasn't like him to project frustration outwardly like that or to unload on another person in front of others. She noted the shame that had marred his face, but wondered where it had come from.

"Ah, jeez, lass, I'm sorry," he began apologizing. "I know how much you hate that word," he continued—looking extremely embarrassed on two fronts, as he graveled. "I said God...," he started and stopped just short of finishing the thought when he saw her hand shoot up and facepalm the air between them. The stop sign had been duly noted and understood. "I won't repeat it," he promised. He often made this promise but never committed to it.

"How many 'Our Fathers and Hail Marys' are you up to this week?" she asked him, reaching out both hands and placing them on each of his shoulders. She was doing her best to smooth out his rumpled shirt. She guessed it was part of yesterday's ensemble by the lines and creases and began looking around the room for a jacket. She knew he felt terrible about his words. At least the GD ones. She didn't know Taylor and made no judgment of her. But she felt a connection between them. She'd have to ask him about it when they had a private moment.

"Father Ian gave me at least 150 last week," he confessed as she finished smoothing down the sleeves of his baby blue shirt and straightening up his ugly, uncoordinated red and black tie. These were the times she wished that he had a wife. She didn't begrudge him his happiness. He needed someone to help him dress himself. The man was a force to be reckoned with, but sometimes, he was like a child. These were the moments when he went from 007 to Barney Fife. Noticing his beard, she grabbed a napkin off a nearby desk and wiped away the crumbles of a lemon muffin that had taken up residence in his mustache and beard. Standing eye to eye with him, face to face, she could now tell it wasn't just coffee that he had sucked down moments before. He smelled as though he had bathed in Glenfiddich. It was his favorite scotch whisky. It reminded him of home and his wife, he often told her.

"She could drink me under the table," he said wistfully one evening after a hard day of trying to parent a daughter who had grown into her independence and was giving him more gray hair. I wish she were here to tell me what I'm doing wrong. And to drink with me until I figured it out."

He really did need a woman in his life, she thought. But she knew the drinking was what had kept him company for many years now.

"Well, then, may I add at least fifteen more of each and a breath mint?" She asked, smiling at him as she dug through her pockets and handed him the same silver tin that Bishop had given her last night. "You'll need one of these. Or maybe two."

THE REPORTER

S heriff McTavish cleared his throat before speaking. She wondered if the drink he had taken was to calm his nerves for the press conference or for another reason. He had become quite a drinker, but it wasn't typical of him to open the day with a drink in hand. There was a tension about him that made Sister feel uneasy. Something in his eyes had changed as well, and she couldn't understand why he wasn't sharing it with her. Whatever it was.

"As many of you may have already heard," McTavish began in his address to the press, "two bodies have been discovered in the past six days. First, I would like to clarify that these two cases are unrelated. There is no evidence to support the claims that have been reported. Therefore, we kindly ask that you refrain from drawing conclusions, as the MAPS Department would greatly appreciate it. Our office has limited time to address and differentiate fact from fiction every time one of you chooses to publish a sensational story."

The first body is that of an unnamed minor, a seventeen-year-old girl from New Orleans. The second body is that of an unidentified adult female, believed to be from the Charlestown area. Initially, both were considered runaways, but we are exploring other possibilities. At this time, we do not have any additional details to share. Further comments on the investigation will be provided after the autopsies are completed."

McTavish paused momentarily, swallowed, and stood up a bit taller. The room was full of people; the air reeked of ambition and a lack of empathy. Each one of them wanted their twenty questions answered in detail and all at once. "I will not be answering any questions at this time," he continued. "MAPS D and all those involved with these investigations would like to express our deepest sympathies to the families of the deceased, and we ask that you respect their privacy. This would be a perfect opportunity to show restraint and boundaries during this time of mourning," he finished.

Reporters called out their questions, all yelling over one another, hoping that when he said, "No questions," he didn't mean it. That's when she heard a familiar voice call out above the others.

"Lovejoy, over here. Miss Lovejoy," she heard a voice shout. "Deputy Lovejoy," the voice persisted, demanding her attention. This caused her to freeze. She wasn't prepared to answer any questions. She wasn't even there to speak, and there was no reason for anyone to ask her anything. She was just another face on the team. Within these walls, her identity outside didn't matter. The special badge she carried and the credentials she had fought hard to earn were kept secretly locked away in Langley. She was meant to be an invisible nobody, doing a job that no one in their right mind would want to do. She hadn't expected anyone to call her out, in a place where, if anyone looked closely enough, they might remember her. She hadn't changed all that much, yet in so many other ways, she had.

"Deputy Charlee Lovejoy!" he shouted, daring her to ignore that. This immediately captured her attention, as well as that of every single other person in the room. Each of his words resonated, causing a hush to settle over the crowd. Sister felt her face flush, and the back of her neck grew hot as all the eyes in the room turned towards her. The only other woman with a badge, who stood next to her, had started to inch away. Sister watched as Taylor slinked off, leaving her in the spotlight.

A young man was staring directly at her. He wore a brown dress coat, tan pants, and a dark brown fedora, reminiscent of a character straight out of a 1930s dime store novel, like Dick Tracy himself. "What about the young girl who was found yesterday morning? Do you have a comment on the apparent links between her and the seven other girls discovered in the surrounding rivers over the past five years? And what about your case?" he quickly added, barely taking a breath as he snapped photos with his camera. She would have been genuinely impressed by his tenacity if his audacity hadn't sent her reeling. Her feet began to itch as she felt the heat creep through her from the floor up. A flood of emotions rushed over her, making her feel like a red-hot, breathing dragon. She wanted to melt into the floor behind the podium, but she couldn't move. She was frozen stiff, not with fear, but with panic. She didn't know how to respond to his challenging questions.

"Please wait," he said, shuffling out of one uniformed grip while dodging another. He could feel McTavish's eyes on him, and he knew he'd be in deep shit later. His charming smile and innocent expression wouldn't help him with McTavish today, but he'd deal with that when the time came.

"Is the body of Mia Ward, the girl found in The Rouge, linked to the Daily-Doucet case?" he asked, carefully not to draw a direct connection between herself, Kathryn Daily, and Caroline Doucet. "Do you have any suspects at all? Please give me something! I know you're working on this case."

Officers were already on their way to collect the young reporter when Mc-Tavish motioned for two more deputies to block his retreat down a southbound hallway. They had the little rat trapped and were about to scoop him up themselves when a hand reached out and snatched the young man by the strap of his camera and dragged him in the opposite direction by his neck.

After the room had been cleared and seeing that the boy was in good hands, McTavish returned to Sister's side. He reached out and took both of her hands into his own. "Just breathe," he commanded. "Stay with me."

Her color had returned, but she needed air. The air in the room had grown too thick, and the walls seemed to close in on her. He nodded his head at the door. He gestured for her to get lost as the boy's outburst triggered the onslaught of questions from the now overly-packed hallway.

Following her out the door, he repeated, "Just take a moment and just breathe. It's been a while since you made an appointment. I'll need you to do that. And soon," he said as he gently placed a finger under her chin and lifted her face so that he could look into her eyes. Are you here? We are worried about you."

The look in her eyes told him that she was listening. She loved how he pronounced "you" in that way. It made her feel gooey inside. As if drawing out the Os made it more personal. It was weird and silly, but when he said, "You," she relaxed. It was like a magic safe word, like Abra Cadabra or something. It sounded ridiculously comical, but it helped her. He was the only one ever allowed to treat her like a mental case, and she knew he was right. She needed to get a grip on this reality. People were watching her, and she didn't need the attention.

"I'll take a minute," she said, thanking him with a quick squeeze of his hands. She needed to gather herself and clear her head.

"Boy, are you out of your ever-loving f-ing mind?" Bishop shouted; his teeth clenched so tightly that they almost cracked under the pressure. His voice boomed like thunder, echoing down the hallway with a pitch so loud that the walls carried his outrage. The intensity of his anger radiated so much heat that anyone standing near could feel it. He gripped the young man's arm firmly, dragging him down the corridor toward an office. Bishop banged on doors along the way, not caring whose office it was as long as it was empty.

The reporter knew that Bishop's question wasn't meant to be answered. If he had, it would have been a sarcastic retort, which would have been met with an equally unpleasant consequence. At this very moment, the current Undersheriff of Marie Anjou Parish, former US Marine Gunny Sgt Badass, and former Secret Service Bishop Bohannon wanted nothing more than to rip off his head.

Bishop is a decent-sized man. He is somewhere near six feet and in decent enough shape. He'd pass for a much younger man if it weren't for the silver touches that ran through his black hair or slightly weathered look to his face. Anyone looking at him would know immediately that he had spent considerable time conditioning himself. His features were dark and complex. But his eyes often betrayed him. They were kind and soft, whereas his words were generally direct and seemed harsh. The reporter felt like a heel next to Bishop and a complete sucker at being dragged around like a bag of shit.

The reporter's face was red and sullen. His embarrassment was on full notice for all to see. But he was not ashamed of what he had done. He was doing his job, just like everyone else in the room. As he passed by, he watched the onlookers nod in disapproval. It was almost like a wave had turned the room. But no one really knew why; what he had done had upset McTavish, Lovejoy, or Bishop as it did. He knew why, but even he had been smart enough to go for the attack underhandedly and not a full-on assault.

By now, everyone had either witnessed or heard about the scene he had caused at the press conference, which showed on their faces. His story would be featured on every news channel and would appear in everyone's newspaper, blog, and social media feed by noon, except his own. That was if Bishop and everyone else in the department had their way. He would be on lockdown until McTavish decided otherwise. And it wasn't fair.

Bishop opened a door and tossed the reporter ass-first into a chair. It was neither his chair nor his office, but Bishop didn't care either way.

"What in the hell were you thinking? Is this the sort of nonsense you have learned at college? Do they not teach time and place? Respect over there?" Bishop narrowed dark eyes at the young man who flashed with amber specks. "How could you do that? Did you think at all about what position you would be putting this department in?" he said, jabbing a finger at the floor. "Not to mention what you did to Sister. What the F, man? How could you call her out like that?" Bishop ran both hands down his face in frustration. "Someday, boy, your ambition will get you caught up in something you can't get out of. You take too many risks."

The young man believed he had just seen lightning bolts crackle across Bishop's eyes, and he had a fear of the man he hadn't before. He swallowed hard and fought back the lump that had formed in his throat, making it hard for him to speak. He hadn't meant to hurt her.

"Bishop," he started to explain, but the words were stuck. "I didn't mean... I didn't mean to call her out directly. Or to draw attention to her. She's here, and I know she's working on one of this state's most notorious cases since Bonnie and Clyde. I know it's not unusual to find bodies in our swamps. But Jesus, who does that to a nun? And it's unsolved. We have a serial killer operating in our town. And I want the story. I'm an investigative reporter. Why wouldn't I want this story? I was only doing..." He was quickly cut off as Bishop's hand cuffed him on the back of the head as he walked past him to sit on the end of someone's desk.

"Take off that ridiculous damn hat. This isn't like the time Mrs. Poole caught you pissing in her birdbath or the windows getting busted out, or the streaking. Or the trespassing, or the umpteen million other things you have done to help your investigation along," he said, throwing quotation marks around "investigation." "She's not a trash can you can rummage through in broad daylight. You humiliated her and threw dynamite on Alister's already explosive press conference. Did you not see the circus going on outside? You just made yourself the chum bucket for those sharks out there," he said, pointing vigorously at the window. That was NOT part of just doing your job."

He removed the hat, smashing it into his lap, and bowed his head. He couldn't look Bishop in the face. He knew he was in trouble and hated feeling bad for going after what he wanted. He hadn't seen Bishop this upset with him since his 21st birthday when he pissed in old Mrs. Poole's birdbath, and she had him cornered in her garden with a hoe. When Bishop showed up, he still had his little buddy in one hand and a bottle of tequila in the other. Mrs. Poole had refused to allow him to zip up, wanting his shame to be witnessed by others. Or his senior year, when Bishop had come to pick him up after he and his baseball mates were caught streaking through Wisconsin Circle after winning state. But in all fairness, that hadn't been their fault. This came after the opposing high school's girls' track team had stolen their clothes, and with no other options, they emerged from the locker room and headed to the bus, flanked by two rows of parents and fans who had gathered to cheer and congratulate them. They had considered drawing straws to see who would be the one to run out and let someone know what had happened to them, but then decided that it was an all-for-one, ride-and-die-together scenario, and they all took one for the team.

"The Birdbath Scandal was a glorious day," he whispered, with a slight chuckle under his breath at the memory. Mrs. Poole still gives him a sideways look when he passes by her yard. She's even sprayed him with her garden hose a time or two, warding him off like a stray cat. But she's given him more than a few grins, too. The old cougar was probably reminiscing about how she wouldn't let him pack it away, and he was so drunk that he didn't mind.

He was trying not to smile while Bishop glared at him. That day was one of the best of his life; he even got the girl he had had a crush on since grade school to tell him she loved him. The baseballs crashing through the windows were how he ended up on the baseball team in the first place, and he wouldn't change it for anything. He had Kyle Rhys to thank for that. Becoming friends with Rhys had transformed him from a social outcast into someone at least somewhat accepted by his peers. They had become best friends around the tenth grade, and he would be grateful for that friendship in the years that followed.

Sister paused at the door, listening as Bishop reprimanded the boy on her behalf. She wasn't sure how much she appreciated the scolding he was giving, as she was quite capable of standing up for herself and had never liked Bishop's overly protective tendencies. However, being angry at either of them wouldn't do her any good. As always, she brushed it aside and pretended it didn't matter. She wouldn't lose control or raise her voice. She would check her emotions at the door before entering the room.

She adjusted the collar of her shirt, making sure the sleeves came all the way down past her wrists, the collar was buttoned correctly, and the lapels were straight. She then smoothed out her jeans and twirled her ponytail to smooth out any flyaways. After addressing her clothing and hair, she wiped the palms of her hands across her cheeks, neck, and ears. She was mentally wiping away all signs of hurt, embarrassment, and outrage.

No matter how angry she felt inside, she did her best not to allow another person to witness that weakness. She handed out grace like candy. It was her way of moving forward, taking the blows and letting them glance off, which was not always easy in her line of work. It was hard to find God in others at times, but she could at least try to see if God was moving in or packing to move out. That's how she viewed her relationship with him. He had moved into her life; it was a death-do-us-part relationship. No matter what. She did her best to keep a soft tongue and to leave all heads attached to their bodies.

As she pushed open the door, Bishop looked up at her with a worried expression. She felt guilty that she couldn't love him as much as he needed or wanted. He was a good man, but she was already in a committed relationship. Just because she was no longer a nun did not mean her vows to serve him faithfully were negated. No husband or children were part of that deal. And if she were being honest, her responsibility to Beast was about all the emotional connection she could manage.

Across from Bishop sat a young man. His face had changed, but he wasn't that far off from the boy she had once known. He nervously came to his feet when she entered the room. He reached out his arms as if to hug her, but quickly dropped them and shoved his hands into his pockets when he heard Bishop clear his throat. His apprehensive demeanor was a tell. The way he shifted his weight from one foot to the other. The way he fidgeted with whatever was in his pocket. He probably wanted to keep his hands busy so he wouldn't reach out again. He held her gaze, never looking away like a game of chicken. He challenged her with his eyes, and she wondered what his words would sound like. Just as challenging, perhaps? His features were soft, but everything about the young man suggested that he was still the spirited little boy she used to know. He had seen things in his young life. And he still faced the world like a bull.

Finally, she blinked first, giving a slight tilt of her chin, as her eyes dropped briefly. She had submitted and let the young man off the hook. She knew if she didn't, he wouldn't. It wasn't a pissing contest but more of a test of will. And she had no desire to break his.

"Deputy Charlee Lovejoy," she said, holding out her hand and introducing herself. He looked at her momentarily, puzzled at the greeting since he already knew her name. He had known her for as long as he could remember, and this wasn't who she really was.

She could tell he wanted to take it, but he looked at Bishop as if asking for permission first. That's when she cleared her throat and wiggled her fingers at him. "Come on, you. I won't bite." Then she smiled, conveying that all was forgiven. "I have Beast for that," she said with a wink.

When he reached out and clasped her hand, she pulled him in and hugged him. She could feel the tightness of his body melt as she held him tight. She fought back the tears that stung her eyelids, fighting the river threatening to escape and fall down the young man's back. She was upset that he had drawn attention to her, but she would also be forever grateful to him for saving her life.

"I'm sorry. I didn't mean..."

"It's okay, Bama. I know you didn't mean anything by it. Just, please, next time, call me, okay? We'll grab beers and talk," she offered.

ROUGH AS FUK ROAD

Sister's encounter with Bama had left her mouth dry and her body emotionally drained. She was exhausted from the tension carried in her upper back and shoulders. Her insides were twisted up like the mangled metal of a car crash that had been left in a heap on the side of the road. With the combination of the flight, the autopsy, the girl's scar, Beast's panic attack, the words on the mirror, and Bama's ambush, Sister was feeling explosive. In less than 48 hours, the blows continued to come. She tried refocusing her energies elsewhere, but even the music raced through her brain like a five-car pile-up.

Pearl Jam's version of "Last Kiss," which usually made her feel good, now felt like nothing more than an irritating noise. As the rain poured, she searched the sky for the promise it might hold. The crispness of the air, which usually excited her, felt dull and lifeless. The rain washed away the dirt and grime that had accumulated over time, but she was stuck in her thoughts and unable to embrace the renewal that the rain could bring. She recognized that her mind's swirling shades of red were misplaced when directed at those around her. However, she had grown weary of her "believe it till you achieve it" approach to life.

She believed that happiness was out there and that good would ultimately prevail. However, she found success only in her work, not in her personal life. She felt overwhelmed by her rage, her insides churning as if a brick had been pressed against the gas pedal while simultaneously holding down the brake. Her emotions were revved up and ready to explode, but she felt completely stagnant.

She wanted to lash out, indifferent to the fact that her loved ones might become casualties in the battle raging in her mind. She yearned to demolish buildings, reducing them to mere pebbles beneath her feet. She wanted to scream at the top of her lungs with such ferocity that the world would crack and shatter under the sheer weight of her voice.

Instead of unleashing chaos in the world with her nonexistent superhuman powers—because God only knew what she would do if she actually had such abilities—she dug deep within herself and spoke the words of a prayer. This prayer began, as it often did, tracing her journey back to salvation from the day she had become sober. It started as a tightly woven string of profanities and grievances directed at the Father. While it shamed her, she recognized that what poured out bordered on blasphemy, yet she no longer kept those words silent. She chose to have an open dialogue with the man upstairs. Opting to express the thoughts that had been left unspoken felt like a lie between herself and Him. After all, He already knew her innermost thoughts, so she figured she might as well let them all fly, like a murder of ravens being released from an overburdened tree.

She hoped vocalizing her anger and discontent would shed her overburdened branches and leave her tree bare. Mostly, she prayed that no bodies would lie in her wake and that she would do no harm—especially to herself. She needed her higher power to center her. She always did, and she never forgot that. Even if her approach differed from others, she loved the Father. Who else could she bear her soul and let her most authentic heart be seen?

As she expressed her grievances, she followed them up with praise and blessings. She was grateful for the air she continued to breathe and felt blessed by the many who loved and looked out for her. Despite viewing her life through dark shades, she could still see the light within it. Then, she turned down another dirt road, planning to sort through her thoughts during the drive.

The rented Jeep shifted and bounced along yet another washed-out, pot-hole-filled, neglected road. The suspension was cheap and worn out, making the ride jarring. She felt the last jolt clear to her teeth, and she couldn't help but laugh as she looked up at the sky and beyond the clouds. Her response came when a lightning strike flashed, and a rumble echoed through the clouds. "Well played, Sir. I hear you. I've been dually warned."

She hadn't quite captured that horror movie vibe, with dueling banjos and a sinister "eat 'em or breed 'em" atmosphere, but she was getting close. She wondered if she had taken a wrong turn somewhere along the way. Bishop had warned her that GPS apps on her phone wouldn't be reliable this far out, but she feverishly toggled and tapped at her screen. Unfortunately, the little blue arrow just spun in a constant, dizzying circle.

When she entered the next intersection, she stopped in the middle of the crossroads. Then, she undid her seatbelt and got out. Standing in the middle of the intersection did nothing to change the landscape, and the rain continued to fall. No matter in what direction she scanned, there was nothing to see. On any other day, she might have embraced the solitude of "nothing," but again, today was not that day.

She hated feeling this far out of control. It left her feeling disconnected. Like her hinges were swinging widely and bashing against her house of cards. This had her looking back down the road from which she came, wondering if she had lost focus and missed a detail. Bishop's pre-kindergarten scribble said she was looking for 1127 Castle Landing, near an old airstrip. Still, she hadn't seen anything indicating that she was even remotely close to that particular spot. There had been nothing but isolation, brown and drowning crops, wet air, and abandoned life.

Looking down at the scrap of paper again, she watched as the raindrops broke up the ink, causing little blue veins to appear. Not wanting to ruin the map, she returned to the Jeep and pulled out a baseball cap. Then she turned the paper in different directions, twisting it this way and that way, and in a circular motion. Unfortunately, he hadn't included a "you are here" box on his crudely instructed map, and she found herself dialing his number.

"Sister?"

Surprised to hear him answer, she quickly hung up and texted him, "Sorry, butt dial. Call later," and slipped the phone back into her pocket. It was just her luck that the GPS wouldn't work, but a call would get through. She had followed the lines that represented the roads. Bishop hadn't written down any other street names, but his drawing seemed reasonably intelligible when he had placed it in her hand. It wasn't until this point that she had questions. A landmark sprinkled in here and there might have been helpful. Maybe that's why he didn't. Perhaps he knew she'd have to call.

As the rain fell, she knelt, and the mud splattered, covering her legs. She had allowed him back into her thoughts again. She couldn't let Bishop take up residence in her mind; it was already overcrowded with thirty-five-plus years of memories. There was no room left for anyone else, and she didn't want to take the time to unpack and make space for him.

As she pushed out the unwanted images of Bishop, she closed her eyes and tilted her face towards the heavens. The rain continued to fall, and she let it rinse away the day. Once she relaxed, she opened her eyes and began looking for new purchase. Looking towards the far side of the cross-section, on the other side of the road, she noticed a sign pole that had its sign ripped off. In its place, tied with a piece of baling wire, was a neatly trimmed board.

The words "Rough as Fuk Rd " were written on it in carefully brushed white letters. Just beneath that, propped up against the pole, was a worn-out piece of plywood that read, in spray-painted letters, "Bess Take out UR teeth & Tightn UP Da bra."

She couldn't help but laugh. She was thinking how that sign would have been better served at the beginning of her trip, but there were no truer words. Someone with a good sense of humor had obviously written the sign.

"I don't have much to worry about there, now do I, girl?" she yelled to Beast as she looked down at her mounds rather than hills of a chest. "Not much 'strapping' required," she continued as she watched Beast's eyes and the tilt of her head. Just for her amusement, she shrugged and shimmied and threw in a jiggle wiggle for good measure. There was zero reaction from her girls. Nor from Beast. "What? That was funny!"

Beast's expression matched that of an eye roll. Throwing her hands in the air, Sister gave up on her comedy routine and returned to her seat, stepping on the stiff clutch. "Well, you clearly didn't write it. You have no sense of humor."

Rough as Fuk Road had certainly lived up to its name. When Sister stopped this time, it was in front of the only mailbox showing any visible signs of life. She was exhausted. Her hands and arms ached from battling the ruts and grooves of the road. She realized that power steering would be a priority next time. The road seemed to either pull her in or send her bouncing off toward the deeply creased ditch. She had forgotten just how treacherous the roads could become. For her, wrestling with the steering wheel had felt like a sport that she hadn't practiced for.

There had been minimal signs of life along the way, but some were off the road along Rough as Hell – albeit abandoned ones. She didn't, however, presume that just because the homes looked disheveled, there were no suspicious and unwelcoming eyes behind the tattered curtains and broken windows. But not one of the lean-tos, shacks, shanties, or discarded buses had a mailbox near them. Nor were there any signs that a child may have once lived there.

She pulled the piece of paper off the dashboard and read off the numbers again. 1127. There was just enough light from the only working yard lamp for her to point out a leaning mailbox on her right, featuring the numbers "112" in black lettering and a "7" created using thin strips of gray duct tape next to it.

"What do you think, girl? You think this is the one?"

She pulled into the connecting driveway covered in overgrowth and low-hanging branches. Just beyond the bushes, hidden away, a nicely kept yard came into view. The vegetation from the driveway had been hiding a home behind its camouflage. The yard lamp illuminated the entirety of a landscape that someone had made the best of, given the circumstances. The only exceptions were a half-crushed baby pool filled with trash and a burned area next to the house.

The baby pool sat a distance from the house, and probably hadn't seen a baby for some time. It certainly wouldn't hold water for wading or escaping the heat. One side was crushed, and it overflowed with garbage bags. It looked as though the local wildlife had feasted, leaving behind whatever wasn't still in the trash or shopping bags, which either floated in the brown muck or were scattered across the yard. The smell of the rotting heap reached her from the driveway, prompting her to press a finger against her nose to block the odor. It made her eyes water, and she was grateful that she hadn't had lunch. She wasn't sure it would stay down. She quickly drove further down the driveway and stopped in front of an old double-wide trailer. Twenty to twenty-five years ago, it was probably a beautiful home. In many ways, it still retained some charm, but time had taken its toll.

"Stay," she said to Beast as her head perked up in anticipation of getting out of the vehicle. "No," Sister continued.

Sister got out and quietly closed the door, standing in front of the home. There, she saw that the right end of the trailer had a smoldering black appearance—evidence of a fire that had once engulfed that end of the trailer. What appeared to be a burned and rusted carriage of a stripped car and a few dead trees also accompanied the space. But there was beauty there as well. Neatly decorated and arranged containers of flowers of all types and shapes turned the rusted and burned frame of the old car into a piece of art.

At the center of the trailer was an attached and worn screened porch. At the left of the porch, the screen had a hole big enough for a small animal to fit through. Although the deck had looked weathered, it had been recently stained. The smell of the stain was faint, but it didn't help the scent that she could taste in her mouth from the trash. Between the headlights and the lamp's overhead light, Sister could quickly pick out something else. Or rather, someone else. She could feel the eyes on her when she exited the Jeep and knew that she wasn't alone. Now she could see her. Sitting behind the screen was a woman—Tia Ward's Mama.

MEETING MELBA

"Mrs. Ward? Mrs. Melba Ward?"

Sister hesitated before placing a foot on the first step of Melba's porch. Then, she cautiously placed her hand on the handrail as she ascended the stairs. As she proceeded, she called Mrs. Ward again, but there was no answer from the woman. Sister kept a watchful eye on Melba through the screen and the way she lit her cigarette. Sister tracked her hands and noted the variables in movement that could lead to something less desirable. Sister nodded her head in the woman's direction, silently greeting her again and trying to elicit a response.

Sister had ventured to the woman's part of the parish uninvited and unannounced. She sure wasn't looking to get herself shot in her efforts to speak with the dead girl's Mama. Not wanting Melba to feel threatened, Sister had left Beast in the Jeep with the window down, just in case Beast needed to make a quick exit. Sister didn't feel any danger. Nothing about the place hinted at trouble, but she proceeded with caution.

Melba's face remained void of reaction as her eyes stared blankly up at Sister through the porch screen. Her features conveyed nothing but exhaustion—the type born of tears and heartache.

The creases along her eyes sat atop her skin as deep, swollen ruts, as her grief wore heavy in her jowls and forehead. But there were no grievances in her stare, and seeing her hands light the cigarette gave Sister some comfort. It was deliberate. Melba's body language had only one design, which helped Sister relax. With her motives somewhat clear, Sister continued to the top step of the porch.

Melba's muddied, salt-and-pepper hair sat bound together atop her head in a heavy, rat's-nest-like heap; it hadn't seen a comb in a few days. By the looks of her, she probably hadn't showered in just as long. The sleeves of the man's t-shirt she wore had been cut off, displaying her thick arms. They looked strong, as if they were used for heavy lifting and hard work. The shirt was covered in stains, and the rest of her frame was hugged loosely as if it had been tugged into place. The shirt hadn't been changed in days.

From her posture, it was clear she wasn't wearing a bra as her girls were resting freely on the width of her lap. She either hadn't been expecting company or hadn't the energy to care for herself. Sister got the feeling it was a little of both. Apathy would have followed the observation of Melba's current state of disarray. However, Sister had seen her sheet and her previous mugshots. The woman in front of her was now the complete opposite of the woman she had been back then. Before motherhood, Miss Melba Jean Lathan was thin as a rail. Almost skeletal. She was strung out, covered in sores, and missing most of her front teeth. By the look of her now, she was no stranger to hard work or a hard life, but she was doing it clean. Her overall appearance had undergone a complete transformation. She wasn't the woman Sister had remembered either.

"The smell offends you?"

Sister watched as Melba reached over and twisted out a smoldering cigarette butt into a plate of what appeared to be untouched grits, fried fish, and okra. "At least someone cares enough to feed the poor woman," Sister thought.

She'd have to figure out who was close enough to the Ward family to bring food this far out. There were the usual suspects: family, friends, and kindly neighbors. The church. Or someone with a guilty conscience. It was just as likely that someone was looking to get their jollies by watching the fallout of their destruction.

With one eye squinted, protecting itself from the smoke that streamed from the newly lit Marlboro that hung from her lips, Miss Melba's other eye pointed at Sister; she said sharply with a snide smirk she didn't try to hide, "You act like you got yourself a delicate nature about you now."

The question caught Sister off guard, and she instantly felt ashamed and seen. She realized she had unconsciously put a finger under her nose again. And the "now" hadn't gone unnoticed either, but she decided to let that part go.

"Oh, no, ma'am. I mean... I apologize if I've offended you," she said. Sister's stomach was stronger than that, and she should have been more aware of her surroundings and who might have been watching her. "That was rude of me. I do apologize."

"I ain't so easily put off as all that," Melba stated matter-of-factly. "And it ain't like you ain't got cause. I reckon I've just gotten a little too used to it," she sighed. "It ain't always like this, you know?" she continued while gesturing with a hand towards the front yard.

"No, ma'am. I suspect not. You do have a lovely yard. You've put a lot of work into it. I don't have one myself. Don't have the patience for it, I guess."

"So, you here about my Mia then? Your sheriff ain't got another rich white woman to dig around for, so you got some time for my girl now? Now that she's dead? Y'all weren't too interested in looking for her a week ago. Is McTavish too good to come out here and explain himself in person? Fucking coward. He already sent a couple of you assholes out here already. No need for another, 'I'm sorry, ma'am, we'll look into it.' I already know what that shit means."

Other than the red blotches of sun that had burned the tops of her shoulders and cheeks, the fact that Melba was as near white as rice wasn't lost on Sister. However, she was married to a black man who was doing time. This, combined with a family history of arrests, led Miss Melba to have a list of grievances towards society and law enforcement.

Mia had gone missing about a week ago and had only been found yesterday. Sister understood Melba's anger. It hadn't appeared as if any of McTavish's deputies had taken Melba's concerns seriously. Melba was bound to be hostile, and Sister kept that in mind as she surveyed the porch, taking note of everything seen and unseen. She noticed that Miss Melba had a sawed-off 12-gauge resting on the floor, just behind the rear of her chair. Under any other circumstances, that would have been enough to detain Melba.

Miss Melba's felony sheets notwithstanding, any shotgun under an 18-inch barrel was illegal, and the shotgun itself was not 28 inches in total length. Sister covertly picked up four unspent shells and slipped them into the pockets of her jeans while Melba focused her gaze out the screen again. She was Creole through and through, so Sister got her meaning.

Rural and uneducated, she knew the statistics would not favor Melba. She hadn't been a priority to anyone her entire life, and she wouldn't believe now that that had changed. To be honest, her daughter probably wouldn't have been either if it hadn't been for the brand on her neck and the gold button in her mouth. That was not lost on Sister either. But that wasn't the sheriff's doing. Sister thought she knew him well enough to know he cared. Even if he couldn't do anything to prevent what had happened. But there wouldn't be any point in trying to convince a grieving mother that they would do their job and find out what happened to Mia. Only time could prove otherwise.

"Is there anyone inside?" Sister asked, looking at the trailer's front door. "Anyone I need to be worried about?"

"No, just me," Melba stated weakly, her words were broken and deafening. "Just me."

Watching the weight of that statement, Sister's heart hurt for the woman. "May I?" Sister asked, gesturing toward a chair matching Melba's. It had a broken arm and looked like a puppy had used it as a chew toy. Small teeth had scarred the legs and one of the armrests, but it looked sturdy enough to use. Melba responded with a nod, but continued to keep her eyes fixed on the distance of the yard and skyward.

"I am Deputy Lovejoy," she said, introducing herself and reaching out a hand. "Or you can call me Charlee if you like. Either is fine with me."

When Melba didn't move, Sister sat and quickly noticed that Melba's bare feet displayed blue nail polish on her toes. The paint was old and chipped. The color had long since lost its shine, which seemed fitting on a woman of her hard exterior. But something melted Sister's insides at seeing it. Trying to imagine the bright, new polish on Melba brought a pain to Sister. It was the same shade of blue that Mia had on her fingers back at the morgue.

"I like the blue polish," Sister said sincerely, pointing to Melba's feet.

Melba quietly looked down at her feet, and Sister watched as Melba self-consciously rubbed the top of her toes with the bottoms of her feet as if she could rub away the memories. Sister saw Melba's energy sink deeper than before, though she didn't know how that was possible. Melba withdrew inside herself and physically appeared smaller. Sister was going to lose her. The woman was deteriorating right before her eyes, and she wouldn't be able to speak if she let this play out any longer. She had to remove the delicate hands.

Sister took a deep breath. Their job was challenging and could be cold. She sought out and eliminated serial killers, mass murderers, crime lords, war criminals, human traffickers, and those involved in other types of crimes that affected people on a level beyond societal norms. Those who thought they could hide themselves across the world and dissolve into the landscape to remain unseen. Some sought protection from their own countries or had friends and the means to get away with whatever atrocities they inflicted upon any country, including their own, evading and avoiding capture and prosecution. Sister didn't like being here. It was rare for them to work together on U.S. soil. This is what the other three-letter agencies were for. There were just too many jurisdictional hurdles to clear and variables to navigate. Too much red tape and politicians with their hands out, looking to trade favors to look the other way. She was meant to be invisible, and by sitting here talking to Melba about her daughter, who had been killed in Baptiste, Louisiana, USA, Sister felt exposed. This put her, as well as the rest of them, on someone's radar.

It had been a very long time since she had spoken to family members about anything. All interviews had been left to the local authorities. Sister got everything she needed from a file provided to her by Bishop or the Old Man. She didn't feel as though she had anything left in her arsenal of tricks that gave her that edge or the skill to deal with loved ones and their emotions. That's why this job was easy for her. She lived in the shadows and always as someone else. There was a distance there, and she felt removed from thoughts and the effects of things that got in the way, like grief and vengeance.

There was no thought to it. She was given a task that required no debate—cause and effect. Being invisible had its privileges and advantages. And it had worked for her for a very long time. Returning to the continental U.S.

to work this case seemed unreasonable in any direction she took. She had to become a real someone. She was being made to show herself among those who knew her face. That wasn't good, and she didn't understand what the Old Man was up to.

"God be with us," Sister whispered.

Sister needed His strength to help her find a connection. She needed to pull that part of herself she kept protected forward, and she knew she would need God's hand on her to do it. She needed to find that part of her that could relate to this woman. She had no children. She was doing her best to keep Beast alive most days, and God forbid someone gave her a plant. It would be as dead as dead could get if left in her care. She doubted that she could truly understand Melba's sort of loss. But she did know loss, and knowing what Mia had experienced gave Sister some sort of starting ground.

"I'm going to show you a picture," she said, pulling a Polaroid from her breast pocket.

Dr. Tomlin had done an excellent job of cleaning up Mia. The photo was in good taste. She looked like Sleeping Beauty. Her hair had been washed and dried. He had combed out her curls and placed them neatly around her head like a halo. She looked like an angel. Sister had seen plenty of dead bodies. Most often, their faces were distorted and disfigured. Some faces memorialized, frozen thoughts of their last moments on earth—that of shock and horror. But Mia's face bore no such terror. Like she had simply just fallen asleep to never wake again. Sister could feel what Mia had suffered. Yet, Mia looked like she had accepted her death and rested easily.

The table that separated Sister and Miss Melba was cluttered and overrun with trash, dishes still full of food, and packs of empty cigarette wrappers. The ashtray had so many butts that they spilled out onto the tabletop and down onto the porch floor. Judging from everything around her, this mess wasn't the norm, and Sister wondered just how long Melba had been sitting there. Maybe she thought that at any moment now, Mia would come walking up the drive. Sister, too, looked down the driveway and envisioned a sweet Mia skipping towards the house. She wanted the whole ordeal to be one big mistake, and for Melba to hug her girl again. Sister shrugged it off and brought herself back to reality. She couldn't allow herself to slip into Melba's mind-space. It hurt too much. Not seeing a clear place to rest the photo and still not getting an answer, Sister gently placed it face down on Melba's knee.

"Take your time," she said, pulling her hand back. "There is no rush. I have nowhere else to be."

Sister watched tears begin to form at the creases of Melba's eyes. They stayed there, daring to fall, but they had latched on tightly and refused to spill. Even Miss Melba's tears were stoic. But her cigarette gave a slight quiver, and that tremble gave her away. The tremble stopped when she tightened her lips to take another drag. Drawing it out, it steadied its movement, and her posture straightened. Sister watched Melba's eyes as she flipped the photograph over. The photo showed the head and shoulders of a young teenage girl with long, black, curly hair pinned back by two purple barrettes—the only child of Melba, Mia Ward.

Sister reached out to touch her hand to comfort her when she saw Melba's posture deflate. All attempts at the "stiff upper lip" were now gone. Melba quickly jerked her hand away before Sister could make contact. Sister was almost grateful for the rejection because she was so far out of her comfort zone that it made her nervous. Melba's sobs were gut-wrenching. The howl that escaped the woman could have called in the dead. Sister had little practice when it came to comforting the grieving. Any experience she had in consoling others had faded over the years, leaving her almost vacant. However, Sister could relate to Melba's rejection of comfort.

Sister let her cry. And once Miss Melba fell silent, she returned to staring out the screens and ignored Sister. Maybe if she pretended long enough that Sister wasn't there, she'd go away. But she would be wrong. Sister may have been vacant regarding the warm and fuzzies, but she had fortitude. This may not have been her choice, but once she started a puzzle, she would see it to the end.

For a ridiculous moment, Sister wished Melba would continue to scream and yell. When the thought entered her mind, she immediately dismissed it and chastised herself for inviting chaos. But anything physical, Sister could handle. Sister seemed to thrive in the mud and guts of it all. It was the pretty parts of life that held her back. Melba's sadness was crippling. Sister had worked hard at keeping that emotion absent from her life. Sadness was something that she didn't allow to take up space. Therefore, she did her best to remain impassive and unattached regarding her work. She knew she'd never get out of bed if she let it in, even a small piece.

NO TIME FOR SHENANIGANS

"My Mia was a good girl," Melba finally said after a while, breaking the silence. Sister observed as Melba gently ran her thumb over Mia's face as if trying to summon her home. Melba had left the image face up, and her thumb mindlessly circled over it. More often than not, a guilty person would have turned the photo over, quickly putting it face down—unable to look upon the face of the person they had murdered. There were some exceptions, though. Sister had dealt with several people who could look at the photo and reveal nothing. However, Melba was not one of them. She wasn't the sadistic type. Sister was confident that Miss Melba had played no part in the death of her daughter.

"She was kind and so smart. She was good in math and science, too. They moved her a grade

ahead, you know. She was a straight-A student over there at that school."

Melba's voice faltered, and then she paused and lit another cigarette before she spoke again. "She weren't like me at all. But more like my Tommy. He's a good man, no matter what y'all say about him. He went to college. She was good and smart like him. Never any trouble to nobody. She was gonna be somebody like him. Before he met me."

"Did Mia have a boyfriend?"

Melba gave a weak laugh at that. "My girl didn't have time for shenanigans. She had to keep her grades up to stay in that school. Boys would have distracted her from all that."

"The Sisters of Holy Souls?" Sister asked.

"Yeah, that'd be the one."

"But there is a boys' school on the same grounds. Were there no interested suitors?" Sister asked, treading slowly, not wanting to imply anything torrid or amiss.

"Yep, The Sacred Hearts of Father Thomas. It used to be a boys' home. They're on that old plantation land owned by the Doucets," Melba said, eyeing Sister cautiously. "But like I said, Mia wasn't into boys. She's a good girl."

Sister knew of both schools; she had visited them many times in the past. But she didn't want to interrupt Melba's train of thought, hoping it would keep her talking longer. She already knew the schools' histories. The Sacred Heart of Father Thomas was erected in the 1930s and served as a boys' home until it was converted into a school for boys in the 1970s. The girls' school, The Sisters of Holy Souls, was built about ten years later. Both schools were preparatory academies that offered education from pre-kindergarten through 12th grade. Each rested on the grounds of an old plantation—the same plantation on which the church, St. Constantine, was built.

It was hard to believe that Mia hadn't noticed not one boy—or that the boys hadn't noticed her. Only about 160 yards separated the two schools, with a decent-sized pond between them. Hardly enough distance to keep the rage of hormones apart. Mia was a cute girl and a budding teenager. But it hadn't been necessary to point that out to Melba.

Melba then reached under her chair and pulled out a tall bottle. Sister had noticed it when she first arrived and had guessed it was vodka or gin, but she couldn't see the label. Melba's words carried with them the scent of alcohol when she spoke, and Sister could smell the heaviness of it once she reached the landing. But who wouldn't be nine sheets deep, given the circumstances? It seemed logical that an addict would turn to something. Melba twisted off the cap and poured herself a mouthful. At first, her cheeks puffed out as though a dam threatened to burst. And then she sucked in as she held it for a bit, swishing it around before she swallowed. By the look on her face, it had gone down like lava. But that didn't stop her from doing it again, and twice more, as if she were punishing herself. She then handed the bottle off in Sister's direction, silently asking if she'd like a tilt.

"No, thank you," Sister said, holding up a hand to ward off the bottle. But then she paused, thinking about where she needed to be and what she needed to do later that night. "You know what, what the hell. Why not," she said, a bit hesitant. She wasn't sure it was a good idea, but then Sister pulled the shield from her shirt and placed it in her pocket. She wasn't an actual deputy sheriff anyway, she told herself. She was only playing a role.

Besides, Melba didn't need a cop as much as she needed a person. So, Sister took the bottle from her and tilted it back. It burned her sinuses and tasted awful. Sister had never understood why anyone liked the taste of gin as she swallowed a mouthful. Vodka was smoother and cleaner. In contrast, gin had a perfumed taste. Maybe she couldn't appreciate the finer points of Juniper, but she was okay with that.

"It's cheap, but it does the job," Melba replied with a slight smirk. She noticed Sister's face, wrinkled in disgust at the taste. Melba took back the bottle and took another long pull before placing it back underneath her chair.

"I'm partial to Scotch whisky myself," Sister shrugged. "But not bourbon—definitely not a fan. I've acquired years of experience to discern the difference," she said with a twinkle in her eye and a knowing smile.

"So, you're one of those, huh? A classy drunk?" Miss Melba said in a teasing tone as she tilted a pinky finger and a thumb up to her mouth and gave the universal sign for "drunk."

"I've been a friend of Bill's for many years now," Sister said with a chuckle at seeing Miss Melba loosen up. Sister figured this was a good time to ask some questions and took on a more serious tone. "Where was Mia before she went missing? Can you start from the beginning?"

Melba lit up another cigarette and let out a long sigh before she answered, handing the pack over to Sister.

"No, thank you," Sister said, "Now that I do not partake."

"Suit yourself," Melba shrugged, placing the pack back on the table among the mess. "It was Sunday morning. My brother came over around eight something. My car wasn't runnin' so good, and I ain't got the money to get her one of her own. So, he picked her up and took her over there to that big church on the other side of Baptiste. You know, the one where her school is. She was meetin' up with her friends for a youth group meeting before Sunday school at 9:30. Friday was her last day of school, and VBS was about to start up. She was volunteering for Victory Bible Study with some of the other girls from her classes, like she did every year since she got too old to be there herself. She loved teaching the littles, you know," she choked out before the sobbing started again.

Melba could barely get out the words. Her tears began to fall, flooding her face and running down her neck and onto her chest. "She was going to be a junior next year. She was so proud and excited. She shoulda come home that evening. She had packed her bag already, but I wanted her to come home and get some snacks and stuff. She told me that they would be campin' there all week and that she would be helpin' to chaperone a few of the younger ones who would be staying there instead of going home at night. I wanted her home with me for just a bit, since I wouldn't be seein' her that week."

"Do you attend this church yourself?"

Sister already knew the answers to most of the questions she was asking. Still, in her experience, people who were facing a traumatic situation tended to forget the small details or have different answers later on after thinking about it. She didn't believe it was due to deception or meant to be misleading on Melba's part. Just stress-induced memory fatigue. That's not to say that people don't sometimes lie. Everyone lies about something. Intentionally or unintentionally. By repeating questions, the details could often be expanded on. New memories or perspectives could be brought forward. Sister understood why Melba hadn't been a member of the congregation. Not much had changed since her time there.

Melba shot back a look that would melt steel. "Your fuckin' kiddin', right? The good folks of the 'Holier Than Thou' don't let former pipe heads like me mix it up with them. They'd probably put newspaper down on the pews before allowing someone like me to sit. And besides," she snorted, blowing out her cigarette and waving her free hand dismissively into the air. "I don't want to be in the buildin' when that one up there," she said, pointing to the ceiling above her, "decides its time, and he sends a lightnin' strike at that bitch, and burns the whole fuckin' house of hypocrites to the ground. That'd be a hoot, right?" Melba laughed and took another drag from her cigarette as she pulled the bottle out from under her chair again.

As she took the bottle for the second time, she sat quietly, mulling over Melba's words, before she asked, "And her father?" Again, she already knew the answer. But she wanted to keep Melba talking as long as possible.

"My Tommy's over in Angola," she said softly. "He was protecting me when he killed that man. But the law around here don't care none about that. He was just another broke-down black man to them."

But he wasn't just another broke-down black man. Sister knew better than that. She had read that the girl's daddy, Thomas Ward, was doing twenty for a murder conviction after he was found guilty of killing a man in a bar fight over a woman. As the facts were laid out, in another world, Thomas would have been hailed a hero for saving Melba's life. They dragged out his trial, giving all appearances that it would be fair and impartial. During his trial, he fell in love with Melba and married her. But the perpetrator of the assault on Melba was a rich man's boy, and white. Melba was the daughter of a local drunk, and Thomas wasn't from the area. Thomas didn't stand a chance and probably shouldn't have gotten involved for his own sake.

Sister asked a few more questions while Melba stroked Beast's head, who now sat at Melba's feet. After the third drink, Sister realized she'd probably be there a while longer and let Beast out to do her business.

She was sure that Melba had already answered the same questions or similar, a dozen times or more with the local authorities. However, not only did Sister want to hear what she had to say, she also really just wanted to sit with her a bit longer. She wasn't too worried about Melba hurting herself, though that had crossed her mind more than once. She did know that impulse all too well. Sister didn't think that would be a problem, but she worried Melba would relapse into something much worse. Sister had been convinced that Melba had only given up the drugs for Mia. And if she didn't have Mia anymore, what reason did she have to stay clean? So, Sister sat there with her. She listened to Melba for another couple of hours, while she cried, screamed, talked, didn't talk, and often sat in silence as she drank herself into slumber.

During a moment of complete quiet, the three of them shared a kind of understanding. Beast, Melba, and Sister watched the stars twinkle. Every now and then, they'd comment on whether or not a star was falling, or a plane was just passing through. The on-and-off rain had ceased, and soon, a noise was heard. Beast's ears perked as the noise came from an old cat that had climbed its way through the hole in the screen. Beast paid him no mind and placed her head back into Melba's lap. That's when Sister noticed that Melba's head would drop and slowly spring back up. She was almost there.

She took this as her cue to leave. She stood and placed an arm around Melba, lifting her to her feet, and walked her to the door that led into the trailer. She used her hip to hold up Melba as she pulled the door open with her free hand. Then she walked Melba up the two thin steps and led her to a couch covered in unfolded clothes, towels, and heaps of unopened mail. She gently pushed everything to one end of the sofa and laid Melba down. An old, red chair sat in the corner of the living room, its seat held a neatly folded blanket. Sister retrieved it and placed it on top of Melba, who was now sound asleep. The old black cat from earlier had quietly curled up next to Melba and purred at her side.

The trailer was a disaster in a forgotten kind of way—the type of neglect that comes from grief. There were dirty dishes everywhere, trash spilled out of its can and covered the floor, and the place smelled as if the litter box hadn't been cleaned in a minute. But it was obvious that it had once—and often—been tidy. She may not have had the latest and greatest, but Melba had done right by her girl. The walls were painted in bright, clean colors, proudly displaying Mia's artwork from kindergarten to the present. There on the wall was a hand-drawn photo of Melba. Her likeness was unmistakable. At the bottom, it read Mia W 1/1. It was an amazing depiction. Mia was a talented artist. These were all the "proud mama" pieces. She wanted everyone to see just how incredible her baby girl was.

Next to the front door, Sister saw three pairs of shoes stacked neatly beside it. They were heavily used but still in decent shape. The shoes next to those were well-worn and most suitable for working outside. Sister wondered if they were all Mia's shoes or maybe Melba's. They appeared to be all the same size. Perhaps they shared shoes. Sister had heard of mothers and daughters doing that. She had been an only child, so she hadn't experienced it herself, but she knew that sisters also shared shoes and clothing. It was clear that Melba's entire life was dedicated to Mia, regardless. She couldn't see Melba wearing the sandals or even the black high-tops. But even so, there was no doubt that Melba loved her daughter more than anything and did her best to provide for her.

There were art supplies, schoolbooks, and a laptop on the coffee table. Sister took this time to gain a better understanding of Mia's home life. A huge bowl of fruit had started to rot, sitting in the middle of a small dining table in the kitchen. Next to the bowl was a framed picture of a very pregnant, younger, and healthier Melba with a handsome Tommy. Sister smiled at the photo. It was clear that they loved one another. Melba still called him "her Tommy." Sister searched the many documents and found no divorce decree of record for them. Melba hadn't divorced him after he was sent up. She had promised her life to him, and she meant every word of it.

Maybe he was the reason she got clean. Perhaps he'd be the reason she stayed that way. Sister knew he had a parole hearing soon. He had already been denied three times, and she wondered if there was anything they could do to help it lean in his favor. McTavish had those types of connections, and she made a note to ask him about it when she returned.

There were cereal boxes and lunch-type items neatly placed on top of the microwave, next to a bag of small brown paper bags—the type school children used to take a sack lunch to school. Sister then pulled open the fridge. The fridge always told a story. You could tell how a person lived by its contents. It was packed with the types of things a family would have; leftovers, milk, eggs, and cheese—some of these, which were probably not edible now, but last week, this household had been thriving. On that note, Sister shut the door and started down a small hall towards the back of the trailer.

There were three doors off the hall. One led to a clean bathroom. No clothing or towels littered the floor. The trash basin was empty. Sister made note of only one toothbrush in the holder, but decided that Mia had probably packed hers when she left for church. Since her bag hadn't been found yet, this wasn't a fact, but a good guess. Sister closed the door and continued down the hall. The door to the left clearly led to Melba's room. Sister had no interest in that room and took a few more steps to the door at the end of the hall. On the door, a metal sign that read "Mia's Domain" was attached to the front.

Sister pushed open the door to find a room resembling that of an ordinary teenage girl. However, this was clearly the master bedroom. Melba had given her daughter a better space. On the right side of the room, a poster of Justin Bieber had been taped to the wall. Next to it was one of Selena Gomez. On the wall behind the bed was a movie poster of "Divergent," with an image of Four standing on a train with a group of kids. Opposite that was another movie poster of "Underworld." Sister couldn't help but remember that Theo James was in both movies. Mia had a type, and Sister couldn't blame her. James was a good-looking man. The room was painted white with yellow curtains. The bedspread was white with a giant yellow puffy sunflower sewn on. It had a 3D appearance.

Next to the bed was a white nightstand. On top was a sketch pad, a lamp, and an empty glass. It was most likely her late-night water glass. There was also an old-school Scooby-Doo lunchbox—a metal one like the one Sister remembered from her own youth. Hers had come with a thermos. Sister opened the lunchbox. She wasn't sure what she expected to find. More art supplies? Old food? What would a teenage girl keep inside a Scooby-Doo lunchbox?

Sister thought back to being a young, dumb teenage girl and the things that she would hide from her parents. If it had been her, there would have been no way she would have left the box out in the open. Whatever was hidden in the box—if anything at all—it and the box would have been buried deep enough that it would take an FBI bloodhound to sniff it out. When Sister still lived at home, she had found a hole cut in the back of her closet, hidden behind her clothes. Her room had once belonged to a teenage boy. Sister remembered thinking that he had probably cut out the drywall and had turned the piece of scrap into a door, hiding his porn collection or drugs from his parents—or both.

Mia had left the box in the open for anyone to see. Either it contained nothing of importance, or Melba wasn't the type of parent to go rummaging through her daughter's privacy. She knew there were protocols for what she was about to do, but Sister told herself that she wasn't doing anything illegal, really. She wasn't even a real deputy, and any permissions she needed were, well, subject to her discretion. Something about the death of a curious cat came to mind, but she hadn't heard of curiosity killing anyone—except those who "heard a noise" in the movies.

She was willing to take the risk, though. Sister opened the box. It held a mass of colored pencils and one Elmer's glue stick. These, along with a handful of different charcoal sticks, had left smudges on Sister's fingers. A few loose dollar bills and a handful of change sat on the bottom. As Sister moved things around, she noticed that the bottom of the lunchbox was covered in what looked like a folded-up piece of paper or a white envelope. It had been secured by taping the edges of the paper product to the bottom. Sister looked at the door of the bedroom. Listening for Melba, she waited. Hearing that Melba was still out cold, Sister poured out the contents of the box on the bed and began to pull back the tape. Once the tape had been removed, Sister lifted out what was now, for sure, an envelope.

Sitting on the bed, Sister opened the envelope. She poured out the individual pieces on top of the box's earlier contents. Sister's stomach felt sick at what she was seeing. They were photos of girls about Mia's age or older, including herself, in various forms of undress and stages of sexual innuendo. In total, there were seven girls and at least thirty photos. Each girl was painted up in makeup beyond their years and wore different arrangements of lingerie. At least half of the images were of Mia herself or with a friend, sexualized and demanding the camera's attention.

Sister quickly picked up the photos and placed them back into the envelope. Then she scooped up the pencils, charcoals, and money and stuffed them all back into the box. After arranging the box and the room back into its original condition, ensuring nothing was out of place, Sister unbuttoned her shirt and tucked the envelope into the waistband of her jeans. Then she buttoned her shirt back up and headed for the front door.

Clearly, Miss Melba hadn't had a clue about her daughter's shenanigans.

BARSTOOLS &
BOURBON

Frankie's Pub had been a downtown staple in Baptiste for as long as anyone could remember. It was nestled between a trendy new hair salon called Dyed Becomes You and Doolittle's, a do-it-yourself pet grooming facility. Frances O'Shea Sr., an Irish immigrant, had passed away some time ago, and now his only grandchild and heir, Frankie the III, owned what many considered the pulse of Baptiste. Frankie had never intended to stay put, but after struggling with college life, had returned home with a sickness and an empty wallet. With nothing left to pursue, Frankie took up the challenge of keeping Granda's sixty-year-old dream alive. That was about twelve years ago. Sister was happy to see that Frankie, once voted Most Likely to Succeed, had managed to keep the old pub thriving.

The after-work crowd filled the place with a chaotic hum of overlapping conversations, making it impossible to discern one from another. In a small town with limited economic opportunities and nothing else to do, she bet her entire month's salary that some patrons had been there since it opened that morning. For many of them, the pre-game festivities had begun before they headed home for dinner and family time. Others seemed to have completely forgotten they even had a home to return to. Despite it being a school night, the bar was crowded, and the staff appeared ready for a long night ahead. Red paper-lined baskets overflowing with Southern fried anything and everything cluttered the tables, alongside plastic utensils and pint glasses.

A blonde server wearing a painted-on jean mini skirt and a red checkered Daisy Duke top giggled a bit too uncomfortably as a man patted her on the ass as she stood near him. This was a little too familiar for Sister's liking. Sister looked away, fearing that her death glare would be deemed as confrontational, and she needed to fly under the radar as much as possible. For all that, Sister's judgy nature soon took over, and she concluded that the woman couldn't have been all that upset with her circumstances, given that she hadn't busted the man in the face with her serving tray, leaving him spitting out his teeth on the table. Then she saw the bubbly blonde wink at the man. Sister had to reel in her short line for that kind of nonsense and shrugged off the situation altogether. "Not my circus, not my clowns," she mumbled as she continued to circle the room. She was far removed from a feminist, but a man should keep thy hands to thyself. She was pretty sure that had been written in the Bible somewhere.

A cook in the back had yelled for the third time, "It's getting cold, Alice!" That snapped Sister back to the task at hand, and she began looking for her boys. She could be offended for Alice, but it wouldn't do anyone any good. A table in the back erupted in laughter as one young deputy told of his encounter with a woman he had pulled over that morning for drunk driving.

"She literally hiked up her skirt, pulled down her underwear, and took a heaping shit on the highway," he said, barely able to get the words out between sobs of laughter as tears ran down his face. "And she was a classy dame. I mean, she was done up all nice. She was small, too. A good-lookin' old broad. And she drove a BMW! A BMW! Can you even imagine?"

"That is the funniest shit I've seen all year," another deputy said. "My boy got it all on his dash cam. All of it. He was chasing her around her car with her panties around her ankles. She was totally out of it and started swinging on him. I thought he was going to have to taser her until she fell over. I mean, she hit the ground hard. I think that knocked some of the fight outta her. The worst part.... I heard that Nichols, over in filing, called his dad to come and bail out his Mama. We only had the one lady in holding."

"Was that Mrs. Nichols? Oh, man! Seriously?!"

"No way! She's been a principal forever. I had her as a principal in like the 6th grade."

"Dude, didn't you bring her in around 11 this morning?" another voice asked.

"Shit, if I had you in any class, I'd drink my breakfast too," said someone in response.

"Damn, that's some breakfast!" said another with a laugh. "Smith, you sure we ain't talkin' about your mama?"

"That would be Daddy to you, Jones," Smith said, laughing and throwing a wadded-up napkin at him. "Or Papi if you like. That's what your mama calls me."

Sister scanned the crowd for Bishop's face amidst the commotion and the flurry of questions flying around the table. However, all she could see were Sunshine, Brick, and McQueen. The three were enjoying themselves, listening to stories and antics shared by the other local deputies. They were trading tales about local happenings and the lack of activities that had fostered an atmosphere of creativity, allowing for entertainment to be had by all. Though she hadn't met the others yet, she quickly made a mental note of their faces shortly after the plane landed. She made it a habit of familiarizing herself with all the key players and essential individuals.

After pushing her way past the jukebox that belted out a Gretchen Wilson song, "Redneck Woman," she spotted Bishop sitting on an old barstool at the front of the bar. He was fully engaged with the beautiful and popular Frankie Frazier. If her doe-like eyes indicated anything, Bishop would be on his way to a preacher if she had her way.

"Can I interest you in somethin' sweeter, Darlin'?" Sister heard her ask.

Sister saw the way Frankie's red lips moved like honey, as her doe-eyes sparkled, dark as charcoal but shining like diamonds. She wasn't referring to anything of liquid substance, as she poured him another drink. Her red lace bra played peek-a-boo behind a white cutoff t-shirt, and the V had been purposefully cut deeper. Sister knew right away that Frankie was pouring him a bourbon. That was his drink of choice when his current mood came to visit. Sister was sure that, given a few drinks herself, Frankie would have no fear of climbing over the bar and wrapping him up in all that honey. Although Frankie held back on her flirtation, she probably only needed an invitation or a very drunk Bishop.

Many of the thirty- and forty-somethings around here were still clinging to their glory days and hadn't progressed as one might hope. Sister recognized this was a cynical perspective on the people around Baptiste, but she understood better than most. Whether it was due to falling on hard times, enjoying good times, managing family life, or just trying to be the life of the party, no one needed a reason to drink or use drugs.

"I'll take a sweet tea since you're offerin'," Sister said in her most charming Southern voice as she sat beside him and laced her fingers together. "Heavy on the tea. But you can keep your sugar, Honey." Sister's smile wasn't missed. Nor were the territorially snarky expressions and inquisitive eyebrows sharp enough to cut glass. Frankie's cheeks blushed redder than her bra, and Bishop nearly choked as he spat out a mouthful of bourbon onto the bar top between them.

"Comin' up, Darlin'," Frankie said as she cleaned up his mess. Frankie looked as guilty as a junkie who had just been caught with her hand in another man's stash.

"I thought tea without sugar was a sin in the South?" He said, giving her a sideways glance. "And that was none too kind, Sister," he said. "I know when you start dropping those G's from your words, people should duck. You might wanna put those eyebrows back where they belong before you cut someone." He tossed back the replacement bourbon that Frankie had placed in front of him.

"Here's your tea, Darlin'."

"Thanks, Darlin'," Sister said kindly, but her eyebrows were still razor sharp. Her gag reflex had been triggered at about the fourth time; the word "Darlin'" had been used. She couldn't help but notice that Frankie's syrupy demeanor had dissolved and was now replaced with some salty bitters. Her eyes had a hard time finding a place to land. Instead, they kept darting over at Bishop, the back of the room, and then back to the bar at Sister. She clearly didn't recognize Sister, and she was enjoying Frankie's discomfort. Although Bishop looked unamused, he had a sort of smile on his face. After Frankie had slid over the red plastic tumbler in Sister's direction, she busied herself needlessly wiping down mats that were obviously fresh out of the washer and smelled of lemon detergent.

"Sister, is it? Okay then, Boss." Her words were hard at the edges, and the wound it left wasn't missed on his face.

She looked at him with her most hurtful expression, attempting to mimic Frankie's big-eyed look, but she couldn't maintain a straight face. Of course, he knew better. Over the years, she had adopted so many names that she felt a bit schizo. Each name came with its own personality. However, the name "Sister" suited her perfectly, and she wore it like a badge of honor. She took pride in what that name represented.

Each of them had played a part in choosing their name. Some handles came to them naturally, like "Boss." He was a natural leader and quickly took charge, making him responsible for relaying the Old Man's wishes. Others spent time finding just the right name. Luke Kidd adopted "McQueen" in honor of the legendary Steve McQueen, his father's idol. The Old Man named Silas Holiday "Sunshine" because he radiated positivity no matter the circumstances. Addison Adler had been called "Addie" in his childhood, but after he stood up to his much older and bigger childhood bully, he earned the nickname "Brick."

"Addison's bully was struck in the face with a red brick from a pile at the construction site near our apartments, where we grew up," explained Brick's wife, who had known him since childhood. "As a result, he went toothless throughout secondary school."

Everyone but McQueen had attended Addison's and Lily's wedding at Old Marylebone Town Hall in London. It was a beautiful affair, and Sister's eyes filled with tears as she witnessed everyone's moments of happiness. Watching the couple gave her hope for better times for them all.

"Addison," Lily continued, her East London accent lightly salted with her parents' Jamaican roots. Sister admired the love shining in her eyes as she looked at Brick. "He was skinny and all limbs when we were kids, but he could be quite mouthy," she said, kissing his forehead. "It's no wonder they liked to beat him up. But that blow would've left even his children born toothless," she joked. "After that, those boys left him alone."

"I call bullshit," Bishop called out, laughing as he raised a glass to the couple. Lily looked stunning in her white, Justin Alexander Cooper-designed mermaid dress, and Brick resembled a Caribbean James Bond in his crisp white tuxedo. "You were never little. I bet you were born built like a brick shithouse—solid and full of it."

"Frankie, there was just offering to take me home, is all. Just being neighborly, of course," Bishop said.

"Oh, of course. Well then, please don't let me stop the good deeds. I'm sure she's awfully neighborly. I'd wager that with minimal effort on your part, she'd let you see the match to that bra. Red is your favorite color, if I remember correctly. Very charitable of her."

Bishop ignored her sharp tongue by leaning over and stirring her drink with its straw. "Just drink your tea and stop whatever this is," he said, annoyed. "You don't get to do that."

"Do what?" she asked, looking at him in a puzzled gaze.

"Don't play games, Sister. That—the jealous—'I'm just playing around, teasing, fake shit.' You don't get to be hurt—fake or otherwise—and you don't get to be jealous. If I want to bang Frankie here on this bar, you don't have a right to say a fucking word. So stop."

They sat in compatible silence for a moment, neither of them knowing exactly what to say or where to start after Bishop's candor. She took to stirring her tea while he nursed another drink. She wished that she had ordered something stronger, but this wasn't the time for that. Judging by the glassy stare of Bishop's eyes, he had drunk enough for both of them. Besides, she was sure she reeked of gin and didn't need another reason for Bishop to look at her sideways.

The last time she needed a drink, she nearly jeopardized her career and friendships along with it. It hadn't just been one drink; it had been many—all of which paired nicely with China's favorite. She had truly embraced the role and had been pretty convincing. Eventually, the operations concluded, but she remained in character, chasing the high all the way to its end. As a result, she got Silas shot, compromised their second assignment, and the Old Man suspended her from the team. He ordered her into treatment, and it took just over two years before anyone trusted her enough to work with her again. The disappointment in their eyes was enough to crush her spirit; she didn't need drugs and alcohol to feel that pain. Rediscovering her faith had helped her regain control of her life.

"You already knew, yeah?"

She had finally decided to open the can. After giving him a moment, she dumped the worms onto the table. Her voice was low; she wasn't trying to draw a crowd, but there was a tone that struggled to remain neutral. When he lowered his head, he had hoped she wouldn't mention it and would leave him to himself for the night. He was struggling, and sitting in silence with his own thoughts was his way of coping. Sometimes, he just liked to be alone.

He had been a decorated Marine and a skilled investigator. This made him a valuable asset to the team, which was why the Old Man recruited him and eventually put him in charge. He was ready to settle down, allowing McTavish to focus more on his family. Deep down, he knew she wouldn't let it go.

"Is this why the Old Man brought me back here? What are the two of you up to now? None of this makes any sense, and you know that." Sister adjusted her seat so she could face him directly. Her eyes narrowed, forcing him to either make eye contact with her or look away. "You know I don't remember anything about what happened. If this is some covert attempt to trigger my memory of something that has already been hashed out a million times over the past ten-plus years, then you two are making a mistake. Nothing has changed."

He wanted to shake her and tell her that not everything was about her. And until he read her file, he had no idea what McTavish may or may not have known about anything concerning her. What he did know was that it was not his place to talk about it with her. He said he wouldn't.

"It's not always about you," he said flatly and ordered another drink.

She could feel the heat rising within her. Her neck grew warm, and she felt as though she needed to remove layers of clothing. She placed her hands in her lap, beneath the bar, and out of sight of others. Then, she pulled back the sleeve of her shirt and began snapping the rubber band around her wrist. The sound caught his attention, causing him to flinch as if he had been shot. He didn't like it when she wore the band, and it was even worse when she used it. It was a coping skill she had picked up along the way, helping her stay present—much like tapping her fingers and counting down. It was her way of staying connected in the moment without losing control of her emotions. She feared saying or doing anything she might regret later, and the possibility of doing so seemed to find her a lot lately.

"Stop," he said as he placed his hand over hers and blocked her fingers from letting go of the band for the third time. The band released, but instead of smacking against her skin, it was caught and silenced between his thumb and index finger.

"You don't need that. Just, please have a conversation. Let it out. Let it go. Scream if you must. But for fuck's sake, is this really any better? You look crazy, and you shut me down. I have never seen you do that with anyone else—just me. I feel like you use that band to throw up roadblocks between us. Why can't you just have a fucking conversation with me?"

"What are you talking about? You act as if I'm the reason we don't speak. I haven't heard from you in almost two years," she said in a tight whisper, wanting to match his intensity but turning it down a notch.

"You're the one to talk. They don't have telephone wires in the frozen north?" he shot back, matching her whisper but still keeping it turned up.

"You made it clear that we had nothing to talk about. Then you ambush me, bring me back here, and send me to see that girl. You did that! Again, I don't know what the two of you are playing at, but I don't like it. I used to live here. You don't think that people are gonna talk," she continued, this time her voice just a bit higher. "And take your hand off me," she said, pulling her hand out from beneath his.

"And you don't get to do that."

Just about the time Bishop was about to tell her why he had brought her back, why the Old Man felt desperate enough to risk her identity, a man bumped his stool. He pulled his hand away from Sister's to confront the man whose nudge had shoved him closer to the bar, not allowing him to swivel in his chair but able to turn his head. Silas looked at him and then at Sister.

"Sorry about that, Boss," he said, giving him a nod and placing both hands on Bishop's shoulders with a pat and a little squeeze. "The carpet grabbed me on my way to the little boy's room."

Bishop looked at Silas Holiday knowingly and sighed. Then he emptied the last of his drink, pushed back the stool hard with his legs—enough to push back Silas—and stood up. He then placed a firm hand on Silas's shoulder and returned the squeeze.

"Good night, my friend. I hear my bed calling me. Don't stay up too late, you two. We have an early morning."

Bishop called for Brick and McQueen as he made his way to the door. "If you boys want a lift and a bedtime story, Papa will tuck you in. Daddy is calling it a night."

"Oh, please, please? Yes, Daddy!" she heard Brick yell back across the bar in a wildly exaggerated Southern drawl, causing eyes to fall on them and the bar to hush in some areas and laughter to break out in others. His sense of humor was always on point. He rarely missed a beat or took much too seriously. His smile and mischievous eyes sold it all. She smiled as she watched the exchange. There had never been anything cross between her and Brick. However, there was an edge to their relationship. He was cautious around her— maybe less connected—which seemed purposeful, as if he did not care for her much. She wished she knew him better. They had never been close, and she had the feeling that if it weren't for their work, they would never have been friends at all. Their only true connection was Bishop. But she was grateful that Bishop had him.

"Princesses and dragons," McQueen echoed, his voice adopting a childlike tone. The two of them then hurried after Bishop. As they reached the door, Brick took the keys from Bishop's hand and put an arm around him to steady him. Bishop wobbled as he stood and greeted the newcomers with a bow. Brick glanced back at Sister and then returned his attention to Boss. She noticed his smile fade, replaced by a look of unease.

"Welcome. Welcome," Bishop said to the ones trying to get past him to enter the bar. His words came out slurred and broken. He was clearly in no condition to drive.

"Looks like Papa tried to find peace at the bottom of the glass tonight," Brick said. Then he looked back at her again and waved a hand overhead, gesturing goodnight and mouthing, "We got this."

"Shut up, Brick. Just take me home."

TREADING DEEP
WATERS

"You alright? That looked pretty intense," Silas commented as he sat down on Bishop's now-empty stool and gestured to Frankie to bring him another. "And one for the lady."

Sister laughed at that. "I'm fine, Silas; really, I've had enough. If I drink another one of these, I'll be up all night. And I, sir, am no lady. You know better than that." Then she tinked his glass with her own.

"Skal!" they said in unison. She took a drink of her tea, and he sipped at an Old Fashioned—neither of them in any hurry to go anywhere.

"I take it Melba Ward had a lot to say," he said finally, looking at her a bit more closely, noticing the smell of alcohol once she started speaking, but wanting to broach the subject.

"You look as if you should've called someone to come and get you."

"I didn't drive," she said with a smirk. "Beast's gotten pretty good at taking the wheel."

"Really? I'll have to ask the old girl how she feels about contributing to your bad inclinations. I don't have to tell you that drinking with the mother of our dead girl probably wasn't the best idea you've had."

"You've taken to that badge kinda serious-like, huh?" she said, tapping at a spot just above his heart where a shield had been earlier that day. "You thinking of becoming one of the good guys now?"

"Are you saying we aren't one of the good guys?" he asked, looking at her with interest. "You're starting to wade out into some heavy waters with that one."

"Frankie," he gestured, signaling for her to bring another round.

Then he turned his attentions back to Sister, curious to hear how she'd explain herself this time around. "You've been clean and sober for ten years now, Sister. What made you decide to break that?"

Sister looked at him for a few seconds before she answered. "It was the loneliness in her eyes, I guess. You know she is still married to her husband after all these years. I read the reports. Did you? Did you notice the blood types? Mia isn't even his. But he gave her his name."

"Melba kept the baby. That rich asshole's family still lives around here, you know. What kind of love is that? He's a good man. Hell, he probably deserved a medal for killing that guy for what he did to Melba. But he gets life for protecting her. Ain't that some shit?"

"She's dedicated her life to being a good mama, Si. No drugs. No booze. She stayed clean. She works hard. Provides well. She keeps a nice place. And all for what? So, she can end up on her front porch, drinking herself to death—or worse, eating her shotgun," Sister said as she reached into her pockets, pulled out the unspent shells, and tumbled them onto the bar.

"Her grief nearly drowned me. I watched her sit there and saw no light left in her. She just stared down the driveway in desperation. Watching a sky that observes everything but doesn't intervene. What kind of God allows this much pain and suffering in one person's life? A drunken father, a suicidal mother, an imprisoned husband, and now, a dead daughter," she said as she reached over, took the rest of Silas's drink from his hand, and drank it.

"You should have seen her, Si. There's nothing we can learn from the death of her daughter, except what she had to say. She's not involved. I felt like the only thing I could do for her was to make sure she didn't hurt herself. So, I had a few with her until she passed out. Then I came here."

Silas watched her as she spoke. A few tears welled up in her eyes, and he looked away as she wiped them clear.

"This girl was definitely into something, though." Then she explained what she had found in the trailer and pulled the photos from her waistband. Looking around, she slid them over to him.

"Don't open it here," she said, nodding at Jamie. "Too many ears and eyes."

Silas slipped the photos into his pocket, nodding his understanding.

"He hates that you shut him out, you know? And that band thing sends him up the wall," Silas counseled, nodding towards her wrist. Seeing his eyes on the band, she pulled her sleeve back down and tucked the band away.

"I know it does. But I can't talk to him without getting upset. And he started it."

"What, are we five again? The two of you really need to get your shit together. It's starting to affect all of us, and no one wants to take sides. You've gone your own way, doing your own thing—and he's here starting over. Don't get me wrong, I've enjoyed the break from the Bishop and Sister Shit-show, but you checked out altogether."

"You've skipped the welfare checks and the call-ins. You sending me a random message isn't checking in. At least once a month would have been nice. You letting us all know you're alive at least. That's what we do. You live in the fucking tundra. How are we supposed to know you're okay?"

She liked that no two of them were alike. It kept things interesting and unpredictable. Because they were all so different in their lives, they continually sought to find common ground and understand one another. She appreciated the Old Man's social experiment.

McTavish had chosen each person to complement the others rather than duplicate their primary traits. The six of them came from diverse backgrounds, with varying skill sets, educational backgrounds, and cultures. Their work united them and made them stronger, yet they didn't have to rely on one another for support or survival. Even when they disagreed, she valued that aspect of their relationship.

"You're not my father, Silas. And you're not my husband. I've kept in touch on my terms. I let you know I'm alive, and I come running when I'm called to do so. I don't need a babysitter, and I don't need you questioning my every move or decision."

"And no, to answer your question, I don't always feel like the good guy. I lie, manipulate, and kill people for a living. Nothing about that is godly—even if it's for the right reasons. And before you say, 'Our job isn't to kill people,' the outcome remains the same. We hunt them, and most of the time, it ends with their death. I'm not saying it's not a win-win, but what bothers me is that I don't feel bad about it."

"That's just it. For one, you do need looking after. No one goes it alone. We cannot survive what we do alone. It's all a mental game. And let's face it—the last time you went dark, I got shot. Two, you didn't come running this time. I had to drag you to the plane and threaten to tie you down. Or did you forget that? And three, you shouldn't feel bad. Our job is to collect the worst our society has to offer by any means necessary. It's their choice in how that ends. Coming along without drama gets them bars, four walls, three meals a day, and a bed. Not coming along without drama gets them dead. I don't cry about it, and neither should you. I certainly won't get all twisted up over the death of a pedo-sicko or anyone who peddles sex by enslaving women and children. And don't get me started on drug dealers or the assholes who use children to terrorize their own damn countries. Those fuckers should be hanged by their nuts in the center of the village and set on fire. It won't upset my feathers one bit."

She didn't know how to respond, but she was tired of defending herself. And he wasn't wrong—except she hadn't gone dark this time. She was living a life far enough away to avoid oversight and learning to live apart from all the bullshit. She was seeking her peace. She loved her work, but she had grown tired of the darkness and endlessness of it all. For every one they took off the board, a hundred more lined up to take over. She needed some light in her life that wouldn't be found in constantly seeking out the worst the world had to offer. Besides, she had been working. But she couldn't share that with the rest of the group.

The light she sought was in solving her own case and finding peace with what had happened to her. She saw the contradiction in her thought pattern but needed to finalize her own story—at least that part. Then maybe she could settle down. Maybe even accept the love offered and reevaluate her choices.

"Women all over the country are being found dead, Si," she said. "They are all linked together—I know it. I've been working it out," she confessed. "And by my last count, five high-profile individuals have been found dead under extreme circumstances. It's an odd case. It has me interested."

"But those are not your cases. Did you find that missing girl in Nome? Randy Harper used to be a Trooper. His brother is still APD. Did the brother help him? Did you finalize your report on those departments?"

"Those were your cases. Look," Silas said, doing his best to keep from becoming frustrated. "I know it's not kicking in doors and the excitement you are used to. You wanted low-key, you got low-key. And we haven't even been asked to look into those five deaths. The Old Man just wants you to be smart about where you step."

Silas wanted to ask her if she had had any visitors of late. But she was already struggling, so he decided it could wait.

Sister watched over Silas as if a thought had entered his mind, but when he said nothing, she continued, knowing yet again, he wasn't wrong.

"I am finally taking time for myself. Time that doesn't require sessions or check-ins. You all take time for yourselves, and I resent that I am unable to do the same without everyone thinking I need some hand-holding. Why am I not able to live my life apart from anyone without one of you having your hand up my ass and marionetting my every damn move? It's ridiculous. I am a grown-ass woman. I haven't been on my own in years. It's one assignment to the next—and always with one of you shadowing me. I don't need a babysitter or a puppeteer. I just want space."

"How was the P.M.?" Silas asked, changing the subject again. Silas knew he wouldn't get far, interrogating her or trying to shame her, so he took the conversation to current events.

Sister adored the man, but she wasn't a child. He did, however, look regretfully pained, and she let her irritation go. She explained what Dr. Tomlin had found in the postmortem and what observation and conclusion he had made off the record.

"His final review will take another week or so," she said, intentionally leaving out the scar behind the girl's ear.

For now, she wasn't ready to discuss that detail. He would review the file soon enough and piece things together, just as the others would. As far as she knew, only the Old Man knew all the gory details of that weekend and the life she had before everything fell apart. Everyone seemed to know a small part of each other's lives, but no one had the whole story. It felt like breadcrumbs had been carelessly scattered on the ground, with no one ever caring enough to intrude into one another's space to follow where each piece led. She hadn't wanted to know their lives any more than she wanted them prying into hers.

"Can we do something about Thomas Ward?" she asked. "He has a parole hearing coming up. I'm sure you can do something about it, right? Ask Alister to do something for him. Please, Si," she pleaded, placing a hand on his. "He'll listen to you if you ask. And I don't want to take this to Bishop—for obvious reasons."

ONE OF THEIR OWN

The last thing Addison remembered before visiting Peter Pan was watching the storms. The sun was beginning to shine through the gaps in the blinds. He hadn't thought to twist them closed before kicking off his shoes and stretching out on the couch—whatever time that had been. He noticed the clock right away. It hung above the couch with its hands frozen in place. Still, it couldn't have been that long ago. He could feel that strange hum circulating in his upper body—the fuzzy kind that indicated he hadn't gotten enough sleep. But it didn't matter. He figured long ago that it would be a regular part of his life until he retired—either tits up or to a seaside villa off the coast of Mexico somewhere.

Lightning had lit up the sky for most of the night. Its thunderous booms echoed through the clouds and rumbled into the early morning hours. He had heard thunder before, but nothing sounded like thunder and lightning in the South. Nowhere on Earth compared to the music the sky made in this part of the world.

He had been here before—not often, but enough to experience the storms. They gave him a jolt he couldn't quite explain. Nothing like fear; it wasn't that primal. It was something more thrilling than that. He felt it pulse through his body each time a boom or a crack lit the sky. It tingled his skin and he liked it.

But that feeling was gone now, and the skies were different. Judging by the amount of light, it might just turn out to be a nice day, even though the weather here could be deceptive—much like people.

Addison felt grateful to be on the ground and alive. The flight here had him nerved up and for a time there, he found himself thinking about all those preflight directions. The ones that the commercial flight attendants gave out through signs, demonstrations, and gestures. Those that he had ignored. The ones that told him where the flotation devices were stored and where the paraglider could be located.

He had been a soldier longer than anything else in his life, and that had taught him not to sweat the small stuff. When his time came, no amount of instructions would save him. He figured he had a better chance of getting shot in the face at a bodega in Queens than he did of being in a plane that fell from the sky.

Yet, that had been the first time he had ever closed his eyes and envisioned the woman's face—the one who looked shellshocked, moving her arms to her sides, then running her hands up and down the aisle, directing them "in the invent of."

He must have pulled out the white card stuck in the seat about thirty times. He also wished he had brought his pack on board—the one he kept the parachute packed in and stored next to his girls' bicycles in the garage.

As he lay there on the couch with his eyes shut, half pretending to be asleep and half avoiding blindness, he waited for his boy to decide whether or not he was going to move.

Bishop had slept restlessly as if he couldn't find a comfortable spot or something was tearing away at his mind. But it could have just been the drink.

They had been mates a long time, and Addison knew that if he got Bishop going too soon, he'd most likely need a toilet as soon as his head lifted off the chair.

Bishop wasn't much of a drinker, and Addison had been a little surprised to find him sitting at the bar, drinking by himself. At first glance, he hoped it had been about the pretty girl doing her best to grab his attention. She was certainly dressed for it.

But he wasn't having it. And judging the way he looked at them when they entered the bar, Bishop wasn't having them either. The guys knew to keep clear of him.

He was set to be alone—and alone he would be. They opted instead to listen to the monkeyshines others got up to. The entertainment value alone was enough to make him consider life in the American South.

Addison had met Bishop Bohannan while in the service of the Queen.

They were both serving in Afghanistan for the same mission and had quite a rivalry going. His team pitted against his. Bishop had heard about Addison's reputation as a solid boxer and wanted to test his abilities against Addison's infamous left-cross. He learned promptly that a blow by Addison Adler was akin to playing chicken with a Mack truck without a seatbelt. The thought of Bishop on the ground still made Addison chuckle with a wide grin. Bishop had been young and cocky. Not unlike Addison, he reckoned. It had been a humbling experience for both of them. But for different reasons.

"You hit like my little sister," Bishop taunted, as a right jab landed square, forcing his chin down and his jaw to pop. Not wanting to give Addison the satisfaction of knowing he hurt him, he continued his barrage of barbs, "Did I tell you her name is Addison as well?" Bishop circled him, tapped his gloves together in between taking jabs with not only his hands, but his fast words. "Come on then little Addie, you big black bastard, let's see you try that shit again."

Addison welcomed Bishop's eagerness to bleed. He wanted nothing more than to shut him up and wonder just how many times he'd have to hit Bishop to shut him down.

"Do all you white boys talk this much shit," he asked, grinning through a Union Jack mouthguard. It wasn't just any smile, though. He grinned from ear to ear like he had a secret and couldn't wait to share it.

"I'm pretty sure all us Americans talk this much shit," Bishop countered, "But is it really talking shit when you're this damn awesome," he said, as he danced around Addison, his cockiness all feathered up like a proud peacock. "I mean, we did win the war. And let's not forget, 165 years later, we saved your asses, not once, but twice. If it weren't for us, you'd be speaking German." He shrugged, tapped his gloves together again, taunting Addison and laughing. Then gestured for him to bring it forward.

"I'm going to enjoy ringing that skull of yours," Addison said as he side-stepped and backpedaled, avoiding contact with Bishop.

Then Bishop launched a solid attempt at a right jab, left hook, and right knee trio. His knee connected squarely with Addison's upper abdomen—knocking the air out of him.

He had to give it to Bishop—that knee got him. But also like him, he wouldn't let Bishop know how bad it hurt him. He couldn't allow him to see how much he wanted to take a minute.

"You've got good footwork there, mate, but your mouth moves much better," he said as he shook off the pain and countered with a double right jab, followed by the infamous left cross everyone except Bishop had watched for. It landed squarely, causing him to fold like an accordion to the canvas. His silence and his ego followed him to the floor. Bishop had left some DNA on the mat that day and took a pretty good concussion back to the barracks with him. "My tip of the day, mate," he said, as he stood over him, grinning. "The next time we meet, wear a mouthguard. It will save what's left of those pretty chicklets of yours."

"To be young again," Bishop said out loud as if he were reading Addison's thoughts. Then he ran his hands over his face before sitting up and then slumping back down again. He looked ill, and he looked as if his head were going to fall off by the way he clutched his temples between his fingers.

"But we're not," Addison replied. "And if memory serves me, mate—which it does pretty well— you didn't handle your drink much better back then, either. You look like shit," he continued, through the side of his mouth, squinting through the narrowing slit of one eye, watching him.

"How you liking that couch there, Addie?" Bishop asked sarcastically as he sat up again, his face twisted up in pain. It was either his head or his back—both were possible. "And why the hell didn't you just toss me in bed? Or on the floor?"

"Boss, had you played those cards right last night, you'd be across the hall, wrapped up with that lass from the bar right now, instead of in that chair starting shit with me. Don't go blaming me for your foolishness —or your sore ass," he said. "I'm too old for that bullshit. It was your back or mine, mate, and that chair was your doin'."

"Her name is Jamie, and we're just friends," Bishop said. "And I use the word 'friend' loosely. There's nothing there. And that couch isn't long enough for a toddler, let alone your giant ass."

"All I can say is you need to be trading more than sugar with that lass next door," he said, shaking his head.

Addison was lying flat on the seat of Bishop's couch, while his legs from the calves down hung over the arm at the other end.

"I don't use sugar," Bishop said flatly, eyeing Addison. "You look ridiculous. And you need new socks."

Bishop reached out with his foot and tapped Addison's right big toe, which was peeking through a hole in his sock.

"I thought that's why you got married — new socks and clean drawers? I'm positive I heard those exact words in her vows."

Addison pulled himself up, scratched his face, and then pulled and tugged his sock correctly back into place.

"We've slept in worse. Your baby couch is acceptable. And just so you know, I did consider your bed. But there's no tellin' what you've gotten up to in there," he continued, tipping his nose toward one of the two visible interior doors in the apartment. "And you wouldn't let me tuck you in—there or with the bartender. But judging by the conversation last night, you've taken on the role of the Virgin Mary. You sat there, drownin' yourself in what-ifs and maybes, instead of booze. Not that you didn't try that too, my friend—but your place is clear. Which would stand to reason, since you don't drink. And I sat here listenin' to you like a ninny schoolgirl until you passed out. But hey, what are girls for, aye?"

Bishop wasn't led by anything levelheaded or logical when it came to Charlee. He was all arms and legs of irrationality and irresponsible left feet. In the beginning, Bishop loved it — the rollercoaster of it all. And Addison had been happy for him.

She made Bishop a different man, less rigid. Protocols had been thrown out the window. He had that sort of baked-in authority about him that made him follow rules to the letter. But with her, he loosened up.

They all had seen it. Even though the two tried to hide it in the beginning, it had been obvious they were carrying on behind their backs. Later, though, he became torn up and emotional anytime the conversation turned her way—raw and bruised.

Mostly, he said it was the unsettling thoughts racing through his mind that made him angry. And they could see that as well. He felt as though his insides would burst under the strain of all the information that ran about uncaged—yet made little sense to him.

"At least for now," he explained, not giving Addison any details.

He would have to make sense of it eventually. And then what? What would happen to everyone involved once the bigger picture had been painted in bold, unforgiving strokes? He worried about that—because whatever had Bishop this twisted up was bound to be bad for all of them.

"She's a fucking mess," Addison said. His words echoed in Bishop's head for at least the hundredth time. "You can't change her, and you'll get run over for your troubles."

Addison had made it clear that he wasn't a fan. If he's being honest, she rubbed him the wrong way. She carried herself like she was better than the lot of them, as if being a former nun gave her some higher superiority. Addison got the impression that she was dangerous—like she had a secret that could get them all killed. But his mate loved her, so he kept his mouth shut on the important stuff.

Bishop was still mad as hell that she had stayed away so long, but Addison didn't think that Bishop hadn't done much to mend what was broken between them. By all accounts, he had been the one to freeze her out. He had accused her of a lot—lying and cheating was the worst of it. Addison hadn't been surprised by any of it. She was wound tight, so he reckoned there had to be something behind those eyes of hers.

Bishop believed he deserved her truth. Instead, he said that she had lied to him instead of trusting him. It was hard to see if things could be good again. Addison had told him, "this is why you don't shit where you eat," but Bishop didn't listen. The best any of them could hope for now was to keep their heads down and try not to get stabbed in the neck.

"Take a shower, mate. You'll feel better," Addison said. "I'll make us something to eat."

Later that day, by the time they got out to the cornfield, a light mist had settled in. So much for the day looking brighter than yesterday. It did nothing to help with the heat, either—only made the air claustrophobic.

The team set out across a new growth of baby corn, begging to be noticed underneath the sheen of deep river water, debris, and mud. Every now and then, one of them could be seen dodging a drive-by nudge from something looking for an escape route —a bass, or maybe a carp that had been washed up into the crop.

Each man was draped in a plastic slicker cover-up and chest waders. Between the muggy, humid air, the trash bag–like plastic, and the neoprene materials, they were all already hating the assignment. Everything had been designed to keep them dry from the rain and to protect them from whatever else lurked in the waters or fell from the sky, but nothing could alleviate the heat.

It was like a sauna in the suits, and Addison felt as though he was being cooked from the inside out.

He knew Louisiana weather was mostly warm all year round, but he had no idea that May would feel this sticky.

"Have you ever thought about what it would feel like to be cremated?" Addison heard Silas call out. "I bet it feels something like this. Or maybe being locked in a trunk. Do you think this is what suffocating would feel like?"

They all laughed, but he wasn't joking.

Between the heat and the air, it was hard to decide if they would burn to death or run out of air first.

"I shoulda went with Sister," Addison said, wiping away the rain and the sweat that clung to his face. His hands swiped twice over a two-day growth that itched mercilessly. His face was irritated by the constant rubbing, and he was tired and coming close to something near pissed off.

"This is bollocks," he said, and started towards a tent, unfastening his waders. He was soaked to the bone.

His clothes were soaked in sweat under the plastic, and he was thinking that he'd rather risk a day in his skivvies than be cooked to death in the human greenhouse.

"There's not a damn thing we can find out here in this water," he called out, gesturing to Bishop that he was done.

Though the other two seconded his statement, they kept their eyes down and concentrated on the ground.

Bishop, who seemed to have acclimated to the weather over the past couple of years, listened to his bitching with a nod. But he could tell by the look on Bishop's face he was somewhere else, and this cornfield full of water wasn't it.

The scene had been preserved as best as anyone could hope for, given the circumstances. Louisiana's SCIS had placed a 10x20 pop-up tent over the body's location, hoping to return later to see if there was anything else useful—even when they all knew there wouldn't be. This hadn't been the original dump site, and the water was still too high to see anything of value. It had been the perfect time to dump a body.

The storm that had raged for days would have destroyed most of the evidence left behind if there had been any to begin with. But if whoever dumped her was hoping she'd stay in the river and float away, never to be seen again or eaten by the numerous possibilities, they had been mistaken. They hadn't figured on a flash flood rushing the area and pushing everything up and out, washing anything not weighted down into a farmer's crop.

Bishop said that the body had already been driven to the medical examiner's office in Baton Rouge but hoped that by bringing them out to see the area, maybe between the four of them, they could determine where the body may have been placed first. He figured it was fruitless, but it had also been a better opportunity than not to get them all together for a little pow-wow—away from any prying ears.

Once they had walked the 100-yard radius around the markers left by SCIS, they all sheltered under the only tent in the field. Silas removed his plastic coat and was the first to speak up.

"This isn't our kind of assignment, Boss. I mean, I feel for the family and all, but unless this has something to do with a cartel dropping bodies in the river or a transcontinental killer, a dead girl in a Louisiana cornfield ain't what we do."

Addison watched Silas eye Bishop with curiosity, as if he were looking for something else in his words, or lack thereof. Addison and probably McQueen had the same thoughts, and Silas was only voicing what they hadn't.

Addison had never really questioned his assignments. He doubted that the others did either, but this one had a particular weirdness to it that made him wonder if he were the only one not understanding the objective. They all lived by their gut, and when something smelled bad, it was bad. "Why are we really here, Bishop?"

He understood Bishop well enough to know that he knew the questions had merit. He wasn't blind to their situations, nor the fact that each of them had their own reasons to be concerned. Addison wasn't even an American citizen. He had no rights here. And if shit went south, he'd be fucked.

"So why aren't the state police, the locals, or the regular Marie Anjou deputies working on this one themselves?" McQueen chimed in.

Addison thought Kidd should have looked more worried than he did, since he probably had more to lose if he got caught than the rest of them. Given that he had a get-out-of-jail-free card, Addison thought perhaps he shouldn't be testing its strength or fate.

"Whose toes are getting stepped on by us being here?" Addison asked. "And how much lying is going to be involved? How many bodies will we be packing back in our luggage or leaving in this river ourselves?"

"This is a request from Alasdair McTavish himself," Bishop said, watching each of their faces to see if they understood the magnitude of what he was saying. Not that it actually mattered. It wasn't as if they knew who pulled his strings anyway. Shit always started high and ran downhill. And they would do as instructed. Besides, McTavish was the Boss before Boss was Boss. Still was. "There is no agency behind this case. This one is close and personal to the Old Man."

"McTavish?" questioned McQueen. He was looking from one guy to the next, waiting for one of them to answer his non-question.

"Yes, Freshman, McTavish. You know, the guy who signs off on our checks," Silas said in confirmation. "He didn't say anything about what was going on when he sent me North for Charlee. However, there was no mistake; it was not a suggestion. Under no circumstances was I to board that plane without her."

Silas is a tall man—taller than any of them by a lot and in extremely good shape for his age. His hand could palm Addison's face, and he couldn't say he'd ever had the desire to find out whose hand-to-hand was better. Though he has strong Nordic features, he is most often mistaken for a Russian, and that has served him well. His look has allowed him to blend in with the lower echelon of the social hierarchy. Put aside the slightly rounded middle, it was hard to believe that he is somewhere near 50 and shows no signs of slowing down. He's got at least ten years on them, but it doesn't show all that much. He had been a Florida beach bum when he decided to do something productive with his life. When the U.S. entered Desert Storm, he ditched the board and signed up to be part of the band of brothers who were "The Few, The Proud."

Being a soldier put him in McTavish's path, which in turn, circled him back around to Bishop. He didn't know the story between the two of them. He was sure it was like the rest of them—teaming up with McTavish opened doors for them that changed their lives.

Addison watched Silas as he played with his beard, listening to the conversation. His glacier blue eyes were intensely focused on Bishop's expressions. Addison could see why the ladies seemed to love his brooding nature—especially with the scar that ran vertically down from the corner of his left eye and stopped at his nose. He was a man's man. You either liked him or hated him.

"But why McTavish?" Kidd repeated. "Does this have anything to do with me?" He had interrupted Bishop in mid-sentence with an impatient squall in his voice. "I'm just making sure I don't have lead suit in my future and having breakfast with Jimmy Hoffa, if you know what I mean. But, I'm down with anything, you know that, I'm just saying..."

"You're covered, kid. Again, this is personal," Bishop said. His tone had become annoyed, but he knew it wasn't McQueen's fault. It was the hangover talking.

Addison had been in McTavish's chain of command during his military days, before transitioning into private contracting. He was one badass son of a bitch back in those days. McTavish had met and married an American interpreter with the US Army. He seemed to settle down, took fewer risks, and stayed closer to home. The familiar drill—tried to be home for holidays and birthdays, kick the kids and kiss the dog, and all that. Tried on the suit of family life. Addison thought he wore it well, remembering him with his beautiful wife and kids only once. He looked happy. Then she was killed in the plane bombing over Lockerbie, and he shut down, packed up the family, and left Scotland. He brought his wife's body back to her family.

"McTavish brought his family here," Addison said, thinking about how long it had been since he had spoken to him. It's been a couple of years—probably not since his wedding.

"McTavish is as straight as they come. We all know that, so if he has us all here, knowing that it has us hanging by the short and curlies," Silas said, looking knowingly at McQueen, "he must have a damn good reason. I mean, shit, I have a fuse lit on that Anderson Dockett case, and if I don't get back to it soon, we'll lose whatever ground we've made in finding the buyers. They won't be around Ramstein for long. I don't need to tell you what will happen if we don't find those weapons. I want heads to roll on this, and that won't happen unless we get the buyers too. So, what's going on here has to be more important for McTavish to risk bringing generals up on charges for selling arms to our enemies. We'll be back in Sudan or Yemen within a month," Silas shrugged in a loyal, defeated optimism. "I'm okay with it. My contact believes the buyers are..."

Addison couldn't help it. It hit him, and just as Silas was about to finish his sentence, he cut him off. "Son of a bitch! Does this have anything to do with Charlee? he asked.

By now, he pulled off his T-shirt to wipe the sweat from his face, which not only conveyed annoyance but also had worry lines etched deep. He had a strong feeling that he was about to get dragged back into something that could get them killed. "Are we about to get tied up in another one of her shit storms?" he asked.

Addison knew that she had lived here once. He assumed that McTavish had recruited her long ago—probably before any of them. If this were Charlee's business, he didn't want to hear it. No matter how he did or didn't feel about her. She was a loose cannon, and he couldn't understand McTavish's fondness for her, nor Bishop's.

"What the fuck has she done now?" he asked.

"McTavish needs us here, and it's complicated," Bishop said flatly. He wasn't holding up well under the conversation and dodged key words. Addison could tell he was leaving something unsaid by the way he hesitated. He watched as the gears in Bishop's head changed direction and Bishop chose different words. "But it's not just about Charlee." That was all the confirmation he needed to hear.

They were here because of her, and he bit back the expletives that found their way into his mouth while Bishop carried on. The words were about Charlee, and none of which he could say out loud out of fear that the weight of them could damage their friendship.

"Greer was supposed to meet up with Bama and McTavish for dinner and pulled a no-show," Bishop continued. "That was four days ago. No one has seen or heard from her since."

DOCTOR WU

"What's up, Doc?"

"Hello, Baby," the doctor said, glancing down at her watch and not making eye contact. "I see you're still keeping late hours. What I don't see is you on my schedule for this evening."

Dr. Scarlett Jolene Wu showed no visible reaction upon finding Baby in her office. As she crossed the threshold, her heart began to race, and her anxiety ramped up to a thousand. She had to remind herself to stay calm, maintain an expressionless demeanor, and appear unaffected by Baby's unexpected and unscheduled arrival.

"I was in the neighborhood, Doc. I thought I would visit an old friend," Baby said with a sheepish grin. "I get around better at night, you know that. I also figured you'd be awake—maybe even missing me—since it's been a while since I've just dropped by. Besides, who else would enjoy such stimulated conversation at this late hour—clothed anyway?"

Wu maintained a composed, neutral expression as she settled into her seat. She removed her glasses and turned to face Baby. Baby sat upright in the center of the couch, her legs crossed and her arms resting over the back of the sofa.

"I doubt there's much talking going on in those situations."

"Touché, Doc. I do prefer most people on silent, in—and out of bed."

"Are you comfortable?" Wu asked. She wasn't sure if Baby sucked the oxygen out of the room or filled it. She had a way of keeping everyone uncomfortably intrigued.

"Yes, very much so," Baby replied. "Thank you. I do like what you've done to the place," she remarked, approvingly looking around the room. It's a lot nicer than your location in Dublin and definitely cleaner than Dallas."

Baby's arrogance both frightened and excited Wu in ways that only a scientist could understand. However, that would never be something she would admit aloud to anyone except maybe a colleague. Only then would it be necessary to have someone with clearance and an understanding of what she was working with.

Baby wore her sexuality like a tiara and her volatile nature like armor. Every moment and step taken appeared calculated and for show. Baby's hair was long and blonde. It was different from the last time Wu had seen her. She had it pulled up into a ponytail, a bright red satin scarf holding it all neatly together. The scarf was the same shade of red as her matching stilettos.

Baby was taller than average, and with her striking features, Wu surmised that her height in heels only added to her appeal. She was dressed in a black, skintight, sleeveless jumpsuit with a collar that ran thin down the center of her chest, exposing a lot of skin and ample cleavage. The ensemble left nothing to the imagination, which Wu believed was the point of Baby's look. She was toned and well-framed. And her clothing choices were deliberate. Each garment was hand-selected for each specific production. It was all theater.

"I see you thinking, Doc. Do you want to share what's on your mind? Are you ready to reveal your darkest secrets yet? Perhaps there's something I don't already know about you," Baby taunted.

She had worn this specific outfit just for Wu's benefit. Baby wondered if she could elicit a different reaction from her this time, so she focused on Wu's body language rather than her face. Wu had become adept at concealing the darker thoughts that occasionally crossed her mind, but her body language told a different story. Although Wu's face always appeared soft, Baby noticed that when she would intentionally relax her jaw, her teeth would unclench. This, however, did not work with Wu's posture, which remained stiff and robotic. Baby recognized the uncertainty in Wu's eyes and the distance she maintained between them. This realization gave Baby a sense of satisfaction. She was aware of far more about Doctor Scarlett J. Wu than any patient should know about their psychiatrist.

"This is your time, Baby. Are you going to waste it by flirting with me?"

"We could be wasting my time doing something else," Baby challenged. "Something—a bit more—fun and definitely more pleasurable—for us both," Baby said coyly. Her tone was seductive and playful. Then she shifted forward slightly on the couch, crossing her arms over her knees. Grinning at Wu. "Am I not your type, Doc?"

"We are not here to talk about my sexual proclivities, Baby. And, to avoid sounding repetitive, I have already asked you not to invade my privacy. My personal life is off-limits. I shouldn't have to ask you more than once. I would appreciate it if you would stick to the rules of our arrangement."

"Oh, for fuck's sake, Doc, lighten up already. Seeing the immovable expression on the doctor's face, Baby sighed with an exaggerated exhale. "Fine," she said, rolling her eyes and throwing herself back onto the couch. "You are no fun at all. Don't go gettin' your knickers in a twist. Where would you like me to begin?" she asked, annoyed at the doctor's disinclination to explore a more enjoyable relationship between the two of them.

Then Baby returned to her previous posture, arms on the back of the couch, sitting up straight, conveying to Wu that this conversation would only move forward because she was willing to do so. "Ask away."

"I'm not here to entertain you, Baby," Wu said, pushing back against the baiting posture. "You've turned the world into your playground, and everyone in it is a toy. I—am not one of your playthings. My purpose is to monitor you and hopefully gain a better understanding of what makes you—you. You have instincts that I find beyond comprehension and fascinating. But there are rules and boundaries to our relationship. A sexual relationship would be both unproductive for both of us and quite unprofessional. Please keep this in mind the next time your thoughts stray off into dangerous territory."

"Oh, I don't know about that, Doc. It could be very productive, as you said," Baby smirked. "Dangerous territories excite me. But that almost sounded like a threat. And that's funny, Doc," Baby continued, laughing. "I knew I liked you.

You've got some moxie to threaten me. I think I like you even more, knowing that you're afraid of me but still willing to show me a thing or two."

It was Doc's turn to laugh, though she was still masking her discomfort. This wasn't the first time Baby had found herself in Wu's office, but this visit carried a darkness that had not been there before—one that extended beyond what Baby brought with her. Wu sensed that the secrets of the past, long buried, were on the verge of exploding, and Baby was the spark that would ignite the fuse.

"We're all afraid of something," Wu said, marveling at Baby's confidence, which went beyond her understanding. Baby seemed to have no fear or boundaries, with little to no social awareness of right and wrong. If she did, it didn't influence her decision-making. There was no chance in hell that Wu would admit to any fear regarding Baby; she had learned how to conceal her thoughts early on. Baby had a knack for reading people far too well.

"Those who are not afraid of anything are not being honest with themselves," Wu continued, her tone firm. "But I will not allow myself to be disrespected or intimidated. You know I had a very different life before becoming a doctor. So if you think you can make me afraid, you are welcome to try. But bigger men than you have tried, and I'm still standing. You won't get what you expect," she added matter-of-factly. "And just so we're clear, you will not find yourself in my bed."

This only made Baby's grin wider. Baby found the doctor interesting—she always had. It hadn't taken her long to piece together the doctor's life. With every new piece of information she uncovered, the doctor became increasingly more intriguing to her.

"Come on, Doc. Be honest. It feels more like you're using me to gather information on the others. You say this is so you can gain some insight into my psyche. But what you're really doing is keeping tabs on Sister. I know I'm right, of course—there's no need to humor me with your answer."

"It's true, after what Sister has experienced, it's my job..."

"What we experienced," Baby cut in. "What we experienced."

"What you both experienced. I apologize. I didn't mean to imply that you were not affected. Nevertheless, it is my job to get Sister to a place in her life that she can navigate without feeling the need to self-destruct or self-harm. She isn't as strong as you are. However, I do find our talks productive. You are every bit just as much my patient as she is. And you are a fascinating study. I've never had a patient like you. There is a great deal to be learned here. And if I may say so, you sound like your feelings are hurt. Have you been experiencing emotions of sadness or sorrow? Or depression, loneliness, or isolation?"

"Whoa, Doc!" Baby laughed, throwing up her hands. "I was just here, tryin' to get you outta that skirt. Not confess my touchy-feelies. You wanna pick my brain, Doc, you go ahead. But let's leave all that other bullshit out of it, Love. I'm not the crazy one."

"Fair enough," Wu nodded with understanding. "Let's talk about Sister."

"What can I say, Doc? The good sister is still as uptight and rigid as ever. She continues to dress as if she is protecting her virtue, unless it's work-related, of course. However, I think she's tryin' to put those days behind her. She is taking fewer risks now. Don't get me wrong; she is great at hiding her true self. She has mastered the art of character, but deep down, she is still a nun. She doesn't quite think like a cop, or whatever her title is. Today she's a deputy; tomorrow, who the fuck knows? I don't understand how she lives with herself most days. She's a tortured soul for sure. On a brighter note, she is clean and sober—well, clean anyway." Baby shrugged. "I can vouch for that. No drugs."

Wu thought about Baby's answers and thoughts on Sister's progress and then asked, "While Sister was up north, what did you do?"

"I kept my distance when it came to Sister, if that's what you mean. I just observed from the sidelines. She didn't seem to need me; in fact, she appeared to be doing quite well on her own. For the most part, she kept to herself. She visited a few churches—Catholic ones, no doubt—and had conversations with a priest or two, but there was nothing particularly noteworthy about it—no men, no women; just the same boring life as usual. I was surprised to learn that she bought a place. I didn't see that one coming. It's a remote cabin in the middle of nowhere. There's no way I could handle that, but it seems to suit her and her damn dog," Baby said. "Oh, and I went hunting," she added with a casual shrug. "Just for small game. I managed to bag three."

"You still haven't made peace with Beast?" Wu asked, interrupting with a smile, already knowing the answer. But then she paused at how dismissive Baby was of the hunting remark.

"Don't laugh, Doc. That fucking mutt hates me. The only reason it is still alive is because I know Sister would probably self-destruct, and I don't know which one of us would survive that."

"I apologize again," Wu said, half-heartedly trying to hide a smirk behind the back of her hand. "I understand. If only dogs could talk. Hearing what she has to say about the two of you would be fascinating. Before we continue with Sister, could you tell me about the hunting trip? Was this small game of the human variety? Say, three friends?"

Baby grinned at the doctor. Up to this point, she hadn't kept anything from Wu, but now she was unsure if she wanted to share everything she had learned while shadowing McTavish's team. Although she could rule out everyone who worked for the Doucets or the Monroes, there were still a few individuals on her list with close ties to all three families. "Ambassador Hadley provided a wealth of information," Baby said. "He was accommodating, and the timing couldn't have been more perfect. It was like hitting three birds with one stone. Wrath, Envy, and Gluttony met with an unfortunate hunting accident," she added, feigning shock and covering her mouth to hide an even more exaggerated expression of surprise.

"You've had an extraordinarily busy eighteen months," Wu remarked, unfazed by Baby's lack of detail or empathy. She had viewed the photos that were highlighted by the hunting parties who discovered the bodies. "It seems you truly surpassed yourself this time. Removing Mr. Delaney's face the way you did seemed like child's play compared to what you did to those three."

Baby shrugged again. "I've had more practice," she bragged, looking almost bored with the conversation. "It could have been much worse. But my hands got cold. I fucking hate the cold. Why would anyone want to—on purpose—live outdoors in the snow? But it made for one helluva backdrop. All that red on that beautiful white canvas. It was art. But I'm happier to be back in warmer weather."

Doctor Wu had seen more than her fair share of brutality and grisly acts of the worst kind very early in life. She was born in China to parents who wanted a boy. By age four, she had been sold to make room for her new little brother's arrival. She was taught to be grateful that her parents hadn't killed her instead. Until the age of seventeen, she had been moved over 100 times, lived in 19 countries, and survived being passed around until the men who had taken her were killed by a group of men like McTavish's team, who were pretending to be FBI agents. But whenever Baby spoke of what she had done, Wu's stomach flipped, and she felt sick.

Wu wasn't sure if she felt sick because Baby had described what she had done in detail or because a part of her championed what Baby was doing. Wu was supposed to be a passive observer. She was supposed to be helping Sister, not carrying Baby's banner of revenge. Wu understood why Baby killed these men; she just wished Baby didn't enjoy it so much. Then maybe, secretly, she wouldn't either. Giving some thought to what Baby had done, she said, "So then, you have two more?"

"Three," Baby countered. "I have the guy calling himself Liam and the last frat boy. I know who he is now. This one will blow up in a big way," Baby laughed, excited about it, knowing the identity of the last remaining frat brother from that night. But I want the guy who helped cover it up. These guys got away with what they did. And that wouldn't have happened if someone hadn't helped them. Not one of them had the brainpower to get away with this, let alone all of them combined. They're not masterminds. They have a guardian angel."

"I understand," Wu said, nodding in agreement. "Let's continue on about Sister. Where did we leave off?"

"She was working on the Ronda Sespe case—one of the missing women from somewhere around the Barrow area."

"Yes," Dr. Wu said, nodding her head. "I reviewed the Sespe file. It details the case of a native woman whose clothing and shoes were found abandoned in her tent, along with her pack and winter coat. It has been over a year since she disappeared. This is yet another tragic story, and I fear it may have a sadder ending. I assume she didn't find her answers?"

"Yes and no. She made good progress. She knows that Ronda is connected to three other missing women from different villages. All four were last seen in the loving arms of one Randy Harper. This information has been kept quiet because he is related to someone higher up in their Garda. He's pretty well-connected, and they have been very effective at silencing witnesses. Nobody wants to talk, at least for the time being. But she isn't finished with the investigation. She plans to return to it once she's finished here. You know how determined she gets—there will be a resolution to this, one way or another."

"I see." Again, Wu understood the unspoken in Baby's words. "And how has she been since Sheriff McTavish sent for her?"

"You haven't got enough paper for all that. She's struggling with it. Probably why it's best I stick around for a while. Do you know what it's like to look at every man who passes by you and wonder if that's the one? Coming back here did her no favors. I sure hope he knows what he's doing. But somehow, I have the feelies that you had more to do with this than the Old Man. Tell me I'm wrong?" Baby said with a smile, not really caring who was at fault here for keeping Sister spun up. "Who's really the puppet master pulling 'ole Sister girl's strings?"

"We consult—nothing more. I can give him perspective. That is all."

"Sure thing, Doc. What you call perspective, I call collusion. I'm sure that's your story, and you're stickin' to it," Baby said skeptically.

Baby knew more about the relationship between the old sheriff and the doctor than they realized. However, she was much better at keeping her cards close to her chest. She never revealed secrets, nor did she genuinely care about the plans the two of them were concocting regarding Sister. At the end of the day, Baby would remain a necessary evil in the world and would be free to act as she pleased. The longer Sister felt out of control, the less attention would be focused on Baby, allowing her to settle old scores.

"So, tell me about Bishop. Are they speaking amicably? What about Silas, Luke, and Addison?"

Baby thought about how to answer that. "Come on, Doc. Bishop's a coward. He bailed on her, and she checked out. I'm pretty sure whatever connection she was able to hold onto there has been severed. She's pretty tight with Silas, but those two are lifers. You know that. Even if that's for obvious reasons, they'll go down together. That is something she is still too naïve to see. I mean, for as smart as that woman is, she is fucking dumb when it comes to men."

And Addison and Luke? Has she been able to maintain the relationship there? Something other than a superficial working relationship?"

The mention of Addison Adler's name made Baby laugh. That prick's obvious disdain for our Sister girl is visible to everyone except her. Oh, the mate tolerates her well enough, but he doesn't trust her. I see how he watches her. He's pretty damn careful in his words and dealings with her as well. If you ever had to put her down, he'd be the one to call. He'd do it for free."

Wu paused for a moment, grappling with her thoughts. She realized she would never have the authority to decide whether Sister should be "put down." That kind of power was beyond her reach. It had taken a significant effort just to arrive at this point. In the beginning, the powers that be wanted her to stay as far away from Sister and Baby as possible, deeming them too valuable for their purposes. As long as Wu promised not to interfere with their operations, she was granted the freedom to study them.

Sister was a good person, coping with her circumstances as best as she could. Wu's only hope was to convince those in charge that, if necessary, she should be given the authority to have Sister removed and detained for both her safety and the safety of others. She pondered Baby's assessment of Brick and felt a wave of concern. Baby's observations were accurate; Wu wasn't sure when Brick had decided that Sister was public enemy number one, but she believed he would indeed kill her if instructed to do so.

"Do you worry that they will come for you first?" Wu asked, not sure why Baby hadn't considered that if someone had to be, in her words, 'put down,' she'd be the one most likely targeted, due to the nature of her crimes—even if they had been sanctioned. Baby was violent in her approach to everything. Wu wondered if that was the difference between the two. Sister was unpredictable, whereas Baby hid nothing. Not even her intentions.

A laugh erupted from Baby, causing her smile to widen and making her even more beautiful. "I'd like to see them try, Doc. I let you see me when I'm coming. Do you think I would extend the same courtesy to them? I've been inside the president's bedroom while she slept. If her top security didn't notice me slip into the most heavily guarded building in the country, I'm pretty sure I can take care of myself. Besides, there are other powerful people who love me—and why wouldn't they? Just look at this face, Doc," Baby said with a mischievous grin. "I'll be alright."

Somehow, Wu knew she wasn't wrong. Baby had a determination about her that would survive most anything. Wu just wasn't sure who would be standing with her when she did. "Have you introduced yourself to Brick?" Wu asked, knowing that she had only shown herself when it was essential to her task.

An evil smile lit up Baby's face. She had introduced herself to Mr. Adler the day before his wedding. Though he wouldn't remember it. As much as he liked to tar and feather Sister for her past misdeeds, he downplayed his own indiscretions. He had a propensity to play hard when it came to the ladies and even harder when it came to the coke and poker, in that order. He seemed pretty emboldened when he did coke, and that had led to a severe gambling problem. "Yes, we have been acquainted. Don't believe all the hype about black men, though. They aren't all as advertised."

Doctor Wu wanted to smile at that. She, too, had the same opinion of Addison Adler. He hid himself well behind his kind smile and good looks. But there was something much more dubious about him. She had considered that it had more to do with their type of work than it did with him being involved in sex crimes, and she tried to back burner her opinions of Brick.

But she did have to ask, "Were you able to take him off your list, then? Do you think he is involved?"

"Oh, he's involved in something. But not this. I don't believe he knows anything about what happened. At least not anything that deserves my kind of attention. Though I wouldn't mind killing him just for fun," Baby confessed, smiling at the thought of shooting him thirty times in the face. She had gotten that idea from him. "He's taken a few bribes to look the other way, but he's not involved in human trafficking—especially after seeing what he did to Alexi Volkov. He put about thirty rounds in the man's face. I must admit, I gained a bit more respect for Brick after seeing that. Volkov will never hurt another woman. He hates Sister for his own reasons, but it has nothing to do with what happened."

"That's good. It sounds like you have started whittling down your suspects. And what about McQueen? Has he taken to her okay? Or her to him?"

"Luke looks up to her. He's like a baby bird around her. He's pretty close to Sunny-love. He stays clear of Brick and idolizes Bishop. The boy is smart, but he's not all there, if you get my meaning. But he don't make waves among the group. He understands the pecking order of things and his role. I can tell by the way he looks at her that he'd follow her to hell if asked. She's like the mother he never had. Cute kid. I can't say anything bad. He's young. I'm trying to figure out his quirks. He's hard for me to read. He's often as crazy as she is, but I think there's more to it. The boy has tics."

"Crazy is relative, don't you think?" Wu pointed out, looking at Baby and waiting for her answer.

"Oh, sure, it is, Doc. But I'm an expert on that. I mean, judging by your profession, anyway. I'm the ringmaster of crazy. But McQueen isn't nuts crazy. He's different, is all I'm gettin' at. He doesn't make direct eye contact when he looks at you. It's more like he looks through you. But what do I know, aye."

"He's on the spectrum. I'm not breaking any confidences in sharing that with you. His IQ is high, but he lacks social awareness. He'll find his way. It'll come with age and experience. You, on the other hand, enjoy killing people, Baby. I think most would find that goes against social norms. But whether or not that makes you crazy isn't even part of the discussion. I'm studying you because of your connection to her. Her mental illness is what is genuinely the topic here. But we can discuss your labels if that helps you in any way."

"That's right. Your lot goes all in on the mental illness excuse. Always trying to sort out everyone's disorder. Pigeonhole everyone into a box. Maybe I'm on the spectrum myself," Baby said with a laugh. "I have an antisocial personality disorder. Or a psychopathic tendency towards homicidal behavior. I'm aware of myself. You're not good at hiding those notes, Doc. But can't we like what we do without there being a diagnosis attached to it or psychopathy of some sort? Mommy didn't love me enough. Dad was never there for me. Got a sneaky uncle who liked to creep into my room at night. Or better yet, seven men raped us and left us to die in a barrel and an old icebox in the swamp. Wouldn't that make anyone crazy?"

Seeing the conversation heading into territory that Wu wasn't ready to cover, she circled back to an old topic. She asked, "Do you feel responsible for Bishop and Sister's failure?"

Baby groaned and rolled her eyes as she sat forward. "It was an experiment, Doc. I knew how she felt about him; clearly, he felt the same. I will take no blame for it going down in flames."

"You don't feel as though you sabotaged them? Even a little bit? I find it interesting that you would go out of your way to get them together, but make a mistake like you did. Unless it wasn't a mistake? Surely, you knew she would be the one blamed? Do you think it was wise to play with Bishop like you did? I mean, why interfere in their relationship if you knew how it would end? Do you not feel responsible?" Wu asked.

"Why would I feel bad about it? He had a thing for her, and I know how she felt about him. I played the best role of my life there, Doc. I pretended to be you. I got them to see each other, didn't I? I got Sister to stop seeing herself as a fucking nun, even if it was for just a minute, and get herself laid."

"You pushed her too far. She married him and moved in with him, but now she is overwhelmed with the pain of hurting him. She believes she made a mistake that she never should have made. It will take a lot for her to overcome that guilt. She feels as though she manipulated him in some way and is unsure of why she did it."

"Like I said, Doc, he's a coward. He could have stayed and stuck it out. But he thinks she's back on the flower and packed his shit and left. I do believe there was some part about 'until death do us part' in those vows. That is on him. He's a believer, too. So I don't feel bad. I got both of them what they wanted, and they shit the bed. That ain't on me, Love. But look at it from my side, I was able to eliminate him as well."

"So, if you had to pick, which man would be standing at the end?" Wu asked, curious to see how she would respond. Baby had gone out of her way to have Bishop in Sister's life and wondered how far she had gone to secure Silas in hers. "Silas spends time with you. I'm just wondering how he copes with your decisions and how they affect Sister?"

Baby stood up and adjusted her clothing, choosing to ignore the question. "As I mentioned, I like you, Doc. It's been enjoyable, and I'll be seeing you again. But now, I gotta go talk to an old man about a drink. It seems our sheriff has overlooked an important detail in his reasons for gathering everyone here. As much as this is about Sister, it turns out his little girl is missing, and he wants Bishop to keep it a secret. But Sunny-love is a wealth of information."

YOU CAN NEVER GO HOME AGAIN

~ SIR THOMAS WOLFE

Sister's run had been met with a clear sky and a beautiful horizon. After days of gloom and doom, the rain had finally stopped, and the clouds dissolved away. Sister was grateful to be able to stretch out a few miles outdoors. The tedious pace of a treadmill did nothing for her. There wasn't enough Gretchen, Disturbed, or Outkast to drown out the mechanical hum and sole-pounding grind that melted her resolve. She absolutely loathed running. To her thinking, she carried a gun and, in a pinch, she could either shoot them or hit a fleeing subject with her car. There was no need to run or give chase.

However, besides needing the distraction, she needed the mental workout that running could provide. She didn't run for the pleasure of it. She'd rather sit through a root canal without drugs than run ten feet. Yet, she had discovered that it was essential to her sanity. Before the assault, she believed that running was only important when being chased by bears. And for all that, she only needed to be faster than the person next to her. Then she found out the hard way that it wasn't enough to be faster than the bear. There were far worse things out there than being eaten alive.

She was grateful that Bishop was able to keep Beast. She had stressed over her 4:30 arrival before the rooster woke up—only to find he was all too happy to hang out with his best girl for the day while she drove to New Orleans. She had worried for nothing. Maybe it wasn't waking him up that had her all knotted up as much as it was seeing him. She put that out of her mind and focused on the meetings she had lined up for the day—ones she had previously avoided.

It had been at least five months since she had attended her last mandatory session, which had been conducted via telephone. She had also been dodging an attorney's calls and hadn't responded to one of the zillion emails that had choked out her inbox. She didn't have the heart to have that conversation, regardless of how determined Archie B. Walton Esquire was to have it.

Sister would meet with the attorney first. Then she would knock out face-time with the psychiatrist she had seen for the better part of six years now. The doctor often pushed for group sessions, but Sister wasn't all that thrilled about sharing her worst moments in life with a bunch of strangers who were—like her—frayed around the edges and prone to self-destruction. She had a hard enough time keeping her own shit together without thinking about those in the group. She knew herself well enough that she would take on every one of their problems as her own, and she refused to do that to herself. She already had enough in her head already, and tried hard to make it a habit not to get involved in other people's lives. It wasn't as if it cost her anything more for the one-on-one.

It didn't seem to matter when and where, the good doctor was always available for a meeting. At first, Sister thought it was just a coincidence that she or one of her predecessors were always nearby when Sister needed them. However, not believing in coincidences, Sister later concluded that she was always being watched and under someone's thumb. Leaving nothing to chance, she was now convinced that "they" had followed her every movement, everywhere she went—training camp—duty stations—assignments. And probably, more than likely, here as well. They were never just a phone call away, but rather within 100 yards.

She parked the Jeep in a department store parking lot, laced up her runners, and began to pound out the nine-mile trek she had laid out from Perlis Clothing to her first appointment in the Garden District. This would take her through the Big Easy and around to the address located off Josephine Circle. She had taken a similar scenic route before—once as a gawking tourist before starting her third year of university. New Orleans' history had fascinated her. There was a time she thought perhaps she'd be a history teacher. But that was the furthest from her mind now. Maybe even an architect, combining her love of both. Yet, designing structures that could put her name in history books could never give her the peace she had found in taking down bad people.

As she ran, Sister was surprised to see how many people were out. Then her mind had drifted off to thoughts of Bishop as one of those people who would be up this morning. He had answered the door in a pair of barely buttoned cargo shorts that hung low on his hips. His hair was tousled in a not-so-unattractive way, and his sleepy eyes gave him an air of youthful mischief. His face still had pressed lines from sleeping on his arm, with a perfectly rounded circle imprinted on his lower jaw, the size of the watch he wore around his wrist. She smiled at seeing the watch, a pang of memory grabbing her.

"I'm here," she said, self-consciously tucking her hands into her armpits as if trying to guard herself against the natural instinct to hug him.

"I see that," he said, looking from her to Beast, who stood glued to Sister's side. Even she looked like it was too early in the morning to be up. Looking at Sister's attire, he was surprised to see that she wasn't in long pants and a long-sleeved shirt. Instead, she wore shin-length yoga pants and a tight T-shirt. He had seen her in less-modest wears before; of course he had—but rarely on her own time. When not working, she dressed as if she were near sixty and afraid of the sun. "You didn't say you'd be arriving at crime time, o'thirty," he continued, glancing down at his watch.

"I'm sorry," she said, only apologizing out of habit. She always apologized for things, even when she had no reason to be sorry for anything. "I should've given you a time. I can ask Silas if it's easier. I wasn't really thinking..."

"Stop," he chuckled. "Take it easy. I'm just messing with you. It's all good. Come in here, girl," he said to Beast, yawning the door open a bit wider for her to pass.

Sister reached down and patted Beast's side. "It's okay. Go on."

"You be safe out there," he said to Sister. "Just find me when you get back. Oh, and don't forget, McTavish wants to talk to you about a personal matter." Then he closed the door, ending all further conversation between them.

******

Sister's face was hit with flashes of strobing sunbeams that had blown through the palms, bringing her mind back into focus on the scene before her. She was now jogging her way through the Central Business District. She had been deep in thought as she ran. Yet, it did not hamper or dull her senses. She had this strange ability to remain on autopilot while deep in thought. Her eyes remained alert. She scanned every face as they passed by. Daniel Gillies, in all his beauty, ran past her. The material of his black jogger grazed her arm as he dodged around her and continued without losing a step or lifting his gaze to look at her. He had his hoodie pulled up tightly over his head, obscuring his features, but she got a good glimpse of him as he turned her way.

His attempt to be just another addition to the mass of individuals running in the herd had been partially successful. Not having a bodyguard helped aid in his efforts to remain invisible in a city that seemed enamored with him. He may have avoided the paparazzi and crazy star-crossed fans and fanatics, but Sister recognized him within a few seconds. Back in her younger days, Mr. Gillies may have been the recipient of a pair of her gently worn panties, and she—most definitely—a restraining order. She probably would have risked the latter in a different time. She was a fan, but now understood his need to remain anonymous. As Elijah Mikaelson, he was a terrifying threat. This thought made her smile as she watched him widen the distance between them. The actor in his $250 running shoes was nothing but a mere mortal. His black running suit, on the other hand, could be his undoing—his white oak to the heart. Seriously, under this sun, a heat stroke would certainly do him in.

She mentally tallied every person who made direct eye contact with her, taking note of their hair, height, clothing, and body language. Then, she quickly evaluated any possible weapons they may have secured on their body, hidden, lethal, or non-lethal. Her training had taught her that any object could potentially harm her, and that she needed to be prepared for anyone and anything.

The French Quarter was a mixture of modern Cajun-Creole cuisine, hotels with boutiques, high-rises, and theaters. Her running sneakers smacked heavily on Canal Street as she made her way towards Market. Environments with high humidity seemed to echo differently than dry places, she thought. Her sneakers made a squishing noise with every step, like soggy slugs being smushed beneath her feet.

She was heading to meet with Mr. Arnie B. Walton, Esq. His voice pierced her the first time he contacted her through the recorded message. It wasn't sexy or commanding, but rather mouse-like. She pictured Peter Pettigrew from Harry Potter in her mind. A tiny round man with a rat face and two bucky front teeth. He'd be clothed in old English clothing and a bow tie to seal the look.

He had called her to let her know her presence was required in New Orleans—something she wouldn't do. He needed her to come home immediately, he said.

"Home," she thought.

It had been a long time since she called this place home, or any place, for that matter. Looking back over the years, she had chosen to live from one job to the next and day by day. She had been nomadic before buying land up north near North Pole, where even the McDonald's looked like a piece of Santa's village. Yet, it would never be home—just another place to lay low.

Sister reached Walton's office thirty minutes before she was due to arrive. She made it a habit to arrive early to every appointment—surveilling the area—marking exits and entrances—counting windows—knowing the general layout of the property and surrounding buildings. Everything was calculable. Walton's office was centrally located between Café De Mundo, a donut shop, two hotels, and the French Market. The top floor of the two-story structure had apartments that ran the length of the block, with each business painted or fitted in its own dramatic flair. Greens, teals, rusty reds, and lots of etched glass.

Once inside the two-story building, Sister stood waiting uncomfortably in the empty entryway. It was so quiet in the room that she wasn't sure they were even open. If it hadn't been for the big ornate etched glass that read, "Doucet & Walton, Attorneys at Law. Lawyers of the People," circled above the top, she would have gone back out and selected a different door. She was surprised to see that Archie Benedict Walton hadn't removed his partner's name from the window. However, the Doucet name carried significant weight in Louisiana, so it made sense that Mr. Walton would keep it for the notoriety alone.

Her eyes swept over the beautifully decorated entryway, with its French-inspired design. Blacks, grays, and pinks sprinkled across off-white walls, with a floor-to-ceiling print of the Eiffel Tower that was most likely a rummage store find. Yet, had the allure of an expensive painting hung as its focal piece.

Sister suddenly felt underdressed as she looked down at her runner's clothing after observing the small white camera in the corner of the ceiling with its blinking red light. She wanted to sit, yet had decided that the chair didn't deserve the abuse—she was hot and sweaty.

"Well, hello there. I do apologize, Miss. I didn't mean to keep you waiting. I just stepped out to get Archie his coffee. These old legs do not move like they used to. Can I get you a cup as well?" The woman who entered the office attached to the entryway had been the office secretary for a long time and appeared to have survived the Ark with Noah. Her hair was in an uptight bun at the center of her crown, and she walked with a hunch. 'Silvie Walton,' read the nameplate on the desk. She was his wife and long-time confidant to his former partner. Silvie paused at seeing Sister's face in recognition. Then, the courteous smile dropped from her face and fell into a look of pity.

"Silvie," the rat-like voice called from an office to the left. "Can you please show Miss Lovejoy in. If she's ready, I'll see her now."

Silvie's kind smile quickly returned as she raised her hand towards the door. Sister thanked her and entered the room. The office was large, but the entryway had been the proverbial hook. The face of the front office was all Silvie and no Archie. Not even his former partner had a hand in the new look of the front office. Sandra Doucet would not have allowed such a cliché.

Archie's office had a thin layer of cigar smoke that floated through the air like wispy clouds. Upon hearing Silvie's demanding ask, "Please shut the door, Dear," Sister quickly pushed it closed—not allowing the clouds to waft out and terrorize the beauty out front.

Archie was not quite the same as Sister remembered him from his visits to the old plantation home. He sat behind his desk, cigar in hand, and flipped through a pile of papers on his desk while he scanned the contents of a book. The book had the same cover as three others on his desk. They read, "Thomson Reuters" on the front cover. Next to it was a book on Entertainment Law and Litigation.

He still looked the same. Just an older version of himself. He was still unattractive and just as arrogant in a pug-faced sort of way. She hadn't much cared for the old man back in the day, and that had not changed.

"Did you know that there were over 300 movies and TV show episodes filmed here last year?" Archie said, still head down while he scanned what Sister could now see to be a contract. "I think I am in the wrong business. Please take a seat."

Archie's desk was covered in files. Stacks of them towered higher than others, while some were opened and laid haphazardly, so that anyone paying attention could read if inclined to do so. Sister glanced over them as she stood in front of the desk. Two divorces, an estate, and a few of them had ring stains from a coffee cup. Probably from the same one that rested at his right, full and still steaming. To his left was the ashtray. Surprisingly, it was the only thing on his desk that wasn't overly dirty or neglected.

"No sir, I didn't know that. That sounds like a pretty good trivia question for Frankie's," Sister said as she looked for a place to sit. A brown loveseat held its own in the corner, covered in newspapers, magazines, and what looked like a week's worth of jackets and mail. Now less afraid of ruining the furniture, she took a seat. She didn't bother to move the newspapers, thinking she might need the barrier.

"You called me Mr. Walton," Sister said directly, trying to get his attention.

"And now you are here. Finally," he said, looking over his glasses at her. She didn't miss the way his tone chastised her as well as the glare of disapproval. He didn't try to hide his annoyance. "Had you made it to the funeral, we could have taken care of this then, but I digress," he said, standing and walking to the end of a bookshelf. "I had this on my desk for a while, expecting you to come and see me, but getting an answer, I finally moved it off my desk to make room for other matters."

Archie rummaged through a seemingly abandoned stack of papers and files that had been tucked away in the lower compartment of a large bookshelf that took up an entire wall of his office. "Mrs. Doucet's will and trust left strict instructions for everything to be handled in person. It doesn't matter much to me, I guess—I get paid either way. No matter how long you want to prolong this."

"Regardless, the house is empty, and I would hate to see it fall to ruin due to neglect. I do have a gardener stopping by every couple of weeks to see to the grounds. Of course, this is only in relation to the house itself. The rest of the property is managed separately. There is a handyman, a caretaker of sorts, though he's not much of one, who goes by and runs the kids out of there regularly. It has become quite popular among teenagers—especially those from the school. He keeps the trash cleaned up and does what he can to keep the place from getting torn apart. The place is still fully intact, per Mrs. Doucet's instruction—all the belongings and household things have not been removed. I did, as a courtesy, mind you, have the refrigerator cleaned out," he said smugly as if that was one of his crowning moments.

"Well, that was awfully kind of you," she replied, carrying the same tone.

"The rest of the property will stay in trust," he said, handing over an envelope with coffee ring stains that overlapped one another—proof that it had at least seen eight cups of coffee. The envelope also had a few gray smudges that looked like smeared ash from a cigar. "I trust you can read this for yourself," he said again over his glasses. "Given that there wasn't anyone else left," he choked out in a strained expression, "she's instructed you to get it all."

Sister held her breath to keep from commenting on the way he had come at her. The way he said Miss Doucet came out as if they were not there to discuss the same person. Sister opened the envelope and pulled out the contents. An inch-thick section of paper filled with lots of words that she did not care about. Nor did she care to read it. Clearly, he had disapproved of the woman she loved, leaving her the plantation, the school, the church, and the family's home. Miss Doucet had left her everything. And all Sister wanted was to pretend she wasn't here and that everything would be okay. She would trade the Doucet Plantation and all its worth to have Mother Agnes Valentine back.

"You will need to secure a long-term management firm to oversee the property," he said, looking at her blank-faced. "That is not my job. That is, unless you plan to stay at home and see to the board yourself. Since you now own the land, you are the board's chairperson," he said as though it pained him greatly. "Though, given what you do, I highly..."

Sister cut him off before he could finish. She had heard enough and was beyond the tone that cut her down like a sword every time he addressed her. "What I do has nothing to do with this," she said coolly. "It seems you know more about me than I do of you. I thank you for your time, Mr. Walton. Clearly, I have taken up enough of it. I will consult with my attorney, and he can handle whatever needs to be done. So that we can be done with this matter completely."

"The property has no real value, Miss Lovejoy," he said, nearly choking on her name as he rolled it past his lips. She cringed at the implication that she was in it for the cash buy-off. "In case you are thinking of selling it to turn a profit. Not only is the Doucet name broke, but the place has a lease agreement firmly in place that not even your great-great-grandchildren's children will see undone. However, the house is livable. And you are welcome to it. You may even wish to rent it out. I'm sure you can find someone who wouldn't mind living in a manor. Though it needs some work, it is still a beautiful home. The keys are in the envelope," he said dryly. Still unmoved by her presence or her circumstances. No matter how late it was, she was there, and he acted as if it wouldn't have mattered when she showed up. Her presence would still have left a bad taste in his mouth as much as it did hers. She had considered that he was offended on behalf of Miss Doucet. If that were the case, there wouldn't be an explanation good enough to change the old lawyer's mind. But she had the feeling that there was much more to it.

"No matter how much you may change," she had read once, "you'll always be seventeen to those in your hometown."

"Good day, Mr. Walton."

COUCH SESSIONS

S ister approached the building with a dread that made her feet feel as though they were stuck to hot tarmac. After she met with Archie, a melancholy seeped into the hollow spaces of her insides. She would have to face heartaches that she just wasn't prepared for. In the past years, she still hadn't wanted to face any of it. Sweat ran down her face as the weight of the key hung heavy in her pocket like an anchor. It seemed to pulsate like a heartbeat against her leg. She could feel beads roll down her back. She wasn't in the mood for a therapy session. However, McTavish insisted that she keep to the contract, especially after that press conference.

She looked up at the freshly white stucco home, clad in its traditional garden-style exterior. The building was a two-story structure with two white balconies and eight large windows—all covered in wrought iron. Most of the outside face was adorned in ivy from the eaves to the garden below. She paused at the front door, unsure whether to enter there or walk around to the back of the house. Years before, she remembered that a rear entrance was how she had previously entered the home. However, she found that highly unlikely now since there was no gate to the newly erected eight-foot iron fence that enclosed the gorgeous structure and its garden. She ran her hand over the doctor's name on the front of the house and placed her hand on the knob. She hesitated for a few seconds before twisting the handle and reluctantly stepping inside.

She drew in a deep breath, fighting the urge to leave and reschedule for another time. She had a knot deep in the pit of her stomach. She wasn't prepared for the interrogatories that awaited her behind the door. She had no good answers to any of the questions.

"I should be used to the experience by now," she thought to herself as she stood directly in front of a woman with a nameless face sitting at the reception desk. The desk sat in the middle of a glass cubicle, in the center of what appeared to be the grand foyer. To call it an actual reception, however, would imply that one would be spoken to, but that did not happen. The woman kept her eyes down—not lifting her head to see who had entered through the front door. She slid back the partition and placed a clipboard in front of Sister.

She looked over the counter, looking at the top of a badly separated hair part that hadn't seen fresh color in about six weeks. Sister wondered what held the woman's attention enough to be so indifferent to her presence. This woman would make a terrible witness if Sister were so inclined to snap and take out everyone in the house. But she knew it didn't matter. It never did.

The most she had ever heard from anyone who had ever occupied the chair was, "Please hold" or "Please sign in." She couldn't remember a time that she had ever been addressed directly or had anyone make eye contact with her. "Good thing I'm not here to kill you," she thought.

Sister took the clipboard from the counter and wrote a string of numbers across the sectioned-out lines on a piece of paper, "DOE14938771." She never wrote her name. Besides, what name would she use?

About five years into her therapy, it became almost impossible for her to make every weekly appointment. Once her job became more demanding of her time and her particular skills were needed elsewhere, she became a ghost. The four years she spent training with McTavish's old unit had taught her how to fight and protect herself. Then, having spent six years with the OIO, England's version of a fugitive task force, she had been trained to find people who didn't want to be found. After that, McTavish's agency allowed her to apply all that knowledge effectively, without relying on bureaucracy.

Being part of the three gave her somewhere to direct her anger and vent her rage. There was no way she could return to her old life. To the world, Kathryn Daily and her friend, Caroline Doucet, had died the night they had been attacked and left for dead. Kate Daily was on every channel for months as the Daily family mourned their loss—while Caroline's death had been nothing more than a subtitle. The Dailys were government royalty, and the fact that the perpetrators were unknown and still at large only sensationalized their deaths. Sister was given a new name and had moved on, never to look back.

She could no longer do the job that she had traded financial security and family for. She told herself that she didn't blame God. She truly wanted to believe that. She told herself that she hadn't lost her faith in the Almighty, but rather, she had no faith in man. She had lost her ability to see the good in others, and she had lost her taste for pious indifference. She could no longer leave it in God's hands, and she settled on taking that up with him whenever it was her time. Until then, something needed to be done for those still upright on this planet and all those who were no longer walking among them due to a violent act so far removed from acceptable that its depravity made her ill.

Truth be told, Sister preferred the electronic method of her therapy. Skyping was so much easier to do. It was less formal and felt the least intrusive. She always felt like the dog in Pavlov's experiment. If she said just the right words and shared the correct feelings, a Cheeto would drop from the ceiling tile, and a hand would reach out to pat her on the head. "What a good girl."

A closed door on the other side of the room quietly opened, and a thin Asian woman with long black hair, bangs, and stylish black-rimmed glasses gestured for Sister to follow. Sister guessed that the doctor was about her age. However, who really knew? Sister wasn't good at guessing ages, especially with how she wore her hair and the edgy, tailored skirt suit that perfectly fit her tiny frame. Whatever her age, she was stunning.

She placed the four-year-old magazine she had been pretending to read back on the table and followed the doctor. She had read the magazine before, several times—a couple of years ago. She wondered how many other people visited this location and had read the same material over and over again, or how often the doctor had packed up, moved and rearranged everything. It felt like a prop. The entire feel of the building was staged. But Sister played her part, learning her role early on.

Dr. Wu pointed at a few seats lined up between a large window and her desk. Sister selected a big, fluffy gray chair that seemed to swallow her when she sat down. She slipped off her running shoes and tucked her feet up underneath her. As much as she hated coming to see Dr. Wu, she genuinely appreciated the effort she made to make her feel comfortable most of the time. Other times, Dr. Wu had a way of making her feel immature, like a child—safe and self-conscious at the same time.

"One to ten?" Dr. Wu asked. Her face was pensive, and her expression conveyed an earnest concern. She didn't like that Sister looked as though she hadn't been eating or sleeping.

"Do you ever get tired of asking that question?" Sister asked her, sounding even more curt than intended. She already knew that part-time Dr. Wu, a former Senior Forensic Psychiatrist to the FBI's Behavioral Analysis Unit, always asked that same question first off—just as her previous doctor had done. And the one before him. Dr. Wu wasn't going to perform any differently. She wasn't new to the program, nor was she new to Sister's therapy, which Sister found unnerving. She never had to relay her experience with the next doctor because everyone already knew her entire soul-crushing life, from the beginning and probably to its end. She knew it was complete paranoia, but she hated that everyone seemed to always have her name in their mouth—trading her story like baseball cards, comparing notes, and analyzing her.

"I'll trade you mommy issues for a near-death," she thought.

Dr. Wu watched Sister over the top of her glasses. She was waiting for her to answer the question and wondering why such an innocent question would provoke Sister's obvious annoyance nearly every time.

"What question would you rather I start with today?"

"I don't know. How about, how's the family? How's the baby? How was the Bobby Flay cooking class? What color's your underwear today?"

Sister sighed in frustration. She was tired of the same script. Tired of being a lab rat stuck on the same hamster wheel that never moved around the cage. Tired of talking about the same bullshit. However, she wouldn't use that word out loud. She never swore. Even in her anger, she never wanted to offend God's ears in that way. She knew this was absurd because he knew her thoughts and that she used the word "F" about 100 times a day in her mind.

Dr. Wu's eyes narrowed—intrigued by the idea that Sister were actually thinking about their interaction and a possible future. By her own experience, Sister would always answer the questions directed at her, but she had never volunteered or divulged any information that didn't require prodding or pulling teeth. If she was, in fact, taking a cooking class, that showed that she was taking an interest in life's pleasures. The baby comment was interesting as well. Dr. Wu wondered if it was meant to be a strike against herself or a spoken misstep. Dr. Wu knew that due to the injuries Sister had suffered, there would be no babies in her life.

"I see," Wu said, placing the pen she held in her hand into her lap. She was resisting the compulsive need to put the pen between her teeth and bite down—quelling her own nervous tic. "Is there someone new in your life? How's the baby? And have you indeed taken on a cooking class?" she asked, more out of curiosity and with a tone of skepticism. "And your underwear choices could be a topic for another session altogether, but I'm going to venture to say they are not super-hero undies."

Dr. Wu was privy to nearly every aspect of Sister's life. If Sister thought she was hiding anything, she wasn't. Sister didn't date—went to mass when she could—avoided therapy sessions—loved books, but only owned a bible. Sister listened to books from CDS or cassettes because of her need to multitask and her inability to sit idly. She claimed not to have had a drink since she was put in rehab, except for a few glasses of wine here and there, but never to excess, and she hadn't taken drugs since she nearly ODed four years back. Dr. Wu knew that this was only partially true. Sister drank like a fish when she had the inclination, and found sobriety during her times of regret. She could field-strip and reassemble an AR-15 in under forty seconds and completely clean and reassemble it in fifteen minutes. She spoke five languages, and she was fascinated by Greek and Norse mythology. There were hundreds of everyday nuances and developments within Sister's life. And Dr. Wu knew pretty much every single one of them—even the ones Sister couldn't see herself—let alone face.

"I thought this was going to be a group session today," Sister stated, knowing its falsity. "I finally agreed to one group session, and you canceled it? Maybe you should be over here so that I can examine your life's choices?"

"I haven't seen you in months. I thought we could talk. Just you and me. And we both know that you knew there were no group sessions here. But nice try. Besides, don't we need to figure out how you are doing?"

"We?" Sister countered. "WE are fabulous."

Dr. Wu watched Sister speak and listened to her words. Her face was make-up-free, exposing the purpling skin under her already dark eyes. She noted her body shifting and stretching. She had even noticed the short yoga pants and the athletic t-shirt that showed her bare arms. Wu wanted to be excited about the clothing options, but would remain skeptical until the end of the session.

"You're not sleeping?"

Sister skipped over the question of her sleeping inabilities. She relayed the events of late—how her "baby's" meltdown coincided with the invasion of an intruder. The message on the mirror— the empty water bottle and why someone would break in, take nothing, but eat her granola bars. She knew it hadn't been Beast. She wouldn't have bothered with removing the wrappers first. She would have eaten them—paper and all. Sister would have had to clean up the mess left after Beast had puked up the evidence later. Sister spoke of the case—the gold button and her feelings about seeing her colleagues and friends back together. She vomited her entire last few days all over Dr. Wu. When she was done, she felt spent.

When Sister fell silent, having nothing else to say, Wu asked, "And what about the divorce proceedings? Have either of you budged on that? Has he signed yet? It's been what, now, two, three years? How are you feeling? Are you finding it difficult?"

Sister shifted uncomfortably in her seat before placing her feet firmly on the floor. "It's been about eighteen months, and you know it. "Nice try, though," she said, returning Dr. Wu's early remarks. "He won't sign them, and I'm too busy to force anything to happen. I know you think that I'm just dragging it out, but he's hurt, and I don't feel like I should poke that wound any deeper than I already have. I still have to work with him, and I'm actually okay with the status quo. We live on separate sides of the globe. It isn't as if I'll run into him with anyone else, living so far apart."

Dr. Wu found it interesting that Sister included "him with anyone else." "And what if you did run into him with someone else?" Dr. Wu asked, again finding Sister's answers surprising. As long as Dr. Wu had been her doctor, she had never once witnessed any forward mobility in Sister's decision process regarding her personal life. She lived her life very simply, with few material possessions and a one-day-at-a-time approach, characterized by a fight-or-flight response.

"I'd like to think I could regard his choices with impartiality. He's a grown man, and he owes me nothing."

"So, what I am hearing is you've chosen to effectively stay married and be unmarried to him at the same time while hoping he stays single," Wu said. "Interesting strategy in getting him out of your life."

"I never said I wanted him out of my life or that he should remain single," Sister said a bit too angrily. She was surprised at the force of her words and how quickly she leaped to defend her relationship. Her words nearly decapitated Dr. Wu. "Why do we have to talk about this anyway? It has nothing to do with anything at the moment. It's all too complicated and confusing, and I've been too busy to think about it. And why do you always seem to feel the need to continue to make me feel bad about not wanting to be married to him? If his feelings on this subject mean that much to you, why isn't he on your couch instead of me? Maybe you should ask him why he cut me out of his life, but won't sign the papers? Really? Who's actually the bigger jerk here?"

Dr. Wu's expression did not change as Sister unloaded her feelings without saying she was upset that her husband and former team member, Undersheriff Bishop Bohannan, hadn't spoken to her directly in that time—especially after she had served him with divorce papers. If either of them had an interest in mending their two-week nuptials, that had been the nail in their coffin. Dr. Wu hadn't been all that surprised, though she had hoped that Charlee Lovejoy had finally stepped out of the shadows and had found love and joy.

"I made a mistake, is all," she had told Dr. Wu, but she never would open up to what that mistake had been. Although Dr. Wu had gathered from previous sessions that she had been quite taken with Bohannan and that maybe, just maybe, this was the guy to bring her out from behind that wall she had sheltered. However, she knew all too well what had happened between the two, and she hoped that with a few more sessions, the problem would finally reveal itself to Sister without Dr. Wu having to tell her.

"I didn't mean to poke at your wounds," Dr. Wu said, using Sister's references about Bishop. "I am just asking questions, trying to get honest responses. "Let's talk about Archie Walton. How did that go? How do you feel about discussing Mother Agnes Valentine? Or rather Renee Doucet?" Seeing Sister shrink a little, Wu continued, "How are you taking Walton's news?"

"I should have been here," Sister said. Tears filled her eyes as she thought about the death of Mother Agnes Valentine. It had affected her more than the deaths of anyone else she knew. She wasn't able to visit, though she did not doubt that McTavish would have made it possible if she had pushed for it. But there wasn't a nerve in her body with the backbone to return. Even after hearing that the woman she loved more than life had died.

Two hours later, Sister woke to an empty room with a handmade white and blue Afghan throw covering her. She was stretched out and surprisingly comfortable. She felt a bit better as her batteries had time to recharge in a safe environment. Her head felt lighter, and her mind a bit clearer. When had she fallen asleep? The last thing she remembered was her crying hysterics and beyond consolation. She had been drained past exhaustion. Maybe the nap was what she needed. Now, she felt renewed energy. Sister sat up and pulled on her runners. Then she quickly gathered up, folded, and placed the blanket beneath the pillows.

Sister opened the door and stepped out into the foyer. The white walls and glass looked elegant and nothing like a place where a psychiatrist would be shrinking heads. Dr. Wu was descending an all-white staircase that wound its way up rather than being straight and boxy. Her heels lightly clacked with each step. She had changed out of her suit and now wore a skirt and a white blouse. Sister imagined herself walking down the same set of stairs. She felt as though she had before. Her hand instinctively cupped an invisible banister and glided across it as she envisioned herself walking the stairs.

"I'll see you soon, Sister," Dr. Wu said, stopping midway along the staircase. She took a long look at Sister before saying, "You be careful out there."

"You too, Doc. I'll see you again real soon. Love those shoes, by the way," she winked with a smile.

PRIDE

CURRENT DAY - BABY

The young woman on the other side had fallen quiet. I wanted to call out her name as her breathing still had that rattling echo that reverberated from her chest. Yet, it was softer now and sounded less hurried than before. At least she was still alive, and she was finally resting. About the only time she was quiet was when she dozed off. I did appreciate that. She talked too much. Maybe her ease into slumber had been chalked up to finally being able to relax, knowing she wasn't alone in here. Once she was out, a silence fell that stilled the stone walls. But we weren't alone, were we?

In the quiet, I listened for anything that could give me a clue to where we were being held. My back had rested stiffly against a wall made of rounded stone. They felt like grapefruit-sized rocks that had been polished at some point in their lives but now felt worn down and porous. I placed a hand over one of the stones, my fingertips searching the inner filling of concrete and grout. It was chipped, jagged, and sparse. The construction felt old and broken. By the dampness of the wall, I was sure that we were underground. The area felt familiar. A vague memory swam around in my head, but I couldn't slow it down long enough to pull anything from it. Maybe a basement area or a root cellar.

Being Louisiana, both of these seemed illogical, but I wasn't sure what other conclusions I could make. Anything built below ground would be an uncommon aesthetic for any home in the area—unless we were being held more towards the south. No clear-minded businessperson would risk their livelihood on a basement or cellar. Most everything, including the dead, were buried above ground due to the amount of groundwater that seeped from the earth.

There were plenty of stories where waters had unearthed loved ones, and caskets raced for space in roadways and lawns. The floor had the same texture as the walls, with just a bit more grit. It made my dress feel damp and grimy—the air smelled of mold and raw earth. It was altogether possible that it was never meant for the living. Thinking about how this all played out and how I got here, I cursed myself for my poor clothing choices as I removed the heels from my feet.

"How about you tell me another story?"

My hands stopped their search at Greer McTavish's sudden, but soft voice as it interrupted my concentration, and my hands froze in place. I wasn't startled by her voice. However, if anyone else were listening in, they might have been at that very moment, and I wanted to listen for any changes in sound around us. Greer's voice was low but direct. Showing no apprehension, though I had noted that she sounded wheezy and in need of a big breath. Hearing nothing of importance in the area around us, I continued my search along the wall and paused as my fingertips brushed at the edge of something that felt like a wooden frame.

"Oh, come on now. You are smarter than that. Do you want just another story, or do you want the story?"

"You sound as if you know me already," she said while keeping in mind that she didn't believe in coincidences or that I had nothing to do with why she was here. Yes, I did know her that well. "Start by telling me who 'they' are. They call you Baby, I got that much, and you kill people for money. But not always," she said in a questioning tone, without asking a question. "You enjoy killing, but only bad men. Well, maybe just bad men. I reckon I shouldn't assume too much about how your victims are picked. Or if they are all just men. Do you kill women as well?"

I had smiled at her directness and the bold assertion that the people I had killed were victims. Thus far, I hadn't killed anyone who didn't have it coming. Whether by the deeds visited upon us, or the many others across the world that had inflicted the same hurt on innocent people. I like that Gears was finding her footing, and her investigative nature was finally drowning out her fear. She was her mother's daughter for sure.

"Ambassador Jonathan Hadley," I stated. "Do you know the name?

She thought for a moment, and then she answered. "Yes, Ambassador Jonathan Hadley of California. He died in Rome, I believe. Maybe two years or so back. He was murdered in his hotel room. I don't think it was ever solved."

"That he did. One year, six months, and two days ago. He's the one I call Pride. Sin number one. Not because he was a prideful man. But because Pride is the first sin enumerated by Pope Gregory the 1st in the 6th century. In truth, from everything I have learned about the man, he was considered an honorable politician from all accounts. If there is such a thing. Well-liked and respected from what I've gathered. Even those who opposed his politics genuinely liked the man. I found nothing in his past that would lead to his downfall politically or morally," I said.

"Roman Catholic? That's interesting. Saint Thomas Aquinas expanded on the seven deadly sins in the 13th century. At least, that's what I learned in catechism lessons. You say that Congressman Hadley was a good man, and yet, I'll take a big leap here, that you took his life anyway," she said dryly. She also sounded confused at the idea that I used Christian doctrine to kill people and did, in fact, murder without cause. And in the name of God? It was unsettling thoughts, for sure. "I gather you are catholic then?" She asked.

"No," I said with a snort. "Catholic? No. I do not follow your God. I have my own Gods. It seemed fitting, is all. In time, you'll understand, I continued. "A simple chance encounter at the American Embassy in Rome put us in the same room together. Later, I followed him to a hotel. I knew his face the moment he lifted his chin.

When our eyes met, I saw a flash of recognition in those eyes of his, and he wasn't able to hide it. He tried to casually pull away, drawing a false smile on his face, but it didn't reach his eyes. His face colored from shades of white and red and settled on a deathly shade of grayish blue as though his life had already left him. He did his best not to cause a scene, though. I give him great props for that. He'd shuffle through his papers, nodded appropriately, and commented when expected. He took small bites of his Caesar, and all the while, his eyes betrayed him.

After seeing me, he was no longer focused on the conference. He was on autopilot throughout the rest of the day. When his eyes would drift in my direction, they held mine longer than I thought he could manage. Then, once they had adjourned for the night, he stumbled over himself, trying to get out of the room. The ghost of his nightmares had been visited upon him like the ghost of Christmas Future. He saw his future ending."

Later, when I slipped into his room, he sat in a chair facing the door. I had taken a key card from housekeeping, but to my surprise, I hadn't needed it. He had left the door unlatched and slightly ajar. He was still dressed in his white button-up and black slacks. But he had removed his shoes and had placed them neatly beside the bed. He had removed his watch, his wedding band, and his phone, which all sat on the table. Interestingly enough, his phone had been powered down. He hadn't reached out to anyone. He had plenty of time to do so. He had worn a beautiful silk tie. A Tom Ford, I believe, which he removed, and it sat folded neatly on the table next to him. He held a highball in his hand. Four fingers high with scotch. I'm sure it was topped off before I entered the room.

"I wasn't sure if you'd need to use this,' he said, eying the tie. "But if it helps, you won't need it. Well, at least if you intend to tie me up. I'm not going anywhere."

His response amused me. I hadn't ever encountered a man willing to offer up his head on a platter.

"Would it do any good to tell you how sorry I am?" He asked me.

"No," I replied, placing a hand on the chair opposite him. "But, I can sit while you finish that drink," I offered.

"Please do," he said. Can I pour you one?" he asked, looking at the decanter and empty glass beside it.

"No, thank you," I replied politely, shaking my head at him, and pulled out a seat. That had surprised me as well. I hadn't expected to feel that calm. "Not while I'm working. But I do appreciate the offer. Maybe under other circumstances, perhaps.

His hand trembled as he lifted the glass to his lips, but his voice was calm and pleasant, really. I hadn't detected any hostility in his words. I wasn't sure how I was going to kill him until I did. Millions of scenarios had played out in my mind, but until I was sitting in front of him, my sidearm resting on the table between us, I really didn't know.

He was actually the only one, since it began, who had recognized my face from that night. He never even tried to argue his side or negotiate his way out of it. He didn't fight me. He didn't cry out for help. He didn't beg for mercy. No reprieve. I honestly thought he looked relieved, really. As we sat quietly for a moment, he asked me if I had told anyone about who they were. I told him that if I had, I wouldn't be there now.

"I didn't know," he said. "I didn't know what was going to happen that night. I don't think any of us did, to be honest. Until I saw the story on the news and the details that followed," he stopped. "I was horrified."

"How many fish did you catch that night?" I asked him. He was confused by my question, so I repeated it for him. "That night, you went fishing after our party. How many fish did you catch?"

"I don't remember," he replied. "I don't remember much of that night. Honestly. Between the booze and the weed and whatever else, I just don't know. But I do remember you girls. And so that you know, I didn't touch either of you. I don't think we all participated. But I don't know that for sure. I just know that I didn't touch either of you. I'm not trying to get out of anything. I'm just letting you know. What happened to the both of you has haunted me to this day."

"Yet, you kept quiet," I said to him flatly. My tone was neutral and without judgment. "You said nothing. Never came forward or turned yourself in. Or the others."

"I didn't," he said. "I was a coward. Liam isn't the kind of person you cross. Once I learned that, there was no way of telling who had been involved. They said that no evidence had been found, and I, I mean we, or us. We all decided to keep quiet. It wasn't as if I really had a choice."

"Didn't you, though?" I asked him. We all have choices, Ambassador. I'd like to think we are defined by them. You took our lives. You killed us. Destroyed and rewrote us. Killed our families and friends. We may have survived what you did to us, but we must certainly have died that night."

"I also had parents and family to worry about. Again, Liam isn't the type of person you go against. Or those he worked for. So, from then on, I did what I could to make up for my lack of heroism. I know I sound like a coward. And I was. I am. Then, as life grew, I got married and had children. I kept moving forward in my life, still a coward," he told me. "But my family went unharmed. I believed that he would kill them. He set us all up for your murders."

I let him talk for a while. Letting him get whatever he needed to say off his chest. Let him finish his drink. When he fell silent, I knew our conversation had run its course. "It's time," I said. I picked up the gun that sat closer to him than me and pointed it toward the bathroom door. "In there," I directed. At first, I was surprised that he never once reached for my gun. He had plenty of opportunities. But as he spoke, I understood better why he didn't.

He smiled weakly, drank down the rest of his glass, and followed my instructions without protest. Slowly, he walked to his execution but never faltered in his steps. Once in the bathroom, he sat on the edge of the tub and folded his hands in front of himself. He was going about all of it as if it were a business transaction, and the terms had been settled on and agreed to.

"What's next?' He asked. "Are you going to shoot me?"

I knew that most people would have felt bad for him. I felt it in my own chest. A pang of sorrow filled me. But that pain didn't belong to me. I couldn't allow it to hamper my resolve—even when I could feel something inside me trying to talk me out of what I was about to do. He had led an exemplary life. He leveraged his position and his status around the world to look out for others. He had truly been a good man. Yet, he and his friends had left us for dead. They thought they had killed us. And even if he personally played no involvement in the rape and assault, he went along with keeping his mouth shut all these years and never betrayed his brothers. I had no mercy for him, and my Gods do not require forgiveness. He was going to die.

I slipped the gun back into the holster and pulled out my knife. As I stepped closer to him, he sat up straighter. His chin was held high, and he braced himself. I gently placed a hand on his face, and then, softly, I placed a kiss on his lips. He did not move or try to pull away. As I did so, I slid my knife in at an angle between his fourth and fifth ribs and pulled my blade left. He flinched, but he did not pull away. He had accepted his fate. As I pulled my lips from him, I placed a hand behind his head, my knife slicing through the fourth and fifth ventricles. When he began to relax, I quickly lowered him into the tub. As he lay dying, tears began to fill his eyes. I knew it wasn't because he felt sorry for himself. He was remembering what they had done. And all his good deeds wouldn't make up for that.

"Am I the first, he asked me with a light chuckle in his voice. I haven't heard that any of us have been found dead."

"You are," I said to him as I sat on the edge of the tub and looked down at him. The others' time will come. I'll find them."

"I can make it easier for you," he said, gently placing a hand on mine. "I owe you that much."

He rattled off the names, and I stored them away. A sort of peace crossed his face as I placed my knife to his throat. I felt no pity for him, but I did not want him to suffer now. He was drowning, and that is a cruel death. Was that human of me? I wanted to be angry that he had taken that satisfaction from me. But he was dead, and it was bloody. Wasn't that the deal? Wasn't that the point? Cowards weren't allowed to enter the Halls of Valhalla. Perhaps, since he was a Christian, his God had forgiven him. Maybe he found peace in that.

As I finished this part of our story, I wished that I could see Greer's face. She was silent as I paused, and I wasn't sure if I should continue. I wasn't even sure that she was still awake. Let alone alive. She had been silent for so long. Part of me panicked a bit, I won't lie, but with a story like that, I had to assume that she was all ears. I would bet that in her line of work, she was kicking herself for not having a recorder in her pocket.

"Are you still there?"

"Uh, yes. I'm sorry. I'm just processing what you are saying. So, did you work at the embassy in Rome? Or, at least, you were there. And you are the one responsible for the murder of Ambassador Hadley? Because he was there when you and this other person were found assaulted?" Her voice carried an edge of incredulity. She was shocked and suspicious of what I had to say. Then, as if a light bulb had exploded in her mind, "Wait! Here? Did this happen here in Louisiana? The bodies in The Rogue?"

THE WAR ROOM

McTavish's War Room was set up similarly to the tent he occupied during his military days in the desert. He had also used the same sort of setup later, after utilizing his contacts to secure a private contract, applying his team's skills to do what governments weren't allowed to do themselves.

Those who didn't know him believed he was a highly decorated retired military man who had proudly served his country and then decided to fill his days policing a small parish in the American South. But those who served alongside him knew better. He never broke cover. Not once. He worked with an intel unit that hadn't exactly been one of them.

McTavish specialized in covert insurgency—creating havoc and backing revolutions while encouraging able-bodied citizens to fight back against their suppressors. He was good at his job, and along the way, he had made a name for himself. That reputation had aided him well when it came to retirement and building his agency. He had secured contracts with governments from around the world. But this time, instead of fighting wars for countries, he fought a war against the worst crimes committed against everyday people.

Sister's eyes fell to the blackboard that ran from the ceiling to about halfway down the wall. He set up his war wall the same way he would if he were gathering intel on a target. On the right, at the top of the pyramid, was a blank sheet of white paper. Below that were photos of six local girls from Louisiana. Among them was a photo of Tia Ward and Stephanie Hollenbeck; the two girls found within a day of each other.

Sister and the boys had spent a couple of days gathering information about the girls in the photos found in Mia's bedroom. Neither Stephanie Hollenbeck nor

Tracy Witman were among the girls in the images, so they were relieved to know that at least The FAB 7, as they were referred to, were alive. And so far, there was nothing that linked either of them to Mia or Sister. It hadn't been hard to find out who the other girls were. McQueen, because of his youthful looks, had been planted at the school as Bishop's wayward nephew. Bishop had painted it on really thick when talking to the Mother Superior—letting the administration know just how grateful he would be if the school did him this solid. His nephew, his sister's kid, wasn't all that bad. He was just a misunderstood youth who required a firmer hand than his single mother could provide. Bishop sold it, and by lunchtime, Luke Bohannan was enrolled in the 12th grade and having lunch with the other kids his age.

By the time Bishop picked him up from school, McQueen had the names of Kari Laney, DeDe Jarvis, Cora Perez, Shanna Gonzalez, Devina Sanders, Lauden Nash, and Lorien Hall. They were all graduating seniors, except for Kari Laney, who was in the 10th grade, and Tia Ward, who was turning junior. McQueen said that Kari had been Mia's best friend since kindergarten.

Sister saw that their photos had been arranged just beneath those of Mia, Tracy and Stephanie. They all looked so young. Yet, they were all made up, each one holding a perpetual duck lip look that seemed to be the rage among young girls and grown women alike. However, their eyes did not sparkle as they should at that age. They looked old and heavy, as if they held secrets far too big to carry, yet unable to put down.

Below the photos of the Seven, Sister shuddered at the blow that hit her, like a gunshot to the chest that nearly had her on her back, bleeding to death from her heart. If it hadn't been for the table behind her, she would have collapsed dead to the floor. Below the photos of the seven girls, Sister saw the pictures of Kathryn Daily and Caroline Doucet.

Kari came from a background similar to Kate's. Though her parents were divorced, living on opposite sides of Louisiana, they were well-to-do—both lawyers and prominent members of their community. The Doucets had been old money—generational wealth that had been around for over 200 years. Doucet Shipping had hit it big bootlegging in the late 1700s. Many assumed they made their money in the slave trade, knowing most of their ships sailed through the

Caribbean, but as much as the patriarch of the Doucet family operated in the pleasures found in the illicit, he hated the slave trade, deeming it a godless act. After Harrison Doucet bought the land and built the Doucet Plantation, he sealed his family's wealth in tobacco and corn. Later, Harrison's grandson, Jack Doucet, a non-believer, built a church to honor his Catholic father's wishes at the behest of his mother, while also keeping up the family's business in the opium trade and moonshining, which was a thriving success.

Years later, the boys' and girls' schools were added to the plantation's grounds, primarily as a goodwill contribution to the growing town built on the dirty money generated. By the 1980s, with most of the land being leased out to local farmers, the plantation existed in name only.

By the time Franklin Doucet married Sandra, he was working a regular 8-to-5 job in finance, while she kept her law practice afloat and raised their children on the Doucet Plantation. She did her best to maintain appearances, but traded on the Doucet name, knowing they were as rich as the average Joe.

Sister had to consider the possibilities of connecting the girls to this history while examining what would cause these girls to become entangled in whatever they were doing.

"Are you okay?" Silas asked, grabbing Sister by the arm and steadying her. The firm grip of his hand brought her back to the room. "Sister, are you okay?" he repeated. She heard his words as if he spoke them through water.

"I'm fine," she said finally, removing her arm from him and pulling herself vertical. She ran her hands over her hair and down her arms. When she reached the tops of her hands, she then ran her hands down her legs and along the top of her boots. As her eyes met Silas', he looked away as she finished her ritual. All the energy had been wiped, and she was now centered again. Then she looked at Silas as if she were seeing him for the first time. "Are we ready to speak to the girls?" she asked, skipping over whatever just happened.

Silas watched Sister's eyes for any signs that something was dangerously amiss. When he was assured that she had her feet underneath her, he then looked over at the two photos at the bottom of McTavish's War Wall. He did not have to ask her anything else. He could feel the hurt coming from her. Maybe even a bit of betrayal. Her face was in one of those photos. She was younger then, but there was no doubt that it was her. He knew she'd be upset when she came to the room and saw the photos. Yet, he also knew it was a necessary evil. He had taped them there himself.

There were too many dead girls to tiptoe around her anymore. The stories were linked, and it was time those stories were told. There would be questions, but that was something that could be addressed as they arose. He didn't want to admit that he played a part in having her here. Neither Bishop, Addison, nor Luke knew the whole story, and it wasn't up to him to tell it. That would be on McTavish to fill in those details. All he had to do was do his part. His loyalties were with her also, and this was the only way he knew to not only save her, but to stop those who hurt her. In the end, Sister would be the bait, and there was no way around it. With Bishop running his own parallel investigation, all Silas could hope for now was to get Greer back safely without Bishop or Sister getting her killed.

YOU SHOT ME, BABY

S ilas Holiday walked through the back entrance of Madam Elle's with all the presence of a man on a mission and all the confidence of a lion. A lone bouncer sat on a stool and looked up from his phone just long enough to greet Silas with a nod and a "Hey" before looking back down at his phone. Nothing about the place had changed, nor had the man. He was the same person every time Silas had come through that door. The place had always been dark—low-lit with an ominous red glow from black metal, velvet-colored lights that ran along the ceiling, while black lace hung loosely from the covers of the lights' sconces. A sultry seduction filled the room and allowed its patrons to be masked in the shadows of scandalous intimacy. Their clandestine affairs were left only to themselves. Well, that and the hidden cameras that lurked behind those beautifully hung tapestries that had once adorned the walls of a castle in Romania—furthering the atmosphere's mystery.

He stood in front of his dresser and stared at the message in the mirror. Trudy hadn't been in his room yet to clean, and it was still there. He had hoped it had been a figment of his imagination, but no such luck. The perfectly formed letters had been calligraphed in bright red lipstick. The beginning of each letter looped as though the writer had created a line of drawn art.

"You know where to find me, lover. See you soon."

If he ignored the message, there would be no telling what other measures she'd delight in taking to get her way. The possibilities would be endless and, most assuredly, unforgettable. This was her being subtle. As long as he had known her, she got what she wanted, or she took a more scorched-earth approach. He had never personally witnessed her, well, being her. So, he wasn't sure what her rage looked like up close and personal. But he had seen what she was capable of. If the three men left on the mountain were any indication, he'd hate to be on the receiving end of her anger. She was seductive, coy, and could be childish. Her humor, at times, came across as that of a twelve-year-old boy. But her wit was unmatched. She could be quiet and calculating. Her words were often deliberate and direct as if she savored their meaning. And she could be unpredictable. That was what worried him the most. Given that, he would show.

Baby watched him enter Madame Elle's through the back entrance. With his head held high, his dark expression was piercing. Back in its prime, the place had been a brothel and a gambling hall. The old building, now razed to the ground, and new walls had been erected to honor the infamous Madame Elaina Albescu, who had attracted the likes of Lucky Luciano, Bonnie and Clyde, and Bugsy Siegel during her rise to fame before her death in 1959. Victoria Hall had once sung there, as had Mae West and Ella Fitzgerald. A hidden room had been built in the 20s on the old site to hide the rum pirated in from Nassau and stowed for distribution during the Prohibition era—all courtesy of the Doucet and Monroe families' hard work.

Silas had seen her as well. Her hair was braided in a mixture of black, blond, and pink dreads that hung loose in the middle of her back. It was probably just a wig, but it looked well done and served its purpose. She wore a short black dress and red heels that added six inches to her height, making her appear slimmer and more powerful. Her skin shimmered under the glow of her tan, suggesting she had been somewhere warm for a considerable amount of time. His eyes couldn't help but trace every part of her skin—seeing the old tattoos, and noticing a few new ones. He watched her closely as she stood at a tall table and took another sip of her drink. Her eyes locked onto his, daring him to look away first. He couldn't help but notice that she looked beautiful in her element. Deadly, of course, but beautiful, nonetheless.

She understood Sister's draw to the tall, dark, and handsome. Bishop's dark hair and deep brown eyes were intoxicating. She loved it most when they turned a dark black when tested. She had seen this happen often. She smiled, thinking how she thoroughly enjoyed the simplicity in which he approached life, the lawlessness of his hacked and rough features, rather than chiseled and GQ. But

Silas Holiday excited her in a way that no other man could. Bishop was a man of high character and principle. He was Sister's type, even though she vowed never to be with him. But Silas Holiday would straight up gut you like a prison fish in the middle of a crowded cafeteria and leave you as dead as a chicken nugget where you fell without a second thought. He was her kind of guy. He made her feel alive as he had breathed it into her himself.

The file she kept on him stated that he had been vacationing in Florida when he developed the itch to join up after the U.S. entered Desert Storm. He knew that London would follow suit. Silas ditched the board and signed up with McTavish. She knew his story, as well as the others, but she'd kept it to herself. She might need that information later and kept it squared away for a rainy day.

Baby scanned over his features lustfully. The broadness of his shoulders and the depth of his chest left her breathless. McQueen had been right. It wasn't hard to picture him with a battle axe and shield, hacking his way through a battlefield. His strong Nordic features were striking. His long, blonde hair, with its strands of silver, competed to be noticed. She liked that his beard was more silver than blonde. His glacier-blue eyes were intense, and she could see why the ladies seemed to love his brooding nature, especially with the scar that ran vertically down from his left eyebrow and stopped at the edge of his nose. He was a man's man. You either like him or hate him, and she wanted him.

He was taller than the others, and for his age, he looked fantastically delicious. He was often mistaken for Russian, which has served him well. It had allowed him to blend in with the lower echelon of the social hierarchy operating in the underworlds. Putting aside the slightly rounded middle, it was hard to believe that he was anywhere near fifty and showed no signs of slowing down.

She smiled, thinking that it was attractive—seeing that he was human and wasn't immune to a growing waistline and gray hair. His scar seemed more pronounced as a shadow fell across him and cast him in that shroud of danger that she found appealing about Elle's. His hairline hadn't moved much, and she envisioned him pulling out the leather tie and watching it fall around his face and shoulders. She liked that he had smoothly shaven the sides of his face but had left a nicely trimmed mustache and beard that hung long just around his lips and down his chin. It glowed white in the darkness of the room. She could not imagine him looking any sexier than he did at that moment, at any point in his life.

As she watched him move, she wondered just how long it would take for her to have him puddling beneath her—remembering just how quickly he had surrendered before. None of those moments had taken much convincing, though he protected heavily at first. He always put up a shallow barricade, "We aren't doing this again," but his eyes always betrayed him as she stepped over his weak defense.

He was in love, and she reveled in the knowledge that she could use that love to get from him whatever she wanted. She could see the times he considered killing her. It was probably the exact reflection he had seen in her eyes as well, but they killed each other with sex instead. She knew that if nothing else, as much as he hated it, he would always protect her, even if he dreamed of killing her at the same time.

She watched him as he drew closer. She liked the ease of his gait and the relaxed confidence of a man with no predators. His expression and posture were unreadable. His assertiveness masked his secrets. He stopped at the bar and ordered a rum and coke with a squeeze of lime before turning and walking in her direction.

Silas watched her as she turned away from him. Her hips swayed purposefully with each step as she walked to a back corner booth—the place where he could find her monitoring the comings and goings of everyone who entered from either of the two doors of the building. The only light that illuminated her favorite table was an electric candle situated at the back of the table, making the booth feel intimate and cozy.

"May I sit?" he asked, pointing to the seat beside her. He was polite, but his undertone suggested he wasn't exactly asking. She knew he could hide a lot behind his eyes, but very little when he spoke. His words had often betrayed him.

She would rather he not sit right next to her. That would be entirely too close for now. She would need to weigh him out first. She needed him to stay at arm's length—creating a safe distance between them. She had her weapons on her if necessary. But she knew he would as well. No self-respecting lawman, or whatever he was pretending to be right then, would be caught with his pants down. Given the new circumstances, she also didn't expect him to come alone. Although, it was nice to see that he had kept to their game. She watched him when he entered. No one trailed him in, and he made no eye contact with anyone in the bar before his arrival. However, she was sure it was only a matter of time before the rest of the gang would be knee-deep in her business—considering they had all swarmed on Louisiana like an unwelcome infestation.

"Of course, lover," she said, pointing to the bench seat across from her. "But over there, so I can look into those beautiful eyes of yours. You don't want me to get a neck crick, do you, Love?"

"You asked for this meeting," he said as he slid into the seat opposite her. "I'm not in the mood for any of your shit today."

"You sound cross, Sunny-love. Are you angry with me?" she said in a fake, sweet voice.

He didn't take his eyes from her. She now wore a white drama mask that covered everything but her lips, which were the same shade that had been cleaned from his mirror. She had purple and gold glitter bursts around her eyes, and big purple, gold, and green feathers streamed from one side. The mask must have been waiting for her in the booth. He never understood why she felt the need to play this part of her game. He knew every part of her face.

"Please place your hands on the table where I can see them," Silas commanded, as he got as comfortable as he could possibly get under the circumstances. After the last few meetings with her, she had left him feeling a bit gun-shy, and he thought he should be on top of his game tonight. She was up to something. He could feel it.

She remembered his eyes from their first night the most. They were deep, like the calm of an ocean, sometimes with just a hint of white-blue that made them sparkle against the darkness. For a second, she thought she could be in love with a man like him. Then she laughed, catching herself, knowing that she was probably not capable of love. Her lips turned up into a smile at his request.

"That's my boy," she said as she laughed out loud. "Always thinking."

She sat down her drink and stretched out her hands, wiggling her fingers as she advanced them forward. Palms up first. Then she rotated them over and placed them palms down on the table, just inches from his hands, resting on the table.

"See, Deputy. I got nothing up my sleeves," she said coyly as she slowly moved a hand toward him and placed it on top of one of his. "Did you miss me, Sunshine?"

He watched her as she lightly circled the top of his hand with the tip of her index finger, but he didn't pull his hand away. He's not sure what kind of game she's playing at, but he was all in. The confidence she displayed was remarkable. She was both a psychopath and unlike any other woman he had ever encountered. The last time he saw her, she wore her hair in a short black bob and a short red dress that barely covered her curves. Tonight, she was wearing a black Vera Wang dress with bell sleeves and a V-cut that exposed the edges of her breasts and cut just below her navel, featuring a small ruby gem. He found it interesting that it was the only piece of jewelry she wore besides the tiny cross around her neck.

He noticed the short, unpainted fingernails as he looked her over. This explained why she left no evidence behind. She was a pro and good at what she did—brutal, methodical and clean. He wondered if he could stop her without killing her. There was a small part of him that wished for her death, knowing without a doubt that she would not stop her brutal destruction on the world, but he was unsure if he could be the one to do it. He has grown fond of her despite the many things she has done.

"Why am I here, Baby?"

"What? No foreplay? Sunshine doesn't seem so sunny tonight," she said, pouting out her lip and taking a sip of her drink. Seeing that he wasn't going to respond, "Fine," she said next. "A little birdy told me that she was meeting with a reporter who didn't show up last week. Someone you may know?" Her eyebrows raised, questioning him with an inquisitive challenge. "A friend's sister, perhaps? Or maybe a sheriff's daughter?"

Silas's eyes didn't change, but she saw the tiniest shift in the way he sat and the slight worry that made the black of his eyes widen in shape, and the white edges turning color.

"A little bird, huh? Do you care to share the name of this little birdy?" he asked, trying to hold his interest in her words.

Baby could tell she had his attention then. She saw the intrigue in his body language as he shifted his weight from side to side. She could see him weighing out his options. He could stay and listen to what she had to say, or he could get up and walk out. But the situation would remain the same. They had too many dead girls on their hands. Only, she knew there were five, and that's just in Louisiana in the past seven months. If they looked closer, they'd find another three in Bossier City, Dry Prong, and Slidell. All women who had gone missing while a certain someone should have been protecting and serving. This isn't information she'd share, though. Silas had his own ideas, and she didn't want to spoil it for him.

"Why would your birdy want a meeting with this particular reporter?" he finally asked. "She's barely out of uni." He knew he wouldn't be going anywhere now. There was too much at stake, and he needed to know what she would do next. He knew what reporter had gone missing. And it worried him even more that she knew it, too.

"To hear tell it, she's interested in spinning quite a little tale about the life and times of the most infamous Baptiste families. What do you suppose she'd have to say?"

Silas eyed her intently. He mulled over her words and wondered where she was going with it all. Her Dublin accent was rather good, and he wondered how long it had taken her to perfect the nuances of each word's melodic pronunciation and the emphasis on certain letters that brought out the specifics that made it a proper Dublin area accent.

"We could be great partners," she said to him seductively. "We could find out together," she hummed with a shrug.

She had already slipped off a heel and was rubbing her foot up the inside of his leg. She stopped only when her foot rested in a deep crevice between the bulge of his jeans and his upper thigh. She could feel his body stiffen up against her. Unsure of her intentions—her eyes smiled bashfully at him, but he saw through her.

The corners of his mouth turned up in a smirk as he picked up his drink and drank down the remaining contents of the glass. He didn't push her foot away. Instead, he pushed into her, causing her foot to be trapped awkwardly between his legs. He wouldn't give her the satisfaction of letting her know she had gotten to him. He also didn't have to say anything. She already knew that he wanted her.

"I have a partner," he said. "You remember her, right?"

She didn't answer the question right away. Instead, she tugged her foot from where it had been pinched and placed it firmly back on the floor. Her face now donned a pouty lip again. He had turned the tables on her. He had finally gotten a reaction that didn't seem practiced and controlled. He could tell by the flash in her eyes that she was angry, but still, the innocent way she looked at him didn't leave her face.

"It's just a matter of time," he thought. "Just a matter of time."

"How is Sister these days?" she asked with a bored slump of her shoulders while rolling her eyes in a fake mean-girl way. All that was missing was the smack of bubble gum while she twisted the sweet stickiness around her finger. She had taken on the appearance of a bored 1980s teenage girl. "Had any meltdowns in the middle of a road lately? I don't think our girl is doing so well being back home. Do you?"

"You would know, I'd imagine. You seem to keep pretty good tabs on her. How is she doing from where you sit? Is she keeping it together?" he asked, watching for a sign—any sign.

"I think our girl is batshit crazy myself," she said in a long-drawn-out laugh. "That press conference had been an absolute shit show. Seeing the look on McTavish's face when that reporter called her out was all I could do to hold it in. I thought Sister was going to shit out a kidney right there at the podium. Her entire body shook like a junkie needing a fix. She's really lost her shit. She was embarrassing us. I'm trying to work with her, but another stunt like that, and I'll have to take over."

"Are you listening to yourself?" Silas groaned, trying to stop the pounding in his head and thinking how much he wanted to choke the life from Baby when she started talking like this. Protecting Sister had been his priority, and he hated it when Baby seemed to find new ways of getting her killed.

"She is fucking nuts, and you lot know it. She got crazy, jumping from tree to tree in that head of hers. And that finger-tapping thing she does—one, two, three," she counted mockingly. "Oh, and that fucking rubber band has got to hurt like hell? Constantly snapping herself with it. And y'all say I'm sadistic? She is cray cray, Sunny-love," she continued, circling her finger around her ear. "Her bell ain't ringin' all the way to the top, Love. You know what I mean? Loco. Folle. Pazza! See what I did there," she said in a proud childish giggle. "I can say crazy in four languages," while she held up and pushed forward at him, four fingers for him to count. "Four."

"That's very impressive," he said, slowly clapping his hands at her. "Bravo. See what I did there?" he asked, giving her a look that caused her to roll her eyes again and the smile to drop from her face. "And you are no one to talk about anyone's crazy being on the loose. You're missin' four out of five strings on that banjo of yours yourself."

"Ouch," she said in faux indignation. "You're absolutely no fun, Sunny-love," she huffed in another pout, as a naughty smile crept across her face. She lifted her foot, slid it again at him beneath the table, and pushed the heel of her foot into the right side of his abdomen, just below his last rib. "Does it still hurt, my love?"

He sat up quickly and pushed her foot to the floor. It didn't exactly hurt, but he was now good and pissed off that she had the nerve to even gone there. The look he gave her could have killed her twice over where she sat, and she covered her mouth with both hands to muffle her laugh.

"I'm so sowry," she said in a baby voice as she giggled. "Too soon?"

"You are one crazy fucking bitch," he said, sitting up straighter, while the anger visibly overtook his features. What the fuck are you up to? Why are you here? I mean, I know why you are here, but why—?" he growled quietly through his teeth, just loud enough for her to hear. He could feel his face grow hot, and the vein in the side of his neck began to throb. He took a deep breath and tried to calm himself. He thought about Sister and the finger-tapping thing she did that drove them all batshit themselves. But he almost understood why she did it. It was to keep her from killing everyone in broad daylight. He considered it as he glared at Baby.

"I said I was sorry."

"You fucking shot me. How do you think it feels? You shot me, and Sister is the one who took the fall."

"If she hadn't wandered off course, I wouldn't have had to shoot you," she said, her eyes were now big and faultless. "Besides, you assholes turned her loose on the world way before she was ready, and I had to pick up the pieces. It's not my fault she liked to fly the dragon," she said, holding her arms out like a kite. "I'm the one who got her out of the gutter. I'm the one who got her clean. You bunch of dickheads just used her to get in tight with another bunch of dickheads and got her fucked—literally. Didn't any of you assholes consider just maybe she was just a bit too good at being someone else? McTavish knew what had happened to her. Yet, he allowed her to take those jobs. What did he think would happen teaching her all that shit? He created a one-man army. Acting like everything was okay, just because she didn't remember what happened to her. Aligning herself with those men, so you all could get slaps on the back. You deserved that bullet," she said, crossing her arms across her chest like an indignant child in satisfaction and smirking at him. "I got another one for you and the rest of them if you get in my way."

"You are going to get Sister killed. We are a team. We all make sacrifices. Dammit, Baby! I won't allow it. Can't you see what you've done to her life? Hasn't she been through enough without your bullshit? You are killing people, and it will come back on her. Can't you see the path you've put her on? What will happen when McTavish finds out what you or she has done? What do you think Bishop will have to do when he finds out? You don't care what vengeance will do to her?"

"Sacrifices, my ass. She's asked to do whatever it takes to get it done. I don't see you giving out blowjobs to get in good with that Anderson guy, now do I?" she said, making the gesture to make a point. "You knew what she was doing, and she started drowning herself in booze and pills - shooting herself up to get through the day or night. Anything to numb her mind. All those secrets, Sunny-love.

They have a way of coming out in the end. I'm not hiding anymore, and I won't let her either. I'll take us both down to get what I want."

"I didn't fucking know what had happened to her in the beginning. I wouldn't know now if it weren't for you. We all do this job because of someone or something. Some of us are hiding, and some just like the gig. But what we don't do is pry into each other's lives. We don't sit around braiding each other's hair and telling sob stories. One thing is for sure: your need for revenge has crossed the line, Baby!"

"It's justice! Get off the fucking soapbox, you twat. Is it vengeance when you go outside the law to catch and kill a target or a suspect? You can call them 'cases' all you want," she said, her fingers in quotation marks, "but you know damn well it's nothing more than a sanctioned hit. It's murder, no matter how many pretty fucking bows you tie it up in. Very few of them see a courtroom. How many of them have you killed yourself, you self-righteous prick? It's fucking justice served up in vengeance. I will kill every last fucking one of them for what they did to us!" she said as she slammed a hand on the tabletop. "Sister is weak. She nearly killed us both with her weakness. She chooses to forget. And then pulls her, poor woe-is-me, shit. I can't remember the faces...blah, blah, blah. Well, I do remember their faces, and I only have two more of those motherfuckers left. Greer McTavish being taken was the best damn thing to happen. Your sniveling Sister would never have returned here if Greer hadn't gone missing. That old bastard wouldn't have called in the big dogs otherwise. Not too hard to figure out who his favorite is."

Silas was now standing. She had finally made her intentions clear to him. Though he hadn't ever wanted to see it—not really. His insides were tortured. How could he have such feelings for a woman who was capable of such madness? His hands balled into fists as he kept the weight of his body onto the tops of his knuckles and pressed hard into the table. His body was now hovering over Baby's head as she looked up at him squarely in the face. The determination and lack of fear further fueled his anger. "What the fuck did you do, Baby?!" he asked, barely holding back the urge to strike her. "What did you do? Where is Gears?"

Baby sat back against the bench top and remained calm. Everything she did was thought out, weighed, measured, and precise. She had gotten extremely good at reading people. Playing the chess game that McTavish taught so well, she could almost predict every move as he did. Almost. There was always the unpredictable human aspect to some outcomes. Some emotions caused people to react differently, which could muddy things up for her.

"I did nothing. You can't possibly blame me for everything going up-shit-down in everyone's world—including the untouchable McTavish clan. Greer McTavish is a fine young reporter looking to finish uni with her name on a byline. She's ambitious, intelligent, and just happened to fall into one helluva story, that's all. What better story is there than the one that single-handedly solves the brutal attack on a young undercover rookie cop and a nun left to die in a barrel? And they're related. Plus, the tot was there! I mean, honestly, can you imagine? I'm a talking Pulitzer! Am I right? You just can't make this kinda shit up! What investigative reporter would pass on this?"

"Come on! Honestly Sunny-love. I had nothing to do with this one. But I can't say I'm disappointed in the outcome. I mean, she is McTavish's daughter. She's like a puppy with a new bone. And I'll be there to make the heads roll when it is time," she said, with a smirk and the face of the devil in her expression. "I got myself a new axe, too," she said, licking her thumb and running it down the edge of an imaginary axe blade. "And please don't make me have to kill ya, my love. That would break my heart if I had one. I haven't spilled innocent blood yet. And we both know you are not all that innocent," she continued with a knowing nod that made Silas sit back and take pause with her words. "You know my secrets, and I know yours too."

He had never been afraid of her. But something about her now gave him time to rethink that. She had never been this open about what she was doing. They had never discussed her plans and how Sister fit into them. He honestly never really considered just how far she was willing to go. He had the protection of those much bigger than either of them. So did she in many ways. Those who employed her kept their team in fat checks as well. What struck him the most was that she couldn't do what she did without a bit of help from the powers that be, and that also worried him. Who else knew of the connection between

Baby and Sister? If he had put it all together, couldn't they as well? He wasn't the brightest bulb in the pack, so it stood to reason that someone else knew. Sister wasn't a part of what Baby was doing. But she would be the one to take the fall once everyone figured out what was really going on. He had a feeling that McTavish and that doctor of hers wouldn't be able to protect her forever.

GREED, GLUTTONY, ENVY & WRATH

PRESENT DAY - BABY

"Baby? Are you awake?"

"Yes, Greer."

"How do you know me?" she asked quietly.

I could tell by the way she asked that she had some idea, but she couldn't bring herself to say it just yet. "You called me Gears, and I don't think that was by accident. You seem like you've got your shit together. I don't think you'd make that kind of mistake. You're too familiar. At least enough to know what my family calls me. You want me to remember you, right?"

I wanted to tell her everything, but not out of some sort of kinship—but out of the need to get a reaction. I wanted that 'Ta-Da!' moment, where I stepped into the light and was like, "Do you see me?" I lived in the shadows while the men who destroyed all their lives walked around free. She had only been a child. In many ways, she still was. And after I got my pound of flesh, her world would never be the same.

She would most likely lose any ground she had gained in healing from the past. I knew that, and I wished that I cared. But I didn't. She was so close to putting it all together on her own. Perhaps, I would become her Boogeyman in the end. Only time would weigh that out. Hopefully, the scales would balance in my favor, but it wouldn't bother me if they didn't.

Instead of answering her question, I asked, "Would you like me to finish our story?"

"That's not an answer," she replied. "But I haven't anywhere else to go."

"Ambassador Jonathan Hadley had been invaluable in finding the others. As soon as I was able, I caught the first flight out, landing in Houston, and took a flight attendant job on a private flight to Dallas. Rich Carter, I call Greed, because he would be the second one to die. His wife Olivia had just been a bonus. Before judging me, you must know she wasn't a good person."

After Hadley gave me the names of the other five men in his house, I looked up each one. I was happy to see that they had all thrived in the lives they had made for themselves. Carter married into a wealthy family; his wife had inherited a substantial fortune. I must admit, he was the most difficult one to get to. You wouldn't think so, but he's a paranoid son of a bitch. I'd probably enjoyed killing him the most. How do you kill three people on a plane without ever being seen?"

"You crashed the plane," she said without missing a beat. "The Carter crash was headlines for weeks," she added.

"But first, you bail out," I said, smiling. "How exciting was that? Talk about having the wind whipping through your hair."

She understood the assignment. She'd eventually figure this out without me saying it. I let the gears turn as I continued to explain how they all died.

"Richard Carter was an arrogant man, with a small mind and an ego that insisted on others calling him Rich instead of Dick. I personally preferred the latter. I'm sure you can gauge that one for yourself. His pilot was also onboard, of course. And before you get your knickers all sorta out over him, he wasn't an innocent, either."

"He hadn't even filed a flight plan. That can only mean one thing—they were up to dirty business. He had ties to a cartel out of Mexico City. With a little effort, finding out what watch list he was on wasn't too hard. I don't feel bad about him."

I wondered if I'd feel the same as Hadley, but the anger grew deep inside me when I realized Dick didn't recognize my face. I even placed my fingers on the scar under my eye—just to see if it clicked for him. I got nothing, which festered the growth even darker within my pit. He slapped my ass when he passed by me, and I nearly gutted him like a hog while we were still on the ground. That would have ruined my plans, so I just smiled. While I poured him a drink, she watched as he ran a hand up my leg. She seemed to enjoy the unwanted attention as humor danced in her eyes. But the smirk she gave me told me that she thought I had a price. That set my teeth on edge, and I had considered stripping her nakked nd tossing her out the door then. But I stayed the course.

Olivia's crimes involved using her charity program for after-school kids and collecting the girls for him. She had been doing it for years and getting away with it. She deserved to burn in the flames.

I left them alive as they plummeted back to earth in a spiraling death roll. I wanted them to understand what was happening. I wanted them to feel the terror of not being able to do a damn thing about what was going to happen. The flames would melt away their skin like marshmallows if they survived the fall. Either way, the fear alone would have been a good death.

"So, what, you only crashed the plane?" Greer asked. "That doesn't seem to have the dramatic flair you thrive on."

I let Olivia think I was more into her than her husband. Once I had her tied to her chair, I moved to his lap. He smiled like a horny teenage boy. Even with me sitting face-to-face with him, he still had no idea who I was. Once my knife came out, the color drained from his fat cheeks. His fear excited me, and I couldn't wait to get back home to my man.

We discussed their crimes, and he was surprised when I introduced myself. They cried and cried some more. Then, the pleading started. His tears dried and faded into shock as he considered what I was about to do. I know he didn't see that coming. I peeled the skin from his face and stuck it to the glass of the window so he could look at himself. So that he could stare into the face of the same man who thought it was okay to spit on me, bite me and disgrace me because he thought I was nothing but a paid whore. He thought I was beneath him. I can still feel the bite in the muscle. The Doc assures me the feeling isn't there, but I can see it and feel it. She called it a phantom pain. But there's nothing phantom about it.

Gears was quiet for a moment, probably thinking over my conduct. Then she asked, "Does any part of you understand that what you are doing is wrong? I mean, I understand why you would want to do this, but it sounds like you need help. I knew someone who had suffered the same as you. When I was a child, someone I loved was murdered. Later, I learned she had been brutalized in a way that no woman should endure. I don't know why that happened to her. But becoming a monster yourself isn't the answer. I mean, it can't be."

"What do you think your loved one would have done had she survived and had the opportunity that I have?" I asked. "Do you think she would've walked away?"

"My father would have helped her. He can help you. He's a good man. His team finds bad people all the time. I want to help you, Baby. I can tell your story. You must stop now. You said that you had two more, right? Can't you let them be and tell the police who they are? Tell my father who they are," she said desperately. The sadness in her voice was caught in her throat as she fought back tears. "I don't hear the brutality in your story, Baby. I hear the pain and emptiness of justice you deserve forgotten about. I hear you crying out for help."

I wanted to laugh at that. There was no desperate cry in any part of my body. But I didn't want to piss all over her attempt at a sencere understanding, so instead, I asked her, "Why do you think you are here? Do you think the man who took you was just driving along and said, 'Hey, why not?'—drove his car onto your sidewalk, broke you, drugged you, and then placed you in here? Do you think he went through all that just for that? Like a target of opportunity? Or would the smart answer be because you messed up?"

"How would I have messed up?" she demanded. "What do you think I did? Seriously?"

"You started asking questions about your aunt's death. You can't be so naive as to miss the connection. Just think about that while I finish with what happened to the next three. Maybe that will help you put all those pieces together you got floating around in that head of yours."

Wraith, Envy, and Gluttony were up next. They were the easiest to take, but by far the most remote. Locating them had been relatively simple. There aren't that many highways to choose from, and because of their connection, all three had made headline news when one posted a photo of them taking their first caribou on Instagram. One of their family relatives had shared it with the world. The photo had a nice picture of the Brooks Mountain Range.

You can't even imagine the level of luck I felt at seeing that. Within hours, I was making my way down the Dalton Highway. I hear it has some of the best caribou hunting around. I don't go in for that sort of thing, though. I prefer hunting things that might wanna fight back. One thing was for sure: that road isn't for amateurs. It's isolated and has only a few amenities around. You really gotta go in prepared.

It took me a full day of driving and a 4-wheeler to find them. Lucky for me, they were the only ones out there. I reckon arriving two days ahead of the season had its advantages. I honestly thought they'd pack it in and head to the nearest lodge when the weather turned. But they were determined to stick it out. I liked that. They didn't seem too quick to get outta Dodge, but I knew they had a plane heading back to pick them up eventually. So, I couldn't mess around.

A .308 made quick work of slowing down the first two. Donald Jacobson and his brother, Merv the Perv. Wrath and Envy. They owned a chain of hardware stores throughout Oregon and Washington—churchgoers with families. Merv had been suspected as the local Midnight Peeper, but no one could prove it. But I could. And his brother always alibied him. That made him just as bad, knowing what his brother was doing. I had considered using something that could leave a bigger hole, but the canvas was so beautiful out there—all that white. So, I went for the knees. I had plans for them. I wasn't so daft that I'd just walk right in there. I figured handicapping them first would give me the advantage.

"Don't you feel for their families? You are ruining people's lives with your need for this twisted revenge," she said in a low voice. It hadn't been judgmental—but rather more loaded in pity. I just wasn't sure if it was meant for me or them.

"No, I do not. They and their buddy, Grant Pritchard, earned that death. I left Grant lying next to them. I got him while he was walking back to camp after bagging up their illegal caribou. He actually took off running in the wrong direction when he saw me coming towards him. I don't know where he thought he was going," I snorted out laughing. "We are in the middle of fucking nowhere. No, I didn't feel bad for them or their families. They set the terms of the game when they left us to die in that swamp."

Once I caught him, he flopped to his knees and started crying and begging me to spare him. He offered me money. Can you imagine? Where would a man like him get that kind of money? Clearly, he was dirty. I guess he just didn't understand my determination to see him dead. Money couldn't buy that. The tears froze on his face while he sobbed. That only made my gut hurt more. The sight of him begging me to let him live was grotesque. So much for the decorated hero, huh? He died like the coward he was."

"Grant?" Greer asked. "Why do I know that name?"

"He was only a detective with CID, working narcotics, back then," Baby said. "But you probably know him as a captain with the LSP."

"Captain Grant Pritchard is a friend of my father's," she said, almost on the verge of tears. "I've known him since I was a child. I think he was also friends with my mother or something. A few years younger, I believe. But I'm sure he's known to the family.

"That they were," I said, wondering if she was getting any closer to drawing those lines. Grant was considered a good guy back then.

"How can I understand you killing people the way you do, Baby? I don't understand how that makes you better?"

Hearing her upset, a part of me was glad that I hadn't gone further into detail about what I had done to them. They were dead, and that's all she needed to know.

"Again, you're not a dumb girl, Greer. It'll come to you. And when it does, you'll have your answers, and you'll understand me. Even if you can't agree with me, you'll understand."

"I'll never understand this. You killed someone I know. This is insanity."

"Every life I've taken was forfeited the moment they crossed the line. I didn't feel bad when I did it, and even with some reflection, I don't feel bad now. If that makes me the psychopathic killer, then I'm okay with that, Greer."

"Your father once said that once I took a life, there'd be no going back. That it couldn't be undone. No reverse. No do-overs. That almost everyone becomes a different version of themselves—often unrecognizable. Something about the risks of my soul turning black and twisting itself up so much so that I wouldn't be able to bear the image of myself in a mirror. Do you know what I say to that? Fuck 'em all."

"I am not real. They made sure of that when they destroyed our lives. I have learned many things over the years. My need is not to seek righteousness but revenge. It's a reckoning that's coming for them, and it has fueled my fire. I have no intention of allowing a single one of them to enter the halls of Valhalla. They did not and will not die as warriors. I will not test their courage or resolve. I only want to hear their screams. I want their pain to be violent and bloody. I want the world to hear their cries. I want them all to die brutally and without honor. My Gods seek this. Yours does not."

"Baby," she said, "God had nothing to do with what happened to you."

"Maybe not, but he did nothing to stop it either."

TAHLEQUAH

"Over here," Bishop heard the woman say, with a wave of her hand. In the middle of a dining room, the woman sat alone, sipping on what appeared to be a martini. The table had been situated in the center of the interior walls and steps from the main bar. If Bishop were a betting man, which he wasn't, he'd say this was a power move. Sitting in the middle of an open room like a baited snare conveyed a confidence that if one wanted to do harm, they wouldn't get close enough.

By lunch, Bishop had skipped out, leaving Charlee and Silas to interview the girls in the photos alone while he boarded a plane headed Northwest. He jumped at the opportunity when he found a message left behind for him in the seat of his truck.

"If you want answers, be at the airport by noon. Your ticket is waiting. Follow the instructions left for you. Tell no one. You won't be disappointed. See you soon."

She was dressed in blue jeans and a pink hoodie with the words "Lake Hair Don't Care" printed across the front. She was a striking woman, her hair pulled up casually and her makeup applied subtly. He thought she was an attractive woman the first time he saw a picture of her standing next to her husband on the Senate website. That picture was of a mature woman dressed in an expensive suit with polished hair and posed assertively beneath the Oklahoma State Seal, nothing like the woman sitting in front of him now. She looked more youthful than in the photo, though perhaps a bit more tired.

The file he held also included a photo of her, a photo of her with her husband, and a photo of their teenage daughter. He should have had his head examined because a sane man would have at least thought about finding out who he was meeting before traveling on a highway to the middle of nowhere on the outskirts of a national park to meet a stranger. It's a good thing he did his homework before getting on the plane.

As she waved, he could see a slight hesitation in her gesture. She had an uncertainty about her movements. But her eyes told him she'd bury him under the porch if he dared. She obviously knew him by sight, which he found interesting yet disconcerting. Considering he was practically a nobody, but with their family connection and his seven degrees of separation from McTavish, he shouldn't be surprised that she would look him up. She had once been Oklahoma's AG and the wife of a governor. Collecting intel on him had to be a hell of a lot easier for her than it had been for him. Surprisingly, there wasn't all that much on her before college.

The drive was beautiful, but he was taken aback by the destination she had picked for their private conversation. It was isolated. He wouldn't have taken her for the "babes in the woods" type. He could have just as easily met her at her office or home. Her need for secrecy prompted him to think of many things. As his mind drifted to what McTavish's team did for a living and all the secrets that seemed to follow them around like unwanted strays, he thought perhaps she often met her adversaries in such places. He wondered how many of them found their way out of these woods and back to safety. And just how many of them had become part of the ecosystem? He still might end up that way, after McTavish found out what he was up to.

Once in flight, he took that time to flip through the files, reading the incident reports, witness statements, follow-up statements, and search efforts to locate the assailants responsible for the attacks that had occurred the weekend, rookie vice cop Caroline Doucet and the nun Sister Mary Charles had been found. There wasn't much in the file. The basics had been covered, but very little of anything else had been completed, let alone documented. It was only pure chance that he had these files on him, and after seeing the woman's face, he was glad that he did.

It wasn't a secret that Charlee was a former Sister, but to find out that she was the daughter of the Daily Duo, who had been murdered years earlier, had done something to him. Just another wedge she had daggered through their relationship. He was aware that McTavish had sent Sister to Europe. However, the bigger picture hadn't been part of their intimate exchange of information. She had left out a lot about herself and her family. He now understood that the bits and pieces she had given him were intentionally meant to be vague and lead nowhere. He wanted to believe that she had done it to protect her parents. But he had shared every detail of his life with her—not wanting barriers between them. When he broke it all down to its most basic foundation, he found it had crumbled to nothing. She hadn't trusted him enough to tell him the truth about herself.

LJ Daily had left instructions that he not deviate from her plan. He picked up the car left for him at the terminal and headed west, three hours to a town called Tahlequah off Highway 51. Once on the road, he didn't understand why he couldn't have flown into Tulsa, given that it was closer to the address left in the car. He wasn't even sure how to pronounce the name, but decided it was best not to try. Especially if he had to converse with the locals. If there were locals, he doubted the name he had in his head was anywhere near what he had worked out in its pronunciation.

"I wondered when we would finally meet," Bishop said curiously, extending a hand that she accepted. "I am surprised by it, however," he continued, eyeing her suspiciously. "So, what's the proper protocol here? Do I call you Mrs. Daily or Senator?"

She smiled at him, but the smile only seemed to mask her unease. "You can drop the polite bullshit with me, Mr. Bohannon, and call me LJ," she said briskly.

"Okay, Senator, it is. I must admit, this is a surprise," he said, eyebrows raised questioningly.

"I figured it was time we met," she remarked, almost as if she wasn't sure it was a good idea.

"I have a lot of questions," he said. "About Kathryn, that is. Or Sister Mary Charles. Hell, I'm not exactly sure what the protocol is there, either—or the proper title and form. Which would you prefer?"

"She is Kathryn or Kate to us. She'll always be that to us. Her name change did not change that. We gave her that name at birth. I don't see why that should change to suit the Catholic doctrine, do you?"

"No, ma'am. I never understood the practice myself," Bishop said honestly. "I'm a Southern Baptist, so we aren't exactly driving in the same lane. We may all get to heaven, but I don't see us all living on the same street," he laughed. "Can I get you another drink?" Sitting down, Bishop could feel the hostility in her words, and he waved over the bartender, hoping that with enough alcohol, maybe the senator would be more pliable. "I'll have a bourbon Coke, and another martini for the lady," he said. Maybe another drink would smooth out her prickled edges and decrease the emotional toll that was about to be paid. However, he wasn't all that sure which of the two would be putting in more of the payment.

After a moment of watching her with the bartender, it wasn't too hard to figure out why she had picked this location. She had an ally here––or an accomplice. However the relationship, they were familiar. The glances and secret looks of communication between the two were not missed, and Bishop felt their personal connection. With the man constantly at his back, he'd need to keep his head on a swivel.

"If you don't mind, please leave your gun with Samuel. You won't be needing it here. Just place it on the bar, if you will," she instructed.

"I'm not in the habit of giving up my weapon, Senator," he said, eyeing them both cautiously.

"And I don't make it a habit of asking twice, Mr. Bohannan."

Bishop surveyed the room, looking for anything out of place. It would be easy enough for another person to hide among the empty tables and dark corners. The stuffed and mounted game trophies were placed throughout the room, but not in an overbearing manner. The establishment wore a rustic backwoods hunting cabin look, yet also had a modern feel. The white linens made the place seem less like a family hunting shack and more clubhouse chic. The bone serving sets and crystal glass gave it a classier atmosphere than the outside exterior had conveyed.

Once Bishop was assured that the senator and the bartender were the only two others in the room, he did as asked. He pulled his Glock from its holster, dropped the magazine, and racked away the unspent ammo before placing it on the table. Then he put the bullet and the magazine in his pocket.

"Thank you," she said. "It's for my protection. I'm sure you can understand. Was it difficult to find the place?" she asked.

"No, the instructions were fine," he answered, raking his eyes one last time over his weapon, thinking that leaving it there went against thirty years of training before turning to look at her.

"Good. I often spend my time here, and thought it would be a good place to get to know one another. We own the property and that cabin there," she said, pointing out the big window towards the water. "It's quiet and out of the way. But close enough so I don't have to cook or make my own drinks," she smiled with a light laugh. "It's funny, really. I used to hate coming here. I preferred the city, or my office. I'm a workaholic and every bit the politician," she confessed with a faint smile of remorse. "But this was Kate's favorite place," she said, with a broad smile that finally reached her eyes at the memory. "My husband inherited the place from his family, and well, Kate loved to come here and hang out with her cousins," she said solemnly. "And a few times over the years, we'd meet up with an old friend I grew up with. Her daughter was about the same age as Kate. Well...," she waved off and sighed again. "That was another time, wasn't it?" She shifted slightly in her seat before asking directly, "What can I do for you, Mr. Bohannan? Or would you like me to start first?"

He wanted to point out that she had initiated this clandestine interlude and that perhaps she should start, but if she were willing to let him question her first, then he would not object. He could also mention that he was an Under-Sheriff or Deputy, rather than a Mr., but again, he thought better of it, figuring it best not to come across as confrontational.

Bishop pulled out the file and slid it over to her. "I came into possession of this a few days ago, and it's not so much about what's in the file but what isn't. It appears that nothing has been accomplished. There's no lead investigator listed. Aside from Kate's written statement, the rest of the statements are all over the place.

The toxicology, the sexual assault reports, and the forensic data sheet are all missing. It is ambiguous at best. It's like amateur hour at the Apollo. It states that you demanded Sheriff McTavish be removed from your daughter's investigation and requested that the state police take over. I don't understand why you would do that. But then, there's nothing. No forward movement. It appears as if it all just went away. I don't know how that is possible when a damn cop was left for dead. Let alone, given at the time, the daughter of a former AG and a governor was left for dead. Why was the ball dropped on this? Why haven't you been beating down the doors to find out who did this to your daughter?"

"Do you smoke, Mr. Bohannon?" she asked, shifting in her seat.

Seeing her skin turn gray under his questions, he wanted to feel some way about her lack of an answer, but instead, he just shook his head no. "No, ma'am. I do not smoke," he said coolly.

"Of course, you don't," she said, rolling her eyes at him. "I should have expected as much. You seem like the type of man who played everything black and white. I watched you stroll in here. All cocky, with your tail feathers wagging behind you. You are a very confident man, but your walk stiff and brittle. You probably starch your socks," she said dismissively.

Turning away from Bishop, annoyed, she raised a hand to get the bartender's attention. "Samuel, if you could please bring me a cigarette, I would appreciate it."

"Sorry, Miss Love, you know I can't do that," he said, smiling nervously and shaking his head. "No ma'am. I reckon not. You told me not to give you another smoke, ever. You're quittin', remember? You said you'd fire me. I kinda like my job, ma'am. So, no. No smokes."

Then he stopped drying the glass he'd been twisting around a towel during their conversation and walked towards them. He pulled a bottle of Precious Vodka off the shelf and poured her a shot. The bottle was crystal with something that appeared blue, like a sapphire gem encased in the top. Bishop hadn't seen a bottle like it before, but guessed it wasn't cheap.

"Miss Love, I don't have any weed either," he offered up, grinning slyly at her. "Before you ask, that is. But I'll get you some sapphire. Do you want the man to have one?" he asked, not looking at Bishop as if he didn't have a say in what she wanted.

"What about it, Mr. Bohannan? Can you still do shots as you did back in high school, or are you going to pretend to sip that mixer like a ninny, while I drink myself stupid during your interrogation?"

"I didn't go to college, but I was a young Marine once," he said with a sly grin, thinking about how he had made a much better soldier than a drinker even then and amused by her use of 'interrogation.' He took the shot from her. "Whatever it takes," he thought.

The senator flipped through the file and pulled out Kate's account of what happened that night. While she read over it, her face grew dark. Her eyes narrowed in on the words, and then she read it all over again. All the while, the air in the room grew heavy. Once she had run through it for a third time, she slid the papers over to him.

"What game are we playing here, Mr. Bohannan?"

Seeing the rays of concern and mistrust on her face, he said, "I'm sorry, Senator. I don't understand what you mean."

"My daughter is dead."

Surprised by her response, Bishop replied harshly, "Ma'am, we both know that isn't true."

He couldn't believe she'd accuse him of playing games when she was clearly playing one of her own. Irritation overtook his face. Taking the statement, he looked it over for himself. This had been at least his fifth time reading Sister's statement.

"I understand the witness protection rules as much as you do. I assumed this is why we are meeting in the middle of nowhere," he said. "Once I figured out who you were, I assumed you didn't want her to know. Well, that, and because you know who I am, and I know who you are. But this is the only account of what Kate had to say about what happened that night. And from what I understand, it took almost a year to get it. They were going to place her in a new church, but she wanted a new start, doing something else. This was long before I came into the picture."

The senator tossed back another shot as a tear ran down her cheek. She quickly wiped it away and waved at Samuel to pour her and Bishop another.

"Mr. Bohannan, my daughter is dead. Like dead, dead. She was murdered—no Wit-sec, no name change, no afterlife for Kate. No future. As much as I wish it were possible, she's not living a secret life as some international globetrotting hotshot agent. I personally sat with her and held her hand while she was bathed after her autopsy. We buried her ourselves. We saw what that monster did to our baby girl. We were there when she was cremated. We were there when her ashes were interred in Guthrie with her grandparents—my husband's parents."

Bishop looked as if he was going to puke. It was like he had been punched in the gut, and he couldn't breathe.

"This doesn't make sense. I know her. I work with her. I lived with her. For fuck sake, lady, I am married to her," he said as he stood up, knocking over the chair. "What game are you playing at? Are you going to tell me that this isn't your daughter?" he said, digging out his wallet and pulling out a picture of him with Charlee, placing it in front of her. "Tell me this isn't your daughter?"

She held up a hand to stop Samuel's advancement, seeing the distress on Bishop's face and the need to protect her on Samuel's. She didn't know if Bishop was the type to lose his shit violently. She didn't get that impression of him, but she knew very well that Samuel was. Knowing Samuel as she did, and guessing what skill Bishop had to possess to garner McTavish's praise, her money would still be on Samuel for the win.

If she wished Bishop harm, she could have had him gone long ago, but that wasn't her style. She did not take the photo or look at it. Even when every part of her wanted to grab it and dared to believe in something she knew wasn't true. "Please sit down, Mr. Bohannon." Then, looking at Samuel, she ordered, "Pour us another one, please."

"Her name is Charlee Lovejoy," he said, stumbling through his words as if they tasted unfamiliar in his mouth. "She was a nun before she was assaulted. We call her Sister. I think Silas gave it to her. If you know of me, then I will assume you're also familiar with him. Since we are being honest," Bishop said sourly, taking the shot offered. "It started out as a joke, but she was so proud of the life she left behind that it suited her. I guess I don't know how you don't know that your daughter is still alive. I admit she didn't tell me who her parents were, but she said you were still a part of her life."

"Mr. Bohannan, do you know what my first name is?"

Confused by her question, he could only stare at her. "Uh, no, ma'am," he said, finally after thinking about it, shaking his head and stumbling to sit back down. "I guess I don't."

"That's good to know. I've spent a small fortune of my husband's money to ensure that any connection to my family was covered up before we got married. Samuel, can you please tell Mr. Bohannan what my name is?"

Samuel looked at her and then at Bishop. "Miss Love's real name is Lovejoy Daily, Mr. Bohannan," Samuel said matter-of-factly and without hesitation. "No middle name—at least, I don't think so. But it's not my business in tellin' you what Miss Love's name was before hitchin' up with Mr. H. But I've known her a long time, ain't that right, Miss Love?"

"That's right—a very long time," she said, smiling fondly at him. "Thank you, Samuel."

Turning to Bishop, her features now soft and careful. She saw that he had matched her drink for drink, but he wasn't handling it as well as she was. His eyes looked sad and broken. Part of her blamed the drink, but she knew it had more to do with her crashing down his wall of pride and blowing a gaping hole through his ego. The ego that made him confident in the facts. The pride that wouldn't allow him to see that he did not have them all.

Pulling the statement towards her, she reviewed the words that had summed up her daughter's life.

"Most of what is here is true," she started. "Kate was popular with everyone, especially the boys, and she always sought validation. We hit rock bottom with her after her fourth rehab stay. It didn't matter how much she was loved or how much we tried; she was hell-bent on living fast and falling hard. She was raised in a good life, but was drawn to things that could hurt her. Men—whoever. It didn't matter."

Bishop waved over Samuel. When he reached the table to pour another shot, Bishop said, "Just leave the bottle. I can pour for the both of us, thanks." He then told her, "You talk, Senator, I'll pour."

"Miss Love?" Samuel asked in confirmation.

"Thank you, Samuel. We'll be okay," she said. "Please set up the guest room for Mr. Bohannan at the cabin. He'll be staying with us tonight."

Smiling at Bishop, she replied, "That's a deal." Then she tossed back the shot.

"I called my friend, Rene. You may know her as Mother Agnes Valentine, and I confessed my frustration with Kate's path. We grew up together, and I figured she could help me. Rene specialized in addiction, and I think she was a lot like Kate. I didn't expect Kate to make such an abrupt change, and when she left for Baptiste, my life was turned upside down. Her desire to become a nun like Rene wasn't something I saw coming. It wasn't what I had planned for her, but I wasn't this mother, either," she said, pointing to Kate's statement. "I won't say I was perfect, but I never put my daughter down. I was never good at controlling my daughter's whims. The tighter I tried to hold on, the harder she struggled to free herself. So, I let her go. There wasn't anything else I could do for her, and I knew it. Finding God saved my daughter's life, Mr. Bohannon. And I accepted it wholeheartedly."

Bishop grabbed another shot and tossed it back. He wasn't sure if he needed to drown himself or if he was quieting the noise in his head. The more he drank, the clearer the past few years became. The more she talked about the family dynamics and the ties that bind them all, the more he understood.

"So, Charlee Lovejoy took your name. Why would she do that? Are you sure that your daughter didn't make it?"

Though tenderness and sympathy had filled her eyes, sadness was competing for space between them.

"This is not my daughter's handwriting. She never made it out of that swamp alive. She lost too much blood, and the damage was just too great. No one knows when she was taken. She could have been taken from campus, as it states here, or just as easily from her bed. There is no way of knowing this. She hadn't been seen since before the weekend. I promise you, it is not my Kathryn Rene Daily. It isn't Sister Mary Charles either. Because they were one and the same. I have not spoken to McTavish since we buried the girls. And I didn't have him removed from Kate's case. He wasn't supposed to be part of it anyway. Caroline was state police. A rookie cop called up to work vice—not a sheriff's deputy. It fell under state jurisdiction. And then, it would have gone to the FBI. Kate's father would have seen to that. He wasn't beyond throwing his weight around. He wanted the responsible man's head on a pike beside his bed. But like you said, it got messed up along the way, and we still have no real answers."

THE COMPANY YOU KEEP

L J gently took Bishop's hand. She could tell that her news had shifted the direction of the conversation. A heartbroken boy had replaced the stable, confident man who had entered the room earlier.

"Samuel is the only one who gets away with calling me that, Mr. Bohannon. So, you don't go getting yourself any ideas," she said, smiling weakly as she teased, attempting to make light of the situation. "Just so you know, I would have been proud to call you my son-in-law. You would have been good for our Kate, I think—had she made that choice. But also, I think you were probably not so good for your Charlee. Though I am sure that's not your doing."

After some thought, she finally offered, "My family name is Monroe, Mr. Bohannon." She watched his eyes to see how that news would settle. Recognition flashed in his glazed look as he understood why that would be important information.

"My father was Henry Monroe. My mother was Miss Simone," she said quietly. "When I left home for college, I never returned. I met Harrison and separated myself from my family to protect him. He was headed for politics, and I couldn't allow generations of illegal activity to affect him. I was embarrassed, really—probably more ashamed. I can admit that now. It was more for myself. It was so much easier to do back then—becoming someone new, reinventing yourself. Not so much now, is it?" she said wistfully, knowing just how much it took in the new age of technology.

"It is definitely much harder, for sure," he replied.

"There is no secret in what my family was involved in, or the Doucets for that matter. It's openly celebrated these days. Miss Simone was the Old Queen of Baptiste, and she loved to hold court. The Monroe and Doucet names carry a great deal of influence in Marie Anjou County, as I'm sure you are aware. Miss Simone sent me off to college with a hope and a prayer. She thought having a lawyer in the family would be a good idea," she said with a chuckle. "Kinda like having a sheriff in her pocket." She waited to see if Bishop would bite on that before continuing. "Rene's sister-in-law, Sandra, fought tooth and nail to unseat Miss Simone, but even with that law degree of hers and the name she traded on, she couldn't quite get there. She became the city attorney, though, and that gave her a new sense of power."

"Most of the money made through the vice trade set our families up for generations. But to tell the truth, other than Miss Simone's stills, the last of our illegal deals died with our parents. And they had rules, Mr. Bohannon. The families, I mean. Both families joined together to build Baptiste. They kept the community small and manageable. Perhaps 'loyal' is a better word for it. I don't know. The two families ran everything that could be run and controlled everything that could be controlled. Everything from drugs to deli—even what crops were planted. I'm serious when I say that the two families could be linked to just about anything, except the death of Kennedy and Oswald. It's just how it was. But there were rules."

"That's no secret, for sure. But if you are Miss Simone's daughter, then that would mean that Bama and Crimson are your nephews. I didn't see you at Crimson's funeral. Or Miss Simone's."

"Again, Mr. Bohannan, there are no mysteries to be solved regarding my relationship with my family. I am grateful that she sought a better way for the last of the Monroe line, but she could have done that for her sons. Instead, I attended my brothers' funerals. As well as the rest of the men in our family, including my father. It wasn't a glamorous life, Mr. Bohannon. And nothing to be proud of. Miss Simone was a revered woman, and she wasn't as poor off as she led others to believe. The Monroes of Baptiste will go down in history someday with the likes of the Daltons and the Youngers, or it will die out and never be spoken of again. They were nothing but pirates, drug dealers, and sex peddlers. Personally, I hope the name is extinguished from the vocabulary altogether."

"You seem like a good man, Mr. Bohannon," she started to say and then paused. She wasn't sure if they should continue down this road. But if it didn't happen now, then the wounds that ate up her hometown would continue to fester, and she would never be able to rid herself of the proverbial cancer that ate at her heart. "You wouldn't be where you are if McTavish didn't trust you. He commands loyalty, doesn't he? He knows your secrets and you his? But I am curious as to why a man like McTavish, who would protect my mother's secrets and clean up her messes, would bring in a man like you. You don't have a criminal mind. You grew up on a farm. You grew up modest, and your parents are still together. You are the youngest of two brothers and one sister. All married, and you have eight nieces and nephews. You did poorly in school, but you scored high on tests. Your highest scores in the social development essay were in the areas of morality and loyalty. You had a solid career as a soldier. Retired as a gunny sergeant and then another five years in Secret Service before moving to Baptiste to work for McTavish. But I venture to guess, and this is only a guess, you were already working, in some small way, for McTavish before coming back to the States," she said through narrowed eyes. "Am I warm?"

"Since we are being candid. Yes, sort of," Bishop said cryptically, not giving a straight answer to her non-question. "I tend to believe he took me on to keep him honest. Or as honest as possible. Maybe to honor his wife? I don't know. I worked with her. She was an interpreter in our unit. That's how they met."

"Something was going on in the Parish before the girls were left in the swamp," she confided. "Miss Simone was only making moonshine, so I don't see how anything she was doing led to what happened to the girls. McTavish's wife died, he left the service of whatever organization he was with, returned her body home, and within a year of him becoming sheriff, all hell broke loose."

"Sandra and her partner, Walton, ran a homeless shelter for women off 3rd. There were complaints that some of the women had gone missing. They just up and disappeared. Kathryn told me that McTavish was informed of the missing girls and that he had passed it on to the state police. Does that sound like a man who runs a side business tracking down just that sort of shit? And we both know, he's not going to let someone else come in and yard dog his territory."

Bishop had nothing to say. He was lost in her words, and his brain felt as though it was on fire. He had to be the dumbest son of a bitch alive. And the worst kind of man. He took a cushy job, and now it might have been all so that he could help cover up something that every one of them hated more than lawyers and used car salesmen.

"Look," she said, adjusting her posture as she worked out the words that needed to be said. "Your team is, well...—well known for what you do. There are no secrets in politics. It's a 'scratch my back if I scratch yours' cesspool of vipers. People in politics have flies everywhere who hear everything. Then, we use those secrets against one another to get things done. That's how it works. Men and women like you have been the fabric of our society since civilizations became fashionable, but you are only chess pieces that are often used to your end and eventually get taken off the board. I'm sure most of you have the best intentions, and if you don't, well then, you've done your duty to your country, and it thanks you with a coffin draped with a flag and maybe a few dollars to your loved ones. Perhaps a lot of dollars if you used your position to get ahead. It happens more than anyone wants to admit. But rest assured, it usually ends with a knife in the back or a bullet to the head—especially if you mess up."

"Our government is very unforgiving when it must admit fault for anything. If you are one of the lucky ones and reach retirement, who are you then? The problem is Mr. Bohannan...—Bishop," she said, finally saying his name. "When you live in infamy and when you are willing to cross the line that many times—even in the name of justice, patriotism, and God and country, what will you do for yourself even given the time and the resources? Let's say you are a decent man, with two children, who has spent your career helping others, and then your wife is killed? The very reason you breathe—the one who makes you want to be a good man. I've spent my career getting dirty with dirtier people."

"Corruption breeds corruption, Bishop. I don't know exactly what got my daughter killed. But I never thought it was random, like our dear friend and sheriff suggested—especially knowing she was with Caroline when she was murdered. Caroline knew something about Alister McTavish. I know she did.

And I think she had something on Walton as well. He got everything except the Doucet property after she and Franklin were killed. Then Charlotte passed—and then Caroline. No one ever trusted him. Rene never trusted him."

"You're seriously suggesting that Alister McTavish is involved in this? He's a lot of things, Senator, but a murderer? Or worse, a killer of girls? He helped cover up a murder? That's a bit far out there, isn't it?" Bishop asked, but only half-heartedly.

Why hadn't it been solved? With the number of resources at his disposal? They could have tracked the bastard to hell and back. The Senator made a good point, and he knew it. "What are you going to do now?" he asked. "What is it that you want me to do? What about Sister? Charlee? Who is she to you?"

"Harrison hasn't got much longer, Bishop. He's in the final days of his life—liver cancer," she said, no longer fighting back the tears. Your Charlee may be your heartache, but she is my saving grace. I don't want Harrison to die knowing he was never able to get justice for his daughter. It destroyed him. It ruined his career, and he's nearly drunk himself to death. It's already started, Bishop. There are things in motion as we speak. Sometimes we are judged by the company we keep. I needed to know that you were not one of them. I only ask that you do not get in my way. I will not wait a minute longer. I will get answers if I must burn every inch of earth between here and that backwater shithole you call home."

HOMECOMING

Sister wasn't sure if visiting the old plantation home was a good idea. She had promised herself that everything here would stay a memory, like a milky fog that drifted in during the early morning hours but would burn itself off by noon. After Sister had dropped off McQueen at the boys' side of the church's property, she turned down the driveway towards the old plantation house, Doucet Manor.

As she drove the path, a sadness wafted in. Various colors of sunflowers lit up the path along the edges. She remembered the walk up and down from the house. Nostalgia could be a cruel mistress when half-truths overshadowed the memories. The ones we tell ourselves to cover up the things we'd rather not remember. Sister had a mind full of good times, such as those critical childhood moments like running in the fields and chasing other children. Her mother's face when she stood on the porch and called for her. The rare occurrence when her father would join them outside, and he seemed happy to do so.

She pulled the house keys from her pocket and unlocked the front door. Piles of mail blocked her way into the house. Proof that Mr. Walton's handyman wasn't coming by as often as he was being paid to do so. She scooped up the mail and entered the main room. As she piled the mail on a table by the front door, the air in her lungs released. She hadn't been in this house in a very long time and had forgotten how it smelled. The first thing that caught her was the smell of tobacco. As a child, she thought all homes would smell of applewood. Tears filled her eyes as the ghosts filled her mind with things that once were.

When she entered the main living room, she noticed that not much had changed since she left. The furniture had dated from her absence, and the dust-covered surfaces revealed the neglect that had befallen the room's beauty. But it was still the grand entry it had been intended to be.

She walked to a wall lined with photos in rows, some clustered together on the mantel and tables. These were new. This room was never meant to be sentimental. She smiled at the knowledge that Mother Agnes Valentine had, in the end, in some small measure, reclaimed her home. Sister pored over the sets of families and better times. A photo of Agnes' parents hung in the center, with the remaining pictures arranged around it. Sister ran a hand over an image of Sandra Doucet, the manor's once queen bee, holding a small boy in her arms.

To her left, her husband, Franklin, was by her side, along with their two daughters, Charlotte and Caroline. She ran a finger over Charlotte's face, and a memory of them as children entered her mind. It nearly broke her heart all over again. The sisters had fought that day. Charlotte was upset with Caroline for copying her hairstyle and demanded that she change it. The photo had been taken long before Charlotte's death. Before the death of Franklin and his little boy in a car accident. Before Sandra's battle with cancer had been lost, a year later. Before the family's tragedies piled on like a bad case of typhoid.

Next in line were photos of Charlotte Doucet with her husband, Alister McTavish, on their wedding day. The wedding had taken place in a castle in Scotland. She remembered the destination wedding and how excited she had been to have been included. She thought they were the most beautiful couple, and after their children were born, she knew they were the most beautiful family. She had never seen Charlotte happier as she picked up a photo of Charlotte with her baby daughter, Greer, and her little boy, Tobias.

The picture had been taken on a beach in Spain. She visited them there once while still in high school. After Charlotte was killed, she was devastated. She grieved the loss as hard as anyone. But she found solace in Alister's decision to retire here and to have Charlotte's children close to the family. She was glad that Charlotte would be buried in the Doucet family cemetery, next to her parents and Caroline's grave, alongside generations of Doucet loved ones, rather than being interred in a foreign cemetery on a cold, stony hillside.

As she roamed the house, picking at the memories in her mind like festering scabs that refused to heal, she opened a door off the great dining room. Her eyes found the old chair in the room. It was still covered by the quilt that Charlotte had sent back from her time in Egypt. Mother Agnes Valentine loved that chair. As did most of the Doucet women. She removed the plastic cover and sat down. She ran her hands up and down the arms as if to absorb the memories of the woman she loved.

Mother Agnes Valentine had always hated the legacy and history that followed her family. Sister understood her distaste for her late sister-in-law, Sandra Doucet. It hadn't been just about her moving in and placing generations of Doucet belongings out for the trash. It was her rumored relationship with Archie Walton. Agnes believed Sandra married the name, not the man. Sandra was cold, and her daughters never felt loved by her. Sister had no true fond memories of her. What there might have been had been redacted by years of tyrannical behavior. Sandra's need for power had destroyed her relationships like wildfire. As she held the keys to the house close to her chest, a light knock sounded on the door, surprising her. She looked up, startled, as the door hesitated open, and a head poked in.

"I'm sorry. I didn't mean to scare you," Silas said, holding up his hands. I just saw your Jeep from the church. McQueen will spend the rest of the day reliving his high school years, and then he'll be done there. I have a feeling with that mouth of his, he spent most of those years in a bathroom stall hiding," Silas said, pushing the door open further.

"Or stuffed in a locker. Something tells me he probably earned both of them. Anyway, I don't think there's anyone left for us to talk to there. McQueen said he'd have his final review wrapped up for you by the end of the day. He's got two male teachers he'd like to dig into. But he promised to be quick about it—if that is possible. He thinks there's something nefarious going on with the Am Lit teacher, Mr. Williams' teaching credentials, and he's convinced that the Algebra teacher, Mr. Barrett, is sleeping with one of the female students. But she isn't one of the Fab Seven. He did well for his first sole mission, don't you think? I'm quite proud of the kid," he said with a wide grin. "He wanted me to tell you that he has a lead on that button of yours."

"Really? That was quick. Did he say where?" she asked, looking away from the keys in her hand and returning to the present.

"No, but you know him. He's not real quick with his words. I'm sure he'll spill it all, after his dots are connected. I finished up the rest of the interviews with the other girls, and they all have the same story," he continued, taking a seat next to her. "It seems this Liam character comes and goes from the area pretty regularly, though the girls haven't seen him recently. The girls all say he's good-looking for an old guy, charming, and pretty generous with his money. But he does have a darker side if crossed. He's known to get rough with them when he feels they've stepped over the line. They've all confirmed that he doesn't make them do anything they do not want to do."

"However, two of the girls do not believe that saying no is an option. Kari said that Mia was meeting with someone. A couple of the girls called her a snitch, but they didn't think she was confiding in a cop. At least, that is the favoring opinion among the group. It could be one of the nuns at the school. One of the girls said the girl she saw Mia meet up with was a bit older than them, like a college girl. So, maybe not a nun. I didn't see many youngbloods in habits at the school. And the church's director isn't any better. Most of those ladies' youthful days are years behind them."

Silas paused, wondering where Sister's mind was. She knew Greer was missing, but she hadn't said anything about it, at least not to him. Sister knew as much as they all did by now, but given the current climate, he wasn't sure if her focus should be on Greer or finding out who killed Mia Ward. He believed that in the end, it would get them there, but did he need to poke the bear? He mulled over the possibility of mentioning his belief that the older girl was likely Greer. Looking over the room as he waited for Sister to respond, he saw she had a distant look in her eyes, as if she were locked in her memories.

"Did you find the papers you were after?"

"No. There are no links here. It's been years now, though. If she kept anything, I haven't found it."

"Well, he's covering for someone. If it wasn't Miss Simone, then who was it?"

"Si, stop already. Don't you think I'd tell you if I knew these answers?!"

"Okay, stop there. Put the crazy back in the jar. Shit, girl," Silas said, holding up his hands in surrender. "I didn't mean anything—damn. Ok, 'the Littles' as you call them, only mentioned Liam. Is there anyone in Baptiste named Liam?"

"No. I don't know. It's not a familiar name, but it could be. I can't say."

"I want to go by Walton's place again. See what I can see. You still got a key?"

Sister dug into her pocket and pulled out a set of keys to Walton's back entrance—the ones she had lifted from his desk while visiting him to get the papers and the keys to the manor.

"I've been over the place already," she confessed. "But you are welcome to it," she said, handing him the key. "One thing he said while I was there had me curious. He said the Doucet name is broke. Mother Agnes Valentine left me the house in her will, but where would the money have gone? Knowing how Franklin and Sandra had made it, she wouldn't have wanted their money. She may have donated it, but you saw the same statements I did. Sandra had masked a small fortune before her death. Either Mother Agnes Valentine gave it away, or someone's telling stories."

"Maybe Archie B. Walton, Esquire, has set himself up for retirement," Silas said, dragging out Esquire as if it were a bad word. "He was her partner. I'll take another run at it."

Sister ran her hands down the arms of the chair again before standing up. Sighing heavily, she walked from the room and towards the front door. Silas watched as a strange expression crossed her face. It was like a light had been switched on and a darkness suppressed.

"I need to see them," she said, pushing through the door and leaping off the porch.

Silas followed her to the back of the house, about 100 yards from the garden, to a fenced-in area lined in rows of six, where seven-foot-long concrete structures used to house coffins, with markers for each family member buried on the land.

Sister opened the gate and walked first to Franklin's marker. She bent down, kissed the palm of her hand, and placed the kiss on the marker. "I love you, Daddy," she whispered. Then, turning to Sandra's marker, she did the same, but said nothing.

Kneeling between Charlotte's box and Caroline's, Sister cleaned the grass clippings from each site. Silas was already there, waiting for her, hoping that maybe this time would be different. Perhaps this time, the switch would last.

"You know she'd be proud of you, right?" he said, hugging her gently. "Your sister loved you like nothing else...even having those kids wouldn't have changed that kind of love. All I can do is help you make right what happened to you and Kathryn."

Pulling away, she had no response. Then she made her way and stood before her Aunt Rene's headstone, which read, "Mother Agnes Valentine, Loving Aunt and Sister of Christ."

She then looked up at him and smiled. She knew that whatever secrets Silas held in that head of his, he'd take them to his grave. He had been the best kind of friend from day one. He had her back, and she knew that he'd protect her no matter what she did.

"I know you will, Silas, and I love you for that."

"Look at me," he said, lifting her chin so that he could look into her eyes. He needed to see her. "When this is done, I need you to promise me you'll get help. I mean real help. See that doctor of yours and stay with her for a while. You can't keep going on like this. Please promise...for me—when this is all over."

He watched her eyes for a long while—watching for a change—waiting to see if she would understand just how worried he was for her. Then as quickly as the started, the tears began to dry—the ones that she shed for the friends and family she had lost. The darkness returned to her features and the sorrow that had once been there faded away.

She wiped away the dampness of her tears, and a much brighter expression crossed over. He saw the change in her expression as the shadow changed her features and the mask returned. He knew then that he had reached someone, but not the one he had intended. As her eyes grew darker, a menacing smile turned up the corners of her mouth.

"Oh, Sunny-love, you worry too much," Baby said, smiling mischievously at him. "She isn't the one you need to be worried about."

PATIENT CONFIDENTIAL

By the time Bishop landed in New Orleans, the ache in his brain had subsided, but it teemed with more information than he had bargained for. Lovejoy Daily had drunk him under the table and then some. He was fairly certain it was Samuel who had taken him to bed, and he woke the following day to find them both already gone, with a return flight home and the set of keys to the rental car on the table.

LJ had answered all his questions. The only thing she didn't do, not even once, was touch or look at the image on the table. Maybe she thought she could drink him stupid, and he'd forget about that very important detail—if so, she had underestimated his resolve. She may have answered his questions honestly, but she had purposefully avoided identifying the woman in the photo.

He had something near disgust bubbling up within him. He just wasn't sure who it was for, or where it originated, or in what direction to send it flying. He had known Sister for years. Charlee Lovejoy was the name she had put on their marriage license, but now he had to consider it just another one of her aliases. That was what got him in the gut.

He understood that knowing absolutely everything about a person was impossible—especially given that over half of the people in their line of work were invisible and lived their lives as someone else. But he had shared his life with her. He had lived it honestly and openly. He never needed to know her story because he knew her. That was all that mattered. It wasn't hard to figure out that something awful had happened. She had scars all over her body. Hell, so did he if they were playing "Show me yours, I'll show you mine."

On the plane ride back, Bishop had one thing on his mind: Rome. He ran over his exit again and again in his head. He knew it wasn't right. He could have done a million things differently, but anything he played out had already been done a dozen times. She had been admitted countless times. He had sat with her through drunken tirades and three ODs. She couldn't explain where she would disappear to. She'd go days without checking in with him or coming home. When she returned, she was evasive about what she had done, where she had been, or with whom she had been with. He told her he couldn't go through another year of her using. He had already been there. They all had. He couldn't fish her out of another den or another man's bed. He had asked her straightforward questions to which she had no straightforward answers. Maybe if she had just owned the fact that she was using again, he would have tried. But she couldn't even do that.

Instead, she pretended not to understand why he would be mad. She was working—just working. But he knew that was a lie. If he didn't know where she was, McTavish would. But he didn't. Nor did anyone else.

She was addicted, and he couldn't live with that. But that wasn't the only problem swimming around in his head, and he couldn't bring himself to give it life. The smell of oranges and vanilla came to him as he fought that feeling. The smell in the hotel. He knew that if he said it out loud, it would be real. And he wasn't ready for it.

As he drove to the house in the Garden District, he tried to work out what he would ask. What would he say? Would he kick in the door and go in guns blazing, demanding answers? Could he do that? Could he take off the badge? His real badge. The one he swore an oath to for the city of Baptiste to wear and beat the hell out of whoever was behind the door to get the answers he needed? He knew now that McTavish had kept a lot from him. He wasn't sure why, but it didn't matter. He was so wrapped up in the surface of it that he couldn't see below it. There was so much more going on, and he needed to unpack it. He felt like a complete moron—like he had been led around by his balls and just took it all.

McQueen was straight. That he knew without question—he had checked him into fake prison himself. Kidd was a good kid. He knew the Kidd's entire life story. He assumed every bit of Silas Holiday was as advertised. Though he had never had a reason to think twice about Silas, he didn't like him. He never would have admitted to that out loud, but he cared for Silas about as much as Addison cared for Sister. Silas was her right hand—just as Addison had been his.

He wanted to be a better man. Jealousy wasn't a good color for him, but he knew, deep down to the bottom of his core, that he hated their relationship. She was more open with Silas—friendlier, maybe—honest for sure—like she kept no secrets from him. Bishop hated that Silas got a part of her that he couldn't even touch, and he hated himself for feeling like a heel.

And what about Addison Adler? What did he know? Brick had been with McTavish before him—even though Addison never had a funeral, he was just as dead to the world as Sister was. The only difference was that Addison had never been on anyone's list, at least not that he knew of. And that was the problem. What did he really know? They didn't have to kill him off. He only became invisible for the protection of his wife and children.

By the time he reached the veranda, an Asian-looking woman dressed to the nines had stepped out to greet him, her palm out as if to stop him from coming any closer.

"Deputy."

"Okay, so we are halfway there. You obviously know me. Now, who are you?" he asked, stopping just before he reached her.

"Yes, I know who you are. You are Bishop Bohannan, but you are not a patient here," she said matter-of-factly. "And you are not welcome. How did you find this place?" she asked, worried that her identity and her work had been compromised.

"The perks of being a sheriff," he said, stepping onto the porch, ignoring her warnings.

Tobias had done good work. The morning that Sister left Beast with him to run her errands in New Orleans, Bishop instructed Tobias to follow her. He had worried that she would catch on, given that she wrote the book on spotting a tail. But if she noticed him following her, she hadn't altered her movements.

Tobias followed her to a law firm and then to this house. Bishop looked up the address and saw that a corporation rather than a person was renting it. From the photos Tobias provided, it appeared to be used as a doctor's office. The front door displayed the doctor's name, but a soft pull had not provided him with much information about the doctor.

Other than finding her board certifications, Dr. Scarlett Jolene. Wu was a blank slate. He had intended to dig deeper into the occupant of the house, but with everything else burning down around him, he hadn't gotten around to it.

Instead, leaving it up to Tobias to take the plunge. He had yet to hear back from Tobias. But given his meeting with LJ, Bishop decided he couldn't wait. He had tiptoed around Sister's life far too long, and if he was going to find Greer, he needed to put all the pieces out there, including this house and the woman inside. It wasn't clear how they all connected, but he had learned a long time ago that if it smelled like shit, it was shit.

"Do you have clients now?" he asked, looking over the name on the door—not waiting for an answer, he pushed past her and went inside. He wasn't sure what he expected to find. But it wasn't what he had envisioned.

"Bishop," she said calmly, "I can't help you. Please stop. You cannot be here."

Seeing her determination, Bishop pulled his wallet from his pocket, pulled out two $100 bills, and placed them on the counter. "I am not a sheriff today, lady. I am a crazed man with thoughts of killing off those who have pissed me off today. How would you like to play this?" he warned.

Dr. Wu shook her head, "No", while her mind determined what to do. She had a duty to her patient, but it had stalled. She was getting nowhere and decided that an alternative treatment might be in order. Bishop Bohannan crashing through her door might just be what the doctor ordered, she concluded.

"Come in," she said, leading him past the glassed area in the foyer to a door right of a grand staircase. "We can talk in here." Stopping, she called to the woman behind the glass, "Shelly, please shut off the cameras in my office. This is a private conversation."

"Will do, Doc," the woman said, reaching over and clicking a button. "You're all set."

Puzzled by Shelly's perfunctory behavior, Bishop noticed that the woman never looked up to see who had entered the room. "She's pleasant," he said, following Dr. Wu into her office.

"She's paid to follow instructions," Dr. Wu offered. "She is my eyes and ears, and I pay her to mind my business, not yours," she continued. Looking up into the corner of the room, Dr. Wu confirmed the cameras were off before she started the conversation with the man who had married her patient.

"It's your time, Deputy Bohannon. Take a seat and tell me why you are here."

Sitting in a chair closest to her desk, "Why are you meeting with Charlee Lovejoy?" he asked. "I gather she's a patient, but I need to know more than that. I think she's killing people, and I have too many dead girls and one missing one in my parish to think that she's not tied into it somehow. And I have this," he said, handing her a profile written in her handwriting. "This was in a file taken from Alister McTavish's house. It seems like the two of you are also connected, am I right?"

Wu considered how to answer his questions without compromising her oaths. She was duty-bound to notify authorities if she believed there to be a danger to anyone's life, regardless of her study. The rub was that she worked for an authority much higher than his badge and could cost her her job and her life.

"I specialize in Dissociative Identity Disorder, Deputy Bohannon. You may have heard it called Multiple Personality Disorder or having a split personality. That's what it's most often referred to."

Bishop almost snorted out a laugh. "And what does that have to do with Sister?"

"I first came in contact with the woman you call Sister during my residency. She had been hospitalized after her second suicide attempt. I believe the attempt was triggered after she had shot her partner during a case she was involved in. She had no memory of shooting him, and she believed that she was either losing her mind or being held responsible for something that she did not do. Sister, or as I call her, Charlee, has moments of lost time. And when I say moments, I mean periods of days, weeks, or months where she has no idea where she went or what she has done."

Bishop shifted uncomfortably in his seat, wanting to laugh at the woman, and then he took a page from Kidd's book. "Where the fuck did you get your credentials? Are you honestly going to pull this horseshit on me and think I would, what? Not laugh your ass all the way to my truck while in handcuffs?"

"Nice try, Deputy. But my credentials trump yours. And if you want to measure dicks, I warn you. You'll need a yardstick," she said confidently. "Would you like me to continue?"

With just a nod of his head, she finished her thought. "It is rare. And it sounds like insanity, but after what was happening was discovered, our government felt that she was an asset and should be left alone. I monitor her. Or rather, I monitor them, would be a better argument."

"Them? What are you saying, exactly?" Bishop asked in outrage. "I should just arrest you now, measuring sticks aside. I know I can't make it stick, but the cameras are off, and I can hold you until you give it straight or wither away. I don't have time for this, doctor."

Opening the file he had handed her, the same one LJ Daily had seen, she pulled out Kate's statement and handed it back to him. "This is an account of what happened to Kathryn Daily," she declared in an even tone.

"No, it isn't. I've already spoken with her mother. Kate did not write this. Her mother said it wasn't her handwriting. And as if this shitshow couldn't get any worse, she said her daughter never made it out of the swamp alive."

"No. It's not hers. It's Caroline Doucet's."

"And how is that possible?" he said, looking over the statement as if he knew she was lying. But he had been so wrong about everything up to this point, and decided to keep his mouth shut as she spoke.

"It is true that there were two funerals held. I wasn't part of that, but a decision had been made. Kate was the one who had died, and Caroline had survived. If you want to call it survival. Her department put her through wit-sec, hoping that, with time, she would remember what had happened to her. If she did, then they could build a case. If not, then, well, she'd have a new life."

"Caroline took the name of Charlee Lovejoy. Her sister Charlotte had often been called Charlee, and she took Kate's mother's name so that she wouldn't forget that she had gotten LJ's only daughter killed. This is not my assertion but her own."

"Caroline blamed herself for allowing the investigation to touch Kate. She felt she had involved her and Mother Agnes Valentine by gathering information that only the two of them were privy to...allowing her to use those names was unproductive to her well-being, and I wouldn't have made that call. However, I wasn't part of her team at the time. Maybe if I had been, this path could have been avoided."

"Caroline spent a year in recovery. The first six months were spent healing from her injuries—I'm sure you are aware of those—but the last six months were spent in a protective environment from herself. When she finally wrote out her statement, it was clear that she still hadn't come to terms with what had happened. She had taken on the identity of Sister Mary Charles. She wrote, spoke, and behaved as though she were a nun. All parts of Caroline Doucet were gone. As a doctor, I am supposed to be understanding. But I am a scientist and a skeptic."

"So, you believed that she was faking it?" Bishop asked curiously. "Why would she do that?"

"I don't know what I thought then. But I had an open mind, and I stayed the course. I have learned a lot since those early days. And I have been allowed to study her and help her find herself."

"And how is that working for you? I've known her for the better part of ten years. How long have you been studying her? Because, for as long as I've known her, she has always been a former nun. So, I don't think it's working."

Doing her best not to feel the personal assault of his words, Wu continued, "I am not sure what you've learned from your meeting with Senator Daily, but I assume you've come to the same conclusion as I? She had been a loving mother. When you read the statement, it conveys their battered relationship, but there was no abuse—at least not between Kate and the Senator."

"Most of their tension revolved around Kate's desire for self-destructive behavior. The drugs, the boys, the outbursts. Her lifestyle choices and the Senator's need to help her. Caroline's mother, however, Sandra Doucet, was, by all accounts, a controlling and manipulative person who ruled her home with an iron hand. From what I've gathered, Caroline was a good student, made good grades, and lived an uneventful life, aside from knowing her parents were drug dealers and traded in sex. After the death of her parents and having no one else to care for her, her aunt moved back into the home. I would venture to guess you know her as Mother Agnes Valentine."

Bishop nodded. "Yes, Rene Doucet. The Senator told me that she was the reason why Kate moved to Louisiana and joined her church. But I still do not understand how this has anything to do with whatever the fuck is going on," he groaned. There were just too many moving parts, and he wondered if he was too close to all the parties to see the complete picture.

"Caroline became part of the LSP while in college. She and Sister Mary Charles, who also attended the same university, were friends. They'd known one another since childhood. Kate stayed in the Doucet Manor with Mother Agnes Valentine occasionally, as did Caroline. Being close, they held each other in confidence. One night, while helping some of the girls at the shelter, Sister Mary Charles was told about another missing girl. I gather this was about the twelfth to go missing in less than a year's time. It was unusual. Sister Mary Charles went to McTavish about it, and after feeling as though he wasn't taking her seriously, she took her concerns to Caroline. Shortly after that, because Caroline lived in Baptiste, she was placed undercover to investigate at the state level. She was to tell no one about what she was doing—not even McTavish. As far as I understand, she never told anyone. Other than the initial conversation about Kate's concerns, Caroline never told her what she was doing."

"So she was investigating what exactly?"

"Caroline's bosses suspected William Walton of trafficking girls and boys for the purposes of sex. Four months into her investigation, a steamboat was detained on the Mississippi. It was supposed to be some big private party event, but Caroline's team got a tip, and once boarded, they found forty-seven girls stowed away. You can guess the rest. But, of course, no one knew anything. And all refused to talk."

"So, how does this link back to Baptiste?"

"Until that morning, one of the men onboard that steamboat had been in a cell in McTavish's jail. He was being held over for the state police on drug charges. McTavish claimed that one of his deputies missed the hold order and let him go by mistake."

"But if Sister, or Caroline...fuck this is crazy," he said, standing up to stretch out the unease in his body. "What am I supposed to call her? If she doesn't remember the who, what, when, and where of this derailed train, then how do you know it?"

"That is where things get a bit more complicated," she replied. "Can I get you a coffee?" she asked, getting to her feet. "You look like you could use a coffee. I could use more caffeine myself," she continued, walking to a small coffee bar at the back of her office.

PAWN F4 TO TAKE THE BISHOP

D r. Wu set a cup down in front of Bishop before returning to her seat. She watched over him while she nursed her coffee. Sipping it slowly, she mulled over her next set of words. She wasn't worried that her admissions would send Bishop down an emotionally spiraling staircase, but she had considered that for a man who didn't drink, he sure spent a lot of time tilting a glass. He may not know it, but Baby could have that effect on a person.

"How can it get any more complicated?" he finally asked, picking up the cup of black coffee and frowning. The impatient nature of his posture was evident.

"I'm sorry. I didn't think to ask. I drink it black. I just assumed you did as well. Would you like some sugar or cream with your coffee? I do have both," she offered, setting herself to get back to her feet.

"Please, don't get up. I can get through it," he said, taking a big gulp of the hot coffee and making another face. "How do you know what happened if Caroline couldn't remember and Kate didn't make it? I'm sure mind-reading isn't part of your abilities. Has another witness come forward?"

Taking a deep breath, Dr. Wu said, "Initially, Charlee Lovejoy wasn't my patient. I had been assigned an agent they call Baby. Or maybe she calls herself that. That part isn't clear, really."

"Baby," he smirked with a shrug. "Okay. So, this Baby was sent to see you. And then what?"

"They believe Baby is a valuable asset who can't be replaced. At least, they'd prefer not to. However, she has co-dependency issues, along with a list of other psychological problems. But that's the only one they are concerned with. It's hard to explain the human mind to someone who doesn't study it. I can do my best, but I need you to listen and not be yourself. I'll even try to dumb it down, and I mean that respectfully. So, please do not be offended."

"I'd rather you talk straight and stop having me chase you around the damn tree. If you need to talk to me like I have only one brain cell, then get to it. I assure you, my feelings will be spared."

"Caroline's mind broke watching the death of her friend. She wasn't able to tell what happened, but Baby could." Taking another breath, working out how to turn her clinical dialogue into language a jarhead could understand, Dr. Wu continued. "Baby is Caroline if Caroline were a murdering psychopath hell-bent on revenge. Baby is the worst part of Caroline's mind. On the other hand, the adoption of Kate's life is her safe space. A place she can hide and move forward without really having to move forward."

"Kate and Caroline shared many memories and experiences since they had known each other since childhood. With a few exceptions, of course. But pound for pound, she can still feel like herself in many ways, but by living as Kate instead of herself—the person she can't forgive. As a nun, she can embrace the solitude and a singular existence. No partner other than God. It's an easier path."

"You're telling me that Caroline has three personalities renting space in her head? That seems far-fetched, even for a head shrinker like yourself. You're actually telling me this with a straight face," he laughed without a smile.

"No, I'm telling you that for the purposes of this conversation and for the sake of a debate, Caroline Doucet is dead. And that there are two completely different individuals living in her mind. A former nun who hides from the world she doesn't want to be a part of, and Baby. Baby keeps Sister clean and sober. Baby does the bad things so that Sister does not have to. Like remembering the faces of the men who killed them. Remembering the case that Caroline was working on and what led up to them being taken to the swamp. I know they both didn't physically die, but they did. Sister's life ended when they buried Kate. But it isn't that simple either."

"Baby enjoys every part of life guilt-free and on her own terms. There are no restraints, rules, or inhibitions...which makes her perfect for her line of work. Her tendencies are tolerated as long as she accomplishes the task. She doesn't ask questions, and she enjoys what she does. And I mean that wholeheartedly. As long as she does her job, they look the other way while she cleans up old business."

"Caroline should never have been released from the hospital. McTavish pulled a lot of strings to get her out and had her sent to Europe. Given her background, it wasn't too difficult to use his connections to get her a job with OIO."

"The Office of International Operations?" Bishop interrupted, already remembering that Sister had done some work there."

"Yes. There, she worked with a fugitive task force. Before that, though I do not know how long, she trained with his old unit, helping to rebuild her confidence and skills. That's when you met her, I believe. Over time, she was able to fake her entry back into society. But we both know how that was going. And then, as if something was triggered, Sister turned a corner, and in walks Baby. And Baby remembers everything."

"And Sister is okay with her mind being hijacked by this Baby character?" Bishop asked, as the gears in his mind began working out scenarios while he thought about every interaction with Sister over the past ten-plus years. As he thought it out, things fell into place, and though it was ludicrous, he was beginning to understand where Dr. Wu was leading him.

"Baby is fully conscious of Sister, but Sister is unaware of Baby's presence. Baby retains and utilizes any and every thought that Sister has for her purposes. In many instances, she has improved Sister's skills, and for a lack of a better term, she has improved her abilities. She makes Sister more aware of her environment and better able to assess her situations. However, there is no evidence that Sister knows that Baby is calling the shots or that Sister is even aware of what Baby—separately—has done."

"In the beginning, Sister was blamed for her erratic and strange behaviors. Many of these, I do believe, were her acting out and her own doing. But, take Silas getting shot. Sister wasn't the one who pulled the trigger. She genuinely was mortified that she had done it and didn't know why. Yes, her hand held the gun. But Baby is the one in control. Since then, Baby has grasped the reality of her situation. And I do say hers. You have to separate them and see them as individuals—each on their own, responsible for their own actions. Baby has come to understand that her volatile nature will have consequences for Sister. The more times she casts Sister in a negative light, the shorter Baby's life becomes. So, she's learning to dial it back."

"And why not just tell Sister that she is Caroline?—not Kate or a nun? Or Charlee Lovejoy or Baby. I mean, for fuck sakes, when I say it out loud, even I hear the convoluted idiocy of what you are implying."

"And you don't think that's happened? She had been told. Many times over and over. She understands that Charlee Lovejoy is the name she uses, just an alias. She has no attachment to the name beyond paying homage. And she's never once referred to herself as Kathryn Daily. Or the daughter of the Dailys, for that matter. In her mind, she was just simply Sister Mary Charles. A nun who experienced something so horrific that she had to flee her life and start over as someone else. Baby knows what they did to Sister Mary Charles for talking. And she knows the awful truth of what they did to Caroline. Make no mistake; the fraternity boys are casualties in this. Pawns, if you will. Willing pawns that will be dealt with. But Liam—well...they did a number on Caroline. She was a sweet and innocent girl, if you understand my meaning."

Bishop knew what she meant, and he could only nod as a hurt came over him. Caroline had been a virgin. His stomach turned at that. These two girls lived each other's lives. He thought about the part of starting over and how he had fallen into the mix. He wanted to be the guy who could shrug it off with a "shit happens" approach, but the "what about me" part of him had risen to the top of his throat, strangling his heart, and he had to know.

"So, which one of them was I with, and who did I marry?" he asked defeatedly as if knowing the truth before she answered.

Dr. Wu wished there was a way to tell Caroline's story without making Bishop a casualty. But she knew there were no magic words or pills that would make any of this settle well within his being—figuring it best to get it over with—she ripped back the band-aid.

"Baby was trying to play matchmaker," she began with the best positive spin possible. "I wish I could tell you it was a kindness she had done, but knowing Baby as I do, I think she did it only to see what could happen. There may have been some altruistic motivation, but I highly doubt it was for your benefit, as much as it was for Sister's. I believe she was running an experiment that backfired. Not understanding what she had done, Sister did her best to go along because she loves you. Perhaps not in the way you love her, but the best she is capable of. I have spoken to Sister in great detail about your situation, and she truly believes she must have had a mental break or had been using again. Maybe acted out after a few too many rounds with the guys. She doesn't even remember starting a relationship with you. I know this doesn't help you, but maybe it will give you some insight into her level of guilt for hurting you."

"Your marriage is not legally binding, if that is your next question—and it should be. But I'd have to explain it again, and for now, it'd do no good. She's still not there. If you sign the papers, the process will proceed as usual. And if you do nothing, then well, she's prepared herself to be your wife on paper until, well, death do you part. The ball's really in your court on this one."

"And what does McTavish have to say about all of this?" he asked. "How is any of this going on behind his back?"

They both knew that nothing happened in Baptiste without Sheriff McTavish being aware of it. And there was no way that Sister was operating as herself or this imaginary friend of hers, without McTavish knowing that either. He's the one who got her released from the mental ward and sent her to Europe. How that was able to fly was another concern. However, only Dr. Wu understood the disclosures regarding that.

"That would presume that he doesn't know. You've been here what, eighteen months? Do you think it's possible that he doesn't know about Caroline's investigation into human trafficking in his parish, nor the fact that he was the one in her crosshairs?"

"But he is her brother-in-law. Even I've been able to put that together. Caroline Doucet was Charlotte's kid sister. I worked with her briefly. I admit I am an idiot for not seeing the resemblances, but I know the relationship. Are you telling me that Alister McTavish had her and the real Sister killed? That's insanity. He's dedicated his life to helping people. You have to be wrong. This Walton guy, okay. Sure, but, come on."

"And I hope that I am. But Baby doesn't think so. She's made her way through each member of your team."

"Including me, you mean? She thought we were all involved?"

"Not you so much as Addison Adler and Silas Holiday. They've been a part of his team for years. When it happened, McQueen was barely out of diapers, so he was never on her list. But they were there with him as far back as when he was wreaking havoc on the villagers. Most people view what he did as heroic, pushing people to stand on their own two feet. And up to a point, I would agree. However, he wielded a lot of power in those days and had just as many connections. He learned how to put it all together to make a lot of money for his business. Isn't it possible that he did the same thing here?"

"Look, Baptiste changed after McTavish's arrival. It seems safer on paper, but look how many more people, especially the number of women who've gone missing out of his parish alone. And what about the ones who have been found murdered? The statistics are far too great to be a typical day in the life of this state, let alone a small parish like Marie Anjou."

"What about you?" he asked, wondering about her role in all of this. "How are you, or why are you so connected? You seem heavily invested in the outcome."

She thought for a moment, wondering if her story mattered in the whole of it. She didn't talk about her life, and only a handful of people knew about it. Considering that, she decided that it didn't matter if just one more knew of it.

"I was on the steamboat, Deputy. I had been sold to the highest bidder and was on my way to Memphis when the FBI raided the boat. I was granted citizenship, graduated from high school, and attended college. Thereafter, I joined the FBI's behavioral unit and am now a private contractor. I'm sure you can guess my current employer. Caroline's investigation saved my life, and I don't want to see her—maybe locked up for her own safety, but I understand her. I even understand, Baby. She fascinates me, to be honest."

Looking down at her watch, Dr. Wu got to her feet. "I hate to end this, but if you don't mind, your time is up. I have another meeting in a few minutes, and I don't think it wise for you to be here."

"Right," he said, standing to meet her gaze. "This is really a lot, isn't it?" he said, still reeling from their conversation.

"I guess it can be," she said, willing to see it from his perspective. "I'll walk you out."

Standing on the porch, Dr. Wu handed him a card, "Here's my number if you need to talk. I can find you someone if you need it."

Bishop laughed, taking her card, he slid it into his pocket. A bit of the tension eased as he wrapped his thoughts around his friend being behind the brutality that had touched the two young women.

"Thanks, Doc, but I'm a big boy, I don't..."

His words were cut short when a sound rang past his ear, and something struck Dr. Wu in the front of her body. Blood spread out in a circling, flowered pattern as her white blouse changed colors, and a panicked expression widened her eyes in surprise as she fell backward through the open front door.

Sally's screams were deafening as another shot rang out, causing Bishop to drop to his knees, paralyzed, as he fought for breath. He hadn't even had time to react as a trained man would. As Bishop sagged to a sitting position, it struck him that his investigation would end there, the conversation he wouldn't have with Alister, and the life he wouldn't be able to repair with Sister. Then, another shot rang out, leaving two holes in the center of Bishop's chest.

SEALS & SHARKS

PRESENT DAY - BABY

I watched Sloth, sin number six, from a rented black Porsche as he pulled up in front of the bar. A woman waited on the curb, and if I didn't move soon, he'd be out of his car and on his way to her. She was probably a rental herself, judging by the way she eyed him like he was the leprechaun at the end of her rainbow. However, I seriously doubted it would have taken all that much to take the big-boobed brunette for a test drive as I ran my hand along the contours of the 911 GT3 and considered just how much cooler I'd look in this car than that old Jeep Sister favored.

The brunette may have been waiting for him, but she flirted with and propositioned every man who walked past her as she waited. I guessed she was shoring up work for later in the night. While she was distracted, I quickly slipped out of my car and hurried to his, knowing that the shit had hit the fan and now I was out of time.

Just as he opened his door, I slipped into the passenger seat, halting his exit from the car. He smiled wildly at me. "You're not Katrina," he said, his eyes excited yet confused.

"Hey there, Tommy," I said, placing my hand on his. Thomas Evans owned the bar across the street and frequently spent time with the women who used his bar to trade services for his own pleasures. He let them come and go, asking no questions as long as they were available to him, free of charge. "You don't need Katrina," I flirted. "I'm here now," I said, rubbing his hand and smiling innocently.

"Well, I have to say you are prettier than Katrina," he smiled, rubbing my hand with his thumb and caressing my exposed leg. "What is your name, little bird?"

My attention was pulled away as I caught a flash of an old Indian World War II replica parked three cars back. I had seen it before, and I smiled. Tobias was so grown-up now and full of surprises. He had found me, though I wasn't exactly sure how. I felt a bit of pride in that. I felt all mushy inside. I knew it wasn't me, but Caroline's love for the boy. I wasn't worried about him. I was almost done and didn't care who knew the truth. The finish line was so close and I think Caroline liked the cover of the backseat now.

"They call me Baby," I said with a sickening, syrupy, sweet smile. "I wish I had time to explain," I said, drawing him to my lips without them touching as I teased him into letting his guard fall. His eyes closed in anticipation as I reached around him and locked his door.

"No need to explain, little bird," he whispered, his voice raspy with excitement. "I've seen you watching me," he said, his accent growing thicker, his pretense falling away. "Were you stalking me, little bird? I think I like having a stalker. This could be a fun adventure, no?"

I laughed at that, brushing my lips across his and pulling away. "You could have just introduced yourself," I said, running my hand down his hair and stopping at the back of his neck.

Yes, he had seen me watching him. He was a self-assured little rat. He was a disgusting hobbit between his trousers, which were too tight, and the combover. He thought that owning a nightclub gave him power. I knew it wasn't the club, as much as the people who visited it. He was nothing more than a minion. He was a man controlled by other me, and that caused him to take out his inadequacies on others. As I drew him in with a kiss, I slid my knife into the center of his throat. His eyes flew open as terror replaced the desire that slipped from him.

"I had so much to say, Tommy," I said, holding his head firmly against the knife as he tried to pull away, "but I am out of time. I'd ask you to think about what you did, but you've done so much, aye Tommy," I whispered in his ear. "Do you see me now?"

The only response I got was a gurgling noise as he struggled against my hold, wanting to cover the hole in his jugular notch. Smiling, I twisted the knife and sliced outward, widening the gap and ensuring more blood loss. I held him there until he stopped moving, and then I strapped him in his seat, pulled out his keys, and left the car, locking him inside.

Greer was quiet as I detailed my rushed execution of Thomas Evans, but I knew she was listening intently. As I spoke, I picked away at the wooden frame, hoping it was my way out. My fingertips felt raw and slippery with blood.

There were some details I didn't give out, though. I hadn't tried to lose Tobias since he first turned up, spotting him on the way to meet with Archie Walton. If he were going to show out his daddy in this business, he'd really need to step up his "tail game." I couldn't believe no one had ever looked at that boy and didn't see my face. Charlotte's children favored her, as did I.

As I diverted my path down a side street, I abandoned the rental where it was parked. I thought back to the night in that Hackney alleyway, really aware of the power I held, and considered that, at that moment, Caroline had found a way to speak. The attack on Charity Martin had triggered something primal—deep down inside Sister as she staggered her way home, spun up out of her head, and thought of ending us for about the hundredth time.

She hadn't been able to face it herself. I became the weapon she needed to do what needed to be done. Part of me knew it was her inability to tarnish the good Sister's name as she sought to reclaim her life. The worst part was that Caroline had been the better person all along. I knew all of her memories. Her life growing up and the impressions that existed in the crevices of her mind. Kathryn Daily hadn't been the person Caroline built up in our head. Kate becoming Sister Mary Charles didn't change who she had been. But to Caroline, the pedestal she placed on her own was infallible. In truth, if anyone deserved to be canonized in memoriam, it was Caroline.

With Tobias only 100 feet from me, I planned what to do next. Silas no doubt had his knickers in a wad as he searched high and low for Sister, unaware that Bishop had followed her since day one. That had made things more difficult for me, but not impossible. Tobias was a pup and still had some training before he could outsmart me. But, word has gotten out faster than I could respond concerning the shootings in New Orleans. Doc and Bishop had been taken to hospital, and no one was talking about what had happened to them.

As I tugged away at the frame, I reckoned I knew, didn't I? By Sister's visceral reaction, she assumed the worst and withdrew entirely. I knew I was in trouble if Silas believed I had any part in it. Or at least, Sister would be. Hearing about Bishop had sent her beyond what even I could reel in. I considered that, too, while I worked. Did I even want to bring her back? She was weak, and I had worked hard to keep us alive all these years. Stepping in every time, she decided she was ready to check out. No, I think it's my time now.

I wasn't sure I had it all figured out until Kidd sent that message to Sister about the button. He's smart, that one. It wasn't a button at all. Not really. Caroline had a pretty good idea who was involved back then, so that meant I knew who was responsible for Caroline and Kate's murder. Still, Mia's had me thinking more towards a different person altogether, and I must admit, I almost missed it.

"Where yous want to go, Mon Cher?" the woman asked, smiling as if she had missed me.

I returned the smile as the cabby pulled beside me as I walked. "Back around the corner," I instructed her from the window. I climbed inside and handed her another tube of rolled-up bills. "It's on Market Street."

"The Old No. 82 Hotel is all that is advertised," I told Greer. "From the walls to the ceiling, a complete gallery adorned the front entrance. The building was built in 1854. Did you know that? It's had many occupants over the years, the last being a slaughterhouse. I may be completely mad, but I appreciate the beauty in that. At first I felt a bit of shame in spilling blood there, but there's been plenty of blood on these floors already. It seems almost poetic, doesn't it?"

"I can understand why you'd see the romance," Greer said dryly, as a tremor shook through her words.

I could tell she was getting worse. I had to work fast and continued talking, giving her something to consider.

"Miss Devon?" he questioned, reaching out his hand for me to take. His hand was limp and soft—like a noodle not yet ready. His voice was polite, but his body language was clear. I'd been paid for it, and he was a retriever.

"Follow me, please," he said, with a twinkle of disapproval in his voice and expression. "He's this way."

I laughed at seeing the bridal suite set up as if I were looking to spend the rest of my days with the old man. His days were short, with one foot in the grave, and he just didn't know it. A sugar daddy on his way out could be someone's dream wedding. When I considered taking that call, I wondered why a man who preferred the younger girls would ask for someone fitting my description.

If they thought I was an idgit, they would be wrong. I'm here knowing it's a trap. But I needed to draw out sin number seven before I could get to that angel. I'm the breadcrumbs on the way to Granny's house. Isn't that what Silas had planned for Sister all along? McTavish thought he was so damn clever, using Sister as bait to get back his little girl.

"Miss Devin," the man said, and I turned to face Archie Benedict Walton Esquire, who had entered from an adjoining room. As I turned, I saw his smile droop slowly, as if it were made of wax and he stood too close to the fire.

"Hiya Archie," I said, watching the color drain from his waxy expression. His eyes darted left and then right. He looked surprised. By the way, his stomach seemed to fall from the sky, he'd reached the same conclusion I had—we were both the bait. But this was like emptying a seal in with a shark. The shark may get trapped up, but at least he won't go hungry.

"Miss Lovejo... Caroline," he said, staring at me as if I had a third eye set high and center. "Why are you here? I have a meeting soon. Is there something I can do for you?"

"I am your meeting, Love. But you can call me Baby. They all do. Baby, Baby, Baby. Say it with me. I love it when a man calls me Baby. Sound familiar, don't it?"

Archie backed up, a look of confusion on his face. He looked at his hand as if unsure of what to do with the cigar it held, and then glanced at his other hand, which held a cigar cutter.

"Your sister called you that," Archie said, now really looking at me. "It was childish then, and it is now, Caroline," he said in an indignant, arrogant tone as if he were superior to me. But I could see the fear that cooled his eyes."

"I bet you wish I'da stayed in that barrel, aye?" I said, smiling at him, removing my earrings and placing them on the dresser.

"Stop talking in riddles. I don't know what you mean. What barrel? And why must you continue to speak in that accent? You are Louisianan-born, not English, girl. What are you doing?"

"You don't like my accent? Why not? Not posh enough? I agree it's not uppish or, wait, let's use a Southern term. What suits you better?" I asked, "acting all high-flutin'," dropping my accent and taking on a Southern drawl, similar to Walton's, Texas. "You sound like a pretentious assclown when you talk like that," I said, looking to take some of the wind out of his bloated arrogance.

As I casually walked toward him, I spotted a flicker of something shiny on the cuff of his wrist. It was a cufflink with a round gold button, identical to the one found in Mia's mouth. "Mia Ward was talking to Greer McTavish about the girls you've been taking," I accused directly.

I slipped a hand into my dress and gripped the blade while I waited for his response. He stammered back as I closed the distance between us. He hadn't been a young man for many years, but I wasn't buying in on the weak old man act, as he suddenly began to move as if he'd dislocate a hip. The only thing wrong with him was the years of smoking that had him coughing as if a lung was about to surface.

"I don't know what you are talking about. I didn't kill Mia," he said quickly, trying to find a direction to go after he had run out of floor space.

"So you knew her," I said.

"Yes, of course. She volunteered at the shelter."

When he fell to the bed, I pushed him on his back and crawled up until I sat on top of him, straddling his hips, pinning his arms at his side. Leaning down, I grazed my nose along his face until my lips stopped at his ear. "How did your gold button there get into Mia's mouth?" I whispered as I gripped his wrist and cut free one of the links. "It looks just like this one," I said, holding it above him before letting it drop and letting it smack him in the forehead. "Crickets," I said in a laugh as he struggled to get up.

"Get off me," he cried. "Have you lost your mind?"

"No, sir, Mr. Walton, but you might. Well, not your mind, but I could take an ear. Or an eyelid. How about your nose?" I asked as I gently dragged the tip of the blade along the bridge of his nose.

He cried out in pain as the blade bit in, and I sliced in a line to his cheek, stopping just below his eye. "What do you want?" he asked, with genuine fear sunk deep into his eyes.

"Oh, that's gotta hurt," I teased, smiling at him. "I want you to die," I said, but they ain't here yet. So, you just count yourself lucky that old Miss Silvie ain't a widow yet."

"Who isn't here? What are you talking about?"

"You really are out of the loop. I'm going to guess that with you about to become fertilizer, your boy has decided to retire you a little early. I don't know if you killed Mia yourself, but those cigars of yours will probably match the burns found on her body. So, if you didn't do it," I said with a smirk, "someone's gone through a lot of trouble to make sure it looks like you killed her. Sick bastard doesn't fall too far from your tree, aye? I guess it's a good thing you only had the one. Whew, that's gotta hurt, huh?"

I heard the door latch as it clicked. I smiled, then looked down at Archie, "That'll be for me, Love," I said, placing the blade to his throat and slicing deep, making sure I hit all four jugular veins. "I'll give Silvie your best regards."

"And that's how you got here?" Greer asked, confirming the timeline. "So, Archie Walton," she said, her voice low and almost sad as she worked out exactly what he was guilty of. "Auntie Rene never liked him much. She said he had a way about him that made her skin crawl. She was always suspicious of him and Grandmother Sandy. She said that after my grandfather and uncle died, Mr. Walton spent too much time consoling her. I reckon I know what that means," she sighed. She fell quiet for a moment before stating the obvious.

"But Archie couldn't have been one of the frat guys. I can't even imagine him hanging out with a bunch of college boys back then. That would be kinda gross. Maybe his son," she said. "William would have been about that age," she stated, but not to me. Greer was finally adding up all the pieces, and if she did her math right, she'd reach the same end as I had.

"Baby, she finally asked," Are you going to kill my father?"

SIN # SEVEN - LUST

L iam watched from the shadows, his breath caught up in the excitement. He watched as Mona, the woman's faithful driver, opened the door for her outside the Old No. 82 Hotel. The driver—a heavy-set woman he had seen before with her dark features and deep eyes—called herself Charlee Lovejoy. Once upon a time, he had known her as the sweet Caroline, the younger sister of his classmate, Charlotte Doucet.

Caroline had grown up and joined the LSP, loosely following in the footsteps of her brother-in-law. Had Caroline been the sort to play along for the sake of the team, this might not have been a problem. But she initiated an investigation into the missing woman who had gone missing from her mother's shelter. She shouldn't have done that. She had been gently warned off. But she just couldn't take a hint.

Liam's eyes narrowed as he observed her every movement. Her blonde hair glimmered under the lights, The dress she wore was cut just below the round of her ass and it showed all the artwork she had covered herself in. That wasn't the Caroline he once knew.

Mona leaned out of the window and called after Caroline. Her heavy bayou voice carried through the still night, "Yous sure yous alright, Cher? Yous want me to call Joe?"

Caroline offered a rueful smile. "I'll be okay, Mon Ami," he heard her say, curious again at the woman she had become and excited at the prospects of finally taking her. "I'll be fine, Love. It's just one more night to go."

Mona gave a skeptical nod, her eyes drawn in as worried lines made her linger with Caroline a few seconds longer, before she drove off—the taillights fading completely before he stepped closer to the hotel's entrance. He caught the eye of the doorman as she sheepishly lowered her head, but held his gaze. She was playing up the shy act as if this were her first rodeo. The good girl caught up in something torrid. He'd seen this before. He had used it before. He had taught his girls the art of seduction, role-play, and how to manipulate a man with just their eyes.

He'd been trailing Caroline for days, knowing that he finally had McTavish's attention. The infamous sheriff was renowned for his swift actions and quick thinking. Liam should have guessed he'd use Caroline as bait, dangling her out there like a carrot to lure him out.

Once Caroline disappeared into the hotel, Liam followed her in. The lobby was large and overfurnished, with art pieces greeting every inch of the space as he passed through. Liam hung back, pretending to check his phone while keeping Caroline in view. She was talking to a snobbish man as he led her to an elevator.

Liam didn't bother looking for a room number; he recognized the man and knew she was on her way to meet his father. He smiled as he worked through the idea of her in the same room as Archie. This couldn't have worked out any better than if he had planned it himself. The betrayal being done was staggering, and he was astonished that he hadn't really played any part in it, though he had or would benefit from it greatly if things continued to play out as they were.

He took his time, slowly proceeding to the suite on the top floor that overlooked the city. His father often brought women here. The hallway was quiet, the only sound was a distant hush that drifted in from the street, through a terrace balcony. Liam's steps slowed as he approached the closed door. He paused, his hand resting on the handle, as he slid his hand into his pocket, ensuring his weapon would be easy to get to. His insides coiled tight like a rusty spring, as the anticipation ran through him. The silence was unsettling. Liam's instincts screamed at him to be cautious, but he had been a risk taker his entire life, and he smiled. He knew what she was capable of. Thrilled by that, he tested the doorknob and found it unlocked.

Pushing the door open, he stepped inside. The room was dark, save for the faint glow of a lamp on the bedside table. Caroline lay on her back on the floor, her body still. For a split second, he chuckled a nervous laugh at the thought that his father had killed her.

"Fuck," he said, putting his gun back into his pocket and stepping over her to check for a pulse. She had blood in her hair, a split lip, and swelling around her throat. Purple and green bruises were beginning to show on her skin. He caught sight of the rise and fall of her chest. She was only unconscious.

Puzzled, Liam's gaze shifted to the bed, where a second figure lay in a pool of blood. His heart stopped when he recognized the man. He didn't think he'd feel anything at seeing his father dead. He had welcomed it for years—knowing that with his father gone, he could do so much more. But something caught in his chest. A pang of sorts, as he remembered the man who was kind to him once. The man who had been a good father to him as a boy. The man who had changed along the way as his desires and greed got the better of him. The man he had mirrored his own image after.

The older man's eyes were blank as they stared sightlessly at the ceiling, his face set frozen in shock. There was no peace in his eyes. His father's throat had been slit, the blood soaking into the bed and puddling to the floor. None of this made any sense. There was no way they could have done this to each other. He did not doubt that his father had died at her hands, but what happened to her?

Liam's mind raced as he pieced together the implications. It had to be Mc-Tavish. This was a trap, and Liam had walked straight into it. But why leave Caroline alive? Why leave anyone alive? What did he hope to gain? It wasn't as if it were even a proper trade. Though he may have considered it. He only took Greer to shut her up. McTavish should have put a muzzle on that little bitch a long time ago. His fucking kids were on his last damn nerve.

Ignoring his father's body on the bed, Liam scooped up Caroline from the floor. She was lighter than he had expected—her head dropped against his shoulder as he carried her out of the room. He couldn't risk being seen, so he took the back stairs, slipping into the alleyway behind the hotel.

His car wasn't far. He'd also been lying low in the last place anyone would have looked. He smiled at thinking how often he had seen a member of Mc-Tavish's team combing the grounds, talking to teachers and students. It was also where he'd been keeping Greer. She had been his insurance—his leverage against McTavish. But now, he had Caroline, and that changed things for him.

The drive to Doucet Plantation had been tense. He worried that at any moment, she'd wake up and he'd be trapped in a car with a polecat. If her close quarter combat were anything like the shit she pulled already, he would be screwed. But Caroline only stirred once. Liam glanced at her occasionally, his mind a whirlwind of inappropriate thoughts. He wanted to kill her one moment and undress her the next. Watching her little charade routine with the doorman had his body on fire.

Liam watched as the doorman's eyes raked over her, and he fought the urge to shoot the man on the sidewalk. She let him run a hand down her bare arm and rest a palm on the low of her hip, just below her dress. Liam shifted uncomfortably, watching the doorman's fingers drift toward the bottom edge and then trespass the line. He wasn't uncomfortable in the way a man would be with moralities on how a man should treat a lady. He was angry that the man had the audacity to touch what didn't belong to him.

Caroline smiled so innocently at him—batting extra lashes in his direction. That only made the ache in him twist harder. The guileless naivety she portrayed had played that man like a fiddle. Liam knew what she had in her eyes, and she wanted nothing more than to kill the man in herself. He liked her restraint, but only in the way of preserving her resolve. She fascinated him—this little monster of his—his creation. His father couldn't take credit for the woman Caroline Doucet had become.

When they finally arrived at the plantation, Liam carried Caroline down a long hall, across the abbey, through a chamber, and down a flight of stone stairs. The surrounding walls were cool and damn, causing him to rethink storing her here, given the dress she wore. But he really didn't much care about her comfort. His plans for her could wait while he figured out what to do with Greer and McTavish. If this were a trap, then McTavish would most likely be on his way soon.

Greer's muffled voice reached him from the adjacent room where she sat in the dark. The electricity didn't work in the cellars below the church. Grabbing a flashlight, he quickly opened the door and slipped inside the small stone cell before her eyes could adjust to him.

The man who hit Greer with his car had been dealt with swiftly and without mercy. His body was probably still floating in the Rouge, and it would only be a matter of time before he would be found. Liam counted on the gators to do their job better than the gator-bait had done his. He wanted her picked up, not harmed. Not only did he not want her dead in case things leveled off with McTavish, but he had other plans for her if they didn't. Playing nursemaid had not been one of them. But until he could get them both out of the church and back to Hong Kong with him, he would have to keep her comfortable.

Handing her a glass, "Drink," he said firmly.

Greer took the glass and quickly drank down the contents. She was so thirsty that she hadn't even thought to ask if he had poisoned it. She coughed at the taste before asking, "What the hell is going on? Please, just let me go. I need a doctor. Please!" she urged. Her tears were fewer now, but the fear was still present and forward.

"It won't be much longer," he assured her in a low and urgent voice. "One way or the other."

LAST MAN STANDING

Tobias pulled up to the church, just as a shadow came from the boys' school side of the property, circled the building, and stopped just below the big windows of St. Constantine's. Tobias got off the bike, pulled out his Glock, and slowly made his way towards the shadowed figure, crouched and on the prowl.

"I wouldn't do that," Tobias said, his voice low, as he touched the barrel of his gun to the back of McQueen's head.

"What a bunch of suckers we are," McQueen said, lowering his arm and pulling back his weapon. "You must be Tobias," he smirked. "I've been watching you, watching her, watching me, for days," he said with a dubious smile.

"And you must be Luke," Tobias said, gesturing with his hand and stepping out of view of the windows. "She's in there?"

"That she be," McQueen offered, shaking his hand and nodding at the door. "With that, Mr. Williams guy. Who isn't a teacher, by the way. His real name is William Walton. Word around town—he goes by Liam. You know the guy?"

"I do," Tobias said. "He's a right piece of shit and I saw him at the hotel."

"Yeah, me too. But I was around back, while you were out front. Did you call in NOPD? I heard over the radio that a body was found in the hotel?"

"That would be her, I reckon. She's been busy."

While the two played catch-up, working their plan of attack, a set of lights caused Tobias to quickly pull McQueen towards him and out of view of the driveway. He recognized McTavish's truck as it pulled to a stop in front of the church.

"Dad," Tobias called out, hurrying to his side and happy to have someone back them up as they laid out their plan to go inside.

"Tobias," McTavish said in surprise as he looked from Tobias to McQueen. "What are you two doing here?" he asked.

Looking back at his son, "Why aren't you in Japan?"—not giving either of them time to answer the first question.

"You didn't think my sister would disappear and I not return home, did you?" Tobias asked, leaving out the other reasons.

"Why aren't you at the hospital with Bishop? Where are Silas and Addison?"

"Sir," McQueen said, interupting him, "Silas and Addison are both at the hospital, waiting for answers. When they are out of surgery, hopefully, we'll know more," McQueen said, taking another look at McTavish, who didn't quite look like the man he had met on his first day in Baptiste. McTavish looked green and had a perpetual stream of sweat pouring from his forehead.

"I'm sorry, Sir. But shouldn't you know that? Have you been by the hospital at all?" McQueen asked suspiciously.

Surprised by the expression on his father's face, Tobias asked, "Why are you here?" Looking over at McQueen, "You didn't call him here?"

"Uhm, no," McQueen said, shaking his head and glancing at the church doors. "But can we talk about this part later? I know I'm kinda low on the food chain here, but..."

"McQueen, you take the front. Me and the Old Man will take the side. We'll meet up in the middle, by the sacristy. Most of the front is wide open. There's a small abbey, if you can call it that, and a library. But the church should be empty tonight. No one really stays on the grounds while the schools are closed for the summer. If you see anything that you think shouldn't be there, shoot it. There's plenty of land here, we'll bury them later," Tobias said, only half joking.

"Fair enough," McQueen replied. I'll meet you where you just said," he confirmed, not knowing what the abbey was or even a sacristy. "I'll find you and kill what needs to be killed."

As they headed inside, each taking their time to make sure nothing was unturned, McQueen followed a noise that he knew wasn't coming from Tobias. With his gun at the ready, he used the barrel to push open a door to a room that looked similar to a coat closet. Robes of different colors hung in neat rows ranging from various blacks to shades of green. He had no idea what they were used for, but there were a lot of them, along with what looked like elaborate and expensive scarves.

As he passed through the library, a door to the right began to open. McQueen stepped behind the door as a man stepped into view.

McQueen raised his gun, aimed, and was just about to follow Tobias' instructions to the letter when Tobias called out, "Stop!"

McQueen lowered his weapon just enough to show he understood. When Tobias circled around, his gun was raised and ready.

"Well, now, isn't this a surprise. Young Luke Bohannon, is it? I knew there was something about you. You had me curious when I saw you get out of the sheriff's truck. I wondered why a boy like you would want to spend your summer babysitting a bunch of snotty-ass little kids. And then I saw you chatting it up with the girls, and I thought, 'Be still my heart, young man!' Damn, boy. You are brilliant. You had those girls eating it up. To be young again, am I right?" he laughed. "What I could do with your looks and my skill—damn. And here you are, one of them," he said, turning to look at Tobias and McQueen.

"Sheriff," he said, nodding. "You got here just in time, I see. I left her bracelet on just for you. That was a nice touch, by the way. I'll have to get those for my pets. Have you decided how you'd like to finish our little arrangement, or are we looking at new terms?" he asked smugly and with a wide smile. He watched as McTavish nervously decided on how to answer him.

"What is he talking about?" Tobias asked, confused. His words circled him as the heat rose within him. What arrangements? Where is Greer? That is all the arrangement we need settled. Where is my sister?"

Liam laughed at that. "You poor, stupid bastard. You are that dense. No wonder your father didn't want you following in his footsteps. You're as dumb as a stick. Your father here was supposed to take care of that LJ fucking Senator bitch for me, and I'd take your dear sweet Aunt Caroline off his hands. Though he should have just told me that she didn't die, and I could have taken care of her years ago. But your sister had to start asking too many questions, and well, here we are. How am I doing, Daddy?" he said, laughing as he watched McTavish's fall from grace—watched as his son got to see what his father was really like all these years.

At the mention of LJ Daily, Tobias' confusion sharpened into focus. Somewhere in the church, LJ—Kathryn's mother—was being held captive, a pawn in the Waltons' twisted game with his father. "Where is she?" Tobias demanded. "Where is the Senator?"

"She's here," Liam said, excited in the knowledge that perhaps pretty damn soon, Tobias would hate his father as much as he hated his.

Besides, if he were going to die, at least he could have some fun with them. "Or there—maybe everywhere," he said, spinning in a circle, eager to throw the three men off balance. "There are a lot of places one can bury bodies around here."

Just as he dove for Tobias, a sound rang out, and Tobias watched as Liam fell to the floor without a fuss at his feet. Tobias stopped moving, and his face turned to McQueen—just like that, William Watson's reign of terror was over. There was no big moment or fanfare—just done. Tobias blinked at McQueen, whose gun rested on his wrist from where he took his shot.

"You said kill whatever moves," McQueen said in his usual deadpanned humor. "He moved," he said, shrugging at Tobias.

"He moved," Tobias seconded, returning the shrug.

"She's here, close by," McQueen said. "I'm pretty sure that's what brought me this way. I heard a woman's voice—a very pissed off woman's voice."

McQueen headed for the door that the now-dead man had come through earlier. As he followed the stone stairs down, the air grew cooler and the voice grew louder. A woman's voice grew more urgent, as she swore out words that the walls of a sacred place should not hear. But if these walls could talk, then they'd probably be bound by some clergy oath of some form or another.

There were four doors total. "We used to play in here as kids," Tobias said. "I completely forgot about this place. It was used as a silent prayer room, or something like that. The Sisters and even the Fathers would come down here when they needed solitude."

Tobias pulled on the first door—it hadn't been locked. Pulling the door wider made no difference. The room was still too dark to see inside. "Hand me your phone," he said to McQueen, holding out his hand. "I don't have a phone on me."

Quickly, McQueen handed over his phone, and Tobias panned the room with the phone's flash.

"You okay?" he asked, his voice gentle and a bit unsteady, as he searched her out in the dark.

LJ nodded, her body visibly shaken. "I... I think so. Did you find your sister?"

"Not yet," Tobias said as he entered the room, his tone grim. "But I think she's in here somewhere with you."

LJ looked at Tobias, her expression a mix of gratitude and fear. "Thank you," she said quietly. "For coming for me. Do you know if Samuel is okay?" she asked, tears filling her eyes as she dared to consider what had happened to him. "I haven't seen him and I am worried. That boy is like a son to me," she said grimly, thinking the worst.

"No ma'am, I haven't seen him," Tobias said, hearing the stress in her voice. "We'll find him. But first, I need you to hold still, Senator," he said, seeing her face pale but defiant. He knelt beside her and carefully cut through the ropes with a knife from his pocket. Once he was finished, he offered, "We'll get you somewhere safe. Then, I promise, we'll see to finding Samuel," he said, looking over at McQueen.

As they moved toward the next door, the weight of what had transpired settled heavily on Tobias' shoulders as his eyes fell on his father. Alister McTavish had always been a rock—the type of man who commanded armies and respect. In that moment, there was something very wrong with what had just happened. He shook off the unsettling thoughts that set his teeth to itch. The man he looked up to was lying in the hospital, probably not going to make it and the best thing since chocolate cake was probably a murdering piece of shit.

Tobias fought the urge to shove his father into a wall and demand answers, but he knew deep down—he already had them. For now, he would find his sister and his Aunt Caroline—then he'd figure out what his father had done.

HE SHOULD HAVE PROTECTED YOU

PRESENT DAY – BABY

The dampness of the stone clung to my skin like a second layer. I listened for any sound beyond the suffocating darkness as I worked at the wooden frame without the luxury of light. I could hear Greer's muffled whimpers on the other side, but they had grown faint and sparse over time. I worried that her injuries had finally gotten the best of her.

"Hold on, Greer," I whispered, my voice unnaturally shaky but determined. I shifted my weight, my palms scraping against the gritty stone floor as I worked at the bottom for a while. Every inch was a battle, as my knees bruised and stung, and my heart—Caroline's heart—pounded like a drum in my chest.

Caroline's memories kept popping in and out, those from her childhood, as I tried to remember where and how I knew this place. Of course, it really wasn't my memories per se, but it was up to me to get us out of this situation. The stone was so familiar, and the feel of the wood-framed door seemed like a puzzle each time I placed my hand to work out how to open it.

Just as I was about to give up and reset myself, I heard a heavy thud, like someone was knocking—not knocking, but banging. Then, from outside, the chaos became palpable as the voices rose and fell—whispers giving way to yells. I knew the voice that rang out the clearest—the voice of Tobias—and then McQueen's voice followed, sharp and commanding, as they tried thundering their way through a door. But it wasn't my door. I could hear the heaviness of their attempts to remove Greer from her prison. But there were other voices, too—and that voice gave me the energy boost I needed to claw my way out—McTavish.

My fingers worked feverishly at the splintered beam, and I hissed in pain as a shard pierced beneath my fingernail, sending a jolt of pain past my elbow and up into my chest. I yanked back my hand, biting down on the nail to stifle a cry. Blood seeped into my mouth as I continued to work. I had to get to Greer before McTavish.

"I'm nearly out of here," I said, hoping my voice sounded reassuring. "Can you hear me, Gears? Can you hear them? Tobias is here. Hold on, okay?" I said.

It wasn't me talking. I could feel Caroline trying to pull herself out of her hiding place, and the panic in her made my body feel as though I had drunk too much coffee. I smiled at that. That's a girl. I knew she wasn't strong enough, but it was Caroline and not Sister who put this heartache in my chest. Caroline's love, not Sister's, made me want to make sure that Greer made it out alive. "I'm coming for you," I boasted loudly, hoping anyone and everyone outside this door could hear my voice. "I'm coming for you."

The blows from outside grew louder. Tobias and McQueen were relentless, as their shouts mixed in with the crunch of breaking wood.

"Greer, are you in here?" Tobias shouted. "Gears! We're coming!"

Tobias's voice carried through the destruction like a lifeline through the darkness that had trapped Greer for days.

"Greer, is Deputy Lovejoy with you?" McTavish asked, his voice carrying a tone of fear.

My stomach churned as I heard no reply from Greer. I clenched my fists as I punched and jabbed hard, making my way through the wooden door. Time wasn't on our side, and I had no reason to stay quiet any longer. As I jabbed again, the air in the room shifted as a crack formed, allowing a burst of clean air and a small, dim shadow of light to filter through cracks in the door.

Using my hands, I dug into the cracks, prying pieces loose—each fragment I pulled away brought me closer to her—closer to McTavish. Sweat began to drip from my face, mixing with the grime already caked on my skin and the blood McTavish had left in my hair. The sound of splintering wood seemed deafening in the confined space, but I couldn't stop. Greer's silence was deafening, as were the cries from Caroline.

"Baby?" Greer's voice cracked, barely audible.

"I'm here," I said, my throat tightening around me with emotions I hadn't expressed before. I wasn't the one Caroline used to shit out unicorns and rainbows. My whole purpose was to kill those who hurt others. "Just hold on a little longer. Can you hear them? They are almost to you."

"Baby, please don't kill him," Greer said, her words fading in and out. "Please don't kill my daddy. I know what he did, but..."

Outside, the conflict intensified. Tobias's furious shouts clashed with McTavish's threats, and McQueen's voice carried a dangerous edge as he tried to help free Greer and control the fire that had been ignited between father and son.

My fingers bled, but my drive to get to Greer had numbed my pain. Finally, I had made a hole large enough that I could get a shoulder through, and I began to press my body into the opening.

"Greer!" I yelled. My voice cracked as the wood ripped through my skin with each forceful shove. "I'm almost out."

"We've got you," Tobias said, his voice firm and reassuring. He glanced over his shoulder, his expression hardening, as he placed his hands around my upper body, securing my shoulder and socket to stay intact as he readied himself for what he was about to do.

Then a hand took my arm. "I'm going to pull," a voice said. It was McQueen. "Okay, Sister, this will hurt. One, two..." Placing a foot on the door together, Tobias and McQueen yanked me hard and pulled me out of the splintered door.

Once I was cleared, I glared at McTavish. I fought my nature to slap him to the floor, crawl on top of him, and rip his head from his neck with my bare hands. I had fear set to me for the first time, and it fueled me like nothing had ever. I pushed past him and began helping Tobias open the other doors.

"Greer isn't the only woman trapped in here with us," I said, looking into each room.

"We have her," McQueen said, offering a slight nod or reassurance. "Senator Daily is okay."

Just then, LJ stepped out into the hall and the light, and she too gave me a nod.

As the door to Greer's cell gave way, I nearly choked out a sob. Caroline was becoming stronger, and I had to stop that from happening. She wouldn't be able to do what needed to be done, and I pushed her back, locking her deep in her mind so that only I had my hands on the wheel.

"Tobias," I said, looking at him. There were no words to say just yet. He knew what I had done. Or rather, what his Auntie Caroline had done. I'm the one he saw in Tokyo. I'm the one who walked past him that night and later unleashed havoc on a few men who had earned a righteous death. There would be a lot of explaining to do. But for now, there were other pressing matters.

"I've got you," I said, my voice firm despite the quiver in my hands. I had packed Caroline away, so it had to be the cold that I felt at my center return.

Greer nodded, her expression a mixture of hope and fear, as she looked into my face. Neither of them was for her or me, as she searched over me. She wasn't able to move, and I worried that if we picked her up, we would hurt her more than she already was. Her Boogeyman was gone, that much I had figured out. McQueen didn't have to tell me—nor did Tobias. That boy wore his kills like tally marks along the edges of his red-rimmed eyes. He was a lot like his mother and a lot like Caroline. He was the sort that vigilantes were made of.

"McQueen, can you call for an ambo?"

"Already done, Sister," he said solemnly before returning to stand next to Tobias. "Whatever you have to do, you better get to it," he said, looking around as if he knew there was still unfinished business and making eye contact with no one.

"You know what I have to do," I whispered as I gently eased my way down to sit next to Greer.

Her sadness could have crippled an elephant. Her tears returned, pleading with me not to kill her father, although she knew what he had done.

"I'm sorry, Love. He trained us to do this job, and he is no exception. He'll get as good as he gave. I can promise you that. The McTavish, I know, would want it that way. And if it's any comfort, he knew this was coming. There's a reason he left me working so far away—kept me from coming home all these years."

"He convinced Sister that she wasn't strong enough to make it here. But he couldn't risk her remembering. He didn't have the heart to kill her the second time. He figured that if she survived all that, then she earned it. So he did her a solid and hid her from the Waltons. Really, they were small-town nobodies. Liam wouldn't have been able to do what he's done if it wasn't for your father and his friends, like Grant," I whispered to her, keeping my voice low, so as to keep my concerns from the others.

"Grant tipped them off. He was working as a clerk while in college. He told Liam that some rookie cop was moving up in the ranks and had been put on vice." "Caroline thought that having McTavish as her brother-in-law would help her. But we know how that turned out."

I wondered why McTavish hadn't busted through the door, demanding to see his daughter as I finished our story.

I hoped, but didn't care if she understood what would happen next. LJ stepped into the room, her flashlight beaming directly at me. "It's time," she said.

"He should have protected you," she said finally, tears streaming down her face as she accepted that if it were anyone else, her father would have sent his own to kill them. She knew what her father did. And if she truly understood what that meant, then she understood why Baby had to see this through.

"Just please wait until I am gone. I'm sure the ambulance is close."

Getting up off the floor, I placed a hand on Greer's head. "Your Auntie Caroline loved your guts," I said, wondering if she'd remember and understand the expression. It was one she used on them as children. It was never, "I love you." It was, "I love your guts."

SINS OF THE FATHER

The old church groaned under the pressure of time, but it hadn't lost any of its shine. I saw the way Tobias' eyes traced the room. He had missed the old church and the stories that had built it—from its pews with their high-gloss cherry shine and their velvety soft seats to the high windows that kaleidoscoped their colors, even in the night, across its floors.

I wondered if he could also see Mother Agnes Valentine sitting in a pew with her big, generous smile, waiting to greet them as they all piled in on a Sunday. Tobias wanted that feeling now, missing Agnes with his whole heart, but he couldn't find it as he stood in the center of the nave, his hands clenched into fists, his set jaw tight as he stared at his father.

"Say it again," Tobias demanded, his voice low but trembling with fury. Again, I fought Caroline for power, holding her back as her hurt pushed its way forward and caught in my throat. Watching Tobias' hurt manifest itself as rage was debilitating.

McTavish, once revered for his unyielding integrity, now seemed smaller in the shadows of his son, his shoulders hunched under the weight of guilt. His eyes glazed over with regret as he looked up to meet Tobias' eyes.

"I covered for them," McTavish said, his voice hoarse. "William and Archie Walton... and the others. I don't know their names or who they are. I didn't want to know, but I did protect them. Kathryn Daily's murder, it was... it was all them. And I helped bury it. I buried the truth. And Caroline, I did that too...." his words trailing off as he looked my way.

The words struck Tobias like a physical blow, and he took a step back, covering his face with his hands. "No, no, no," he said, near tears as he began to slap his face. "Don't say that. You wouldn't do that. What are you saying?"

His breaths came out short and fast, and his mind reeled as memories of his childhood flooded back—the unanswered questions, the whispers of corruption, the gnawing suspicion that something had always been off. Now he knew why. His father had become the sort we had spent our careers trying to end.

"You did this to us? You knew this whole fucking time," Tobias hissed, his voice rising to the point of shattering glass. "You knew what they did to her. You let them get away with it! You betrayed everything I was taught to believe in. You betrayed her. You betrayed all of us. You killed Bishop!" he screamed out in a roar, his rage distorting his features as his face took on that of something unrecognizable.

I felt Caroline crumble at Tobias' words—Bishop was dead.

"I didn't have a choice," McTavish argued weakly, his hands raised to placate his son. "They... they had power, connections. If I'd spoken out, it would've destroyed everything. Our family, our name..."

"You had the power!" Tobias yelled as McQueen and I pushed our way forward, LJ close behind. I wanted to step in and end the conversation and get to the killin' part of the show, but I thought it best to let it all come out—let the cancer out. "You are the great Alister McTavish. You could have ended them all with just one directive. But you wanted the money. Say it!" Tobias roared, his voice echoing through the empty church. "You think this is better? Living a lie? Covering for murderers who hurt your own family? We were only fucking children!" he spat, his eyes bulging red as fire.

McTavish flinched at the venom in Tobias' tone, but he didn't move. Behind them, McQueen stood near the heavy wooden doors, his sharp eyes darting between the two men and looking as if he was going to interfere. LJ reached out and clutched at his arm, whispering quietly, "Let it be," she said. "This is a long time coming."

"I'm just watching the doors," McQueen said, folding his arms over his chest, his gaze never leaving McTavish as he guarded the door against anyone coming in or getting out. "I'm not as slow as everyone thinks I am," I heard him say, his eyes resting on mine.

McQueen was smarter than I gave him credit for, and I thought he was brilliant from the start. By the way he spoke to me, carried himself, and asked no questions, I had to assume that he knew more than he had ever let on. He never said a word; he just watched and listened to us all.

"I'm saying that I was involved," McTavish said, his voice breaking. "I'm telling you the truth. Do you think I would have brought you all here, knowing this wouldn't come out?" Turning to me, he said, "Caroline, please. I know you can hear me."

"I called you back here to help me find my little girl. I know what I let them do to you, and I've done everything I can to help you over the years. I made you stronger and better. You can protect yourself now. You were my only hope of finding her, and I knew you would figure it out once you invested the time."

"My name is Baby," I said, glaring at him as if he were already dead.

I did not pity him; the old man was reduced to nothing more than a sniveling coward. "And you did not save her—I saved her. I was the one who helped her get clean and dug her out of the gutter you sent her to. You only locked her up, calling her crazy because you feared what Caroline would remember. That's the only reason you've kept tabs on her—just waiting and watching. I bet when I came along, you thought it only helped you," I said, smiling. "You're a fool. We played your game, and we finally beat you. She knew it was you helping them take those girls. It was you who buried the dead ones, too. That was the catalyst that broke her mind. The great Alister McTavish, the man she loved and adored, let them rape her, mutilate her and leave her and her friend to die. And they did, didn't they? Kill them both."

"It's twenty years too late," LJ screamed, her rage growing as she quickly moved toward McTavish and spat in his face. "You could have prevented this. And for the sake of argument, let's pretend you didn't know it was going to happen; you could have buried those son of a bitches in the fucking ground for what they did," she yelled as she struck him across the face.

"But it wasn't until your girl was in danger that you did anything. That doesn't bring my Kate back. It doesn't undo the pain her family went through.

You destroyed her father. It doesn't erase the blood on your hands. Look at Caroline. Look at what you created," she said, now looking at me as if I were to be pitied. "You broke that poor girl's mind."

"Tobias..." McTavish said, his tone firm but wary. "How is your sister? Can I please speak to her before, well... before you..."

"McQueen, get the Senator out of here," Tobias ordered, cutting off his father's words, his voice brutal and venomous. "Take her somewhere away from here. She can't be party to this. And see if you can find Samuel."

Then, turning his attention to the Senator, "You have to go."

"What do I say to Silas and Addison?" McQueen asked, unsure if he was to say anything at all.

"Nothing," I said. "You are to say nothing. Avoid their calls. Just help the Senator and look for Samuel."

"You're sure?" McQueen said, stepping forward, Tobias. "This is what you want to do? He is your father. I understand her," he said, not looking at me as he spoke. "I think he's earned whatever he has earned, but..."

"But nothing," Tobias growled. "Just go!" Tobias barked, his eyes blazing. "That's an order." Softening his tone, "Hey, can you check on my sister? Let her know I'll be there soon."

"I'll sit with her," LJ offered as she stepped away from McTavish.

She knew what I was going to do—what she had asked me to do. LJ Daily had reached out to me some time ago after she had heard of my reputation and my ties to McTavish's team. She was surprised the first time we met, her mind unable to wrap itself around what I had become—what Caroline had become.

It broke her heart to see her daughter's friend become a psychopathic murderer. Yet, I was what she needed to kill the man who had let all of this happen. The Senator gently pulled McQueen toward the door. "Please, McQueen," she said, giving me a weak smile of understanding, "I need your help elsewhere."

As the door creaked shut behind them, I turned back to McTavish, a maniacal smile crossing my face as I inched closer.

"Tobias," McTavish said, his voice barely above a whisper. "Please, I never wanted any of this to happen. I've tried to make it right. To make up for my one lapse in judgment. After your mother died, something happened to me. The loss of her..." his words falling off as he stopped the line of thought, unable to blame his betrayal on the loss of his wife.

"I never wanted any of this."

"How dare you shit on my mother's memory with that bullshit," Tobias said as spittle fell from his mouth, his hand inching toward the gun holstered at his side. "You made your choices. You ruined my life."

McTavish's eyes widened as Tobias drew the weapon, leveling it at his father's chest. "Tobias, don't, please..."

McTavish wasn't one of my seven. I had killed many in my path to get to where I was, and I would have killed him for sure, but I felt no pull to stop Tobias from seeking his own revenge. What kind of person would I be to take that from him? I was many things, but a hypocrite I was not.

What McTavish had done to them as children was almost worse than what he had let happen to us, and I would not stop him.

"Don't what?" Tobias snarled. "Don't do what you've done my whole life? Kill dirty pieces of shit?"

For a moment, I watched as Tobias' eyes softened, as if he were having second thoughts. The boy in him, the love of his father, was written in his expression as his features fell and the gun lowered so slightly. The only sound was the distant rustle of the wind that circled through the old bones of the church. Then the gunshot rang out, shattering the silence.

McTavish staggered, clutching his chest as the blood flowered out and seeped through his fingers. He fell back into a pew and sat down, his eyes locked on Tobias's face; a mixture of shock, sorrow, and peace was etched into his features.

"Tobias..." he rasped, but his voice faded as his hand fell and a shadow fell over him.

Tobias's eyes widened in tears as he looked to me for something. I don't know if he wanted words or a hug. This is when Caroline could have made herself known. I wasn't the one who cared about people's emotions. That wasn't my job.

As I considered giving him some reassurance that what he had done was okay, a hand slipped into Tobias's and gently took the gun from him, and then Tobias was engrossed with big arms that circled around him as his tears fell. I hadn't even heard him creep into the building.

Silas Holiday let go of Tobias, handed him the keys, and sent him out of the building. "Take these and go be with your sister." Then he turned to me.

"Baby," he said, not as a question but as if identifying which one of us was present.

"Just in time, Sunny-Love," I said, smiling at him.

"It's done," he said, again, not a question.

I knew what he meant, and I wasn't looking to run. I had made him a promise, and I wouldn't go back on it.

"You got a shovel in that truck of yours?" I asked. "I'm too tired to find the river, and I know of a pretty good cemetery not too far from here. You can decide what to do with him," I said, gesturing a nod at McTavish, "while we put that asshole in Caroline's spot. She's not using it anymore."

THE PROCESSION THAT WASN'T

TWO WEEKS LATER

B y midday, only a handful of mourners had trickled into the small town of Lockerbie. The skies had settled on a light blue with moderate cloud cover and no rain in sight, welcoming them to at least a dry ceremony—if not exactly a warm one—at least not warm by Louisiana standards. Only a few cars had passed through the front iron gates of Dryfesdale Cemetery. Dr. Wu had been one of them. She had taken an empty seat next to Silas Holiday. Wu was one of about twelve mourners who attended Alister McTavish's funeral.

Seeing her take the seat next to him, he reached over and gave her hand a light squeeze without saying a word. The looks exchanged between them conveyed that words were unnecessary at the moment. The sober atmosphere set a tone that only a few had shared, but the rest would follow along. They would have words, but that would come later.

Wu looked at the car parked parallel to the greens, so lush in color that it signified the beginning of their summer. Wu saw that the windows were still rolled up, and she wondered if the passenger in the backseat could observe from their viewpoint. She looked back at Silas and smiled dubiously, wondering if he was thinking the same thing. She had observed him taking the same glances as she had.

As the rear doors of the hearse opened, Silas stood, pressed out the legs of his suit, and slowly made his way to join the other five men tasked with the honor of carrying the casket of the man loved by so many.

There had been no public announcement made of the passing of Alister McTavish. Those who made the big decisions found it better to bury the man quietly and without a press. His deeds would be swept quietly under the rug while others cleaned up the ash left behind by his fire. Those who knew his crimes were the only ones to attend his funeral—either for appearance's sake or because they felt they owed him a debt of gratitude, regardless of what he had done.

Of all those in attendance, no one's grief was felt harder than that of Greer McTavish, who hid her swollen and battered face behind wide-framed, blacked-out glasses and heavy concealer.

Wu wanted to be surprised by seeing her in attendance, knowing that Greer's injuries would have mandated a lengthy stay at Ochsner Medical Center. But with Bama at her side, Greer stood on her crutches, hard-casted to the hip, as she leaned on him for support.

Wu watched the two, thinking that perhaps this would make them stronger. Whether together or apart had yet to be determined. Wu also hadn't been shocked to see that Tobias hadn't attended his father's funeral, opting to return to his work in Japan instead.

With the help of three unknown individuals on loan from the church, Silas, Addison Adler, and Luke Kidd lowered Alister's casket through the opening and let it rest at the bottom. Once Father Murphy, the same Father Murphy who had married Alister and Charlotte so many years earlier, had finalized his words, the gathering of people quickly dispersed.

The ceremony had been short, with no one except Father Murphy to speak on his behalf. After, like dead leaves on the wind, they scattered to each process the day on their own terms.

Walking to the car, Silas slipped an arm through Dr. Wu's, helping her as they headed back to the black sedan waiting for her.

"Always a gentleman," she said, smiling softly up at him. "You are a good man, Sunshine."

"I do my best, Doc," he commented. "But don't let my secret get out," he said, smiling back at her. "You wouldn't want to ruin my reputation."

"Are you headed back to the East?" she asked, already knowing his bags were packed and his ride back to Camp Arifjan was waiting for him. From there, only he knew his final destination.

"Yes, ma'am," he said. "You? Where are you off to now?" he asked. "And her?" he gestured to the sedan.

"We are headed back to London. She'll be okay, Sunshine. I found her a room at Broadmoor. It's not open to women anymore, but I have pull there, and I've earned more than a few favors over the years."

"For the criminally insane," he said, sucking back the air that nearly came flooding out and, with it, something that sounded almost like a sob.

"That's where she needs to be for now—you know this. I'm not sure there's anything that can be done to help her right now—especially with what happened to Bishop. But I can at least ensure that she's safe. And hiding her in a men's nuthouse seems the best place, don't you think?"

Silas chuckled at her use of the word nuthouse. "Careful, Doc. You're starting to sound as uncouth as the rest of us. Have you seen Sister since Alister's death?"

Wu sighed, taking a deep breath before answering. "No. I'm afraid Sister is gone. I don't know if Caroline thinks she's served her purpose or if Baby has outgrown them both and is now stronger than even Sister. Bishop's death was more than she could bear. I had hoped that figuring out who had hurt her and killed her friend would bring her back and that she would no longer need Baby or Sister, for that matter," she confessed, looking up at Silas to garner a reaction. Seeing none, she continued. "I know you love Sister, but she's so far buried in Caroline's head now that only Baby is present. I don't know what she'll do now that she's in control."

"I think you're wrong, you know," Silas said with a smirk. "I think Sister was always Caroline. I think she figured out a way to stay close without giving herself away—just another identity she took on—another role. I think Caroline was working on her own case all this time, and she stayed in character. But hey, what do I know, you're the doctor; I'm sure you know better than I would."

Sighing heavily, "Well, on a brighter note, I hear Bama is running for Sheriff," Silas continued, laughing at the thought of Bama trading in his camera and brown hat for a badge and a cowboy hat. "I just wanna see him in the hat," he continued with a wide grin.

"That boy is going to make Elliot Ness cool again," she said, smiling back at him.

"That I think he will," he said, watching in the distance as Bama hugged Addison and made his goodbyes with McQueen. "He's a good kid. Now that Miss Simone and Sister Agnes Valentine's dreams of ending the family's legacy of ill-repute, maybe it'll be uneventful for him. There's no one left to take girls, so he's got that going for him," Silas said sadly.

"Hell, maybe the next time we go back there, it'll be for a wedding," he said happily, doing his best to put on a better face.

"Oh, aren't you the hopeless romantic?" she said, patting him on the arm. "You know, you were pretty convincing through all of this," she admitted, looking up at him. "I can't imagine how hard it was to stay in character yourself, report to LJ, keep Baby from, well... self-imploding, and all the while, maintain some sort of sanity in it all. You are quite a remarkable man, Silas. It sounds like you'd make one helluva double agent."

Wu was just about to comment further on the idea that either of them would even return to the swamp when the sedan's window lowered, and the two turned to look at the car. Silas waited to see who would greet him, while Wu placed a hand on the door as if her touch could prevent it from opening.

"I'm getting pretty hungry in here, Doc," Baby said, eyeing both of them curiously. Squinting her eyes at them, she continued, "You two look awfully chummy. You two talking about me, are you?" she asked as a devilish smile crept to the corners of her mouth and danced joyfully in the spark of her eyes. "That's my favorite topic."

"Hey there, Baby," Silas said, placing a hand on the window frame and leaning into the window. He couldn't help but wish he were talking to Charlee Lovejoy, the woman he had met in the desert, in the sun's heat, who smelled like vanilla and oranges. He missed her. As he thought back to the beginning, he wondered just how much of his interaction with Charlee had been with Baby or even Caroline.

He shrugged off the thought and let it pass over him. Baby had never hidden herself from him. And he knew for sure that Charlee Lovejoy was just as fictional as Baby was—just another role she played to get by. The Sister persona had been nothing more than a crutch that had allowed Caroline Doucet to live without having to face that her best friend had died so horrifically and that her brother-in-law had caused it all. At least, that is how the great doctor had explained it.

"Hey there, Sunny-love," she said back, placing a hand over his. "You gonna miss me, ain'tcha?" she said, her dirty Cockney accent returning. "I hear Doc there is carting me off to the looney bin," she said, her words unfazed by her predicament. "You gonna visit me?" she asked, coyly dragging him in once again.

He couldn't resist that smile of hers, whether it belonged to Charlee, Caroline, Sister, or Baby. It sucked him in, and like Bishop, he devoured it. She had a way of making you feel as if you were the most important person in her life with just her eyes.

Silas fought the lump in his throat at the thought of Bishop and how tragic his death had been. They were never great friends, but Bishop was a standup guy, and he didn't deserve what had happened to him. He knew McTavish's level of admiration for Bishop, and he still hadn't worked out why he would have Bishop killed. It didn't fit, but then again, none of it had made sense.

Even if Bishop had known what McTavish had done, McTavish had already taken steps to have Bishop take over as sheriff and let things unfold as they may.

He never would have brought them all to Baptiste to find his daughter, knowing that they were the best at what they did. He knew his deeds would come to light and that his days were numbered.

"I'll let you get settled. Then we'll see what the Doc has to say," he said, smiling fondly at her through the window. "How is Sister in there?" he asked, seeing the turn of her expression grow darker as she pulled her hand back.

"She's on holiday with Caroline, Sunny-love. A very long holiday. Will you miss them or me?" she asked in a voice that sounded hurt. "I thought we had something, you and me? She belonged to Bishop. You belong to me," she said, now looking at Dr. Wu. "So you keep your hands off my man," she warned.

"You're safe, Baby. You know you don't have to worry about me and Silas," Wu countered, feeling the need to get into the car while she still had Baby's confidence. "We'll get burgers on the way to the airport," she offered. "Say your good—"

Before Wu could finish the words, Baby grabbed Silas and placed a kiss on his lips. Hard at first and then softly, she held his lips to her, feeling his warmth. Silas did not pull back as she slid her arms around his neck, bringing him closer to her.

He needed that kiss. His heart felt torn, watching Baby and seeing the human in her struggle against her nature.

"You be careful with that, Addie," she quickly whispered in his ear, dragging her lips along his cheek. She had looked past Dr. Wu, and he watched as her eyes fell on Addison, who was looking back at her.

As he pulled back, he saw the worry in her eyes. Baby didn't worry, and Baby didn't show fear. Baby nodded at him in a slow yes, almost pleading with him to understand.

"See you soon, Sunny-love," she said with a smirk before rolling up the window.

MEET THE WRITER

J onie Nikole is a writer of psychological thrillers, crime and mystery whose life story brings compelling depth and authenticity to her work. Born in Casper, Wyoming, and raised in Guthrie, Oklahoma, she grew up in an unstable environment—a challenge that shaped her resilience and sharpened her insight into human nature. After high school, she made Alaska her home for nearly three decades, earning degrees in criminology, paralegal studies, history, and accounting in both Alaska and London.

Before turning to writing full-time, Jonie enjoyed a long career as a private investigator, working with individuals and agencies across the country. She has been happily married for 26 years, is the proud mother of four adult children, their partners, and "Yaya" to two grandbabies. When she's not writing, Jonie is an avid bow enthusiast, axe thrower, and marksmen.

For over 30 years, she has volunteered for a wide range of charities, serving on boards and fostering community partnerships. Now, she hopes her own volunteer organization will help nonprofits meet their goals. Drawing on her wealth of life experiences—from her challenging upbringing to her investigative career—Jonie's writing captivates readers with its dark suspense, deep empathy, and evocative explorations of the human psyche.